(For more acclaim, please turn page . . .)

THE
IMMEDIATE
PROSPECT
OF
BEING
HANGED

Walter Walker

AN ONYX BOOK

ONYX
Published by the Penguin Group
Penguin Books USA Inc., 375 Hudson Street,
New York, New York 10014, U.S.A.
Penguin Books Ltd, 27 Wrights Lane,
London W8 5TZ, England
Penguin Books Australia Ltd, Ringwood,
Victoria, Australia
Penguin Books Canada Ltd, 2801 John Street,
Markham, Ontario, Canada L3R 1B4
Penguin Books (N.Z.) Ltd, 182-190 Wairau Road,
Auckland 10, New Zealand

Penguin Books Ltd, Registered Offices:
Harmondsworth, Middlesex, England

Published by Onyx, an imprint of New American Library,
a division of Penguin Books USA Inc.
Published by arrangement with Viking Penguin.

First Onyx Printing, September, 1990
10 9 8 7 6 5 4 3 2 1

 REGISTERED TRADEMARK—MARCA REGISTRADA

PRINTED IN THE UNITED STATES OF AMERICA

PUBLISHER'S NOTE
This is a work of fiction. Names, characters, places, and incidents either are
the product of the author's imagination or are used fictitiously, and any
resemblance to actual persons, living or dead, events, or locales is entirely
coincidental.

BOOKS ARE AVAILABLE AT QUANTITY DISCOUNTS WHEN USED TO PROMOTE PRODUCTS
OR SERVICES. FOR INFORMATION PLEASE WRITE TO PREMIUM MARKETING DIVISION,
PENGUIN BOOKS USA INC., 375 HUDSON STREET, NEW YORK, NEW YORK 10014.

To my mother, who has never stopped striving to do her best and to make sure her children were able to do the same.

Depend upon it, Sir, when a man knows he is to be hanged in a fortnight, it concentrates his mind wonderfully.

—Samuel Johnson
September 19, 1777

The body of Rebecca Carpenter was found late one October night at an overlook in Woodedge that was popular with teenage neckers who drove there from Nestor or Walmouth. But Rebecca Carpenter was from neither of those places. She was from Woodedge. And she was not a teenager. She was forty years old and had been married for sixteen of those years to a prominent local golfer named Wylie S. Carpenter.

When found, Rebecca Carpenter was propped upright in the front passenger's seat of her Mercedes SEL. There were few signs of struggle inside the car—and that was thought to be a little puzzling because Mrs. Carpenter's pantyhose were torn and her $150 silk scarf had been twisted so tightly around her neck that she had died of asphyxiation, which is neither a quick nor a passive way of dying.

This was not the only unusual death ever to occur in Woodedge. It was not even the only one to involve me. It was merely the first in many years that anybody seemed to think important.

1

The town of Woodedge, Massachusetts, was founded in 1640. Founded may be too strong a word, but the town's inception dates from that year, when a group of nine colonial families were given permission from the leaders of the Watertowne plantation to seek "fresh woods and pastures new" by pushing their way further up the Charles River. The names of those nine lucky families were Pendleton, Eire, Stowers, Browne, Whitney, How, Norcross, Mayhew, and Patterson.

They traveled until they reached the edge of a great wood, and then they spread out individually, each seeking the best possible farmland and claiming whatever they saw in the name of the Watertowne plantation. Homesteads were established, paths were beaten from one to the other, and a community of sorts was formed. By 1685 there were 118 inhabitants of what had become known as Woodedge, and the largest contingency by far was the Patterson family. It was in that year that there appeared the first recorded instance of the penchant for isolationism that would mark Woodedgians for the next three centuries.

It seems the frontiersmen were tired of journeying all the way back to Watertowne for their church services and they petitioned to be relieved of the taxation imposed on them to support the ministry in Watertowne. There followed a debate which lasted thirteen years. The debate no doubt was taken seriously by those involved, since on at least one occasion a meeting to discuss the issue had to be adjourned in order "to prevent such inconvenience as might justly be feared by reason of the heat of the spirit that seemed to prevail."

In any event, permission was ultimately granted for Woodedge to build its own church, or meetinghouse, and in l700 the town applied to the Reverend President Mather of Harvard College for advice as to choice of a minister. What Reverend President Mather gave them was Thomas Chesley. What Woodedge gave Mr. Chesley was a home and firewood and 125 acres of land tax-free. What Woodedge got was the inception of a mini-dynasty.

By 1757 there were 156 names on the Woodedge tax lists, and more of those names were Chesley than Patterson or anything else. There are no surviving official records between that year and 1896, and so demographics have to be pieced together from other sources. Some people have done that, using church records, gravestones, and the insides of family Bibles; but the conclusions I have seen, published in town "histories," vary on every point except the prominence of the Chesley family.

In 1860 Woodedge's first town hall was built, or consecrated if the plaque that marks the ruins of the foundation is to be believed. Five years after that a statue of a Union soldier resting his hands on the open-barreled end of his rifle was erected in the middle of the lawn of the town hall. The base of the statue lists the names of the twelve Woodedge residents "who gave their lives in the holy cause of freedom." One of those men was named Chesley. Two were named Patterson.

Among the things controlled by the Chesley family at this point in time were half a dozen taverns that lined the Boston Post Road, which served as the main thoroughfare linking Boston to Worcester, Hartford, and New York. Although this road ran through the heart of Woodedge, it brought Boston no closer than a two-hour ride to the east for Woodedgians, who preferred to satisfy their commercial needs at the string of shops that flanked their town hall and Civil War memorial.

There were other alternatives, of course. If they wanted, Woodedgians could follow the Post Road over the bridge that spanned the Charles to the already industrialized city of Walmouth, or they could ferry across the river to one of the villages in the city of Nestor, where they could board a train and "take the cars" to Boston. But like their predecessors, the townsfolk of this era took pride in keeping their distance, both literally and figuratively, from their neighbors.

An 1890 autobiography by one William Francis Chesley entitled *Life of a Yankee Squire,* while primarily a paean to the author's ability to breed horses, green plants, and children, nevertheless sheds some light on attitudes of the time. It makes a strong, if grandiloquent, plea for self-reliance and appreciation of nature by extolling the beauty of Woodedge's wooded hillsides, hidden ponds, and sylvan glens. But after painstakingly describing the virtues of his beloved hometown to his somewhat obscurely targeted audience, Squire Chesley was then forced to concede that the vast majority of people are, lamentably, simply not capable of either self-reliance or appreciation of nature.

Such people, the book explains, are simply better off living together. The closer together the better. The problem recognized by the squire was that these people often do not recognize their need to live together and so persist in the mistaken belief that each and every one of them deserves his own plot of land. The squire's book is dedicated to correcting that. It argues that if all men got their own plots of land, the majority would only be made to feel lonely and inadequate. They would, inevitably, end up destroying the very thing they thought they wanted. They would sell off whatever space they were not actively using. They would cut down their trees so that they could see what was being done with the land they had sold, and they would start building and not stop until they had made of Woodedge exactly what they had left behind in places like Walmouth—thus destroying it for those who really deserved it. The only solution, besides barring residency to all non-natives (which Squire Chesley, being a graduate of the Harvard Law School, suspected would be unconstitutional), was to limit ownership in Woodedge to ten acres per household.

Again, no record exists today as to whether the Woodedge board of selectmen, of whom Squire Chesley was one, ever considered this proposal. The loss of records is due to the fact that in 1896 Mr. Chesley's son, William Francis Chesley, II, also known as "Wild Bill," burned down town hall, and only a handful of books survived. Woodedge had not, as of that time, deemed it necessary to have a fire department.

Wild Bill, whose motive for such an anarchistic act is not recorded in any documents I have seen, did not get off unpunished. Although he was not prosecuted, he was forced to leave town and spend the next several years roaming around Europe. A gravestone behind St. Mark's Episcopal Church indicates that Wild Bill was killed in action in 1918, at the age of forty-four. Where he died, how he died, and on whose behalf he was fighting at that rather advanced age are not indicated.

Wild Bill's banishment aside, the Chesleys were repentant enough to build Woodedge a new town hall on land donated by the Chesley family not more than a mile and a half from the site of the previous town hall. At this point the records become complete again, and among the earliest to be found at "the new town hall," as it is still occasionally called, are those of the town clerk showing the sales of Chesley land along a five-block strip running due west from the new town hall. Most of these sales seemed to have been made to the merchants who formerly had been located in the immediate vicinity of the old town hall. One, however, was a little different. It involved one-third of an acre of Chesley land immediately adjacent to the new town hall and sold to the town itself. Board of selectmen minutes for April 10 of that year show the sale was approved by a vote of four to nothing, Mr. Chesley abstaining. The purpose of the sale was to provide Woodedge with the location for a firehouse.

The hold the Chesley family had on the town diminished over the next twenty-five years as Woodedge got its own train service and became more accessible to certain Boston types who brought with them their own sources of money, power, and social contacts. A Mr. Clare Ransom built the town's first $100,000 estate on land he bought from the last of the Pendleton heirs. Mr. Ransom owned a series of textile mills in Georgia, Rhode Island,

and Maine. He belonged to the Longwood Cricket Club and the Brae Burn Country Club, sent his children to the Fessenden School, Groton or Miss Porter's, Harvard University or Wellesley College, and cared not a fig whether any of the Chesleys invited him and his wife to dinner—which, of course, they fell all over themselves doing.

William Francis Chesley's proposal of ten-acre zoning was never enacted, but by the early 1930s Woodedge had scores of estates of at least that size. They were owned by industrialists and bankers and other financial types whose only connections with the founding families came when they wrote them checks.

The Pattersons, what was left of them, sold fast and, at least in the case of my great-uncle Frank, often. Frank Patterson pled guilty to fraud and was forced to live under the pains of probation for three years. It was not the family scandal that it might have been only because by then my grandmother Emily had already brought shame on the Patterson clan by fleeing to Gloucester and marrying a common fisherman named Jared Starbuck. By the time my father was born, the Frank and Emily branch had simply slipped away from the rest of the Pattersons, with Frank selling real estate in Florida and Emily remaining on the North Shore painting seascapes.

To the best of my knowledge, Emily Starbuck never expressed any regret at leaving Woodedge. My father, however, was nowhere near so willing to let the family heritage pass. It was his idea to give me the Christian name of Patterson as a means of reestablishing ourselves. It was his goal, often voiced during Sunday drives through the town, to return "to the land that was rightfully his." It was his constant frustration never to be able to do so. His announcements of my birth and baptism went unacknowledged. His Christmas cards, addressed, I suspect, to people whom he had never met, went unanswered. His pursuit of fortune went unrealized to the point that, on his death, after twenty-two years in the insurance business, he had been able to move my mother and me no closer to Woodedge than the village of West Nestor, several miles and a social world away from where he wanted to be.

My father's irrational and increasingly bitter longing
for the town in which he had never lived was probably
the central theme in our house while I was growing up.
He would, with regularity, rant about his second cousins
Parker and Frost Patterson, Yale men whom he claimed
had never worked a day in their lives and yet lived in
splendor on Woodedge's shady hills. Parker, who called
himself a writer, occasionally had an article published in
Reader's Digest, and my father maintained a subscription
to the magazine for no other reason than to ridicule, line
by line, whatever Parker wrote. But even worse than
Parker, according to my father, was the reprobate Frost,
who did nothing more than play the stock market.

They were men of about my father's age and, as he
constantly reminded my mother and me, they were not
one bit smarter than he was. It was just that they had not
had to take a job straight out of high school and stay with
it day after day to make ends meet. My mother, who as a
teenager had been a waitress at a lunch counter my
father used to frequent, who had never been ten miles
from Gloucester until she met my father, would dutifully
agree and damn Parker and Frost right along with him.
My mother generally supported my father whenever he
railed against the raw deal life had given him. She generally defended him, even when he wasted all his weekends
working on short magazine articles that never got published, or when he lost all our money dabbling in the
stock market.

So it was that I spent most of the years of my youth
being vaguely convinced that the Pattersons of Woodedge,
and Parker and Frost in particular, had somehow robbed
my father and me of our rightful inheritance. But whereas
my father would constantly complain of his lost opportu-
nities to buy or be whatever struck his fancy at a given
moment, I remained blissfully confident that somehow,
some way, the Patterson family fortune (millions, as I
understood it) would sooner or later descend to me. That
fortune, once lodged in my name, would allow me the
green Jag with the tan interior I saw on Route 128, the
trip to Jamaica advertised in the travel magazine I was
flipping through at the dentist's office, the girl ahead of

me in line at the bank who was pretending I didn't exist. That fortune, and all it inevitably brought with it, made it unimportant if I studied hard or got into a good college.

It was, for a while, a comforting inspiration and on occasion I even managed to put it to good use, as when I was able to talk Mary Marie Gastonatto into taking down her pants while we were making out in the front seat of my mother's Ford. Mary Marie, unfortunately, was so carried away by her misperceived prospect of being married to an heir that she told her sister Angeljean about my impending wealth, and Angeljean told half the high school.

Not wanting to jeopardize Mary Marie's affections, I did nothing to discourage the story. It swelled and spawned rumors that became increasingly ridiculous. That was okay as far as my friends were concerned. They knew what it took to score with a girl like Mary Marie and they understood my inheritance to be simply a line I had used. But among people who didn't know me so well, who didn't know Mary Marie so well, the rumors persisted. They continued right up to the day the article appeared in the *Courier* about my father's body being found in the woods behind the Patterson family home. After that I didn't hear them anymore.

2

John Michael Keough was thirty-six years old, which made him two years younger than I. He was also district attorney of Exeter County, which made him my boss. As near as I can tell, John Michael, although born with that name in Walmouth General Hospital, did not become known as John Michael until he started practicing law. His yearbook at Walmouth High, which I made a point of finding, simply identifies him as John M., nickname "Jack." His yearbook biography, run out beneath the picture of a very serious young man sporting a hairstyle noticeably shorter than those of his classmates, says he lettered one year in football and was a member of the debating team. It also says he was president of the junior class. It says nothing about him being a class officer in his senior year, nor is his unsmiling face included in the picture of that year's class officers.

After graduation from high school, John Michael commuted to Boston College. His campaign bio, now his "official bio," says he worked in a laundry to help pay his tuition. When I asked him what laundry it was he told me it was the Pilgrim. When I went down to the Pilgrim nobody could remember him; although, to be fair, the Pilgrim is a big place and not that many of the workers speak English.

John Michael also went to Boston College Law School. His campaign bio says that he was a member of the team that won the National Moot Court competition. He has a round medal bearing the engraved image of Supreme Court Justice Powell to prove it and he keeps the medal on his desk at the Exeter County Courthouse.

John Michael took a job with the Commonwealth attorney general upon receiving his law degree, and it appears he did quite well. He was in the organized crime division and the newspaper clipping he has framed on his wall shows he was instrumental in putting a local Mafia chieftain in prison.

John Michael then became deputy district attorney for Exeter County. With just four or five years of legal experience behind him he was put in charge of criminal litigation. That was when I met him. He hired me as an office investigator. It was a bold move on his part because D.A.'s investigators are supposed to be members of the state police force. But the chief investigator for the office was an affable detective lieutenant named Libby and John Michael told me in confidence that he did not trust Libby because he was part of the "old boy" system. He was going to phase Libby out, he said. Bring in new people, his own people, people he could trust. People like me. I needed a job. I told him that was great.

Three years later I was still working and John Michael wasn't. He had fallen into disfavor with the then district attorney, a man named Phil Burns. "Burnsie" was liked by most everyone who is supposed to like a D.A. He could drink with the best of them. John Michael didn't drink. He made allies in other ways. One day Mr. Burns sobered up long enough to realize that John Michael had developed as many allies as he, Burnsie, had friends. The next day John Michael was fired.

This proved to be a mistake for Phil Burns. John Michael held a press conference. Whereas Burnsie had seen nothing newsworthy about letting one of his deputies go, John Michael turned the incident into the lead story on the six-o'clock news. With cameras snapping and whirring, he sat in his dark blue suit, blue shirt, and red tie, like some implacable John Dean, and gave straightforward, noteless testimony for fifteen minutes about the corruption and incompetence in the Exeter County district attorney's office.

Taken by themselves, the Keough revelations were not that remarkable—a dismissed drunk-driving charge against one of Burnsie's Knights of Columbus buddies, a reduction of a burglary charge against the son of another buddy, some lost evidence in a construction-fraud case against the contractor who built Burnsie's swimming pool— but orchestrated as they were by John Michael, the cumulative effect was quite disturbing.

John Michael explained that the morale of the office was devastatingly low, and that all but a few fawning toadies were incapacitated in their ability to do the people's work. Cleverly, he named no names, thus mitigating the willingness to rebut his charges by anyone who did not want to be accused of being a fawning toadie. Piously, he announced that as a public officer he could take Mr. Burns's abuses of power no longer, and that it was his ultimatum to Burns to stop running his office as a private fiefdom that had caused him to be dismissed.

KEOUGH BLOWS WHISTLE, belched the headline in the *Walmouth-Nestor Courier*, which had always liked Burnsie but was nevertheless obliged to play up the story to keep from getting scooped on its own turf by the Boston papers. The *Globe* and the *Herald* had squadrons of young reporters foraging through the file rooms at the county courthouse, and the *Courier* was reluctantly forced to tap its own sources. All these newspapers found dirt, of course, and in their eagerness to outdo each other they managed to keep the story going for a couple of weeks.

Under such competitive scrutiny, Burnsie's most endearing little qualities, like his willingness to show up at any gathering of two or more people where liquor was being served, became cause for criticism. A felony trial of no particular interest to anyone other than the people involved was lost by a very capable member of Burnsie's staff, and the *Courier* said, NO WONDER.

Stung, Burnsie went out and tried a slam-dunk murder case himself. He had not tried a case in years and he should not have tried this one. He should especially not have tried a case in which the outcome was thought to be a foregone conclusion. His every move was criticized, his every mistake magnified. John Michael stood on the sidelines like a color commentator, somberly and almost patriotically providing the *Courier* with a running analysis that made the daily reports of the trial sound like law review articles.

The jurors, who were prohibited from reading the newspapers' accounts, returned a verdict not of first-degree murder, as Burnsie demanded, but of voluntary manslaughter. One of the jurors, when interviewed after the verdict, spoke of mens rea, a term never once used in the courtroom but discussed at length in one news article. It did not matter. Burnsie's career as D.A. was over. The public, even those who did not know who he was, had lost confidence in him.

John Michael, meanwhile, had taken a job with the county's largest law firm. His name was added to the firm's letterhead and then he was essentially freed to go off and orchestrate a campaign for the next year's election, where he beat Phil Burns in a runaway and became Exeter County's youngest district attorney in a century. This should have made John Michael happy. But John Michael, as I came to find out, was not easily given to happiness.

Among the things that displeased John Michael once he became D.A. was that he was not president of the United States, or even a senator or a congressman. He also did not like the fact that he was not wealthy, famous, absolutely respected, and right in his opinions one hundred percent of the time.

John Michael, however, did like me. This was in no small part due to the fact that it had been his idea to create my position as "litigation coordinator" and the success I had experienced in that role reflected favorably on him. It was also due to my willingness to tell him he was famous, brilliant, infallible, and ought to be president-senator-congressman.

There were other people, of course, who told John Michael these same things. But there were only three of us whose words he really believed. One was Royster Hansen, whom, like me, he had brought into the office and on whose legal advice he was dependent. For all his accomplishments, John Michael Keough at thirty-six was not a tower of legal knowledge. Hansen, ten years older, had been John Michael's mentor in the attorney general's

office. John Michael's first move as D.A. was to make
him chief deputy in charge of the criminal division.

The third member of John Michael's triumvirate of
advisers was his wife, Jessica. People in the office had
many names for Jessica. One was the Bitch. Another was
the Ice Queen. She is a platinum blonde who would be
beautiful if only her features were not so rigid. Still, she
photographs well.

The dynamics were interesting. Royster pretended to
like me and really did not. Jessica pretended not to like
me and really did.

We would meet regularly, the three of us and John
Michael. We would meet in John Michael's paneled office on Friday evenings or whenever Jessica happened to
streak in. Sometimes I would be summoned to the lounge
at the Roadhouse Restaurant; and sometimes we would
gather at the Keoughs' house in Nestor Heights. The
home meetings would usually be characterized in their
invitations as a dinner or a cookout, and Royster would
usually bring his wife, Patty. I would be encouraged to
bring a date so that Patty would have someone to talk to
while the rest of us discussed important things. If I didn't
bring a date then Patty would have nothing to do. She
would get sloshed in relative silence while the rest of us
discussed important things around her. We were a fun
group.

Sometimes the important things we discussed had to do
with other people, such as a bombastic Waterford city
councilor named George Constantinis who was always
stirring up the blue-collar folk of that fair city with his
demands for a new dump or a new senior-citizen recre-
ation center or resident parking permits or whatever
seemed politically opportune at the time. George Constantinis was a hack, but he was young and aggressive
and he had a knack for generating publicity, and John
Michael worried about him constantly.

Sometimes our concerns would be rather exotic, as
when we would fret over the latest rumor that one of the
Kennedy children was moving into the area and would
soon be seeking the congressional seat. We knew there
were plenty of Kennedy children out there and their

possible arrival was a fear the Keoughs had to live with from day to day.

And sometimes the concerns of the moment were more personal, as when an editorial appeared in the *Courier* on the use and abuse of plea bargaining. Any publicity that was not absolutely favorable tended to spawn rage, gloom, and intricate plans for vindication in our little gatherings.

"The voting public is fickle," John Michael would constantly remind us. "They'll turn on me in a minute if I give them the chance."

And then Jessica would tell us, "What we really need, what John has to have, is a big case. Something that will give him some exposure."

At this point John Michael might say something like, "Wouldn't it be great if we could catch some Russian spy stealing secrets from one of the defense contractors out on 128?" And if Royster, being more experienced in dealing with that sort of thing, pointed out that a spy case would probably be a federal matter and handled by those assholes in the U.S. Attorney's Office, it would be up to Jessica or me to modify John Michael's wish accordingly. The Route 128 belt of contractors and computer companies was arguably the leading high-tech spot in the nation, and much of it lay in our county. John Michael was always trying to figure out ways to cash in on the attention the Route 128 companies generated.

Jessica, however, preferred to think in more basic terms. Her constant refrain was that what the American people love is scandal. "Sex, wealth, and foul play," she would urge.

We had plenty of cases dealing with those subjects in the office. But the sex usually came in the form of rapes and child molestations, the wealth in the form of corporate fraud, and the foul play in the same mind-numbing forms experienced by every other county in the country. What we were looking for, what John Michael and Jessica were looking for, was one case involving all three elements. What we got was the death of Rebecca Carpenter.

My first knowledge of the Carpenter slaying came on a beautiful mid-October morning when I arrived in John Michael's office and found him parading from wall to wall and happily waving a file over his head. John Michael looked young to begin with, but when he smiled he looked even younger. On this particular day he looked like a Boy Scout. "This," he crooned, "is it."

The file had been prepared over the course of the night by the Woodedge police department. It contained a sketch of the scene, a detailed listing of photographs and prints taken and evidence inventoried, and a lengthy note of what the investigating officer (a Roland Tagget) had observed. Officer Tagget was meticulous in detailing that the victim showed no visible signs of having been raped or sexually molested, other than the fact her stockings were torn above the thigh.

Officer Tagget had contacted his watch commander, a Sergeant Roselli; and the Sergeant had gone first to the scene and then directly to the Carpenter home, where he had interviewed the new widower at one a.m. Sergeant Roselli's report was considerably less detailed than that of Officer Tagget. One gathered, on reading it, that Mr. Carpenter was quite surprised to learn that his wife was dead. Other than a notation that Mrs. Carpenter's pocketbook was missing, it contained little of interest.

The part about the interview read:

> Proceeded to home of victim, 6 Bulham Road. Engaged husb. of vict., Wylie S. Carpenter, in pajamas. Infd. him of event. Became distraught. Thought wife was with friends. Had been at Stonegate C.C. until 10:00 p.m.

I agreed with John Michael. I told him this was it.

John Michael clasped his hands behind his back and strode across his office. "And I don't," he said, addressing me while he faced his rows of bookshelves, "want those palookas out there fucking it up."

I was not sure what he meant. Not much happened of a serious criminal nature in Woodedge, and I had no particular reason, other than the lack of information in Roselli's note, to think that the Woodedge police department was any more incompetent than any other in the county.

"There's some reason why a woman like this would be in a place like that, and whatever it is, it stinks," John Michael said. He turned from his books. He looked at me with a fiery glint of pleasure in his eye. "That's the part I want you going after, Patt. The part that stinks. We'll let Chief Tuttle worry about the dusting and the tracking and the fibers on the seat covers. I want you finding out what kind of woman this was, what kind of man her husband is, how she could have let herself get in the position she was in. You follow me?"

"You want the dirt."

"I want the dirt."

"Where do you want me to start?"

"Friends, neighbors, fellow club members. Start with the husband, of course, and work your way out from there."

I tucked the file under my arm and headed for the door. As I reached it my boss stopped me with one more remark.

"This time we're really going to get them."

I turned, knotted my fist, and pantomimed a short punch to the gut. I did not even bother asking who "them" was.

3

There are several roads that lead from Walmouth to Woodedge, but the main one emerges from the traffic lights of Walmouth's busy downtown shopping area, runs past a former movie theater that is now a Pentecostal church, and then past a bowling alley and a McDonald's, a Papa Gino's pizzeria, a bar or two, and a string of glass-fronted shops that sell doughnuts or insurance or windowshades. Gradually it leads into a neighborhood of single-family homes with overgrown hedges and bare spots in their front yards. The houses have mongrel dogs that bark, and large American cars that back dangerously out of their driveways, and posted sidewalk signs that say CAUTION CHILDREN AT PLAY.

If you follow this main road, which appropriately is called Main Street, you will eventually come to the river. The bridge over the river is, in fact, a traffic circle. You can exit the traffic circle onto 128 going north or south, or you can go exactly halfway around the circle from Walmouth and enter Woodedge. At this point Main Street becomes Old Boston Post Road.

There is a very old, partially broken, stone wall that runs along the Old Boston Post Road, and for the first mile or so there are simply no houses at all. Then there is the hint of one, a dark spot in the trees on the other side of the wall. A few more houses appear, well camouflaged if they are old, intrusive if they are not. There is a roadside farm stand, where, depending on the season, the world's best corn and apples can be purchased. There is a florist with a greenhouse and a gravel turnoff in front of his door. The road goes deep into the woods after that and then emerges into a meadow that begins with an old Presbyterian church and ends with a fairly new Catholic church. The latter has a long paved driveway that runs between planted trees, and a fifteen-foot crucifix at the junction of the driveway and the road. The Presbyterian church, however, divides the road itself. The right-hand fork becomes Woodedge's Main Street. It rises uphill to the town hall–fire station–police station complex, and then runs gradually downhill for two miles until it rejoins the Post Road.

For several blocks Main Street goes past a row of shops selling fabrics, apothecaries, women's dresses, books, hardware supplies, pastries, and real estate. The string of shops ends at the post office, and since Woodedgians pride themselves on having no home mail delivery, the post office has the largest parking lot in town.

Next to the post office is a restaurant called Adolfo's, a converted home with patio dining and white table umbrellas that are used more to keep leaves and twigs out of the food than to ward off sunshine. Across the street from Adolfo's is the town library, a three-room affair patronized by no one between the ages of fifteen and sixty; and next to that is the Woodedge Woman's Club, its function and membership as much a mystery to me once I became a county investigator as it had been when I was a child and used to cruise this street with my father.

Beyond the Woodedge Woman's Club are a few more houses that, like Adolfo's, have been converted into business establishments, most of them travel agents' or realtors' offices. Then there is the original town cemetery, with its eighteenth-century headstones and its haphazardly mown lawn. There is a Christian Science church and a Congregational church and then there is nothing until the statue of the Union soldier standing forlornly on what used to be the grounds of the old town hall. When I drove past there on my first trip to the Carpenter home I noticed a yellow wreath on a wire stand jammed into the earth in front of the statue. It looked as if it had been there for some time and I wondered why it was there at all. I wondered if it was the work of the elusive Woodedge Woman's Club, perhaps some one hundred neofeminists strong, marching ten abreast down the center of Main Street in their tartan skirts and sensible shoes to plant a lousy wreath in front of an obscure memorial as part of their cryptic annual rites.

There was no particular reason why I was driving down Main Street on my way to the Carpenters' house, it was just something I had not had reason to do in a number of years and I felt the urge to see if anything had changed. Once Main rejoined the Post Road I turned right and followed that west to Rotten Row, a country lane with a name that supposedly had honorable English derivations.

Rotten Row led me south onto Highland Street, which is lined with horse farms; and then the horse farms ended and the wood thickened. I passed Whitehall Road leading to the old Patterson place and a half mile beyond that I turned off of Highland Street and entered Bulham Road. The number 6 was set into each of a pair of stone pillars that stood on either side of the entrance to a twisty driveway that ran uphill past a couple of hundred fruit trees. The drive ended by bending into an elipse at the Carpenters' front door.

Just outside the door a young cop whom I did not recognize was seated in a Woodedge police cruiser with the door open and his feet on the ground. He eyed my little Alfa Romeo suspiciously. He eyed me suspiciously as I got out. He eyed me as if he thought I might be the killer.

"Starbuck," I said, walking directly up to him and showing him my I.D. "D.A.'s office."

The young cop went from eyeing me suspiciously to eyeing my I.D. suspiciously. Nothing was going to escape his scrutiny.

I knew how to handle guys like this. "What's your name?" I demanded.

"Griffin," he said.

"What are you doing here?"

Surprised, Griffin said, "I'm with the chief." He pitched his head toward the house.

I grunted and simply walked in the front door without Officer Griffin asking me anything at all.

It was, of course, a very large house. It had three

stories, although the top story tapered with the roof. There was an attached three-car garage. There was a separate cottage off to one side, a grape arbor and a gazebo and a murky little fish pond. Everything was in place and everything was painted the same off-yellow color that probably had some fancy name like Mojave.

I guessed the main house had about fifteen rooms, but I didn't get a chance to count them because Chief Tuttle was sitting in the very first one I entered. Sitting with him was a well-tanned, slim fellow in a Ralph Lauren knit shirt, khaki slacks, and deck shoes with no socks. He was, in an aging and vaguely unappealing sort of way, quite handsome. I figured if he wasn't Wylie Carpenter, local golf hero, he should have been.

Chief Wembley Tuttle had gotten dressed for the occasion. He had on his full police uniform. His plastic brimmed hat lay next to him on the sofa, turned upside down. His stomach was launching the buttons of a jacket he probably had not worn since the last parade. On the table in front of him was an empty coffee cup. He looked both relieved and a little upset to see me.

"Patt," he said, without getting up. The chief was in his late fifties and on the home stretch. He knew the easy part of being chief of police in a small town and he knew the hard part. He had grown comfortable with the easy part.

Carpenter was leaning forward in his overstuffed chair. His knees were apart, his hands were together as he waited to be introduced.

I had to do it myself. "Patt Starbuck," I said. "D.A.'s office."

Tuttle realized then that he had missed his cue. He waved his plump hand in my direction. "Patt's the D.A.'s personal investigator," he said. "We don't usually have the pleasure of his company in a case this early. We don't usually have the D.A.'s investigators involved in our little town too much at all." He still did not give me the man's name.

"You're Wylie Carpenter?" I asked.

The man nodded.

"You have my condolences."

The man said thank you because he assumed I was talking about his wife.

Tuttle was still speaking. "They're usually spending all their time out in Waterford or Walmouth, that's where the real crimes are. Even Nestor, get some good crimes out there every once in a while. Not too often we get much around here except the occasional burglary. Not too often we get anything like this."

I stood in the center of the room and looked around. It was some sort of den, and while everything in it was reddish or brownish in color, I couldn't help but think it was all rather a mishmash. There was a small bar built into a set of bookshelves and there was an elaborate set of cabinets, which I suspected hid a large-screen television set.

Chief Tuttle stopped rambling and we exchanged looks with each other. I noticed he did not have any notepaper in front of him. He just had the coffee cup, and that told me he must have gone through all the preliminaries, all the niceties. I looked from him to Carpenter. "So who do you think did it?"

Carpenter's head snapped back. He turned to Chief Tuttle for help and Tuttle said, "That's what we're trying to find out, Patt."

"Uh-huh." I walked over to one wall and inspected the pictures I saw there. One was a signed Meyerowitz photograph of a Cape Cod scene. I had the same scene on my wall calendar. Next to it was a small, overly green oil painting of a golfer teeing off in front of a large gallery. Then there was a set of three antique hunting prints. As I said, things were a mishmash.

"This seems to be a man's room," I commented.

"We called it our sitting room," Carpenter said. "It was . . . it was both of ours. We tended to close it off when we were entertaining, I suppose."

I turned and saw that he was pointing to a pair of wood-paneled sliding doors. "Reason I'm asking, Mr. Carpenter, is I don't see much that reflects Mrs. Carpenter's personality in here. What was she like?"

Wylie Carpenter waved his hands. "She was kind," he said.

The chief was surreptitiously shaking his head at me.

I pressed on, even though Carpenter had now covered his eyes. "I'm more interested in her activities. Was she, for example, a golfer, like you?"

Carpenter shook his head. His hand stayed on his brow and moved as his head moved. "Not really. She played, but . . ."

"Yachting? Was she a yachter, Mr. Carpenter? Or a tennis player?"

"Tennis occasionally, when the weather was good. She swam, she skied—"

"In good shape, was she?"

Carpenter was giving me a list and he stayed with it. "—rode horses, danced."

"Where would she do all those things, Mr. Carpenter?"

He sniffed and dabbed at his eyes with the pads of his fingers. "Well, at the club, mostly, or with friends. It depends, I guess."

"What club are you talking about?"

"Bollingbrook. It's our country club. We've been members ever since we got married—or I have, at any rate. Becky's family have always been members."

"Mrs. Carpenter grew up around here?"

The chief spoke up. This was something he felt qualified to handle. "She's a Chesley, Patt."

"I see. They're well known, are they? The Chesleys?"

The chief bubbled over on the couch. If his breath had been spittle it would have dribbled down his chin.

"They go back to the *Mayflower*," said Carpenter; and even though I knew from my father's research that that was not quite true, I let it go by.

"What other clubs did she belong to? What did she do with her days? Did she work outside the home? Can you help me with any kind of information like that, Mr. Carpenter?"

"Oh, the usual," Carpenter said. "Junior League, League of Women Voters, Woodedge Historical Society, I suppose. But she wasn't really active in any of them except Bollingbrook. How did she spend her days? Oh, I don't know. The same things all women do, I suppose. Go out with friends, take care of the grounds—she was

very concerned about the grounds lately because she was
just breaking in a new caretaker—I don't know. We have
a place down the Cape in Osterville and another up at
Stratton Mountain, and there always seemed to be something that had to be done at one or the other. I don't
know, Mr. Starbuck. I don't know what she did."

Chief Tuttle sighed heavily.

"You mentioned Bollingbrook, Mr. Carpenter, but I
saw in the police report that you spent last night at
Stonegate Country Club. Did they have that right?"

Carpenter nodded. "Yes, I belong to both and I played
yesterday at Stonegate. I tend to do that, you see, if I
just have a golf game. It's a lot less formal than Bollingbrook. I had some snacks at the bar, a few drinks, and
then played cards with the fellows until about ten." He
smiled, or came close to it. "You wouldn't do that at
Bollingbrook."

The chief smiled with him. The chief had probably
never been to Bollingbrook in his life.

"You mentioned that when you got home you thought
your wife was with friends. Who were you thinking about?"

Carpenter had his thumb and his forefinger pinched
over the bridge of his nose. He answered with his eyes
closed. "Oh, Molly Barr, Hannah Babcock, Gretchen
Patterson."

"Males? Any male friends you're aware of?"

On the couch the chief started, doing untold damage to
the timing of my question.

Carpenter said, "Oh, their husbands, I suppose. Dickie
Barr, Dodge Patterson. Um, Jim Babcock."

"You've got a picture of your wife, do you?"

He made a half-point toward the chief, who got something out of the inside of his jacket and handed it to me.
It was a photograph of Rebecca Carpenter standing next
to a magnificent-looking horse. Rebecca's blond hair was
pulled back and her brown eyes were steady on the
camera. She was a good-looking woman, if you liked the
kind that stared right through you. I gave the picture
back.

"No children?"

He shook his head. "We wanted to, but . . .no. None."

I got out my notebook and took the names and addresses of the three couples he had mentioned. I asked about the help the Carpenters employed. He waved in the direction of the cottage I had noticed when I was coming into the house.

"We had a couple living there, Dominic and Gina, but we had to let them go. We caught her stealing our liquor." He snorted and wiped quickly at his nose. "Big deal, huh?"

"Last name?"

"Marconi. I don't know where they went, if that's what you're going to ask next."

"That's it for help?"

"We have a black gal who comes in Monday through Friday to do housekeeping. Sarah Mitchell. She's been with us for years."

"And you said there was a new caretaker?"

"Oh, that's right. What's his name? Doug Rasmussin, from Walmouth. He's been working here since the Marconis left. Becky took care of all the arrangements with him, so I never paid much attention."

Wylie Carpenter was covering his brow again and the chief was glowering at me when I switched to the subject of the missing pocketbook. "Any idea what was in it?" I asked.

"Near as we can figure, a few hundred dollars," the chief said.

"No jewelry missing?"

"None that Mr. Carpenter is aware of."

I nodded as though that was significant. I narrowed my eyes just to make the chief nervous and then I thanked the new widower and headed for the door with a promise that I would be in touch.

I was just starting my Alfa when the chief came bustling out after me. His white hair was blowing in the breeze and his chubby cheeks were red from the effort of running. I smiled up at him as he planted fingerprints all over the side of my car.

He made an effort to compose himself before he spoke. "Did Keough send you out here?"

"Of course."

"Did he think we couldn't handle it? Is that why?"

"He didn't say anything of the sort. He wants me handling a parallel investigation because he knows you're going to find the murderer and he wants to get a jump on trial preparation."

The chief made his last pant for air. He cleared his throat and tried to smooth his hair. "Yeah," he said, "well, if that's the way you're going to go about it we're going to be stepping all over each other's feet. The way you were talking to Mr. Carpenter in there, that may be okay for your common criminals out in Waterford or Walmouth, but it isn't right with people in this town. You gotta be more respectful." He put his hand on my shoulder. He gave me a fatherly smile. "Believe me," he said. "I know these people. They're different from you and me."

Inadvertently, I gunned my engine. Startled, the chief withdrew his hand. Nothing further was said as I let the car roll forward. Apparently I missed his toes.

4

Rebecca Carpenter's car had been towed to a garage known as Samuels, which the Woodedge police used for an impound center. There was precious little impounding that went on in Woodedge, and so the police simply contracted with Samuels to do both the towing and the storage. Samuels's tow trucks were painted yellow and had the AAA insignia all over them.

The Mercedes was silver in color and appeared to be in perfect condition. It looked thick and strong; as handsome and potentially dangerous as a sleeping lion. The police had secured it by isolating one corner of the garage with a yellow ribbon of tape.

Four cops were gathered in and around the car when I arrived. I saw little Lester, Woodedge's lone inspector, standing like a movie director with a clipboard and pen in his hand. I saw Browning, Woodedge's lone policewoman, perched in the front passenger seat, the focus of everyone's attention. The other two people were young men in uniform, neither of whom I recognized. One of the young men had a camera and stood outside the car. The other sat behind the steering wheel. Up close, all four people looked very excited by what they were doing. Their excitement was manifested by the quickness of their movements.

Browning, I saw, had a long scarf around her neck.

"Okay, lean over slowly, Tompkins," Lester called out in his rapid-fire, heavily accented voice; and the young uniform behind the wheel dutifully inclined toward Browning, who was positioned with her back between the door and her seat.

"Okay, hands on her shoulders."

Tompkins did as he was told. Lester yelled, "Okay, snap it, Morrison," and the flash of the camera held by the second uniform went off.

"You across that console? You can do it, Tommie? Okay, both hands on the bloody scarf. Okay, snap it, Mo. Now knot it, Tommie. One time, hup, that's it: over, round about, up, and through. That's it. Pull it now. That's it, lad. Not too tight. Snap it, Mo."

The flash went off on command. Lester noticed me and pretended he didn't. I moved behind him so I could get a good angle on the proceedings and stood with my arms folded.

"All right, Elizabeth, what are you doing now, you bloody cow?" Lester was from Zimbabwe (Rhodesia, he would tell you), by way of England; and because he was he could get away with a lot that nobody else would dare.

"I'm fighting," Browning shouted, and crooked both her arms at the elbow to pummel poor Tompkins.

"Not bloody well yet, you're not. Put your arms around him. Tommie's hand goes on your thigh. All in the name of the law now, children. That's it. Snap it, Mo."

The actors hung frozen, waiting for the next direction from their tyrannical director. I noticed what appeared to be a growing area of wetness under Browning's outstretched arm and suspected that of the four she least liked her role.

"Now, let's give this a think, shall we?" Lester said, moving up and resting his hand on the roof of the car. "The two of you are embracing. The bugger wants that pot of honey. He's moving his hand ever closer. Move it, Tommie. That's quite enough. You don't want him touching it, Elizabeth, so what do you do?"

Browning raised her fist as if to crush Tompkins' skull.

"No," cried Lester, slapping his clipboard against his leg. "You wiggle that bloody big arse of yours, that's what. You're struggling with him. But you wouldn't have come here in the first place, him driving your car, you over here in the passenger seat, if you didn't like him a little bit. So you're not going to bloody crown him, you're just going to try to keep him away."

Browning promptly pushed Tompkins to arms' length. Lester barked at Tompkins to get closer, and Tompkins, who was a big but rather lardy-looking lug, whose face would have resembled nothing so much as a marshmallow if it were not for the fact that it was transected by a mustache, leaned in until Browning quite clearly was straining to keep him away. Her position began to crumble and Lester ecstatically leaped out of camera range. "Snap it, Morrison, you bastard. Snap it."

The flash went off. Lester rushed forward to inspect his subjects and then jumped back again. "Now, go for the scarf, Tommie. What are you going to do, Elizabeth? Righto, now maybe you'd hit him. Where, now? On the side of the face. Snap it, Mo. But now he's tightening the scarf. And again, Mo. What are you going to do, Bessie? You push his shoulders. You rake his face. You punch him in the stomach. You're slipping down. Keep shooting, Mo. Keep leaning in, Tommie. Now you've got it. Where are your feet going? Kick them, Elizabeth. The bugger's trying to kill you, isn't he? Get the feet, Mo. Get 'em now, lad."

Finally, Elizabeth Browning screamed and everything came to a sudden halt. Tompkins sat up straight, a look of surprise on his simpleton's face. Officer Browning shoved open the door and emerged from the car coughing, hacking actually, her face and neck bright red as her fingers tore at the scarf on which Tompkins had been tugging. She was a good-sized woman, about five foot nine and 140 pounds, and she made quite a sight as she bent over and grabbed her knees and struggled for air. I noticed that the tops and toes of her shoes were covered with white chalk.

Lester nearly knocked her over in his effort to get to the car and stick his head in the well where her feet had been a moment before. "Balls!" he yelled.

He stood up angrily and glared at Morrison, the photographer. He did not pay the slightest attention to Browning, who was still bent over and was now gobbing drool onto the floor of the garage.

"Shoot it all," he ordered. "And see if you can get the

white marks and the green marks in the same bloody frame, will you?"

At last Lester turned to me. "Starbuck," he said as he patted his shirt pocket and went inside his rust-colored double-knit sport coat for a cigarette.

I stood with my arms folded and nodded at him.

"Figured somebody from your office would show up sooner or later. Didn't figure it would be you, though."

I let Lester have his moment of superiority. I knew what he made for a living. "What else do you figure?" I asked.

"I figure," Lester said, making me wait while he lit his cigarette, sucked on it, and waved it at the car, "that there's no bleeding way this woman got strangled in there."

Officer Browning dropped to her hands and knees. Her head was down close to the floor. By the change in the sounds she was making she seemed to be getting better.

I walked over to where Morrison was working and looked inside the car. I could see the white marks of Browning's shoes all over the dash and the console. I could see lines of phosphorescent green as well, but they were only on the underside of the dash. I said, calling back over my shoulder, "You see the body, Les?"

"What a godawful sight that was. Lips and ears purple. Tongue hanging out, white stuff all over her nose and mouth."

I asked if he saw any petechiae and Lester looked confused.

"Burst blood vessels. Little red spots?"

"Oh, that. All over the face. Eyeballs, too."

"Then what makes you think it wasn't strangulation?"

"Oh, it was strangulation all right. They took an X ray first thing and she had a broken bone right there in her neck." Lester checked his clipboard. He turned a page of notepaper. "The hyoid, I think it's called. What I'm saying, if you open your ears, Patt, is that she didn't get strangled in there." He thrust a pointing finger at the car.

Browning switched over to a seated position and was at last breathing close to normally. Lester stepped around her and came up to where he could jab with the eraser end of his pencil at the green marks. "If she was, she didn't put up much of a struggle. These things we've colored here are the only marks we've found."

Somehow, I wasn't that impressed with Lester's evidence. I looked over at Browning and said, "Elizabeth's a big woman. How big was Mrs. Carpenter?"

Lester put the cigarette between his lips so he could blow smoke while he talked. "Well, I haven't seen the autopsy and I didn't exactly get out my own tape measure, but I'd wager she was about five six, five seven." He, too, looked at Officer Browning. "About half the size of that one, I'd say."

We both looked at the green marks again, doing our silent approximations.

"The guy leans over," I said. "He's being amorous. He puts his hand under her skirt. She pushes him away. He grabs her scarf . . . and then what? Does he knot it?"

Lester shook his head. "It was a simple over-and-under. She probably did it herself when she put it on and he just grabbed the ends."

"Okay, can he do that?" I demonstrated what I imagined to be the maneuver. It called for me to spread my hands apart. "She could be whacking away at him. Tearing at his face. Was there any flesh under her nails?"

"I didn't see anything. Maybe the autopsy . . ." He shrugged and let the sentence dangle.

We continued to stare at the car. "So you think the murderer killed her someplace else and then put her in her own car and drove her out to lovers' lane and abandoned her there?"

Lester was silent. This was, after all, his investigation. It was up to him to write the report.

"That would mean that the killer then would have had to manipulate her legs after she was dead to make her feet put the marks on the dash."

Lester shrugged again. "It's possible."

I opened the back door on the passenger side and slid onto the seat. There was a moveable headrest on the top of the front seat where Mrs. Carpenter's body was found, but it still could have been possible to get around it.

Lester saw what I was considering and ordered Officer Browning back into action. Taking a deep breath, she stood up and replaced the scarf. Then she silently assumed the position.

I patted her shoulder and whispered thank you. She nodded without turning around.

"Place the knot exactly where you saw it, Les," I asked.

Lester didn't move. He glanced at where Browning had the knot, in the middle of her throat, and said, "It's there."

I reached forward and took one end of the scarf in each hand. Browning tensed, but I did little more than move my hands apart. I watched as her back arched and her feet pushed deep into the well beneath the dash. Lester saw what I saw and I dropped the ends of the scarf.

"It's just a thought, Les," I said, getting out. "I assume, before you started creating evidence of your own, you scoured both the front and back to see what the killer might have left behind."

Lester was still staring into the car. He kept staring even when I asked who was performing the autopsy.

"Dr. Havens is doing it at Filbert and Tweed mortuary."

"Let me know when you get the results, will you?"

I took his grunt as an assent and headed out to my own car. As I reached the door to the garage I looked back and saw that Lester had Tompkins in the rear seat and Morrison kneeling with his camera on the outside edge of the driver's seat. I suspected that poor Browning was in for another bad time of it.

5

I had an apartment in Boston. It wasn't the smartest thing to do, renting an apartment in Boston—paying big-city rates and commuting to and from work—but I liked the anonymity it provided me.

My building was on Commonwealth Avenue. It was a renovated mansion with a wood-paneled entranceway and none of my neighbors knew, or apparently cared, anything about me. We would nod when we bumped into each other. We would say such things as, "It's going to be tough driving today" when it snowed and "Looks like a beautiful day" when the sun shone. Like the single women in the building, I had my name posted on the mailbox, but not next to my doorbell, so it was quite possible that nobody other than the manager even knew who I was.

On days when, for one reason or another, I could not make the commute to Boston, I would stay at my mother's house in West Nestor. It was the house I grew up in, and in that neighborhood everyone knew me. The kids playing football in the streets would temporarily halt their game when my car approached and yell "Hi, Patt," when I passed by. If Mrs. Graham in the house next door to my mother's was sitting on her porch when I pulled into the driveway I would be obliged to go over and exchange a few meaningless sentences with her. I was always anxious to avoid seeing Mrs. Graham, and yet I almost always would go over to speak with her. While she was as sweet and kind as she could be, usually there was a slight note of desperation in her voice, a tacit admission that she knew I wanted to get on to someone or somewhere else. And so she would do her best to rapid-fire her questions or stories at me, and I, in turn, would answer or listen, mostly because of that note in her voice.

Mrs. Graham was not visible when I went to my mother's house on the evening of my first day's investigation into the Carpenter slaying, but Kelsey was. Kelsey was a friend of my mother's, although he was much younger than she. He was, indeed, closer to my age than to hers, and she was very sensitive about that. She did not want me to think they had any sort of relationship, and I went along with that because I told myself it was none of my business whether they did or not. Still, I remained uncertain as to what my mother and Kelsey managed to see in each other.

My mother had gotten married to my father when she was twenty years old. For their honeymoon they went to Boston and my mother took along her Brownie camera so that she could snap pictures of all the tall buildings. Even now, when she knows Boston intimately, she remembers that trip as a wondrous adventure. From what I can tell, there were few points of comparison during her twenty-year marriage.

Widowed at forty, she inherited a ten-thousand-dollar life insurance payment from her husband, the insurance salesman, and a sixteen-thousand-dollar mortgage. She set out to find work for the first time since my father had swept her away from the lunch counter in Gloucester and came home with a job as a sales clerk at Van Dyne's department store, the pride and joy of Walmouth's downtown shopping area.

She regarded working at Van Dyne's as a privilege, and someone there recognized that. She was made a floor walker and then promoted upstairs to the corporate offices. She was made assistant personnel manager and, eventually, personnel manager itself. All the while, she viewed this progression rather distrustfully, as though she was the mistaken recipient of someone else's good luck and soon would be skittering back to where she belonged— selling ties or cookware or handkerchiefs with initials on them.

This reluctance to accept her own accomplishments may account in part for Kelsey, who seemed to have none of the refinements, none of the ambitions, and of course none of the troubles of my father. Kelsey was head of shipping and receiving at my mother's store, and while that was no small position, it meant he worked in laborer's clothes and spent his days on the docks checking invoices and bills of lading and making sure trucks were loaded and unloaded correctly. Still, he seemed content with his job, content with my mother, and generally content with everyone and everything except me.

When I walked into the house and found him sitting alone at the kitchen table playing solitaire he grinned uncertainly at me as if he was afraid I had come to kick him out.

I said "Hi," as I went past him to the refrigerator.

"I've got beer in there," he said.

I nodded. I could see it and I knew it wasn't my mother's.

"If you'd like one."

I drew two bottles out and slid one over to him. He took it gratefully, as if I were the giver.

"Your mother's upstairs exercising. You want to sit here?" he said, half-rising from his seat.

It was a foolishly sincere gesture and I answered it simply by pulling out another chair and dropping into it. Very faintly I could hear the whir of my mother's stationary bicycle coming through the floorboards. She had taken what we used to call the spare bedroom and transformed it into her own gym. In addition to the bicycle she had a small Nautilus bench attached to various pulleys and weights and a big mat on the floor that she used when she worked out to a series of Jane Fonda tapes that she played on her VCR.

"She's getting real strong," Kelsey said.

I said that she was, even though I did not know that for a fact. Like her relationship with Kelsey, my mother's recent devotion to physical fitness was more a subject of denial than discussion between us. "Oh, I just fool around," she would tell me whenever I asked her about it.

"Tough day at the office?" Kelsey asked.

"Yeah."

"Yeah." He drank his beer. "What were you up to?"

"I was working on that Carpenter murder over in Woodedge."

Kelsey's pleasant face lit up. "Oh, yeah, I was reading about that. Boy, that must be kind of interesting, going around to all those big Woodedge houses asking questions."

I said, "I'd appreciate it if you don't mention it to my mother."

Kelsey looked surprised. Then he grunted. "Yeah, I guess she doesn't need to hear any more about that place if she can help it."

Kelsey grew up in Walmouth, where he developed a reputation as a fine baseball player. He made it into the minor leagues, got kicked around for a while, and then was sent back home, a washout in his chosen profession at the age of twenty-two. Some time after that Kelsey got involved in softball and became a legitimate star in the local leagues. Even now, in his middle forties, he still played regularly and well. That tended to put him in touch with a lot of people, and in my search for a subject of conversation I suddenly wondered if that couldn't be put to use.

"I'm told the caretaker of this lady's estate was a kid from Walmouth named Rasmussin. You wouldn't know him, would you?"

Kelsey rolled the name around in his mouth. He rolled his eyes around in his head. "There's a guy, used to play outfield for Balducci's, I think."

"Balducci's Tavern?"

"I think. I seem to remember that guy's name on the back of a uniform and the reason I remember it was we were razzing him, calling him Rasputin. 'Course, it could be his brother or something." Kelsey shrugged. He smiled. He wanted very much to be helpful, if only to keep us from having nothing else to say to one another.

He need not have worried. At that moment there was a footstep on the stairs and I turned. My mother came into the kitchen wearing a gray leotard that nearly matched the color of her hair. Beneath the leotard she was wearing a white body stocking. She had a towel around her neck and a sheen of perspiration on her forehead.

"Oh, hi, Patt," she said. "I didn't know you were here."

She touched me lightly on the shoulder as she went to the refrigerator and got out some kind of whipped drink she had cooling in a blender jar. "Kelsey just dropped by a few minutes ago."

I looked at Kelsey, who no doubt had been there since he got off work, and he nodded solemnly.

"Working out?" I asked.

"Naw," she said. "Just fooling around."

I nodded solemnly, just like Kelsey. The two of us sat there with our heads going up and down while my mother asked what I was working on.

"Nothing," I told her, and Kelsey and I bobbed our heads some more.

John Michael was delighted with my first day's progress. He liked especially my report of my visit to the home of Molly and Dickie Barr. Sitting in his overly large leather swivel chair, his ankle crossed over his knee, his fingers steepled, he practically had me act out the scene.

"Big house," I said. "Not an estate, like the Carpenters', but a big place on a corner lot, set on top of a knoll. White with green shutters, and the lawn just kind of rolls away from the front door, going down the hill to a thick stand of pines that separates the yard from their street."

"Dead end street?"

"Oh, but of course, monsieur. Leetle black maid in maid's clothes answers the door." I did a curtsy, even though the maid had not done one to me. "She says Mr. Barr isn't home, Mizz Barr can't be disturbed. I let her know that I'm the law and she goes scurrying off to disturb Mizz Barr just as I asked.

"A few minutes later Molly Barr comes toward me from the back of the house. She's got blond hair that must cost her a fortune to get colored and fluffed. She's got white sunglasses and what looks like a bathrobe and tennis shoes with half-socks that have little bobbins on them. The robe's tightened, but it's cut so you can see the tan on her neck and upper chest and it only comes about three-quarters of the way down her thighs.

"I'm standing there looking as studly as I can in my tweed sport coat and she greets me like I'm the plumber or something. 'Yessss?' I'm starting to explain to her about Rebecca Carpenter and then I realize she already knows. That's what the dark glasses are for. She's in mourning.

"The whole conversation takes place in the little entranceway. She says her husband heard about Becky on the radio on his way to work. Called her on the car phone. She hasn't known what to do since. She's not asking me or anything. I mean, I'm only the professional investigator, who you would think has dealt with this situation before.

"I ask her how long she's known Mrs. Carpenter and she tells me they went to school together at Wheaton."

"Where?"

"Rich girls' school. I just asked how come they both ended up living in Woodedge. The sunglasses go down. She peers at me over the top. 'Becky was a Chesley,' she says."

"What's a Chesley?" asked the man who would be the congressman for Woodedge, who was already the elected district attorney for that town.

I explained that they were a leading family.

"How about the Barrs? They a leading family too?"

I said that I believed they were. I said that Becky grew up with Dickie Barr and Becky introduced Molly to Dickie while Molly was working in Boston after college.

"How nice. Becky and Dickie and Molly. And the Carpenters, they a leading family, too?"

I shook my head. "Wylie S. was a trust officer at Boston Union, where Becky had her trust fund. That's how they met. He grew up in western Mass and went to Bowdoin."

"Bowdoin?"

I threw up my hands. "Hey, that's the way these people identify each other. I ask Molly Barr to tell me about

Wylie and she tells me where he went to school twenty-five or so years ago."

"He's not still with Boston Union, is he?"

"Resigned while he was going out with Becky. Took a job with First Yankee and eventually became an investment banker. Quit that some years ago and became one of the directors of Woodedge Savings and Loan. Molly was vague as to times and details, and when I was pressing her—this was the fun part. She's in mourning, right? Got the sunglasses, the little ball of tissue pressed to her nose, the catch in her voice. This is the scene when all of a sudden Mr. Tall-Dark-and-Handsome appears at the end of the hallway coming from the back of the house. Not only is he dressed in full tennis whites, but he's got a goddamn Prince racket in his hand. 'Molly,' he calls out. 'Are you coming back? There's only twenty minutes left before I have to go to my next appointment.' "

A smile crept over John Michael's face. These Woodedgians were turning out just as he suspected.

"She says, 'I'll only be a minute, Cliff,' and turns back to me. But for all intents and purposes the interview's over. Old Cliff is standing there swatting the palm of his hand with the edge of his racket, and she's in effect told me to wrap this thing up."

"So what did you do?"

"So I did. I asked her one more question. I asked her how long the Carpenters have lived on the estate. 'Oh, that,' she says. 'That's Becky's family home. She grew up there, and then when her mother died about four years ago she and Wylie moved in.' "

John Michael leaned forward in his chair. He carefully placed his elbow on his desk and waved a finger back and forth at me. "So when she dies the estate goes to him, the man who was in charge of her trust and who has had no ownership in anything up to now."

I raised my shoulders and held them for a count or two before dropping them. It was always best to let John Michael think he was figuring things out for himself.

"I think we've got our suspect," he said.

6

Jessica Keough had her own ideas about how I should conduct her husband's investigation. They were conveyed to me at a hastily convened cocktail meeting at the Keoughs' house on the evening of my second day's effort. I got the order to appear when I called in to the office switchboard late in the afternoon.

Given the hour of my notice and the fact that dinner was not included in the invitation, I made no effort to get a date; and when I arrived at the Keoughs' I could see the disappointment in Patty Hansen's eyes. Already she was halfway through a tall glass of amber-colored liquid.

Her husband was there in his suit, swirling some sort of highball, but John Michael had changed from his office clothes into jeans and a short-sleeved shirt. He was seated in the middle of a huge couch, with his ankle crossed over his knee just as it had been when I reported to him that morning.

"Good news," was Jessica's greeting when she opened the front door for me. "Autopsy report is in. Point one eight blood alcohol and enough Valium to sedate a horse."

She was very serious about her good news and so I was very serious about receiving it. In the living room, however, both John Michael and Royster were grinning, so I grinned back at them.

"Don't you just love it?" John Michael asked.

I nodded enthusiastically.

"Fix him a drink, will you, honey? What do you want, Patt? Beer? I got some Beck's on ice for you." John Michael rolled onto his hip and began addressing me with both hands in motion. "Can't you just see it? He loads her up on Valium and liquor, piles her into the car when she barely knows what she's doing, drives her out to the overlook, throttles her when she can barely resist, and then sneaks away on foot so that it looks like anybody but him did it."

I wondered which of the three of them had put this together. The theatrics quite obviously were John Michael's, but big Royster was standing there with a self-satisfied look on his face as if he had done something well and was trying to be modest about it. Jessica's degree of gravity showed more than a touch of smugness. Only Patty Hansen showed no proprietary interest in the theory that had just been put forward. Her chestnut-colored hair hung straight and limp as her dark eyes stared transfixedly into her glass.

I took a cold green bottle and a drinking mug from Jessica and stood with what was left of my grin. "Why anybody but him?" I asked.

Jessica sat down next to her husband. Instinctively he put his arm around her. "The only person you would not expect a married woman to go with to a lovers' lane would be her husband," she explained. "No need to."

I poured the beer and everybody waited, knowing that my failure to say "Oh, yeah," meant that I was going to be trouble. "What's the story on clothing fibers?" I asked. "Were there any?"

Royster spoke up. Like Patty and me, he was standing. "A few. They're still being checked out."

"And fingerprints, they provide any help?"

"Wiped clean on the steering wheel, shift, and hand brake, but in other places they found some latents of hers and a couple of his."

"And those were to be expected, weren't they?"

Nobody answered. John Michael was no longer grinning.

I said, "Stanley Lester told me he thought she wasn't killed in the car. That maybe she was put there after she was dead and then had her feet manipulated by the killer."

"That's not what he put in his report," snapped John Michael. "He put in his report that he thought she was strangled from behind, by somebody in the back seat."

He snorted and withdrew his arm from its resting spot on the back of the couch. "The idiot. He thinks, what?, she's sitting snockered by herself in the front passenger's seat of her own car and the killer gets in the back to do her in? Does that make sense to you?"

I agreed it sounded preposterous.

Everybody except Patty grumbled for a few moments.

"Unless maybe there was more than one person," I offered.

John Michael's eyes flicked like a pair of headlights turning on high beam. "A guy in front and another in back?"

"It would be one way to commit a robbery. The police report noted her pocketbook was missing."

"Her husband could have thrown it out," Royster said quickly. He demonstrated what he meant, by flinging his arm to one side, and when he did his drink spilled on the front of Patty's dress.

It was, I felt certain, not a dress Patty Hansen was wearing when she got the call to muster at the Keoughs' for cocktails. It was black with a burnt umber print and a roll collar, and it looked new. The liquid from Royster's glass had gone almost entirely on her right breast and as she stared down at the wet spot it seemed she was on the verge of tears. Although Royster said "Sorry," he did nothing other than wave his free hand ineffectually in front of her, as though he wished to rub the spot dry but dared not.

We were all staring at Patty's right breast and somebody should have said something to make light of the moment, but nobody did. We were discussing important things, and her wet breast was merely a distraction to the discussion.

"If Carpenter was going to fake a robbery, he would have at least covered that detail," said John Michael, still staring.

Patty looked about helplessly.

"There's some club soda on the table," Jessica said, pointing to where she had set up a little bar. "Use a towel from the guest bath." She pointed toward the opposite end of the house, where there was a half-bath in an alcove beneath the stairs leading to the second floor. She made no other move to help, and Patty went wandering off in the direction indicated.

"Well, which is it?" I said. "Was Carpenter faking a robbery or a lovers' tryst?"

"It doesn't make any difference," said Royster, as though he really wanted me to understand and thought I was being just a bit too obtuse. "See, that's the beauty of it. Maybe the cops go looking for some punks who jumped her while she was getting into her car somewhere, or maybe they go looking for a suitor or somebody who was obsessed with her. Either way, they're not going to be looking at him."

I finished my beer in a swallow that was too large for mixed company. I had to wipe my mouth with my fingers. "What time did the medical examiner say she died?"

"Can't tell exactly, but based on the rectal temperature he took around one A.M. he thinks she was dead between nine and ten."

"Anybody know where she was supposed to be at that time?"

Royster Hansen struck quickly. "That's what you're supposed to be telling us."

I gave an expansive shrug and headed for where the beers were kept. Hansen would zing me whenever he could and I had to be careful not to react to it. "Nobody I've talked to seems to know," I called back over my shoulder.

"That's because she was at home," Jessica pronounced, and I felt a little twinge in my chest.

I snapped the top of a fresh Beck's and poured myself a second glass. "I talked to the maid today," I said casually. "Housekeeper, I guess she's called. Said she left at six. Made a light dinner for Mrs. Carpenter to eat alone. Said nobody was expected to visit and she knew of no plans to go out."

"So we know she was alive at six—" Hansen started.

"You knew that already from the medical examiner."

"—and alone," he concluded with exasperation.

I smiled at him. "Maid says Mrs. Carpenter was alone at six in the house. Husband—realizing he's a possible suspect and all—says he goes home at ten and she's not there. He's not even alibiing after that."

"So what we need to find out," snapped Royster, "is what she was doing between six and ten."

It was my turn to pay Royster back. "And what you're thinking, Roy, is that if she wasn't doing anything at all, then that means her husband must have killed her. Is that it?" We were playing subtle games here, getting our digs in before the boss, but my question was enough to make Royster blush.

It was the district attorney himself who spoke next, and it was me to whom he spoke. "Hey, we're not putting on the trial here, you know. We're trying to ascertain which way we go with this investigation. If Wylie Carpenter didn't do it, he didn't do it. But until we figure that out for certain let's use our brains and our experience to try to anticipate what we can. We're working on suspicion here, and suspicion doesn't require any due process that I'm aware of."

Now I was embarrassed, and because I was embarrassed I imagined how John Michael would look with that quote on his campaign posters: SUSPICION DOESN'T REQUIRE ANY DUE PROCESS.

Jessica tried to resolve things. "What we really need is to find out what Wylie was doing between six and ten."

"That much I can tell you," I said. "The starter at Stonegate confirmed that Wylie came in from the course at about six. Guy said Carpenter played eighteen with three people named Whitman, Teasdale, and Patterson. Checked in his golf cart just before dark."

Royster smiled his most vicious smile. "Sergeant Roselli talked with the bartender in the clubhouse this morning and already got that information. The bartender said Teasdale, Carpenter, Whitman, and Patterson came in. They bought some drinks, some sandwiches, and they spent the evening playing gin. Them and a guy named Butcher. People were coming and going all night, but the bartender remembered Carpenter and his buddies being there when he closed up at ten."

"So Carpenter's covered until then," said John Michael disappointedly. "Plus whatever time it would have taken him to get home."

"Not exactly," I said.

"Why?" asked John Michael.

"Because I located Mr. Butcher and interviewed him about three hours ago. He swears he left the clubhouse before eight. Even told me about the show he watched on television at nine."

I tried not to look at Royster. I tried not to look as though I had just kicked ass in the points-with-your-boss department.

"So the bartender can't be relied upon," said Jessica, summing things up nicely.

"This Patterson, is he the same one who's married to one of Rebecca Carpenter's friends?" asked John Michael, surprising me as he sometimes did with his excellent memory for details.

"D. Dodge Patterson, yes."

"Have you interviewed him yet?"

"No."

Royster charged back into the fray. "Then I'd say he's your next step."

"My next step," I said, "is to go to the bathroom."

It had been a long time since Patty Hansen had gone off and, frankly, I had forgotten she was even in the house. I remembered only when I got to the bathroom and saw it was closed. I stood outside the door for a minute or two waiting for it to open and when I started to get uncomfortable I knocked and called her name. There was no answer, so I tried the door and it opened. There was no one inside.

I shut the door behind me and went to the toilet and lifted the seat. I was thinking petty thoughts while I urinated into the bowl. I was wondering why the district attorney of Exeter County had flocked pink and white striped wallpaper in his guest bathroom. I was imagining pissing on Royster Hansen's head.

Suddenly the door opened again and a woman's voice said softly, "Patty?"

I turned. Half-turned.

Jessica Keough's head and shoulders were inside the

room. She was looking directly at me and she was not looking at my face.

I turned back, thinking she would excuse herself, thinking she would close the door. She did both, but she stepped inside before she did either one.

I cut off in midstream, but I was still standing there holding myself. "Jessica," I said. "I'm not done."

"Never mind that. We have to talk."

I shook, dressed, and hit the flusher. As I moved to the sink I could see Jessica in the mirror. She was standing with her arms behind her waist and her shoulders against the door. "About what?" I asked.

"About what we need to do."

I wasn't sure what she meant. She seemed a little breathless. I nodded and continued to watch her in the mirror while I spent an unnecessarily long time washing my hands.

"John told me he wanted me to get the dirt."

"That's good," she said, and this time I was sure she was breathless.

I wondered if she knew that the way she was standing emphasized the fullness of her breasts, and decided that she did. I shut the water and turned for a hand towel from the rack on the wall next to where she was standing. Our eyes met. "Anything else?" I said.

She hesitated and then changed her position. The floor space in the bathroom was small, no more than seven feet from the door to the far wall, where the room's only window was located. Part of the ceiling sloped because the stairs leading to the second floor ran directly above our heads. With the sink and the toilet and the green leafy plants that Jessica had hanging from the ceiling, there was not much room for the two of us to maneuver.

"I think you ought to go back to Wylie Carpenter's hometown. I think you ought to trace his life as much as you can. Up to Maine, down to Boston, out to Woodedge. I think you're going to find this man is the ultimate golddigger. I think you're going to find he's spent years plotting to get his hands on the Chesley fortune."

"You knew Rebecca Carpenter was a Chesley?" I said, taken aback.

"You mentioned it to John and John asked Chief Tuttle about them. He said the Chesleys were the oldest and richest family in town and she was the last of them. You see, it's a natural. And that's what's going to give us the hook we need to get some national attention. The richer she is, the longer and more intricately he plotted to get her money, the more fascinating everyone will think the case is."

"You're forgetting a couple of things."

Jessica looked as though she didn't believe me.

"He already had access to her money. He was living on her estate, working a couple-of-hours-a-week job, playing golf all the time—this guy had everything he could possibly need already."

"What he had was another woman."

For the second time that evening I felt a twinge in my chest because I thought Jessica knew something I didn't. "How do you know?" I asked cautiously.

"Because that's the way it always is in these situations. Look at all the great rich-wife murders in this country. It's always the social-climbing husband who kills his wife so he can get her money and marry some young beautiful woman."

"Rebecca Carpenter wasn't exactly a dog, you know, and she was only forty."

"Look," Jessica said a trifle impatiently, "I guarantee you that if the other woman's not more beautiful she's at least a whole lot younger than forty."

I tried to imagine what had made Jessica so cynical. She herself was only in her mid-thirties. She had been married to John Michael for ten years and had no reason of which I was aware to doubt his fidelity. Yet here she was, nodding at me with total conviction as she explained the rotten core of man's nature. Men cheat, she was saying. Men take what they can get and it is best to understand that and live with it and attempt to use it to your own advantage, because that's the way it is.

A knock broke against the door and both of us, each about to say something, froze.

"Honey?" a husky voice called softly, and by process of elimination I knew it had to be Royster.

"It's me," Jessica called back sharply, loudly. "I'll be out in a minute or two, Roy."

"Oh," he said, and I suppose we expected him to take that news and go away. But he didn't. "I'll wait."

"Use the bathroom upstairs, Roy," she told him, her eyes a little wide and fixed on mine.

"No, no, that's fine. Take your time. I wanted to speak to you anyway, Jess."

This tiny bathroom seemed to bring out the words in people. Both Jessica and I looked at the window. I had to get close to her to ask about it. I had to put my mouth next to her ear. My body touched hers and she rested her hand softly on my arm as she strained to hear what I was saying.

"Where does it go?"

"To the side yard."

"I'll do it."

Jessica hit the flush and I pushed upward on the opaque glass. It did not move as far as I would have liked, but I stood on the toilet seat cover and put my head and arms through the opening as best I could. It did not work.

Panic was now coursing through me, panic that far outstripped the situation. It wasn't my fault Jessica had come into the bathroom while I was using it. If her intention was innocent we both should have been able to walk out together with a smile and an explanation. But now she had spoken as though she were alone. Now she had flushed the toilet. I thrust my right arm and right shoulder outside. Jessica hit the water faucet and turned it on full. I got my head through and wiggled. I had my left shoulder and my left arm far enough along so that I was more out than in. My feet had to leave the toilet seat and Jessica, reacting quickly, grabbed my legs to keep them from banging against the wall. She held them, lifted them, guided them, and clipped them of one shoe as I went headfirst, straight down the outside wall.

I landed in the grass with my hands out in front of me and did a forward roll onto my back. A moment later my shoe came flying out and landed on the turf next to me. The window slid softly shut and the light I was getting was cut by at least half.

I lay in the darkness, trying to catch my breath, trying to feel for my shoe, and only gradually realizing that something else was wrong. Slowly I sat up and squinted around until I saw what it was.

Patty Hansen was standing in the shadows of the hedges that marked the property line between the Keoughs and their neighbors. We stared at each other in silence as I continued to pat the ground blindly for my shoe. We could have, perhaps, exchanged greetings, but there were questions neither one of us wanted to have to answer. When my hand at last touched my shoe I looked down to secure it, to put it on my foot. When I looked up again she was gone.

7

The funeral for Rebecca Carpenter was held on a Friday morning. Her casket was closed and the service was private. I stood in the street across from St. Mark's Episcopal, wearing a blue blazer because it was the closest thing I had to black, and watched the people arrive. There were nowhere near as many as I would have expected for the services of the last survivor of the leading family in Woodedge history, and in that small a crowd it was hard for me to look inconspicuous. But I, at least, was trying—which is more than can be said for Stanley Lester of the Woodedge Police Department.

Lester was wearing a sport coat that was a vicious shade of lime green. It would have been appropriate to wear on Arbor Day in the New Hampshire woods, but Lester acted as though it was the perfect disguise as he stood at the base of the steps to St. Mark's and gave everyone a thorough beady-eyed going over. The purpose of this exercise was not readily apparent to me, and it was made even less so when I happened to observe an unmarked Woodedge police vehicle on my side of the street containing one un-uniformed Officer Morrison with a video camera and a long-range lens.

Seeing the police in action made me feel silly. It had been my intention to watch for single men between twenty and fifty years of age, to look for anyone who appeared to be out of step with the rest of the crowd, to try to identify what I could about those who were invited to the ceremony. But I determined relatively quickly to abandon the field to Lester.

By the time the last of the invitees arrived I had

already slipped away to Brigham's to buy an ice cream. Mocha almond fudge with jimmies. I took off my blazer to eat it and waited for the mourners to head for their homes.

Rebecca Carpenter's friend Hannah Babcock was blond and chubby. Her eyes were very blue, her face was very round, she smoked long cigarettes, and seemed to have more than a passing acquaintance with demon gin. She and her husband and their two children lived in a brand-new house in an area that had been nothing but woods the last time I had seen it. The house had a brick front and a bay window that gave it a middle-class air, but inside it proved to be expensively appointed and much larger than it appeared from the street.

She greeted me at the door in a distinctly unsorrowful orange blouse and a pair of fresh white cotton slacks that would have looked much better on a smaller woman. She acted annoyed, even angry, that I had come to ask her questions on the afternoon of Rebecca's funeral, but I was polite and I had the force of law printed on my card and so we spoke across the threshhold until gradually she relented and invited me to come in and sit in the sun room.

It was a beautiful room, beautifully planned. It was built onto the rear of the house and was almost entirely glass-enclosed. It faced a back yard of lush green grass manicured to a long but uniform height and surrounded on three sides by a crescent garden of hardy flowers. Beyond the crescent were the lucky survivors of a grove of ancient oaks that had been cut back far enough to minimize the amount of leaves that would blow onto the lawn.

As I glanced around the sun room my eye fell on a plate containing a fork and the remains of a very large slice of multilayered cake. Hannah Babcock saw me see the cake and said, "Oh, I eat when I get depressed." Then, to be polite, she added, "Would you like some?"

She was obviously surprised when I said yes, but after fluttering for a second or two she went and got me a piece that was nearly as large as her own. She directed

me to a white wicker chair and she herself moved to a
chaise longue. We ate in silence except for the click of
our forks against the china. When she was done she put
her plate on the floor and lit a cigarette, inhaling deeply
as if she had just undergone a long sexual workout. Even
though I was not done I put my plate on the floor as well.
The experience of shared confection seemed to relax her
and I chose to wait to see what she was going to say
before I resumed my questioning.

"Do you cook?" she asked.

"No."

"But you like to eat."

"I like good food."

"Me, too. That's my problem."

I didn't say anything.

"How do you stay in shape?"

"I work out."

"Where?"

"At a fitness club, near where I work."

"You use weights, that sort of thing?"

"Nautilus, mostly."

She took another long drag on her cigarette. She was
not looking at me. "Why do you do it?"

I could have told her my job required it. I could have
said something zenlike, told her it made me feel better
about myself. Instead, I said, "Because it makes me
more attractive to women."

This particular woman, only hours from the funeral of
her friend, wearing orange and white and binging on
cake, looked at me appraisingly. "Chesley would have
liked you," she said.

"Why?"

"She liked men who take care of themselves."

"Her husband's an athlete."

"Maybe that was the attraction."

"You weren't sure what it was?"

Hannah Babcock shrugged as though she begrudged
the effort.

"You don't like Wylie." There was no inflection in my
voice, no question mark at the end of my sentence.

"Wylie is"—she waved her cigarette around—"different."

"What I had heard, I thought you were old friends—you and your husband, Wylie and Rebecca."

"Chesley and I were old friends. She was my best friend when we were little tiny girls in ruffled dresses. Our parents were best friends and so we were, too. We grew up together, like cousins."

"Can I ask you a very sensitive question, then? One that I could only ask someone who knew her as well as you did?"

Hannah rested her head on top of the longue's back cushion and fixed her eyes on the ceiling.

"Would you say," I hesitated, waiting until she looked down at me, "that she was a happy person?"

"Chesley?" Hannah Babcock's eyes opened wide. For a moment I thought she was going to tell me that Rebecca Chesley Carpenter was the happiest woman who ever lived. But then she tilted her head back once again and said, "Ches was not really what you would call the happy sort. I mean, that's not the way you would describe her."

"Was she always that way?"

"Oh, who knows when you're little kids? There was always something planned for us back then, always so much going on that you didn't have time to figure out if you were unhappy or not. I mean, Ches and I went to summer camp together in Switzerland, we went to Rosemary Hall together, we did show riding, our parents took us skiing and sailing. You know how it is."

I nodded. "Sure."

"She seemed to me to be happy enough back then."

"So what happened?"

Hannah stubbed out her cigarette even though there was still an inch of tobacco above the filter. It was a very long cigarette. "I don't know," she said. "Maybe she ran out of things to do."

I nodded again. "What about in the past few months? Would you say she was more happy, less happy, or about the same happy?"

Hannah Babcock answered promptly, without smiling. "About the same happy."

"And her husband, would you say the same about him?"

"Of course."

"Why 'of course'?"

"Because," she said indignantly. She shifted her heft. "Because why shouldn't he be?"

The white wicker chair in which I was sitting almost required me to rest my arms on its arms. I sat forward and clasped my hands down low between my calves. "You have no reason to believe they were having marital problems?"

Hannah flipped her hand. "Not really."

"Then"—I sat back, slumped back, as though I had to think this problem through—"can you think of any reason why Rebecca would have been where she was on the night she was killed?"

"There could have been any number of reasons."

I responded appreciatively. "Really?" I said. "Can you tell me one?"

Hannah Babcock swung her feet around to the floor and flattened both her hands on the cushion beneath her oversized buttocks. "Look, I know what you're getting at. Chesley was an attractive woman and I'm sure she was perfectly capable of having affairs, but she would hardly need to have one in the front seat of her car, now would she?"

"Was she having any affairs that you knew of?"

"No." The answer was emphatic.

"Was Wylie?"

"Wylie? Wylie has an affair with his golf clubs." She said it as though she had come to grips with human perversity in its purest form.

"Is that what you don't like about him?"

"I didn't say I didn't like him. I said he was different and, yes, that's part of the reason why he's different. If Ches wanted to have an affair she could have had it right in her house because the chances are nine out of ten that Wylie would have been off at one of his silly country clubs."

We were staring at each other now. All my various efforts to be charming, convivial, honest, and inoffensive had come down to this. "Can you think of any reason why Wylie would want his wife dead?"

Hannah Babcock did not so much as blink. "Not a single one," she said. "He had it made."

Gerard Whitman also could not think of a reason why Wylie Carpenter would want his wife dead; although I did not put the question to him in quite the same way as I had to Mrs. Babcock.

"Hell of a guy," said Gerard from behind the big desk that he used to run the Whitman Orthopedic Supply Company. "On his worst day he's a scratch golfer. He could make money on the seniors tour, not a doubt in my mind about it. I'm out there twice a week, three times if I can get away, and I can't come within ten strokes of him. That's what he's giving me now, ten. And I still can't beat him." Whitman shook his head sadly.

"Usually play for money, do you?"

Whitman grinned a bit. He held out his freckled hand and tilted it one way and then the other. He recognized me as a sporting kind of guy, but he wasn't sure how far the long arm of the law extended.

"Other than that, did you ever get involved in any financial transactions with Wylie Carpenter?"

"Wish I had," said the man whose wholly owned company had a forty-eight-state map on the wall in its main lobby showing distributors in 112 locations. "Wylie's a financial genius."

I smiled indulgently. "How do you know that?"

Whitman raised the stakes on indulgent smiles. "Let's just say that if Wylie Carpenter had been doing for Whitman Orthopedics what he was doing for First Yankee Bank and Trust at the time they were putting together the financing for Quincy Market, there'd be a statue of yours truly right behind Faneuil Hall at this moment."

I made sounds designed to indicate that I knew what Whitman meant. Then I asked him, "If he was so successful at First Yankee, why did he leave?"

"Exactly because he was so successful. He had made his mark and he didn't feel the need to go any further. So he bought into that little S and L of his and went home to do what he wanted."

"Play golf, you mean."

Whitman shrugged. Then he drew himself up straighter in his chair and looked at me sincerely. "I hate to think what this is going to do to his game."

I agreed that it was a tragedy.

"Nice girl," he said. "His wife. Lovely funeral service."

"Did he say anything about her during your golf game that day? Anything about having to be home at a certain time?"

"No," said Whitman, pushing out his chin and scratching it with one delicate finger. "He didn't say anything like that before he left."

"Left? You mean he left before you did?"

"Oh, sure. The only one still there when I left was Dodge."

"What time did he go? Wylie, I mean."

"Can't tell you that because I wasn't playing him. Gin rummy, you know. You go one on one. It's where we duffers get Wylie back. He always loses, always goes out early." Whitman chuckled. "Let me see, there was me, him, Dodge, Ben Butcher, and Bud Teasdale—five of us. So we played round robin. Started off I played Dodge and Wylie played Ben . . . Is that right? Yes, because then Ben and I played winners while Wylie played Bud. Then Bud and I played and then Dodge came back and challenged the pot." He chuckled harder, wanting me to ask who won.

Instead, I asked, "And you don't remember Wylie being there after the second game?"

"Well, I don't, but that doesn't mean he wasn't."

"Bartender seemed to think he was there at closing."

"He'd know, I guess. Unless he got Wylie mixed up with Dodge—who was staying around to drown his sorrows." The chuckling this time was accompanied by an eyebrow raised in anticipation of my congratulations.

"Why would he do that? Mix them up, I mean?"

"Well . . ." Whitman paused. "They were both wearing club sweaters, as I recall. White V-neck jobs with the club emblem on the breast. But, look," he let his face soften a bit to show me that he meant no harm. "Obviously you can't expect the bartender to be the brightest kid in the world."

"Obviously," I said, and this time Whitman and I chuckled together. It seemed a small price to pay.

There was no reason for my mother to expect me on a Friday night. She knew that Friday nights usually meant office meetings with John Michael and Jessica and Royster. But John Michael wasn't going to be around this Friday evening and it was nearly dinner time when I got out of Whitman's office and I thought my mother might have something on the stove.

The house, however, was dark when I got there. I only stopped because Mrs. Graham saw my car and waved me down. I only went in because it was a way to escape from Mrs. Graham. I went over and chatted first, of course, just to be polite.

"Have a date tonight, Patt?" she asked, leaning forward in her chair so that she could talk to me over the porch rail.

"Yes, I do, Mrs. Graham," I fibbed. "Just coming by to grab a bite to eat and then I'm off."

"Anybody special, Patt?"

"Not really. Just someone I met."

"Big strapping boy like you, I can't believe you haven't stolen someone's heart yet."

I sighed. This was a little ritual I had to go through with Mrs. Graham, who had a tendency to forget past conversations.

"Still," she said, nodding in consolation, "at least you've got a job. That's something."

She gestured toward Charlie Curren's house, catty-cornered from her own. "I guess young Charlie's still having a hard time of it."

"Young Charlie" was nearly my age. To the best of my knowledge, the one and only job he had ever had was boosting cars for an outfit that stripped them down in Providence. He had gotten caught once and I had put in a good word for him with the arresting officers. I owed him that much. He was home a lot during the day and he was always willing to do lawn mowing and minor maintenance for my mother and Mrs. Graham.

"And that little Sharon down the street, she's pregnant again, by the looks of her."

I knew the girl Mrs. Graham was talking about. I remembered when she herself was born. Her mother had been a schoolmate of mine and had introduced Danny Spinelli and me to the joys of manual sex in the woods behind the junior high. Later, she had married a kid from the trade school and moved into my neighborhood. I always waved when I saw her, but we never spoke. I always looked at her hand when she waved back.

"Is Sharon married this time?" I asked; and Mrs. Graham said she wasn't sure.

"I sit here sometimes, Patt, and everything just blurs together. I've been in this house now forty-nine years and I've seen so many young people come and go, I get them all mixed up. Was it Sharon that used to play that rope game in the street, or was she the one that had all the boys who used to leave their car radios on?" Mrs. Graham's voice trailed off. "I don't know."

I murmured a meaningless response because I knew that Sharon was both but I did not want to get into a discussion about it.

"I remember your father, though, Patt. Always such a serious look on his face. You're a lot like him, you know."

"I'm really not, Mrs. Graham," I said. "I'm really not serious at all."

"I'm still blessed with good eyes," she said. "I think it comes from not reading."

"I guess I'm going to have to go now, Mrs. Graham."

"I used to see him come and go. Always as if the weight of the world was on his shoulders. That wasn't good, you know. That's what caused him to do what he did."

I was turning, I was trying to say good-bye.

"This one she's got now," Mrs. Graham said, pointing

to the house, "he's better for her. They get along just fine."

"Yes, Mrs. Graham. Well, I have to go in there now. Lots of things I have to do."

"That's good, Patt. A young man like you should have lots of things to do."

I hurried across the lawn before she could think of something else to tell me. I went up the stairs and through the door as quickly as I could get it unlocked. Then I went straight to the kitchen and drew one of Kelsey's beers from the refrigerator. I unscrewed the cap and stood drinking from the bottle in the middle of the kitchen floor.

Aside from the beer, there was no sign of my mother's friend; but from up on the second floor came the sounds of movement and I assumed they were coming from my mother's exercise room. I assumed they were the sounds of her Nautilus machine. I finished the beer about the time they stopped and went up to say hello.

The second-floor hallway was relatively small. At one end was a door leading to the attic stairs. Then there was my room, then the little gym, and then my mother's room at the opposite end from the attic door. The bathroom was at my mother's end of the hall, directly across from the gym.

As I reached the top of the stairs I started to turn in that direction just as the door to my mother's room opened. Kelsey walked out, shirtless and fumbling with his belt. I was too stunned to move and Kelsey did not even notice me until he was into his second step. He froze without completing it. Behind him the door was semi-closed, the room was dark.

What I wanted more than anything else that moment was to disappear, to slip silently down the stairs and out of the house without my mother ever knowing I was there. I even had my index finger halfway raised to my lips, but apparently Kelsey didn't see it because he was not quiet about my exit. He was not quiet at all.

"Hey, Patt," he said, and already I was heading back down the stairs. My cover blown, I was trying to get out of there as quickly as I could.

I was taking the steps two and three at a time and Kelsey was still calling after me. "Patt, I found out about that Rasmussin guy."

I had the door open and Kelsey was calling louder. "A kid on his team told me he took off for California the other day. He's not around anymore."

By the time Kelsey got out those last words, I wasn't around anymore either. I could hear his voice, I could hear Mrs. Graham calling good-bye to me, I could hear one of the neighborhood kids saying "Hi, Patt," and I was flat out running for my car.

8

My father was arrested in Woodedge once. Wembley Tuttle was on the police force then, although he was not yet chief, and since he never mentioned the incident I assumed he either had forgotten about it or did not associate me with the wild man named Starbuck who had broken into the Patterson family home on Whitehall Road. I also assumed he did not associate me with the stunned little boy who had watched four squad cars of Woodedge policemen surround the Patterson home and forcibly evict him and his mother and father from the property. I would have thought Wembley Tuttle would have remembered. For it was not just the break-in that was bizarre, it was the fact that my father had moved his family into the house and refused to let any of us leave until he was taken away in handcuffs.

I had not been back to that house since that day, but I had not forgotten anything about it. Most particularly, I had not forgotten the view from the living room window, where my mother and I had stood as the police cars assembled, their blue lights flashing and their radios snapping warlike messages, while my father shouted defiance from an upstairs bedroom.

The police did not know if he had a gun. They did not know he was only my father. All they knew was that Mr. and Mrs. Gordon Patterson, parents of Frost and Parker, grandparents of D. Dodge, had returned home from their Palm Beach vacation to find the house occupied. And so they assembled behind their squad cars with rifles and canisters of tear gas, ready for a full-scale assault if need be.

My father's claim to the house was based on no legally
recognized concept, even though the house had been
built by his great-grandfather Frederick. Frederick had
passed it to his son Alfred and Alfred had passed it to his
son Gordon, who ultimately would pass it to his son
Frost, the reprobate stock marketeer. My father, however, was descended from Alfred's brother John, who
had his own property, which he had passed to my father's
uncle Frank, who of course had sold it several times
over.

The Pattersons had made numerous additions to Frederick's house over the decades, and it had come to form a
layout that comported with no commonly used descrip-
tive phrase in the English language. In my brief time
there it had seemed labyrinthian, with each wing present-
ing its own mystery and sense of adventure. Now, as I
approached it, the house conveyed the same potential
but little of the majesty with which my memory had
endowed it. The paint on the front door was peeling and
the stone lions that guarded it were crusted with bird
droppings and barnaclelike shells that indicated the statu-
ary had not been tended in some time. I assumed, as I
drove up, that the front door was not the entrance of
choice for the family, but it sat at the crest of the semi-
circular driveway and it deserved more attention than it
reflected.

The driveway itself was unmarked and began as a
break in a stone wall. It swept behind a small grove of
trees, past the front of the house and past the entrance to
a detached garage barn. After that it forked: a left turn
returning to Whitehall Road, and a right turn running
behind the barn and along the rear wing of the house.
Beyond the wing the yard was filled with leaves and
branches and small stands of decaying firewood. Beyond
the yard were the woods, and in the woods was a path
that if followed long enough would lead all the way to the
Charles River. Or at least it did when I was a kid.

The rear wing contained an entrance that looked used.
Parked near it were a battered Country Squire station
wagon and a dusty Mercedes sedan of a similar color and
model to Rebecca Carpenter's. As I pulled up behind

those cars a Bedlington terrier began barking madly from behind the screen door of the entrance. As I got out of my car a man appeared behind the screen. The mesh obscured his features somewhat, but I could still tell it was my father's hated second cousin Frost Patterson.

He stared at me through the screen and made no move to stop the antics of the beast at his feet. His stare was not exactly imperious, but I had the feeling that if I turned around and walked away it would have no effect whatsoever on his expression.

I had a moment's fantasy of yelling, "Cousin Frost, it's me, Patterson Starbuck," and rushing the door with my arms thrown open. But what came out of my mouth instead was an almost obsequious, "Pardon me, but I'm looking for Dodge Patterson."

Frost's ice-cold blue eyes measured me as I approached. Age had robbed those eyes of their sharpness, made them soft around the edges, but the loss of his hair and the sweep of his spotted scalp gave them a background that enhanced both their size and color. "He's not here."

I stood on the doorstep looking down at the frantically yapping dog and thinking he needed a good kick, either a gentle one by Frost or a hard one by me. "When do you expect him back?"

"Don't know."

It was Saturday morning. It wasn't unreasonable to think that D. Dodge might be around or that his father might know when he would be back. I decided that it was probably Frost who needed the good kick. "I'm from the district attorney's office," I said.

The old man said nothing.

"It's kind of important I speak with him right away."

The old man still said nothing.

I extracted a card, one that said "Patt Starbuck, Litigation Coordinator, Office of the District Attorney for Exeter County," and held it out to him. He did not open the door. He tried to read it through the screen.

I was wondering if the name was going to mean anything to him and my hand was beginning to shake a little more than the weight of the card required when there came the sound of a woman's voice from inside the

house. "Dad? What's going on out there? What's Tennyson making such a racket about?"

Frost Patterson turned, a maneuver that seemed to
require several distinct movements on his part. The dog
barked even louder and hurled itself against the tin base
of the screen door. Behind man and dog appeared a
woman's shape. I saw a head of luxuriously thick black
hair; a face of smooth, naturally dark skin; a pair of huge
dark eyes that looked friendly and sultry and intelligent
and vulnerable—and whatever I was about to say strangled in my throat.

Frost took a half-step out of the way and the woman
reached down and hushed the dog with a single stroke of
her hand. She opened the door with one long, beautiful,
slender arm bared by a loose-fitting, short-sleeved white
blouse, and said, "Can I help you?"

She was bent, holding the dog's collar with one hand
and holding the door open with the other. I wanted not
to look down the top of her blouse. I wanted to be
professional. But I looked anyway. Quickly. Her breasts
were small but rounded and incredibly firm, and they
weren't covered by any bra.

I stammered. I tore my eyes away. I was looking at the
side of the house, staring intently at an oleander bush.

"Pardon me?" she said, changing her position so that
now she was propping open the door with her hip and
more or less looking at me over her shoulder while she
held down the dog.

I was able to look back. "I'm Patt Starbuck of the
D.A.'s office," I said, handing her the card I had tried to
give Frost Patterson.

She read it and cocked her head as if to say she did not
understand. Her black hair fell with the tilt of her head,
falling front and back and springing up again.

"I'm looking for Dodge Patterson." I was beginning to
perspire. I was wishing I could start this process all over
again, appearing at the door cool, calm, and collected,
the way I had intended.

"Well—stop it, Tennyson—he's out playing golf right
now, but I'm his wife . . . if there's anything I can help
you with."

Frost Patterson stood to the side watching the two of us with what struck me as a faintly disgruntled interest.

"Are you Gretchen Patterson?"

"I am."

"It's about the death of Rebecca Carpenter. She was a friend of yours, wasn't she?"

Gretchen's lower lip tucked beneath her brilliant white teeth. She glanced at her father-in-law, who discreetly looked away. "She was," she said. "But what does that have to do with Dodge?"

"We've got some leads, Mrs. Patterson. What we're trying to do now is develop a big circle of information so that we can get an idea of everything that would possibly be relevant. See what's in the circle and what isn't."

I wasn't fooling Gretchen Patterson. She knew I had just given her gibberish for an answer. I smiled, and it changed nothing. I waited, and finally she invited me in.

She and her father-in-law had been standing inside a small porch that served as a bootroom. To get to the main part of the house we had to step around a child's vehicle. "My son's," Gretchen said simply.

She led the way and I followed. She was wearing pale pink pants that were of such thin material and fit so snugly around her hips that they molded her buttocks and showed the skimpy lines of panties worn very, very low. The shape of the pink pants may have exaggerated the narrowness of her waist, the slimness of her hips, the length of her legs, but I was trying not to inspect those things too closely.

We went into a paneled room occupied with bookshelves, a desk, a few pieces of overstuffed furniture, and a large stone fireplace. I knew the story of those panels. They had come from one of the Chesley taverns that had served as a coach stop along the Post Road in the eighteenth and nineteenth centuries. They had, as I understood it, been a source of pride to my great-great-grandfather. In my memory of my brief childhood stay in this house, those panels were extremely imposing—almost holy relics. "George Washington looked at these very panels on his way to Boston to take command of the Continental Army," my father had told me; and I be-

lieved him. Now, in the sunshine of my cynical adulthood, I could see that the panels were marked and chipped
and desperately in need of oiling. Their importance had
been so lightly regarded that someone had actually
verithaned a map onto that portion of them that was
above the desk. I found it shocking and tried to pretend
the map wasn't there.

In general, the whole room was in a state of disrepair.
The carpet, an antique Oriental, was threadbare. Books
were piled sideways in the shelves. The fireplace was
filled with ashes. The desk was overflowing with papers,
and a black cat occupied the single best chair. I recognized that chair. It was on a list of antiques that my
father had cataloged when he was in the house, a list that
was still in a cabinet drawer in West Nestor.

Gretchen directed me to a seat on the couch and sat
herself in a rocker that could have used some extensive
restoration. "My father-in-law's study," she said, gesturing toward the man who had followed us to the room and
who now stood in the doorway resting his weight on a
carved walking stick that I had not noticed previously.
"This is his house," she said, and I accepted that as an
explanation for the condition of things.

I nodded. I looked around as if I had never seen it
before. "Our understanding," I said when I was done
looking, "is that Dodge, your husband, was playing golf
with Wylie Carpenter on the day Rebecca was killed."

She nodded, her dark brows arching slightly.

"Do you remember what time your husband got home?"

She turned to her father-in-law. She shook her head.
"No . . . well, I mean, it wasn't anything I thought about."

"You remember the night, don't you?"

Again, Gretchen Patterson looked at her father-in-law.
I liked when she looked at me. I liked looking at her.

"From what I understand," I said, drawing back her attention, "Dodge played golf and then stayed at the clubhouse
to play cards. He might have gotten home around ten."

She spread her hands. "I think I was upstairs in bed
reading. Ian, that's our son, would have been asleep
already. That's right, because Dodge stuck his head in
Ian's room before he came in to see me."

"Is that what he usually does when he comes in late from golf?"

She nodded her head once. Her dark eyes spoke wondrous messages to me that I could not really understand. She struck me as being innocent and inviting and desperately in need of protection from someone like me.

I forged ahead. "And Dodge acted as though everything was usual that night, did he?"

"Is my son a suspect, Mr. Starbuck?" rumbled the old man, chilling me by the fact that he used my name.

"No, sir, he's not."

"Because if you're trying to tie him in with her, you can forget about it." He grunted with a great deal of ugly self-satisfaction.

"Dad," Gretchen said, moving her fingers on the arm of her chair and looking at him worriedly.

"Well, I know these policemen fellows," he said, poking his stick in my direction. "They operate on old gossip and rumors. That's what fuels 'em. Keeps 'em running from one place to another."

"Is there a rumor I should know about?" I asked brightly.

"No," said Gretchen.

The old man smacked his lips and looked away.

Gretchen Patterson was fidgeting, trying to ignore both Frost and his noises. I looked from one to the other and asked, "When was the last time you saw Rebecca Carpenter, Mrs. Patterson?"

"Saw her? Well, saw her, I don't know. We talked on the phone at some point not too long ago."

"This is Saturday. The murder was Tuesday night. Any idea what she was supposed to be doing that night?"

Gretchen Patterson shook her head.

I waited, expecting something more.

"You don't have any reason to believe my husband was not playing golf that day, do you?" she asked, trying to sound casual.

Now the old man leaned in, his face twisting unpleasantly.

"No," I said, looking at him.

Frost Patterson twitched as though he had not heard right. Then he leaned back patiently.

"Dodge and Wylie played regularly, didn't they?" I asked.

"Golf?" croaked Frost Patterson.

"Golf," I affirmed.

"They played," Gretchen said, "they played."

"Golf?"

Gretchen's eyes heated up quickly and I was instantly sorry I was such a clown. I went to put up my hand to tell her I was just making a joke, but already she was flicking her glance between her father-in-law and me and already she was snapping, "Look, everyone has probably made a mistake at some time or other. And I don't see where there's any sense trying to make something out of ancient history just because certain people don't have anything better to do than go around stirring up old trouble."

I cleared my throat. My heart picked up its pace. "This mistake you're referring to, did it involve Rebecca Carpenter?"

Mrs. Patterson stared her answer.

I was wondering what kind of man D. Dodge Patterson could possibly be to mess around with Rebecca Carpenter when he had this exquisite creature available to him, but I asked the next question anyway. "Do you have any reason to believe a mistake was still being made?"

"None," she said firmly.

I let my eyes wander to the old man, but his expression was now stoic.

"Do you," I said, throwing the question to either one of them, "have any reason to believe Dodge was not playing golf on Tuesday—not playing cards Tuesday night?"

"None," Gretchen Patterson said, virtually challenging me to ask another impertinent question.

I chose not to do that. I chose to get to my feet instead. I said I was sorry I had intruded on them, but I was going to have to come back at some point and speak to Dodge.

"Should my son have counsel here when you return?" asked Frost. "He's a lawyer himself, you know."

"I don't think so. I'm neither a lawyer nor a cop, so I don't see where I'll be any real threat to him."

He nodded as though keen for the confrontation between his son and me. I looked back at his daughter-in-law and she nodded without any encouragement whatsoever.

"Thank you again," I said and turned to leave. Frost Patterson stepped out of the doorway and let his walking stick flare upward in a half-point toward my exit. As I squeezed by him I said, "Nice place you've got here, Mr. Patterson."

It's possible Cousin Frost's head would have snapped even if I had not said anything. It's possible he was just being informative when he said, "Yes. It's been in my family for generations."

There was a message on my telephone answering machine when I got home. It was from my mother. She said she had made a huge tray of lasagna and she wanted to know if I was interested in coming by to help her eat it. She did not mention Kelsey.

I, however, had other plans. I wanted to spend the evening with a dark-haired woman with wondrous eyes. I thought of calling a friend of mine named Deirdre, who had neither dark hair nor wondrous eyes but who was available. I liked Deirdre all right. She had an impressive body that she held in place with clothes that were always a little too tight. But Deirdre was also a divorcee with two kids and if I failed to give her enough advance notice she would be unlikely to get a baby-sitter and we would end up sitting around watching television until the kids went to bed.

Then she and I would have a glass or two of wine and make mad, silent love on her living room couch. By eleven thirty I would be anxious to leave and she would know it.

I never thought of calling Deirdre except when it was too late to call anyone else, and I chose not to call her this time. I called Robert instead.

9

"Rule number one," said Robert, who figured to know about such things, "is always look for a woman with small hands."

We were in a fashionable singles bar called Hadley V. Baxendale's and I found myself looking at the size of women's hands as we made our way through the crowd in search of an open place to stand. "Why?" I said at last.

"Makes it look bigger when they hold it," Robert called back over his shoulder.

He was obviously a familiar figure in this bar. The doorman knew him, called him by his first name, and let us in immediately even though there was a long line of people waiting on the sidewalk. One of the waitresses knew him, pushed him gently on the chest as he walked by and meaningfully smiled at him as if they had some secret in which he had been naughty and she was being forgiving. A young woman in a low-cut blouse knew him. She stopped him and kissed him on the cheek. She introduced him to her friend and he introduced me to both of them and I tried to act as though I was not feeling awkward about the fact that I was at least fifteen years older than they were.

I should not have felt awkward. Robert was older than I was and he was feeling plenty comfortable. This was his turf. Nowhere on earth did Robert look better or function so well as he did in singles bars.

I had known him when he was called Bobby and aspired to nothing more than a job as a printer. He had left that career when he was in his early twenties because he was having difficulty getting the ink off his hands and because he found it immensely better for his social life to sell drugs. By the time he was thirty, Bobby had turned his marketing skills to real estate and before long he was transformed into Robert.

We were friends because we had grown up together in West Nestor and because we now lived four blocks away from each other in Boston. We were friends because I had once advised Bobby that it was no longer very wise for him to visit the home of a certain Colombian art dealer, regardless of how much interest he had in that gentleman's pottery. Bobby Greenberg, now known as Robert, considered me a very good friend indeed, and he was more than happy to have me accompany him on his Friday-night rounds.

"Rule number two," he said when he had returned from getting us a couple of wallbangers from the bar, "is never stand next to a guy who's more than three inches taller than you." He motioned with his head toward the man standing directly behind me, and then he motioned me away.

As we moved along, Robert was scanning in every direction for likely prospects. He bestowed a lingering smile on a very young, rather Rubenesque woman who responded by sticking out her hand and introducing herself as Chrissie.

As Robert traded intimacies with his new friend I began to regret that I had called him. I regretted I was not with Deirdre. I regretted I had not stayed home alone. And while I was in the middle of all these regrets I glanced across the room and saw the most unlikely sight I could ever possibly see.

There was a woman who looked amazingly like Jessica Keough. She was sitting at a booth in a corner with several other women, all in their thirties, all attractive, all well dressed, and all seemingly out of place.

I did not want it to be Jessica Keough who was sitting there and I did not keep looking for fear it would be. I let Robert drag me into the conversation with Chrissie, even though she was far more interested in Robert than she was in me.

"Patt's a private investigator," said Robert.

"Oooh, maybe he could investigate us!"

"He only investigates privates."

"Robert! I don't believe you said that!"

Robert laughed silkily. He took Chrissie's plump arm and directed her attention to me. "Tell her the kinds of things you really investigate, Patt."

"I specialize in the theft of eggs from fish hatcheries."

"What?" she said, the word coming out like the sound of metal brakes being applied. She looked to Robert for help.

Robert, however, was doubled over with laughter. He thought I was funny. It was another reason we were friends.

Suddenly she was standing there at my elbow, the woman who looked like Jessica Keough. The woman who was Jessica Keough.

"Thank God you've come," she said. "Now I can escape."

I stared at her and her expression changed.

"Didn't John send you?" Her eyebrows rose. Her forehead tilted back.

"Jessica, it's Saturday night. I don't work around the clock, you know."

She watched me as though registering what I was saying for future use. I looked at my drink and sensed, rather than saw, that Robert was waiting for an introduction.

I said, "Jessica, this is Robert, Chrissie."

Chrissie said hello and looked away. Robert said hello and waited for something more. An explanation, perhaps.

"I'm here for a bachelorette party," Jessica blurted. "Karen Coe, do you know her?"

Of course I knew her. She was one of the better attorneys in the office. I looked again at the booth in the corner and realized that not only did I recognize Karen, but I also recognized a couple of others. I recognized all the ones who were waving to me. I recognized Patty Hansen, who was not waving.

Jessica said, "If you really didn't come to get me, will

you at least say you did so I can get out of here?" She moved her head in close to mine, close enough that I could smell her perfume. "It's really not my kind of place," she confessed.

Somehow the option of saying no did not seem available. I told Robert I had to go.

He regarded me as if I was crazy. He excused us from the two women and pulled me off to one side. "Hey," he said, "she's not bad, but there's all kinds of young stuff here. We've just gotten started."

"She's a friend," I said, finding myself irrationally wanting to defend Jessica against the "young stuff."

"Well," sniffed Robert, studying her, "she looks rich anyway." He clapped me on the shoulder, as though bestowing his blessing, and I went back to free Jessica from the strains of trying to make conversation with Chrissie, who was a word processor but was hoping to become a travel agent.

Jessica slid into my Alfa as though she were slipping into a comfortable Japanese tub. "Whew," she said, throwing back her head, "that was quite an experience."

I was mad at her, mad at myself, mad at the course of the night's events. I said nothing.

"Where would you like to go now?" she asked.

I had been attempting to put my car into reverse. Something failed, either my hand or my foot, and the gears made a horrible noise. "I thought you wanted to go home."

"I just wanted to get out of there, plastic-people-land."

"They're not plastic people. They're just different from what you're used to, that's all."

"Oh," she said, meaning the same as "Have it your way." Then she asked me again where I wanted to go.

"Isn't John expecting you?"

"Oh, he's at a dinner tonight for Mayor Mackey in Waterford."

"Will Constantinis be there?"

"You think he'd pass up a chance to make a speech?

Can't you just hear him? 'Mayor Mackey has fought long and hard over the course of his distinguished career to bring public transportation to the point where it is today. We must make sure that we carry his torch forward, that we provide appropriate shelters for the poor, the lame, the halt, the mentally deficient who wish to use that transportation.' By the time he's done everyone will think they're at a retirement dinner rather than a fund-raiser."

We had swung onto Commonwealth Avenue and I was heading for the Turnpike.

"Oh, don't take me home, Patt. It's so rare that I get to be out on an unofficial sort of thing."

"What is it you want me to do with you, Jessica?"

There was a good deal more silence than the question required. "Stop somewhere," she said at last, and it was up to me to figure out what she meant.

"A drink? Would you like a drink?"

"Sure, that would be all right, although I've really had about all I can handle."

"How about some dessert? Some ice cream, something like that?" I was thinking of an ice cream parlor in Cleveland Circle. I was thinking we could get in and get out of there and it would not be any big deal.

"I don't really feel like eating," she said. "Why don't we just go somewhere where we can talk?" She put down the window and filled the car's cockpit with cold air. She tilted her head back. "I love your little car. It makes you feel so close to the road. It makes you feel so . . . almost wild. Take me somewhere in it."

"I am."

"Take me to Newport or down the Cape. Take me to the beach. That's what I feel like doing. I feel like hearing the waves crash and feeling the sand between my toes."

I could not believe she was serious. We were heading in completely the wrong direction and there was no beach even reasonably close. I took her to the Charles River instead.

We got off the Turnpike near the Marriott River Inn at the Nestor-Woodedge line and I drove in a big semicircle that took us to the base of what had once been a small bridge. The bridge had stood burned and broken throughout my childhood, a relic of wooden construction that had not been designed to carry multi-ton metal vehicles. Now all that was left was the foundation on either side.

I had been to that same spot numerous times, and not once in more than twenty-five years. I had smoked my first cigarette there, perhaps heard my first dirty joke there, launched half a dozen ill-fated rafts and homemade boats from there. I remembered it as being a much prettier spot.

But Jessica acted as though it was wonderful. "Patt," she said, her eyes sparkling in the darkness, "where have you brought me?"

"You said you wanted to go to the beach and this was the closest thing I could think of. The waves aren't much, but they lap against the shore. There's no sand, but we can walk along the embankment if you want."

She did not immediately accept my invitation. "It looks muddy," she said. "How did you know about this place?"

"There used to be an abandoned bridge here and my father used to walk across it to get to Woodedge."

"Whatever for?"

"He wasn't supposed to be going where he was going." Jessica waited.

"He was afraid if he drove the main roads someone might recognize him or his car and so he used to walk overland."

We were both staring at the river and I was awaiting the next question when she said, "I'd probably ruin either my shoes or my pantyhose."

I looked down. She was wearing a thin gray leather jacket, a pink striped blouse, gray slacks, and narrow gray shoes. I asked her what she was talking about.

"If we got out and walked along the river."

"What were you planning to do if we went to the beach?"

"If you had a blanket or something I could put it over me. Then I could take off my slacks and my pantyhose, put my slacks back on and walk barefoot."

The thought of the district attorney's wife removing her pants in my car, however briefly, brought back the memory of Mary Marie Gastonatto and the last time I had been parking—eighteen or a hundred years ago. I reached behind Jessica's seat and pulled out a neatly folded plaid blanket. She may or may not have seen it when she got in the car, but it was something I had to keep passengers' legs warm at night if I drove with the top down.

Jessica reached out her hand and for two seconds we both held the blanket, our eyes locked on each other. Then she took it. She faced forward and slid off her shoes.

She flipped open the blanket so that it covered her lap and her knees. She put her hands under the blanket and undid the snaps to her slacks. I heard a zipper open. Her hands moved slightly apart. "Don't look at me," she said.

I looked straight ahead again. My fingers tapped against the steering wheel. Jessica pulled the blanket up higher and tucked it under her chin. She was starting to wiggle, trying to get her slacks or her pantyhose or both down over her hips.

Suddenly she stopped. "I can't do this," she said.

I didn't turn, but my fingers ceased their tapping. "You see how easy it is, though," I said.

"How easy what is?" An edge crept into her voice.

"If I just turned now. If I put my arm around your waist, brought my face close to yours, would you resist me? What if I—knowing your bare ass is on my seat and not being able to control myself—reached down under that blanket, would you push me away?"

She did not try to get her slacks or her pantyhose back in place. She did not rush to say or do anything. "What are you talking about, Patt?"

"I'm just trying to tell you how it could have happened with Mrs. Carpenter."

Mrs. Keough exhaled slowly. "Oh," she said.

"She was with somebody—they could have run into each other or they could have been riding together innocently enough, and they stopped just like we did. Then the guy got the wrong impression because of where they were and the way they were talking. He tried to kiss her, he tried to put his hand between her thighs and she resisted him. Maybe he got angry, maybe he felt misled or he couldn't understand. Maybe he was a jerk. Maybe all of the above . . ."

Jessica said nothing.

"Or it could have been, you know, that she really wanted to be with somebody—this person she was with. She's a married woman with a big old house, but she has no idea what time her husband is coming home. He's out, that much is clear. He's playing golf and she knows he'll have a snack or a drink and play some cards, so she's got no problem getting out of the house without any questions being asked, but she can't meet with her friend inside the house because her husband could come walking in at any moment."

"She could have gone to her friend's house," Jessica said softly.

"Of course. Unless the friend was married himself or something like that. Maybe all it was, she didn't really want to go to his house. She wasn't that committed. Maybe she was attracted or interested, but she wanted to see how things developed. Maybe this guy was just a little fantasy she had and she didn't really want to go through with anything, she just wanted to get as close as she could to see what it would be like. A guy can't always tell those things, you know."

There was just enough light to distinguish the various ripples across the surface of the water. It gave us something to look at as we sat.

"Should I start the engine or do you still want to get out and walk around?"

"I think," she said, "it must be getting pretty late."

I nodded. I reached for the ignition key.

Jessica let the blanket drop away from the upper part of her body. It bunched in her lap. She straightened her legs and arched her hips and the blanket fell away from her legs. She was reaching beneath her thighs and I saw that both her pantyhose and her slacks were much lower than I had thought. I saw a brief glimpse of a thick triangle of blond hair and then she was covered again. Her slacks were snapped shut.

"I guess you can start it up now," she said, without looking at me.

I flicked the key and the engine roared to life. I let it warm for a little while, even though it was not necessary, and then I backed out of our parking space. Jessica rolled up her window. On the way back to her house she took the blanket and covered her legs.

10

On Monday morning I was asked to step into Royster's office by Anita, Royster's secretary. Anita wore very short skirts, had very muscular legs, chewed gum, and generally acted as though being Royster's secretary was the second or third most important job in the office. Anita abhorred typing. She loved clicking around in her heels dispensing orders.

Royster had a high-backed leather swivel chair like John Michael's. He had a large desk like John Michael's. His office, however, was a good deal smaller than his boss's and so its furnishings tended to throw things out of perspective. If you were in front of Royster's desk and he was seated behind it, it was virtually impossible not to focus your attention on him.

When I opened Royster's door on Monday morning I saw that Ralphie Libby had taken up the one position in the room where he did not have to look directly into Royster's face. He was standing behind and slightly to the side of Royster's chair. He was standing at parade rest, with his forearms bulging and a crooked smile on his cracked and lined face. Ralphie was the state police detective lieutenant who had been assigned to our office as an investigator for more years than anyone could remember. He was the one whom John Michael had wanted to replace with me when John Michael had been a deputy in charge of criminal litigation. It was, indeed, the inability to get rid of Ralphie that had caused John Michael to create for me the parallel position of "litigation coordinator."

Everyone, of course, knew that I functioned as John

Michael's chief investigator, and had Ralphie Libby been of a different temperament he never would have allowed the situation to exist. But Ralphie had little ambition and even less interest in getting his skinny old butt out of the office in the heat of summer or the cold of winter. He liked drinking coffee, reading the *Herald* from cover to cover, intricately planning his picks at the dog track, and bantering inanely with the office personnel about whatever had been on television the night before. The unwritten agreement that everyone followed was to call Detective Libby our office investigator and to let me do the work. That was what made it disturbing to find Libby in Royster's office in the middle of a big investigation.

"So," said Royster, by way of greeting, "how was your weekend?" Like Ralphie, he was in shirtsleeves; but his were long where Ralphie's were short.

I chose to focus on Sunday in my response. "Not bad. I watched the Patriots get the shit kicked out of them down in New York. Then I went out and ran about five miles along the Charles until I didn't care anymore."

"Wasn't that awful?" said Ralphie, who may already have forgotten the reason he was there to meet with Royster and me.

Royster smiled impatiently. He had a pencil intertwined among his fingers and was tapping it on the glass top of his desk, first one end and then the other. "You didn't get a chance to do any work on the Carpenter case, did you?" he asked me.

"Yeah, as a matter of fact," I said, to Royster's obvious disappointment. "I was out to the Patterson house on Saturday and interviewed the last of Rebecca Carpenter's close friends. You remember, you thought that should be my next step."

"Learn anything?"

"I'm not sure. They're all pieces in a puzzle, Roy."

Tap-tap-tap went the pencil. "What was he like?"

"Gretchen Patterson was the one I talked to. Her husband wasn't there."

The pencil beat faster. "He was the one I said you should interview." Royster was excited now. He had found something about which he could complain. "Patterson's our key to learning what Carpenter was doing between six and ten Tuesday night."

"I'm working on it."

"And what have you done to learn what the victim was doing between six and ten that night?"

"Since we last talked? Nothing."

Royster silently threw down his pencil and looked at Ralphie. His look was obviously a cue for Ralphie to say something, but Ralphie was into the ceremonial aspect of his role and he was busy grinning and trying to look sharp.

Royster did a double-take. "Ralph here's been working on the case himself. Tell him what you've been doing, Ralph."

Put on the spot, it took Ralph a moment to remember. He broke parade rest, scratched his arm a bit, and said, "Well, I located the gardener."

"Rasmussin?" I said in surprise. "I heard he split."

Ralphie's brow crushed under the weight of his thoughts. "Rasmussin? No, this guy's name was Marconi."

"Oh, the old caretakers, Dominic and Gina."

"That's right," Ralphie said, brightening.

"Tell him about them," Royster ordered.

"Well," Ralphie said, holding out his hands, palms inward. "You should see the guy's wife. Tits out to here. I'm not kidding you."

I made a show of getting my notebook out of my jacket pocket. Royster shoved his chair back from his desk and delivered a glare that even Ralphie could interpret.

"Well, all right," he said, scratching some more. "They're sort of a middle-aged couple. The guy's about five-five and speaks broken English. The woman's got the heavy accent, but she speaks better, you know? I guess they both come over from Italy about ten, twenty years ago. Right now, they're living in a room at their daughter's house in Waterford and they're pretty pissed off about it, if you know what I mean." He waited for some sort of affirmation that I did, indeed, know what he meant.

When I nodded to his satisfaction, he went on. "It

seems they'd been living on the Carpenter estate since
Rebecca Carpenter's mother had the place, doing all the
gardening, all the landscaping, tending to the orchards—
even hiring all the fruit-pickers. It wasn't just him, it was
her, too. Both of them working and never any complaints, according to them. And they sort of thought of
the place as home, you know? I mean, they lived there
and all. Then one day a couple of weeks ago Mrs. Carpenter comes to them and tells them they're fired. Three
days notice, month's severance pay, and boom, they're
gone."

"Thing is," Royster said, trying to move Ralphie along,
"Mrs. Carpenter won't give them a reason. She just says
their services won't be needed anymore."

"Wylie Carpenter said they caught Gina Marconi stealing liquor."

"Stealing liquor, huh?" Ralphie hitched up his belt as
though contemplating whether stealing liquor was a firing
offense. "Well, they claim they don't got the slightest
idea what it's for. So they wait to see who replaces
them."

"Doug Rasmussin."

"They don't got his name, but what they can plainly see
is he's a young kid. Good-looking, early twenties. And
they're saying, 'Hey, the property's so big the two of us
could barely do it all before, and now we're getting
replaced by one young kid?' Now, remember, these guys
are Italian and all, but they think they know why. They
say Mr. Carpenter, he's not home a lot." Ralphie leered,
giving us a hint as to what was to come. "They get to this
part and the two of them really start getting excited.
They're both waving their arms around and yelling, some's
in English, some's in Italian, and some's somewheres in
between. But I get the sign language, you know?"

With that, Ralphie put his hands on his hips and began
thrusting his pelvis in and out while he grinned unabash-
edly at Royster and me. As performed by Ralphie, it was
the single most obscene gesture I had ever witnessed.
Royster must have felt the same way because he waved
violently at Ralphie and told him to cut it out.

For one moment Royster and I looked at each other in

communication of unspoken, sympathetic misery. Then Royster blinked and we resumed our old adversarial positions.

"Get the picture?" Royster asked me. "She sees this young hardbody and wants him. She hires him to replace the faithful family retainers, starts a little thing going with him, husband finds out about it and kills her."

"Let's arrest him right away, Royster," I said.

Royster Hansen stared at me with eyes that were as blank as a wall. Perhaps inside his head he was counting to ten. "What I suggest," he said at last, "is that this is a new lead. If you don't want to follow up on it, I can have Ralph, here, do it. He can go find this new yardboy—"

"Caretaker. Rasmussin."

"—Rasmussin, and have the pleasure of learning whether he was sticking Mrs. Carpenter in between tree trims."

"Rasmussin's disappeared. I'm told he went to California."

"When?"

"A few days ago."

"A few days ago. Like, you mean, right after Mrs. Carpenter was killed?"

I shrugged. I tried not to look happy at Royster's sudden consternation.

"I'd like you to follow up on that," he said slowly.

John Michael and I played squash at the fitness club down the block from our office. We had a regularly scheduled time of Monday at six, but more often than not John Michael was unable to keep the date. On this Monday, he made it.

John Michael did not look good on a squash court. He wore matching wristbands and headband. He wore white sneakers, high white socks with horizontal stripes at the top, and white shorts that emphasized the whiteness of his skinny legs. He wore a gray T-shirt that bragged about the fact that Boston College had gone to the Cotton Bowl. He looked as though he was eighteen years old and undergoing a fraternity hazing obligation. He also was not a very accomplished squash player.

For a while John Michael had played racquetball. It

was something he heard everyone was doing. Then he observed that there seemed to be a class distinction between those who played racquetball and those who played squash and so he took up the latter. Where John Michael went, I was sure to follow—because I was the person with whom he played. I suppose I could have refused to switch from one sport to the other, but the matter never came up for discussion.

So now on Mondays at six, whenever John Michael could make it, we met on a little wooden court where he would flail away at a little black ball and sweat and curse and generally drive himself into a provoked state of anger and frustration that he mistook for the fun of competitive athletics. On this particular Monday I beat him two straight, 15–12 both times. The score was not coincidental. I could have beaten him by almost any amount I chose.

As his last shot blasted into the tin base of the front wall he let out a roar of pain and drew back his arm as if he were going to throw his racket. Then he thought better of it and slumped into a corner. I slumped down next to him.

"You almost caught me there at the end," I lied.

"My foot slipped as I was hitting that last one," he claimed.

"Maybe you ought to try a new pair of court shoes," I suggested. "Maybe they have special ones just for squash."

John Michael grimaced at the soles of the sneakers he was wearing as though considering whether he could get away with blaming the outcome on them. "Jessica tells me you've got some new ideas about the case," he said.

Unsure as to the detail with which Jessica might have described our conversation, I said nothing.

"She tells me that you think Rebecca Carpenter could have voluntarily gone to that lovers' lane with her killer. Then Roy tells me you're thinking it might have been the gardener who killed her. Is all that true?"

"I haven't come to any conclusions of any sort, John."

"Reason I'm pressing you is that public attention seems to have already passed on this baby. You see what's on the front page of the *Courier* today? The whole thing's taken up with the latest brainstorm of Constantinis, that nitwit."

I had seen it. At Mayor Mackey's dinner on Saturday night Constantinis had unveiled a sweeping proposal for the gentrification of Waterford. He wanted the city to issue a bond which would allow it to buy up a huge section of riverfront property in order to re-create the original Watertowne plantation of the 1600s. The newspaper carried artist's drawings replete with little figures wearing Pilgrim-era costumes. It also had economic projections indicating that such a tourist attraction could bring tens of millions of new dollars a year to the city.

"Poor Neil Mackey thinks everybody's there to put feathers in his cap, and goddamn George sharpens his quill to a stiletto point and drives it right into Mackey's skull. 'The mayor,' he says, 'has worked tirelessly to bolster the economy of this great city of ours.' I'd like to know what the hell's so great about it. You ever heard of anybody who was born in this country who wanted to move to Waterford?" John Michael resumed his imitation. " 'But the Mayor cannot do it alone. Like any great craftsman, he must have the tools he needs to work with. He cannot spin gold out of straw. But if we give him those tools there is no telling what Mayor Mackey might do. One of the tools we must give him is increased funding. Where can we get the increased funding our city government so desperately needs? Not from our citizenry. They have been taxed to death. They spoke out years ago on Proposition 2½ and said "No more." The funding must come from outside our great city. How? By giving the people outside our city something they can get nowhere else. What can they get nowhere else? Our history. Our heritage. That's what. It is as unique to Waterford as a fingerprint. How can we give it to them? Well, I have a proposal . . .' and out comes this whole stupid plan about turning the city into a theme park.

"I'm telling you, Patt, all around the room people are barfing into their tapioca. Anybody who knows anything, that is. Of course, they've got some yahoos there, the people maybe who're friends of a building contractor who's bought a table for ten, and they're applauding like crazy. That's what the press picks up on. 'Constantinis Proposal Greeted Enthusiastically,' that's what the headline said today. You have to read two paragraphs to find out it was Neil's dinner."

The district attorney got to his feet and looked down at me. "That's why I'm concerned about where we're going with this Carpenter thing. We don't come up with something fast everybody's going to forget we're working on it."

"Well," I said, getting up to stand alongside him, "the murder didn't get all that much attention to start with. What happens in Woodedge tends to stay in Woodedge. It doesn't affect anybody other than Woodedgians."

"You think anything that happens in Waterford affects anybody anywhere? But look what Constantinis is able to do with his harebrained schemes. You have to catch the public's fantasy. That's the key, Patt. In his position he can get people to fantasize about what can happen in the future. Me, I've got to get them fantasizing about what happened in the past. If I get everyone believing that the rich people up in Woodedge have been fornicating and plotting and killing each other, then I've got something they're interested in. Otherwise, you tell me this is some stickup artist whose gun goes off accidentally, or some handyman shoots his boss, you don't give me much to go with in terms of fantasy. That kind of crap can happen anyplace. I've gotta have something that can only happen in Woodedge. You know what I'm saying?"

"I'm working on it, John."

"Well," John Michael said, and he gave me a grin that was meant to indicate he was not really a bad guy, "work a little harder."

11

Mrs. Violet Rasmussin of 1429 Merrymount Avenue in Walmouth had already been interviewed regarding the disappearance of her son. A nice little man had come by, she said. Had an English accent. Reminded her of a pint-size Prince Charles.

"Inspector Lester?" I asked.

"That's the ticket," she said, and promptly lay down on the couch.

Mrs. Rasmussin had a headache. She also had a backache. She didn't mind being interviewed again, but she only wanted to talk from the prone position. I accepted her hand gesture as an invitation to sit in a modified rocker with a fixed base and a cheap colonial print cover on its cushions. I left the front door open even though Merrymount Avenue was the main thoroughfare between Walmouth and Waterford and the noise from the passing traffic was terrific.

Fourteen twenty-nine Merrymount Avenue was a small red brick house perched very high on a cement foundation. It was separated from the street by a sidewalk, a short hurricane fence, fifteen feet of grass and cement walkway, and six fairly steep cement stairs. The house had an air of wanting to be cozy and neat and modern, and that made it sad. The front door opened directly into the living room, where there was a fake fireplace and a picture window that looked out onto the traffic.

The fake fireplace was useful because it had a mantel. The mantel was useful because it held several framed pictures and several elfin figurines that were either Hummels or imitation Hummels. Either way, the figurines, in their supposed jollity, were every bit as sad as the house they decorated. I pictured one of them being hurled against the wall, breaking into pieces, and still maintaining its sickly little smile on its glazed face.

The house made me feel claustrophobic. It reminded me of a hospital room. I had to take deep breaths, but when I did I inhaled the otherwise abeyant smell of heavy ethnic food—boiled cabbage, perhaps. So I kept the front door open and we talked over the noise.

Doug, Mrs. Rasmussin said, had indeed gone to California. No, it wasn't anything sudden. He'd been talking about doing it for some time. "So finally I said to him, 'Why don't you stop your yapping and just go?' "

"When was this, Mrs. Rasmussin?"

She was lying on the couch with her head closest to me and her feet propped on the distant arm. It was not a very becoming position. It made her patterned dress fall away at the knees and revealed the varicose veins in her lower legs. The back of the couch was to her right. She took the arm that was next to it and crooked it so that she could cover her brow with her hand.

"I know what you're thinking," she said, "but you're wrong. That little Mr. Lester told me all about how that lady who got strangled was the one Doug worked for, but Dougie couldn'ta had nothing to do with that because that happened on Tuesday night and he was already gone by then. I already went over that with Mr. Lester."

"I'm confused, Mrs. Rasmussin. When did you have your talk with Inspector Lester?"

"What's today?"

"Today's Tuesday."

"So he's been gone a week, Dougie. Lester was here, I don't know, maybe two, three days after that."

"Do you know why Doug chose to leave on the day he did?"

"Well, he was planning to all along, you know. That was his plan, he was going to leave at the end of the summer. After the kids went back to school and the pool closed down. And then they offered him this job, just until he got all the leaves up and everything, but he told them from the start he wanted to be outa here before the snow came. What's the date now?"

"October twenty-second."

"So he told them he was going to leave around the middle of October. That was the deal. Me, I get so one month looks pretty much like another. You got your hot months and your cold months and your in-between months going one way or the other. That's all that really counts. You know, is it hot or is it cold? What else is there?"

I didn't tell her. Instead, I said, "Mrs. Rasmussin, let me go back over a few things. What was it you were saying about the pool closing down?"

"The pool where he was a lifeguard. At the club."

"What club?"

"The country club. Stonegate Country Club over there in Woodedge. You gotta know that place. Dougie was the lifeguard there during the summer. Taught the little kids to swim. But it, you know, it closes down September sometime. He coulda gotten another job at the club for the fall, but he said, 'Nope. This year I'm going to California.' So he went. It didn't have nothing to do with that lady dying. You can ask anybody."

"But before he went he did take the job with Mr. and Mrs. Carpenter."

Mrs. Rasmussin took her hand away from her brow and twisted around to get a look at me. She quite clearly thought I was dense. I smiled at her.

"You woulda too," she said, "if they offered you what they offered him. Twice what he was making at the club. But I guess they were desperate, you know? So he said, 'What the heck? It don't make any difference if I go in September or October and I can use all the money I can get.' I mean, he'd saved up, but if he's moving out there for good then he couldn't have too much, could he? So this was the deal, he'd work for them for a few weeks, get things ready for winter and all, pick up a few extra bucks, and then he'd take off."

"And your understanding was that he was going to take care of the property all by himself?"

"What's to picking up a few leaves? Pruning a few bushes?"

"Have you seen the size of the Carpenters' property?"

Mrs. Rasmussin returned to her previous position, feet up, hand on her brow. "Doug's a big strong boy. He could do it."

"He say anything about the orchards the Carpenters had?"

"He didn't say nothing about orchards. Why, did they have orchards?" From the tone of her voice, she might have been asking if they had bunions.

"Would you have a picture of Doug, by any chance, Mrs. Rasmussin?"

She pointed with one of her feet at the mantelpiece. I got up and walked over to look at the array of framed photographs. One was a black-and-white of an unhappy looking young man in an army uniform. "Not him. That's my husband," Mrs. Rasmussin said. "He's dead."

One was a color photo of a bull-necked grinning blond man in a chief petty officer's uniform. "That's my son Alex," she said. "He's in the navy. Goes all around the world in submarines."

Next was a high-school graduation picture of a young man blond and grinning like Alex, but decidedly more slim and handsome. He had a perfect set of white teeth and one charming dimple that told you he was delighted to be photographed and made you feel delighted along with him.

"Good-looking boy," I said.

"Doug could be a movie star," she told me. "If he wasn't so soft in the head."

I asked if there was a picture I could have to take with me and Mrs. Rasmussin suddenly sat up.

"Why?" she said, clinging to the top of the couch with one hand, the bottom with the other.

"Because I may need it as part of our investigation."

"Oh, no. I told you, I already had this talk with that inspector guy and I explained to him how it couldn't have been Doug had anything to do with this. You just go talk with him, you don't believe me."

I told her I would do that and she nodded as though I had damn well better. I asked if she had heard from

Doug since he left and if she had any address where I could reach him out in California.

She told me no on both counts. "Dougie's hitchhiking out there and I don't expect to hear from him until he gets settled in. If he's anything like his brother I don't even expect to hear then."

I propped a card against Doug's photograph. I said, "Since Doug didn't have anything to do with what happened, you'll have him call me as soon as you hear from him, won't you? Have him call collect, or at least get a number where I can reach him."

She thought about it for a moment and then told me what she knew I wanted to hear. "Sure," she said, and flopped back onto the cushions.

I closed the door behind me on my way out, knowing I wouldn't hear from her again.

Chief Wembley Tuttle's office was too small for its accumulation. It had a desk covered with papers; a credenza covered with papers; a tall set of bookshelves that contained half a dozen large books, twice as many manuals, some syllabi from various law enforcement conferences, and more papers. The chief had a swivel chair with a cushion on it. There were two other wooden chairs and a blue couch. About half the blue couch was covered with papers.

Hanging on the wall were photographs of Chief Tuttle shaking hands with various people. There must have been a dozen such photographs and most of them hung crookedly. In one he was shaking hands with Willie Mays. Willie was wearing a golf hat and looking at the camera. The chief was wearing plaid pants pulled high on his belly and he was looking at Willie. In another picture the chief was standing with Burnsie, my former boss. Burnsie's mouth was open, his tie was loose, and his eyes were glazed. The chief had his hand on Burnsie's back and might have been holding him upright for the photographer.

"I thought it was time we compared notes on the Carpenter investigation," I said when the chief, Inspector Lester, Detective Lieutenant Libby, and I were all seated. The chief was in the chair behind the desk, the one with the cushion. Lester was on the couch smoking a cigarette. They exchanged looks.

I was in one of the wooden chairs, penned in by a couple of heavily loaded cardboard boxes. The chief's desk was on my left, the couch was on my right, and I was facing Libby, whom I had brought with me and who was leaning forward in his wooden chair with his elbows on his knees, his feet spread, his hands loosely clasped. Alone among the four of us Libby did not have out a pen and a notepad.

"How are you guys coming?" I asked when enough time had passed without anybody saying anything.

"Good," said the chief, nodding wide-eyed and blank-faced at Lester.

"Good," responded Lester quickly. "Good, good."

"Good," said Libby as though it were a password to get into the conversation.

"Figured out who did it yet, Chief?" I asked with my pen in my mouth.

"We're working on it," he said, unknowingly echoing what I had told Royster the day before.

"That's right. We're working on it," said his able inspector.

Libby nodded. He was ready to leave now that we had gotten all the essential information.

"Got a list of suspects?" I asked.

The chief again looked at Lester. All he had to do was stare straight ahead.

"Everybody's a suspect," cracked Lester.

Libby kept nodding. This all made sense to him.

"Ralphie, here, did some digging and located Mr. and Mrs. Marconi, the former caretakers at the Carpenter place. After talking with them he's come up with a theory. Tell the chief what it is, Ralph."

Libby looked confused for a second. Then he straightened his back and I had a flash of fear that he was going to put his hands on his hips and start that horrible pelvis-thrusting thing again. I moved quickly to head him off.

"The information he got from the Marconis leads him to believe that Mrs. Carpenter might have been the philandering sort, that she might have hired this young guy

Rasmussin for reasons other than his gardening ability, that maybe Mr. Carpenter found out about this and didn't take kindly to it. You guys looked into this possibility?"

"Well . . ." The chief spread his hands.

Lester waved his cigarette. He did it by holding the cigarette at the bottom between his thumb and other four fingers. "The kid's a suspect," he said.

"Everybody's a suspect."

"That's right."

"Including Wylie."

The chief's hands and the inspector's cigarette did their little dance again.

"I was out to Rasmussin's house today," I said. "You're aware he's gone, aren't you, Les?"

"Hitchhiking out west." He looked the conversation back toward his boss, who picked it up from there.

"We've notified the state police in Nebraska and Kansas to be on the lookout for him. You knew that, didn't you, Patt? Ralph did it last Friday."

It must have been readily apparent that I had not known that. Ralphie and I had just driven from Walmouth to Woodedge without him ever mentioning anything about it.

"You been in touch with the FBI or anything?" I said. "Done anything about trying to get a warrant issued? Anything else I should know about so I can do my job?"

The chief regarded me contemplatively. "No, nothing you should know about."

"We figured, chances were he'd be going through one of those states," offered Libby. "And he could be picked up for vagrancy or something until we got out there to question him."

"We told 'em he's a suspect in a murder. But obviously they can't arrest him for just being a suspect," explained the chief.

"Just hold the bugger, that's all we want them to do," added Lester. "Let us have a go at him."

I doodled ugly pictures on my pad. "What about Ralph's theory?"

The chief looked at Ralph for several seconds. Ralphie

responded as though he were waiting to be selected by the captain of a sandlot baseball team.

"We'll consider that, Ralph," he said, and Ralphie beamed.

"Let's consider it now, Wem," I said. I pointed at Lester. "As Stanley has no doubt told you, the young Mr. Rasmussin was a former lifeguard at Stonegate Country Club. As you'll recall from our conversation with Wylie Carpenter, he was a member of that country club."

"That's where he was when his wife was killed."

"Well, we're not entirely sure about that, Wem—unless you know something I don't, which you've just indicated to me isn't the case. What we have been told, however, by Wylie himself, is that he didn't pay much attention to the grounds. He left that up to his wife. What Mrs. Marconi told Ralphie was that she and her husband were going along just as they had always been and one day Mrs. Carpenter walks up to them out of the blue and fires them."

"Wylie said Mrs. Marconi was stealing liquor."

"Wembley, look. The Marconis have been there for years. They were living there before Wylie and Rebecca moved in, right on the premises. And suddenly one day they're fired because she supposedly took some liquor? In September? On the eve of the fall season, leaving Mrs. Carpenter so desperate for somebody to pick up the leaves and everything that she's got to hire away the lifeguard from one of their country clubs? Give me a break, will you? The lifeguard's the handsomest kid you ever saw. He goes to work for a couple of weeks and then disappears on the very day Mrs. Carpenter turns up dead. This should at least raise some suspicion in your mind."

"It bloody well does in mine," said Lester, his face long with sincerity, his eyes on Wembley Tuttle's. "Makes me think the kid must have killed the lady, else why would he have disappeared like that?"

"Well," I said calmly, "one reason could be that he was made to disappear."

For a long moment nobody reacted. Then the chief

shifted in his chair. "You mean, like, if Wylie killed him?"

"I'm asking if you've looked into that possibility."

The chief looked from one of his fellow officers of the law to the other. None of them spoke.

"Let me give you another possibility," I said. "Les, you talked with Rasmussin's mother, what did you learn about him going away?"

"That he was going to California." Lester gestured with his thumb. "Shank's mare."

"And she made it clear to you that he had already worked that out with the Carpenters, right? He had planned to leave last Tuesday and they knew that beforehand, didn't they?"

Lester's laughter came out in little hacks. "It's his bloody mother, for God's sake. What do you expect her to say after I tell her the lady's been murdered?"

Wembley Tuttle leaned forward. "What are you getting at, Patt?"

"Just this. Wylie could have known that Rasmussin was planning on leaving last Tuesday. He could have known that his wife and Rasmussin were fooling around. He could have figured that Rasmussin would be your main suspect if anything happened to Rebecca on the very night Rasmussin took off."

Tuttle's face became very serious. His voice took on a tone of maximum gravity. "It sounds to me like you're out to get Wylie, Patt."

"I'm not out to *get* anyone, Chief. I'm trying to learn what happened and I just want to know if you've looked into these possibilities, that's all. Since Les talked with Mrs. Rasmussin last week, have you, for example, asked Wylie if he knew her son was leaving? Did you find out if it was all prearranged, like she claims? Is any of this even of any interest to you?"

The silence grew to a point of tension before Tuttle said, "Wylie Carpenter is an important member of this community. His wife was an important member. Around here, we don't just throw accusations at such people. We don't just make up things to investigate, either. Stanley and I are handling this matter as we see fit." He paused for a long moment and looked over at Ralphie. "With Ralph's help," he added.

"We're looking for the caretaker and if we don't find him in the midwest, then we expect he'll be contacting his mother or one of his friends once he gets to California. Or maybe the local authorities there will help us locate him. But right now we've got no reason to believe that he's dead or that Mr. Wylie Carpenter is somehow using his departure as a cover-up for his own crime."

"Besides," muttered Lester, "you've got your basic bloody facts wrong."

I cocked my head. "Oh?"

"Your Mrs. Carpenter that you think recruited this young hardbody wasn't even a member of the Stonegate Country Club. She and her husband had a family membership at Bollingbrook, but he had a single membership at the other place." Lester checked with the chief to see how far he could go. "Unless," he said, "unless you think Mr. Wylie Carpenter brought this fellow into his service just so he could boink his wife."

Lester spoke too fast and his voice was too accented for Ralphie to be able to follow easily, but Ralphie knew a joke of sorts had been made and so he offered a willing, if somewhat uncertain, smile. Chief Tuttle, however, did not think his town's rich people should be held up to even fanciful ridicule. His puffy, double-chinned face remained stern.

"I take it," I said, gazing at each of them, "that someone has asked Wylie if he was the one who offered Rasmussin the job."

The chief cleaned his nose. First he used his thumb and his forefinger, then the side of his thumb, then the back of his hand. "We can do that," he said.

"And I take it that if he admits he's the one who asked Rasmussin if he wanted a job, then you'll ask him why he contrived to give us the impression that he didn't know anything about the guy."

The chief spread his hands.

"Now, let me ask one more question. Who's checked the Carpenters' phone records?"

Lester got permission from Chief Tuttle to answer.

"Three calls made from the house on Tuesday. Sarah Mitchell, the housekeeper, verifies two of them as being hers. The other was to the Patterson house at one in the afternoon. Nothing between six and Sergeant Roselli's arrival in the wee hours of the next morning."

"How long was the Patterson call?"

"Short. One minute."

"I think it would be a good idea to obtain the phone records from the Patterson home. Tuesday, Monday, Sunday, Saturday. Also, see if you can get the phone records from Dodge's office. You know where that is, don't you?"

"Law Offices of Hill and Patterson." Lester jerked his head. "Just down the road."

"Now you're saying Dodge Patterson might have had something to do with it? Is that what you're saying, Patt?" The chief sounded disappointed in me.

"Did you ever hear that Dodge Patterson and Rebecca Carpenter might have been more than just good friends, Wem?"

The chief exhaled audibly and slumped back in his chair. "I don't think this is any way to conduct an investigation, Patt."

"Fine," I said, getting to my feet. "I'll have one of the assistant D.A.'s subpoena Patterson's records and I'll review them myself."

As an exit line it had its merit, serving as a none-too-subtle reminder of my position. It was unfortunate, therefore, that most of its effect was lost when I had to return a minute or so later to get Ralphie, who had forgotten to get up and leave when I did, who was still sitting there with his knees spread, his fingers folded, and his prematurely wizened features crossed with bewilderment.

12

When I got out of high school there did not seem to be any major league teams interested in a slow outfielder who hit .250, and I had not prepared myself for many other options. I thought of joining the merchant marine. Somebody I knew told me you got to see the world and avoid the draft at the same time. Unfortunately, everyone else seemed to have heard the same story and the merchant marine was impossible to get into. I went to junior college instead.

Walmouth J.C. was not a difficult school. Its student body essentially consisted of three types: young men like me who did not feel a patriotic urge to die for our country's policy of Asian containment; women in their late twenties to early forties who had missed college for one reason or another on the first go-round; and some very dumb people of both sexes who could get in nowhere else. The admixture was not inspiring. I soon learned, moreover, that it was not really necessary for me to go to class in order to get the B grades to which I aspired.

That left me with some serious time on my hands. My father eventually noticed this and became quite upset with me. Although he had never mentioned the matter, he told me he had just naturally assumed that I would be going to a "good" college. Yale, he thought, would be nice. He asked me what I was going to do with a Walmouth J.C. education and I told him I didn't know. Shortly after that he arranged for me to be employed with his company as a field adjuster.

It was, I am sure, a move made with the best of

intentions by my father. He was certain that a taste of the real world would send me scurrying back to my books and propel me on to the Ivy League education he had previously neglected to discuss with me. Unfortunately, I proved to be fairly adept at insurance adjusting. I started with banged-up cars and did my work quickly and gave my superiors absolutely no indication that I was interested in becoming a claims supervisor, a manager, or anything else. This made them very interested in me. By the time my father took his last walk into the woods of Woodedge, I was already doing residential properties and was pegged by my father's company for the fast track. Company representatives told me so at his funeral.

"Work hard," said a sour-breathed regional supervisor named Winterhalter, as he put his arm around me and rested his sweaty armpit against my shoulder. "Work hard and the world will be your oyster."

I didn't tell Winterhalter how ironic I thought it was for him to be saying that at my father's funeral, but I remembered his words. I remembered them on the day I parked outside the Main Street building of my cousin D. Dodge Patterson. It was three doors down from Adolfo's on the same side of the street, a small gabled house that had been modified to serve as the Law Offices of Hill and Patterson. A new deck and a sturdy flight of stairs had been added to the existing structure to accommodate the hordes of clients who could be expected to park their cars on the vast paved-over space of what had once been somebody's front lawn.

I walked up the stairs and presented myself to the receptionist of Hill and Patterson, who was most disturbed that I wanted to see D. Dodge without an appointment. I had difficulty getting her to be impressed by the information printed on my card. "You will have to wait," she said, spitting out each word as if it were an unpleasant object that had balled in her mouth, "while I see if he is available."

I took a seat on the mini-couch that was there in the reception area for people who had to wait to see if their attorney was available. It was located in the pocket of a bay window, set between a small magazine rack and a tropical fish tank. The fish looked at me. I looked at the magazines. There was nothing in the rack that appealed to me, since I was not interested in sailing, horses, or kitchens.

The receptionist, meanwhile, had turned her back, cupped her hand to the telephone, and whispered into the receiver. When she hung up she pretended I had disappeared.

"Two-person firm?" I asked. I was dangling my right foot over my left knee, showing her that I was comfortable in her frosty presence.

"That's right," she said, without raising her eyes from something she was writing.

"What kind of law does the firm specialize in?"

"General practice of law," she said. A few moments later, perhaps after writing some particularly difficult word, she added, "Mr. Hill does a lot of bank work and some real estate law. Mr. Patterson specializes in real estate law."

"Is Woodedge Savings and Loan one of your clients?"

The woman's voice became singsong. "I'm not at liberty to divulge our clients."

I had nothing else to do. I was killing time until D. Dodge could decide if he was available to see me and I reasoned that this woman probably had not had any good fun since her last kickball game in elementary school. So I asked her why she wasn't at liberty to divulge that information.

She sighed angrily. "Because I'm not, that's why."

"That's no answer," I said.

"I'm not going to argue with you," she told me.

"Why not?" I asked; but she was spared from a further battle of wits by the appearance of Dodge Patterson.

"Mr. Starbuck?" he said as he descended on me with his hand out and a smile of curious greeting spread across his face.

He was wearing neither suit nor tie, but was dressed in a tattersall shirt and a brown crewneck sweater. His thick hair was yellow and wavy and combed straight back. His jaw was rugged, his chin clefted, and his teeth were as uniformly white as a mouthful of Chiclets. He was everything one would expect from the husband of Gretchen and the lover of Rebecca and he seemed abundantly sincere in his welcome. He reminded me of a television game-show host.

"Yeah," I mumbled. "Hi." I withdrew my hand from his as quickly as possible.

"Hold my calls," he said to the receptionist, who either chose that moment to roll her eyes or was experiencing a petit mal seizure. Then he led me down a hallway that took us past a dining room that held a conference table, a galley kitchen that smelled of coffee, a powder room, and a den that held a word processor and a photocopying machine, until at last we entered a room that I assumed had once been a bedroom and was now Dodge Patterson's office. The drapes were drawn and the only light came from the center of the ceiling. The desk looked a little too delicate for a man as big as Dodge, but it had a leather-edged blotter, a gold pen stand, and several little games, including a clown figure on a set of parallel bars and some swinging silver balls that would bang into each other in perpetuity if they were started properly. What was not on the desk was anything that looked like legal work.

I surveyed the four walls before I sat down. There were two large golf trophies and one tennis cup on a shelf. There was a framed bar certificate and two framed degrees announcing that D. Dodge Patterson was a graduate of Amherst College and Boston University Law School. There might have been more items of passing interest, but I stopped scanning when I saw the photograph of Gretchen Patterson. Her face was pressed close to that of a brown-haired, big-eyed little boy who matched her in every way but the darkness of her complexion.

"My wife and son," Dodge said.

"Yes," I said, realizing I had been staring longer than I should have. "I met Mrs. Patterson on Saturday."

"Oh?" Dodge looked puzzled.

"I was out to your house to see you about this Rebecca Carpenter matter."

"That's right," he said, snapping his fingers. "She and Dad did mention something about that." He sat down, his hands folded across his stomach. This was not a man who was greatly on edge as to what I was going to ask him.

"Nice offices," I said. "How long have you been here?"

"Four years."

I glanced at his law degree and saw that he had been out of school eleven years. "Where were you before that, if you don't mind my asking?"

He gave me the name of a firm that sounded prestigious. Crosby, Stills, Nash and Young. Something like that.

"Boston?" I asked.

"Big Boston."

"I guess they don't do criminal law."

Dodge chuckled. He might have been talking to an idiot. "No. They don't do any of that."

"It's a criminal matter I'm here about, you know."

My cousin spread his hands. He smiled. His time was my time.

"You were close with Rebecca Carpenter and her husband, weren't you?"

"Pretty close, yes." A piece of paper caught his eye. He read it, frowned over it, crumpled it into a ball, and lofted it toward his wastebasket. I noticed the wastebasket had a miniature backboard and rim attached to it. "Bird," he said, as the ball of paper dropped cleanly through the hoop.

"You were with Wylie on the night his wife died."

"Yeah. Awful thing. Terrible thing."

"You played golf with him at Stonegate that day."

"That's right."

"And then cards afterward in the clubhouse."

Dodge pushed his hand back over his forehead and held it in his hair. "Did we? I guess we did."

"You and Wylie and Butcher and Teasdale and Whitman."

"Okay."

"You played the last game against Whitman."

"Right. I remember now."

"What time did you leave that night?"

"We closed the place. The bartender was trying to get us out of there, if I remember right."

"Who's we?"

"Wylie and me. I think Gerry Whitman had already gone home."

"Wylie was there when the place closed?"

Dodge hesitated. "I thought he was. Why? Did he say he wasn't?"

"No. He said he was."

"Then he was." Dodge seemed pleased that we had solved that problem. He was playing with a rubber band now.

I looked deep into Dodge's eyes and wondered if he thought this interview was at all strange. To me it was like talking to a stranger who was wearing my shirt.

"How did Wylie get home?"

Dodge's head drew back. "He drove."

"You saw him do that? At the end of the night, I mean."

"Sure. I walked him to his car." Dodge angled his gaze, as if waiting for the trick to emerge from my questions.

"And you, yourself, were in the clubhouse the whole time, six to ten or whatever?"

Dodge nodded slowly, carefully.

"You didn't go home for dinner and then come back, or anything like that, did you?"

"No. In fact, I ate there at the bar in the clubhouse because Gretchen said she wasn't going to be home that evening. She was going shopping or something."

Dodge's rubber band snapped. He looked at it as if it had betrayed him. He looked at me to see if I was through.

"You're a member of that club, aren't you?" I asked.

He nodded. "Ever since they raised the dues at Bollingbrook."

"You know the people who work there."

"At Stonegate? Sure. Most of them."

"Know a fellow named Dougie Rasmussin?"

"The lifeguard at the pool? Taught my son, Ian, to swim."

"You're aware that he left that job to go to work for the Carpenters as their caretaker, aren't you?"

"I think my wife mentioned that, yes."

"But you never discussed it with Wylie."

"Wylie? No. What did I care?"

"You know Dougie Rasmussin left the area just about the same time Rebecca was killed."

Dodge Patterson stopped fiddling with things. His expression changed. He licked his lower lip. "That doesn't make sense, if you're saying what I think you're saying. The Dougie Rasmussin I knew was just a happy-go-lucky sort of kid."

"Good-looking guy?"

"I guess you'd call him that."

"You couldn't see him getting angry or flying off the handle if, say, his advances were rejected by someone like, say, Rebecca Carpenter?"

It took Dodge a moment to answer. "Well, I don't know. I couldn't really see that sort of thing happening."

"Is that because you couldn't really see Rebecca resisting a handsome man's advances?"

"What's that supposed to mean?"

"I'm just trying to learn something about Mrs. Carpenter. Please don't take offense. There's nothing personal about what I'm asking—really, it embarrasses me sometimes—but the circumstances of her death are such that I have to ask some questions that normally would be none of my business."

Dodge pulled at his lower lip with his thumb and forefinger. He could not be a game-show host, I decided. He lacked the resiliency.

"Do you know," I asked, speaking slowly and deliberately, "if Rebecca Carpenter was sexually active outside her marriage?"

Dodge kept his thumb to his lip, but temporarily opened his fingers. "Not that I'm aware of."

"In your opinion, was she the type who might encourage the attentions of a young man like Rasmussin?"

Dodge's eyes narrowed. "I don't think so."

"Do you feel it's more likely she would have rejected his attentions?"

"I mean, that's presuming there are attentions, right? I can't really answer these questions." He smiled. He wanted out of the discussion.

"Didn't you know her pretty well yourself, Mr. Patterson?"

His smile grew broader. He picked up a pewter letter opener and began slicing at some envelopes. "Me? Becky? I've known her all my life."

"Didn't she try telephoning you on the day she died?"

"I don't think so," he said, still slicing, occasionally examining the contents of the envelopes he was opening. "Why would she?"

"Perhaps because you had a relationship with her."

"No," he said. "No. Who told you that?"

"That's not important. I'm not here to gossip or anything. The point is, I was told that you and Rebecca had a relationship at one time."

"A relationship, sure. Like I told you, I've known her all my life. But Becky is, or was, a few years older than me, and if you want to know the truth, she wasn't really my type."

"She seemed very attractive from the pictures I've seen."

Dodge Patterson smiled a between-us-guys sort of smile. His head tilted in a modified shrug. He lowered his voice to just above a whisper. "She was kind of wide in the hips."

"Oh."

He nodded. He apparently understood me to be a guy who could relate to a problem like that.

"So you have no idea why she would have been calling your house that day?"

"My house? I thought you meant she called me here. If she called my house she was looking for my wife. They usually get together, got together, about once a week. Hen party or whatever." He threw me a humorous glance. "Gossip, chew the fat, complain about their husbands." He had found a letter to his liking and he read it as he spoke.

I said, "Well, I guess you've pretty much told me everything you know."

"Hmmn?" Then he realized that I was getting up to go. "Oh, well then, fine. No problem, Pete."

"That's Patt," I snapped, unable to control myself. "Just like your name. Patterson Starbuck."

"Oh, really? How about that?" But already his attention was elsewhere. He was making a note on his letter, he was throwing away the envelope, he was getting up to shake my hand and telling me to come back anytime.

I told him I would do that and tried not to show that I hated him with all my heart.

13

They were all sitting in the corner booth. John Michael felt the corner booth in the lounge at the Roadhouse Restaurant belonged to him, and he had no qualms about asking management to move people if he arrived with any sort of group and found it occupied. Management almost always obliged. They liked having the Roadhouse known as the district attorney's hangout. They liked it so much that when John Michael would send a round of drinks to the displaced persons they often would not charge him.

John Michael had his tie loosened and a tall glass of Coke in front of him. A red plastic straw was still in the drink. Next to him sat Jessica, wearing a dark green blazer and fondling a glass of white wine. Next to her the space was open. Across from her sat Royster, still in his suit, a beer growing warm in his hand; and next to him was his wife, her hair in her face, her eyes hollow, and her drink glass already empty. There was a space next to her as well.

I took the seat beside Jessica and smiled around. No one spoke until I settled in.

"How was your trip?" John Michael asked as he placed his plastic straw between his teeth and chewed it like a toothpick.

"Leaves are still beautiful, although they're going fast. A lot of reds now, not so many oranges."

"What did you learn?"

"That Lee, Massachusetts, is a quaint little Berkshire town just off the pike. A bunch of hotels, motels, and bed-and-breakfasts to take care of the foliage tourists in

the fall, the theatergoers and music lovers bound for
Stockbridge and Tanglewood in the summer, and the
skiers passing through to Vermont in the winter. I learned
that Wylie's father was the town doctor and that Wylie
did not leave there for lack of room. His old homestead
is one of the bigger spreads in town. I was told by one of
the local innkeepers, who purported to know about things
like that, that Wylie was the smartest kid around until his
father sent him off to prep school, where he was president of his student body and a three-sport athlete."

There was silence at the table and then John Michael
jabbed his masticated straw at an ice cube in his drink
and slopped soda all over the table. "The credit check we
ran on him indicated he has seven figures of assets in his
own name, not counting anything he gets from his wife,"
he said glumly.

Jessica, who had not looked at me since I sat down,
took a napkin and began mopping up her husband's spill.
"His motive had to be jealousy, then."

I glanced up in confusion. "I'm sorry . . . ?"

"He found out his wife was fooling around and so he
killed her. Poetic justice. Did it in a lovers' lane."

"I thought we discussed . . ." I hesitated, not sure how
much of our discussion I was free to mention. It had,
after all, taken place in a locked bathroom. I amended what
I was saying. "I thought you felt he might have killed
her because he had another woman. A younger woman."

"Either way," said John Michael. "You were supposed
to look at both angles. What do you have that would
support jealousy?"

The waitress came and took my beer order. She swept
the table with the stub of her pencil and only Patty
Hansen indicated she wanted a refill.

When she was gone I said, "One possibility is Rebecca
might have been having a fling with this Rasmussin, the
young stud she hired as a caretaker, who's now disappeared. Word has it that she liked guys in good physical
shape and this kid was the lifeguard at Stonegate Country
Club before she hired him. Not an unreasonable question
to ask why she hired a good-looking young lifeguard to
do a caretaker's job."

"Any other possibility?"

"Well," I said, and suddenly my stomach felt funny. I raised my arm as a sort of disclaimer. "She may have once had an affair with Dodge Patterson."

"Her husband's golf partner?" asked John Michael.

"Her friend's husband?" asked Royster.

I told them Dodge denied it.

John Michael thought for a moment. The red plastic straw was back between his teeth. "What's he like?" he asked.

I admitted that he was handsome and athletic-looking.

"A lawyer, isn't he?"

I nodded. "Has a firm called Hill and Patterson right there in Woodedge. Before that he was with a big Boston firm."

"Sort of like Wylie? Made his mark and then moved out to the more leisurely paced life of the idyllic country-side?"

"I don't think so. He's only in his mid-thirties. I gather he was with the Boston firm about seven years."

The two lawyers looked at each other.

"Seven years is the traditional make-it-or-break-it time," said Royster. "You get made a partner or you get pushed out."

"Doesn't make him a killer," I snapped, and all four people turned to look at me in surprise.

"Didn't say it did, Patt," John Michael said softly.

I blushed and looked down at the table.

A minute later the drinks came and while John Michael was signaling to have them put on his tab I told him, "Dodge has been identified by several people as being in the clubhouse that evening."

"What about Wylie? Have you got anything screwed down about how long he was there?"

"It's confusing. Apparently five guys started playing two-man games about six o'clock. I've got Wylie placed for the first two rounds of the games. Then nobody remembers seeing him until about ten, when Dodge confirms that Wylie helped him close the place down."

"What time did the second round end?"

"Well, Butcher played in the second round and he's

the one who told me he left around eight. Okay, you say, so Wylie's unaccounted for between eight and ten. Still, that presents us with a logistical problem if we want to make him our killer. You have to figure fifteen minutes to drive from Stonegate to his house and figure another ten minutes from his house to the overlook where Mrs. Carpenter was found. From there he could drive back to Stonegate in about ten minutes, but it would be at least an hour if he walked it in the dark. And I have to figure him walking it because, after all, his wife was left in the car. So that's cutting it pretty close if we want to have Wylie going from one place to the other to the other, killing his wife and wiping off prints along the way."

I looked for my companions to share in the comfort of my logic, but John Michael was staring at me and the rest were staring along with him. I sought to persuade them further. "Also, unless Wylie walked in the first instance from Stonegate to his house, we're left with the question of how he could have had his car at Stonegate at ten. Dodge, you see, says he saw Wylie drive off at closing time."

John Michael had gone from poking at his ice cubes to curling his cocktail napkin. He kept curling until a piece of the napkin tore off. "You know, Patt," he said, "I get the feeling you don't really want to resolve this case. I get the feeling that if you did you'd be looking at the evidence in a whole different light. Is it possible, do you think, just maybe, could the guy have had his wife's Mercedes parked at the overlook all along? Couldn't he have brought her to it? Hey? Wouldn't that be the perfect cover? The guy throws the card game, drives home, dusts his wife, drives her to the parked car, and then drives back to the club. Then he waits for someone like you to come along and conclude that he couldn't have done that. That he had to have driven from his house to the overlook in her car."

I was stunned by John Michael's words. He had never before criticized me in front of others. I looked around the table and saw that Jessica still was not looking at me. Royster was, but he was wearing the blank look he used to hide malicious glee. Patty was looking at me from behind her hair. Then she was looking at Jessica. Then she was looking at me.

"Wembley Tuttle seems to feel that it's far more likely the missing caretaker killed her," I said.

"Wembley Tuttle's an asshole."

"Still, he's got a point, John. The kid is missing."

"Wembley just doesn't want me to get a big hit out of this. He's probably already cut a deal with Constantinis."

"A deal to do what?" I said, genuinely curious, hoping the answer would provide me with some clue as to John Michael's peculiar mood.

"We work on loyalty around here, Patt," he said. "We work on trust and mutual respect. That's why I've always felt comfortable with you, with Roy . . . with Jessica. I know I can depend on you, rely on you, be sure you're not going to cut my balls off the moment I've got my back turned. A man in my position has got to have people like that, somebody I can tell what I want and need without worrying that it's going to get spit back in my face."

John Michael's eyes were probing mine, making me feel guilty of spitting things at him and a myriad of other sins.

He said, "I obviously can't feel that way about Wembley. He's of a different generation, a different school. He's got his loyalties all fucked up. He's like, he's like the head butler in an English manor house. I mean, he's just a poor boy from Nestor Lower Falls." John Michael snickered, a short snicker that brought faint smiles to the faces of his audience. "He thinks it's the height of honor to be working for those rich people. He thinks it's his job to protect them no matter what. To protect their lives, their wealth, their good names. So he's going to do anything he can to keep this thing from blowing up. If that means diverting attention to some non-Woodedge person like the caretaker, then that's exactly what he's going to do. If he thinks it means attacking me because he sees me as the enemy of his charges, then that's what he'll do."

"By attacking you, you mean—"

"I mean giving Constantinis ammunition to attack me.

Because that's exactly what will happen if everything comes down the way I think it's going to. I can't have someone like that, Patt. That's why I need you. I know that with you whatever I say or do stays right here in this little group." He swept his hand around the table. "If any of us makes a mistake it stays here. It doesn't get out. Isn't that right?"

The speech was going right through me, but he most definitely wanted some kind of commitment and so I gave it to him. "Yes, that's right," I said.

"Now I told you before I wanted you to find out what you could about Mrs. Carpenter. I see this missing stud, this Rasmussin, as being another angle you should be working. Was something kinky going on there? Did Wylie find out about it? Those are the questions you should be asking. Don't worry so much about where the kid is, Wembley will be looking into that, if nothing else. But I want you to concentrate on digging up whatever relationship there was between Rebecca Carpenter and Rasmussin. Like Jessica said a few minutes ago, we're looking at jealousy at this point if we're going to support what we've got on the husband."

"Have you got something new?" I asked in surprise.

John Michael thumbed Royster, who cleared his throat and said, "The fibers found on the driver's seat have been positively identified as coming from a white wool sweater, just like the one Carpenter was reportedly wearing on the golf course that day."

"The club sweater," I said, my voice flat.

John Michael smiled wickedly. "Think you can get us some evidence on this Rasmussin relationship?"

"I think I can."

"Got an idea of how you're going to go about it?"

"I've got an idea."

"Good."

John Michael took a major swallow from his soda. Jessica and Royster threw back their own drinks. Patty might have joined them, but her glass was already empty.

14

The scene could not have been more awkward. I tramped hard on the steps and did a lot of unnecessary rattling of the front door. My mother and Kelsey were sitting at the kitchen table playing whist and they immediately put down their cards.

My mother smiled steadily at me, but her eyes were busy searching mine. She offered me chicken soup, French bread, a cup of tea, a bowl of Jell-O with fruit in it. I told her I wasn't hungry. I said I was only there to ask Kelsey to run an errand with me.

Kelsey said "Sure," without waiting to hear what it was. He got to his feet and spared me from having to sit down.

"Are you well, Patt?" my mother asked.

"Yeah, sure. I'm fine." I spoke while I watched Kelsey punch his arms into the sleeves of his plaid L. L. Bean jacket.

"Will you be coming back to spend the night?"

"No, no," I said. "I don't think so. Not tonight."

My mother nodded and turned to Kelsey. "Thank you for coming by, Harry," she said.

Kelsey dipped his head and side-glanced at me and thanked her for having him.

They parted without a kiss or even a touch; and I, feeling guilty, said that I thought I would only need to be borrowing Kelsey for an hour or so. My mother's response was to tell me to keep my coat buttoned. She called me "honey" when she did so, and the term made me flinch in front of her boyfriend.

My mother had always called me things like "honey"

and "sweetie" and "dear" when I was a child, and I had taken those words for granted. She and my father were not given to many demonstrations of affection between themselves, and so such names were a mother's prerogative in my family. They were part of the natural order of things in our household, where my mother and I were the closest of allies in dealing with my father and his whims and convictions and illusions. They were part of an order that no longer had the same purpose once my father was gone and we were left, a forty-year-old woman and a nineteen-year-old boy, with barely a clue as to how to proceed without him. Perhaps because it was easiest we made a tacit agreement to try to carry on as though nothing had changed—something that was only possible to do if we never discussed my father or the strange circumstances of his death.

Questions went unasked and unanswered as I continued to live at home and my mother continued to call me "honey" and do my laundry and cook my meals. She went off to work and I returned to school and we would come home at night and tell each other everything had gone well. It was an arrangement made with the best of intentions, and one that no doubt was even worse for my mother than it was for me. I, at least, had buddies and dates and weekend trips and summer vacations. But, at best, my mother's social life consisted of introductions made by others—a field necessarily restricted by the fact that as a couple she and my father had not had many friends. The men to whom she was introduced tended to be older and were prone to wearing hats and inviting her to dinner in places that didn't require reservations. She would go out apprehensively and come back sadly.

And then she met Kelsey, and I was suddenly freed of the responsibility of having to worry about her ability to come to grips with the rest of her life. He was a nice, physical, semi-intelligent, caring man whose company she obviously enjoyed—and he was an apologetic intrusion into our carefully constructed relationship.

I could not look at him as we drove from West Nestor to Walmouth in his black Jeep Cherokee, even though I talked most of the way. He did not seem to mind, but concentrated on the road ahead, as though driving the Cherokee was one of the harder things a man could do. He listened as I explained generally about Doug Rasmussin and what I was trying to learn, and he asked occasional questions about what I expected of him. By the time we pulled up in front of Balducci's we had the game plan fairly well set.

Balducci's was not the sort of place that attracted many strangers. It had a red brick front and a coach lantern hanging next to its door. It had two windows, but both of them were six feet off the ground and both were covered with black iron rails. In one of the windows was a cardboard sign for Schaeffer beer, in the other was an electric sign for Narragansett.

A green scalloped trim board ran along the top of the building. It read BALDUCCI'S TAVERN COCKTAILS. But Balducci's was not the sort of place where you ordered cocktails. Balducci's was beer and a shot.

Patrons of Balducci's did not limit their activities to the inside of the bar. Weather permitting, they tended to stand on the sidewalk in front of the door, swinging their arms and swapping stories and watching the traffic go by. That meant that I would have been spotted right away as somebody who did not belong if we had driven up in my gray-green Alfa. The Jeep Cherokee, however, was okay. It meant we had money to spend, but probably did manly things on the weekends.

Kelsey fit the image perfectly. Besides his L. L. Bean jacket, he had on work boots and jeans. Emerging from the car, he strode the sidewalk with confidence and yet nodded in a friendly way to the two or three guys who were openly checking us out. They made just enough of a pathway for us to get through the front door without anyone having to say "Excuse me."

It was dark inside, but I could see two coin-operated pool tables, a jukebox with a rainbow façade, a couple of sets of tables and chairs, an oak bar, and a single bartender. One of the pool tables was being used for a game by a mean-faced man with long black hair, a long black mustache, and a cigarette dangling from his lips. He was playing against a fat man whose beltless dungarees were slipping far enough down to reveal the crack in his be-hind. The other pool table was being used as a perch for two women, both of whom had beer bottles and ciga-rettes in their hands, both of whom had very tight jeans, and one of whom was considerably younger than the other. The women were talking to a group of guys who were seated sideways on their barstools. They all turned to see us. The men and the women.

"You got a pitcher, buddy?" Kelsey asked, leaning onto the end of the bar closest to the door. I did as Kelsey did. I leaned onto the bar with both my forearms, my hands clasping my elbows.

The bartender was a very big guy wearing a white knit shirt that was too small for his arms and that more or less rolled over his belly in little waves. He had a hawklike face with a curlicue scar under his cheekbone. He stopped his walk toward us and said, "Bud or Mich?"

"Bud," said Kelsey.

The bartender, without moving his feet, drew out a pitcher and thumbed on the tap. "Three fifty," he said.

Nearest to us was a man with thick, curly hair, an unruly mustache, and a jersey with a football number on both its front and back. He was watching us over his shoulder.

"How's it going?" I asked, nodding at him.

He tilted his bottle to his mouth and let his eyes slide to his companions while he drank. When he put the bottle down he said, "All right," and cleaned his mouth with the back of his wrist.

Nobody in the place was speaking. The jukebox was carrying the sounds of the Beach Boys singing "Good Vibrations." The pool balls were whacking and whirring and reverberating into rubber pockets. And then the bartender, the pitcher nearly full, said in a very loud voice, "Say, don't I know you from somewheres?"

Kelsey grinned. He put a thumb under his chin and propped it there. "Not unless you remember every guy who ever took you over the wall at Morrissey Field."

It took a moment for the nickel to drop, but then the bartender's eyes popped wide and he sputtered as the beer he was drawing overflowed the pitcher and ran down his hand. "Kelsey!" he shouted. "I'll be a hot shit." He hit the tap to shut it off and put down the brimming pitcher. "I know this guy," he told everyone in the place. "Harry Kelsey from the Bombardiers." He reached over and slapped the curly-haired guy on the shoulder of his football jersey. "You know him, Billy. Last guy to get cut from the Orioles one year. Only hits the ball about nine hundred fuckin' feet."

Billy tried to say hello, but Kelsey had to pay attention to the bartender, who had rushed over to shake his hand. Kelsey introduced me to Buzzy Balducci and I got a beer-soaked paw thrust at me.

That was all I got. Buzzy was looking around. "Who else is here? Duane, you know this guy? Sure you do." Turning back to Kelsey, he said, "Duane plays the shallowest third base in the league, but he don't play that way against you."

Duane leaned forward from near the other end of the bar. He had short blond hair, a pockmarked face, and tattoos on his forearm and bicep. He waved a stiff-fingered hand and said, "Whadyasay?"

Balducci went back to get our pitcher and a couple of glasses. He said it was on the house. He wanted to know if we were there because Kelsey was thinking of jumping teams.

Kelsey said no, he was a little old to be doing something like that. He claimed he was lucky his own team still let him play.

Buzzy said, "Yeah, I don't know if I'll be coming back myself. Haven't played since I busted my hand against the cops."

"You busted your hand?" said Kelsey, pouring us beers. "I didn't know that."

"Yeah. You didn't know that? We're playing out at that tournament, O'Brien Park? And that douchebag shortstop they got, what's his name? Finnegan? Drives the cruiser? Claims I don't go down fast enough on the doubleplay. He low-bridges me, you know what I mean? I mean, he really low-bridges me. I'm lucky to be a-fuckin'-live. So I says something to him. He says something back. I give him a shot right in the head. Cleaned the cocksucker's clock, 'cept I broke three knuckles doing it." He showed us the damage, but I couldn't see much given the light. "Still can't grip the ball right. And a guy my age, my size, I can't play noplace else but pitch. Then, get this: Finnegan, right? Being the little prick he is, he can't leave the game on the field. Here I am, my hand's all busted up, he still claims he's gonna get me. I catch him one day out here giving parking tickets to my customers. I mean, gimme a break, will ya? Parking tickets? In this neighborhood? What, I pop the guy, he's gonna drive me outa business? I'm the one with the broken bones, for Chrissake."

Balducci grabbed his belt with two hands and hoisted his sagging pants. "First time, you know, I take everybody's ticket. I go down the traffic court to complain. You know what the court says? You know what the fuckin' judge says to me? He says I don't got standing to talk to him about other people's tickets. I goes to him, I goes, 'Standing? I'm standing right here. What are you talking about?' The guy doesn't listen to me. He tells me I raise my voice again he's gonna throw me in the jail. Me. I haven't done nothin' but try to run a barroom and all of a sudden he's gonna throw me in jail. You know what I ended up havin' to do? I ended up having to pay all the tickets myself. I think it's like seventy-five bucks. I can't keep doing that, you know. So now I tell people, 'You got a car out there on the street? Watch out it's not parked illegal because that little bastard Finnegan'll come along and give you a ticket.' "

"He still doing it?" I asked.

Buzzy Balducci looked at me with a trace of irritation. He had, after all, been talking to Kelsey. "Yeah," he said.

"You collect the tickets you got and give them to me. I'll take care of it."

Balducci took a half-step back from the bar. "You a cop?"

"No. But I know people. If you want, I'll take care of the situation." This was not part of the game plan. This was ad-libbing.

Balducci cleaned his hands on a bar rag and considered

me for a moment. Then he looked at Kelsey. "He mean it?"

Kelsey said, "He says he can do it, he can do it."

Balducci still hesitated. "You a ballplayer?" he asked me.

I shook my head.

"You oughta be. You're big enough. What did you say your name was again?"

"Patt Starbuck."

"Used to be a guy by that name played center field for Nestor."

"You've got a good memory if you can remember that far back."

Buzzy Balducci studied me for a minute before grunting. Shouting over his shoulder, he asked if anybody had any Finnegan tickets.

"Tell me about it," shouted back Duane. He was heavily involved in conversation with the younger of the two women on the pool table and he did not bother to look up.

"You got one with you?"

"Fuck no," said Duane. "I threw it away."

"Anybody else?"

The woman speaking with Duane slid to the floor and walked over to us. She said she had gotten one the same night as Duane and thought she still had it in her pocketbook. As she got closer I saw that she was perhaps a hard thirty, maybe a real hard twenty-five. She fished around in a purse that was slightly smaller than a steamer trunk until she came up with the ticket. She handed it to Buzzy and Buzzy handed it to me.

"Guy says he'll fix it," Buzzy said skeptically.

The woman looked at me and shrugged as if she had heard better lines. I watched her go back to her perch and wondered how she had managed to preserve such a nice butt in light of whatever tragedies had ravaged her face.

"I still don't see how you're gonna do that," Buzzy said.

"Hey, Buzzy," I said, putting the ticket in the pocket of my coat, "you don't really care how I do it as long as I do it, right? The way I look at it, you're a a friend of

Kelsey's and you're getting screwed over. I know some
people who can help. I take this ticket to them, I explain
about the Finnegan problem, and maybe I can make it go
away. If I can't, well, what have you lost?"

Balducci held up his hand. "You can take care of it,
you got my gratitude. You know what I mean?"

"No problem," I said. "In fact, you could call it even if
you'd just tell me where I can find Doug Rasmussin."

"Dougie's not around no more. He split. Where did he
go, Billy, Florida? Someplace like that?"

"Who's that?" demanded Billy.

"Rasmussin."

"He split."

"Right. But where did he go?"

"California. L.A. Hollywood. 'S gonna be a movie
star."

"Talk to Billy," said Buzzy Balducci, thumbing in his
direction. "He's one of Ras's best friends."

With that introduction, Billy welcomed me onto the
stool next to him.

"When did he take off?" I asked.

Billy thought about it. "I don't know. A week or two
ago. He should be there by now, but he hasn't sent a
card or nothing. I wanted him to send one, you know,
with one of those beach chicks on it with their tits hanging out. I like those cards."

"Yeah, those are great. With the Hawaiian chicks and
all that? Lying there in the surf?"

"Yeah. I'm surprised they let those go through the
mail, you know? I would have thought there'd be laws
against that."

"I guess it's all right for the Hawaiian women. They
say it's part of their culture. Like the pictures in *National
Geographic*."

"Yeah, I guess. So you a friend of Ras's, or what?"

"Not really. I promised a guy I'd look him up. But I
went out to this country club where I was told he worked
and they said he didn't work there anymore."

"Oh, yeah, he quit there in, like, September."

"He was the lifeguard, wasn't he? What, did the job
run out or something?"

"Nah. He wanted, he could have done groundskeeping until they closed for the winter. That's what he did last year. But what happened was, he really wanted to go to California. Only, one thing and another, and he never could get it together until he meets this rich lady from Woodedge who, like, works out the perfect deal for him."

"What, more money?"

"That's only part of it, what I heard," said a voice on the other side of Billy. A guy I hadn't noticed before, a guy with hair combed three inches high, was smirking at Billy.

Billy smirked back. He looked over at the two women on the pool table so that he could make sure they weren't listening and then he leaned in close to me and said, "I heard he had his hand in more than this lady's rosebushes."

"I hear it wasn't his hand," said the interestingly coiffed smirker.

He and Billy had a good laugh over that and I joined in. "You mean," I said, when the laugh was over, "he was working at the country club and some lady hired him to . . . you know?"

"Well," said Billy, "alls I know is that Ras said he got to be friends with this real horny rich bitch who used to go to his club. He said she'd do anything, you know?" Billy's eyebrows soared up and down. "The way I heard it, she offered to pay him, like, in six weeks what he coulda earned in twelve weeks at the club. Promised he'd be outa here before winter. Right, Jack?"

The guy with the hair waved his hand. "Something like that. I think all she wanted him to do was fuck her brains out. Only, maybe she didn't want him to do it forever. She was married, is what I heard."

Billy and I were staring at Jack and he shrugged. "That Ras was a good-looking guy, say what you want about him."

"So," I said, after allowing time for all of us to sip our beer, "he was only planning on working six weeks all along?"

"If you call that working," said Jack.

"The reason she gave him the job, see," said Billy,

"was to help him earn the money he needed to go to California."

"That was one reason she gave him the job," said Jack. "The other reason was she wanted to get herself racked up and screaming at the moon." He put back his head and howled into the ceiling.

From down at the pool table came the sound of one of the women howling back at him. She may have just wanted to howl, but she had her head tilted and her eyes closed and her howl was at least as long and loud as Jack's. When she was done somebody else picked up the sound, and pretty soon almost everyone in the bar was howling. Buzzy Balducci beamed at Kelsey, as if he was sure that all this good fun was going to convince Kelsey to jump teams after all.

"So," I said, when the last warbling note had died out, "you guys weren't surprised when Ras left, I take it."

"Cripes, I wouldn't a done it," said Jack, shaking his head. "Get some rich bitch paying me to do that to her, you woulda had to explode me offa her place. But what I heard, this broad he's working for was the one who was encouraging him to go. Always telling him shit like if he was ever going to make something of hisself he had to get as far away from here as possible. Can you imagine anybody believing that?"

Billy, however, gave my question some thought and said, "Well, I sorta was surprised he actually went. I mean, the guy had been talking about going for a long time and he could never quite get it together. There was always some reason, you know? Like, once he couldn't go because the Red Sox were in the pennant race. Can you think of anything more dumber than that? I mean, what the hell, he coulda watched them blow it out in California as good as here. Another time it seems to me he didn't go because somebody offered to take him hunting instead. One weekend, right? So, yeah, I was surprised, I guess."

"So how do you know he really went?"

Billy looked at me as though I was pulling his leg. "Well, he ain't around here no more. Where else could he be?"

I told Billy he had a real good point.

We left shortly after that, Kelsey and I. I gave him the high sign and he broke off his conversation with Buzzy. Kelsey got a chorus of good-byes and I got a big index finger leveled at me along with a reminder to take care of the ticketing.

Kelsey and I walked silently back to the car. It was cold and we were shivering and I sat on my hands while the engine warmed. Then he said, "I didn't know you played ball."

"I didn't know you were the last guy cut by the Orioles."

He snorted. "I never even saw the big club."

"Well," I said, "you fooled them."

Kelsey looked at me for a long time. It was a look he had never given me in my mother's house. "So," he said, "did you."

Thinking about it later, I had to wonder if there wasn't just a trace of disappointment in his voice.

15

It was easy to imagine Doug Rasmussin. Half the guys I grew up with were like him. Maybe they weren't all good-looking, and maybe some were brighter than others, but they all liked sports and beer and they all lived within the confines of old friendships and familiar places. What I could not imagine was Doug Rasmussin having an affair with Rebecca Carpenter.

She was, after all, about fifteen years older than he was, and probably wealthier than anyone he had ever known. Her attractiveness, or at least what I had seen in her photograph, was not the sort that I suspected would play well in Balducci's Tavern. I could see her offering him a job, I could see him taking it, but I could not see him coming on to her. A guy like Robert, maybe, he would come on to her; but a guy like Dougie Rasmussin would know his place.

On the other hand, after ten days of thinking about her, Rebecca Carpenter remained as elusive to me as she had been when I first learned of her murder. She had a husband who seemed unable to describe her. She had a friend from childhood who seemed unsure as to how well she actually knew her. She had a friend from college who would not let her death interrupt a tennis lesson. She had a friend from adulthood whose husband she may have been screwing. For all I knew, she was a temptress who entranced young men like Doug Rasmussin, enticed them into her Mercedes and forced them to drive her to dark overlooks where she teased them into potentially murderous frenzies. It was time for me to find out more about Rebecca Carpenter.

Once again I started with her husband. On Friday morning, I showed up at Woodedge Savings and Loan and was ushered into a small but expensively furnished office where Wylie Carpenter reluctantly greeted me. He was not dressed to meet customers, but was wearing a pale yellow V-neck sweater over a lime-green polo shirt. He was obviously hoping this interview would not take long because, although he allowed me to be seated in a highbacked, tufted leather chair, he remained standing behind his antique English desk, his hands pushed into the pockets of his moss-green slacks.

No, he said firmly, he did not know Doug Rasmussin when Dougie worked at Stonegate. While Becky did identify Rasmussin as the lifeguard at the pool, he rarely, if ever, used the pool himself. His understanding was that Rasmussin had some landscaping experience and that was the reason he was hired. The subject of him only working until October 15 never came up, but the idea didn't make any sense. "Unless," he cautioned, glancing at his watch, "that's how long Becky gave him as a probationary period."

"Did he do a good job?"

Wylie shrugged. "The summer fruit was all in by the time he started, so what was to do? Cut and rake, and I think he did that well enough. At least I didn't hear any complaints—and that's probably significant. Surely, if my wife was planning on sacking him on the fifteenth she would have said as much to me, and she never did." He was rattling the coins in his pocket when he said that. Then he caught himself. "On the other hand, I asked Becky once if she was planning on having him move into the caretaker's cottage and she said she hadn't decided yet."

After a few seconds of silence the coins began to jingle again. I was strategizing a setup for my next question, but as the jingling grew louder I abandoned the setup. "Do you think," I asked, "it was just a coincidence that Rasmussin disappeared on the day your wife was killed?"

Good old Mr. Carpenter gave me the glare I deserved.

I spread my hands. I opened my eyes wide. I made my expression as innocent as I could. "Have you been able to learn anything about the relationship between Rasmussin and your wife?"

"Oh, Jesus." Carpenter stared out the window, his coins silent. He had a lawn to stare at, and in the far distance he had the town hall. "My wife is dead," he said at last. "The only things missing are her pocketbook and the young caretaker she hired six weeks before. That's what I know, Mr. Starbuck. That and the fact she was found where she was. You want me to speculate? You want me to guess? You want me to torture myself with all kinds of things that might have been going on? I can do that, you know. I can do that or I can try to hold myself together as best I can. Now which is it you want?"

A chill came over me. I could not see the expression on Carpenter's face, but I recognized the tone of his voice and I knew all too well what he meant by holding himself together. It was a phrase with which I felt very familiar.

"I understand what you're going through, Mr. Carpenter," I told him, choosing my words carefully, "and I'm sorry if I've made it more difficult."

There was no response.

"Believe it or not," I tried again, "it can be better to have people ask questions rather than make assumptions."

He nodded this time, but still did not turn. The coin jingling, the watch checking, all the signs of impatience were gone; and I no longer felt like grilling him.

"There's just one more question I have to ask you, Mr. Carpenter," I said, rising to my feet. "And that's a question about what you yourself were doing that night." I hesitated, hoping that would be enough. It wasn't. "I know you were at the club at about eight and I know you were at the club at ten. But I can't seem to account for you in the hours between."

By the time Wylie Carpenter completed his turn from the window to me he was no longer showing a trace of emotion, and whatever feelings of empathy I had been feeling drained away from me.

"I was there," he said calmly.

I asked him if there was somewhere other than the clubhouse he might have been and he insisted there was not. Then he corrected himself. "Well, I might have slipped away to use the facilities."

"But, of course, that wouldn't have taken two hours."

"No. No, it wouldn't."

"Would you keep that in mind, Mr. Carpenter?" I said as I walked toward the door. "That I need help with that one?"

"I'll keep it in mind, Mr. Starbuck."

Feeling somewhat less than pleased with the way things had gone in Wylie's office, I drove to his home, determined to do better with Sarah Mitchell, the housekeeper, an overweight woman whose skin was so dark and smooth it was able to reflect the light of a hallway lamp. I knew from experience that Sarah Mitchell was a very tough interview. She kept her eyes lowered, she spoke very softly, and she hardly ever volunteered information. It was that last trait that made me suspect she had plenty to say and that I had simply failed to ask the right things when I first interviewed her a day or two after the murder.

I started with easy enough questions. I asked her what a typical day was like in the Carpenter household before Rebecca was killed.

"Mr. Carpenter," she said, her voice barely audible, "gets up around seven and putters around with his coffee and his newspapers. Financial pages mostly. He might be on the telephone a lot in the early hours, or he might not. Depending. Then Mrs. Carpenter come downstairs about nine and Mr. Carpenter goes off to work while Mrs. Carpenter has her continental."

"By work you mean Woodedge Savings and Loan?"

"Yes sir."

"What were his work hours?"

"He would usually get there about ten. Then he would go to one of his clubs in the afternoon. Sometimes he would come home for lunch first, sometimes not."

"Did he come home for lunch that day, the day Mrs. Carpenter was killed?"

"I believe he did. Yes sir."

"You don't happen to know if he took the Mercedes anywhere, do you?"

"I don't know. Most of the time he'd drive the other car."

"And Mrs. Carpenter, what was her typical day like?"

"Usually do some things around the house or the grounds."

"And that particular day?"

"I don't remember her doing much of anything special."

"I see. Tell me, did you know Mr. Rasmussin very well?"

"Not really. He's outside. I'm inside."

"Did he and Mrs. Carpenter seem to get along?"

"Pretty well, yes sir."

"Did they seem to enjoy each other's company?"

"Seemed to, yes sir."

"Did he come into the house ever?"

"The house? Once in a while, maybe. Like for lunches, something like that. Uh-huh."

"Would he come in for lunches if Mr. Carpenter was here?"

"Un-unh."

"On those days when Mr. Carpenter was not here, would he eat lunch with Mrs. Carpenter?"

"Mrs. Carpenter? Sometimes she would bring his lunch to him."

"Were lunches the only reason he would come into the house?"

"Maybe to use the bathroom."

"Did you ever see him go up to the second floor?"

"No. There's a bathroom right off the back pantry. No need for him to go upstairs."

"Did Mrs. Carpenter ever invite him upstairs? For any reason?"

A long silence preceded her answer. "No."

"Did you ever have conversations with Mr. Rasmussin?"

"Not really. Just about whether he likes lettuce in his tuna fish sandwiches, something like that."

"Did he ever tell you how long he was planning on working here at the Carpenters'?"

"No. I just assumed, you know, that he took the Marconis' place."

"So you expected him to show up for work the day after Mrs. Carpenter was killed."

"Yes. I did expect that."

"When was the last time you saw him?"

"The only way I remember it is it was payday, okay? And he wanted to get to the bank soon as he could. That was ten, ten thirty, and he come in to wash up before he went. Whether he ever come back after that, I couldn't tell you."

"And you left . . ."

"Around six."

"Was Mrs. Carpenter's Mercedes there when you left?"

"I suppose it was in the garage. I didn't look."

"And you don't know anybody she was supposed to see that evening?"

"I don't. No sir."

"There was a phone call made around one to the Patterson house. Do you know why?"

"Maybe returning a call Mrs. Patterson made earlier."

"I'm told Mrs. Patterson and Mrs. Carpenter used to get together once a week. Is that true?"

"Lately, past couple of months maybe, yes sir."

"What would they do when they got together? Do you know?"

"Drink, I expect."

"You mean, like, get drunk?"

"I don't know what they do."

"Then, if you'll forgive me, how do you know they drank?"

"Because that's how Mrs. Carpenter discovered the Marconis been stealing her liquor. Mrs. Patterson wanted some Scotch, she said, and Mrs. Carpenter told me how they turned the house upside down looking for some and then they thought the Marconis might have some so they went out there. 'Cept the Marconis wasn't home because it was Bingo night and when Mrs. Carpenter opened their door that's when she seen they had all her liquor."

"Did that surprise you?"

"Yes."

"Why?"

"I didn't know what the Marconis would want with all

that fancy stuff. I never seen them drink nothing but red wine."

My visit to the Carpenter home improved my spirits immensely. It was a clean, clear, crisp October day and I was cruising the leaf-spattered back lanes of Woodedge, Massachusetts, in my Alfa Romeo driving machine with a whole new set of prospects in front of me.

The enigmatic Mrs. Carpenter had a drinking buddy, and in my experience a drinking buddy was about as likely a candidate to know a person's secrets as you can get. Mrs. Carpenter had a drinking buddy who was going to require my further investigation, and there was nobody I wanted to investigate further than the sultry Gretchen Patterson.

But first I had to get back to the office. It was nearly noon and I wanted to catch Royster before he broke for lunch. Royster was friends with the traffic commissioner and I knew that if he could speak to the commissioner in the time between his double Manhattan and his return to the bench for the afternoon session my chances of wiping out the Balducci ticketing problem would be greatly enhanced. I suspected that a well-placed favor for Buzzy Balducci was my best means of ingratiating myself with anyone likely to be hearing from Dougie Rasmussin, and Dougie was still very much in need of being found.

I wheeled along Highland Street, downshifting at the corners. At Rotten Row I had to be more careful because it was barely wide enough for two cars, but Rotten Row was empty and I drove it the way I wanted. On the Post Road I had to fit in with the speeds of the other cars, but there was no appreciable amount of traffic until I crossed the river and then Main Street was almost bumper-to-bumper. I drove Main to Liberty and Liberty to Court and it took longer than I had expected.

I turned off Court and parked in my usual spot behind the great yellow stone building that housed the criminal courts on the first and second floors, the district attorney's office on the third floor, a branch of the county jail on the fourth floor, and the public defender's office tucked in next to the boiler room and storage area in the basement.

I saw the crowd in front of the elevators and elected to run up the stairs. I took them two at a time, two flights. In the third-floor hallway I bumped into some of our staff people. In our reception area the relief crew was on, and that usually spelled disaster. A woman named Delilah was standing behind the counter ready to give wrong information to anybody and everybody who made inquiries.

There was a door in the wall behind the counter and I was lucky to have Delilah buzz it open for me. Behind the door was a large room that served as the secretarial pool for more than a dozen women who did the work for the various staff attorneys whose offices lined the walls and corridors. Only John Michael's secretary and Royster's secretary had different arrangements. They had doors to their offices and doors behind them to their bosses' offices. Anita, Royster's secretary, had her door closed. I knocked and nobody answered. I opened it and saw nobody inside. The door to Royster's office was also closed and my spirits plummeted.

I stood in the empty room, breathing heavily, and thought about leaving a message on Anita's desk. But Anita's desk was a mess and I thought it would be safer to leave one on Royster's. I thought it would be no big deal to open his door.

I was wrong.

Anita was bent over Royster's desk. She was bent forward and her short red skirt was flipped across her back. She still was in her heels, but her finely muscular legs were spread apart and her white lace panties were hooked around one ankle. Behind her, wedged against her buttocks, was Royster, fully dressed except for his suit coat and his open pants. His hands were on Anita's hips and his skin was slapping against hers.

Anita's own hands were wide across Royster's desk. The side of her face was pressed into his blotter. Her mouth was making little gasping sounds, but her eyes were open and she was staring directly at me. Above her, Royster's head was thrown back and his eyes were screwed shut as he continued his rhythmical thrusting into his secretary.

I expected a scream or a cry or a break in the action, but there was none. Royster continued his movements and Anita continued her staring, and there was nothing for me to do but ease the door closed, as if hiding the sound of the latch would somehow erase my presence. Then I turned and fled.

I went out through Anita's office, through the secretarial pool, and through the reception area. This time, unlike at my mother's house, no one called after me. Only Delilah seemed to notice how fast I was moving, and all she wanted to know was if I was going to lunch.

16

I went to the fitness club. It was in my flight path.

I could have returned to my car and driven straight back to the Patterson house, but after seeing Anita and Royster I no longer had quite the same enthusiasm for doing that. It was not that I cared particularly about Anita, with her finely muscular legs and her white lace panties hooked around her ankle, or Royster, with his big mouth and his stringy-haired wife, it was just that I no longer felt prepared to interview Gretchen Patterson. I felt the need to work out instead.

One of the squash courts was open and, although I had not reserved it, I took my racket from my locker and went into the court to bang a few balls off the wall. Playing squash by yourself is not a fun thing to do and some may even question its value. It was, for example, very hard to sustain a volley and practice difficult shots at the same time. But since the only person I ever played was John Michael, it was not really necessary to practice difficult shots. I opted for trying to keep the ball going for as long as possible and working on my rhythm.

A knock on the door interrupted me and I, thinking it was somebody who had reserved the court, started to gather up my balls. The door opened and a man of about my own age poked in his head.

"Excuse me," he said, "but are you waiting for anyone? I thought if you weren't maybe you might like a game. I was watching through the window and I think we're about the same level . . ."

"Fading intermediate, you mean?"

It took a second for the intended humor of my remark

to register, but then the man smiled and stepped into the court with me. "Skip," he said, holding out his hand.

"I beg your pardon?"

"Skip. That's my name."

He was a fair-sized man, who looked as if he had been in very good shape at one point in his life and was now battling a softening stomach. His hair was a little long at the ears and in the back, his nose appeared to have been broken on at least one occasion, and he wore a soft brace on one knee. Other than that he looked like a fine fellow. I offered him my hand, my name, and a place on my court.

We warmed up a little and his game appeared to be about the same as mine, a little weak on the backhand, a little erratic on the serve, very physical in terms of establishing position in the center of the court. And then we went at it.

He got out to a six-point lead and then I came back and knotted it at nine. At twelve I put a shot directly into the corner and it dropped like a rock on him. I aced my serves for the thirteenth and fourteenth points and then he jumped in front of me and ricocheted a shot off three walls to take back the serve. He tied me at fourteen and I told him we would play for three.

His chest heaving, Skip lofted a serve off the front wall, the back wall, and into the service box. I scooped it softly forward so that it just kissed the front wall and he had to race for it. He got his shot, but I drilled my return and he never had a chance. My sixteenth point was to his backhand and he returned the ball low, directly into the tin. He got a clean return on my next serve and I played the carom off the back wall. He dinked one, as I had done to him a minute before. This time I had to sprint forward, but my shot was perfect, forcing him to turn his back for the return. I charged for position in center court just as he came up from the other end. We hit head-on, crashing to the floor in a tangle of arms and legs and a clattering of rackets as the ball bounced harmlessly around us.

My head was against his chest. My cheek seemed stuck to his soaking wet T-shirt. My arm was under his back.

"Jesus Christ," he said, and when I pulled myself back I saw that he was staring at me incredulously, as if I were a madman.

"Interference?" I asked innocently, and all of a sudden he was laughing. We were both laughing. We were rolling on the floor roaring with laughter, and for that moment I was as sure as I could be that we were both great guys, kindred spirits, and totally without need of worrying about office romances, missing murderers, or misspent lives.

We played for over an hour and then he told me he had to get back to work. We walked to the locker room together, dripping with perspiration, and neither one of us spoke as we stripped and grabbed our towels and went into the showers. There was camaraderie in the silence as we massaged our aching muscles beneath the hard spray of the faucets. We had played as even a match as two men could play, and although I had won two games to one, he had scored more total points than I. When at last we shut off the water we were grinning at each other.

"Have to play you again," he said, before burying his face in his towel.

I told him he would have to give me a week to recover and he laughed.

At this time of the afternoon the locker room was almost empty and we could talk to each other easily across the distance that separated our respective lockers.

"I've been looking for somebody to play with," he said, putting on a pair of tapered boxer shorts. "Nobody in my office seems to be interested."

"Maybe we can set something up," I said. I put on a pair of yellow briefs, tan socks, brown corduroy pants.

"You work around here?" Skip asked.

"District attorney's office," I told him.

"Oh, yeah? I'm an attorney, too."

I glanced up. He was toweling his hair. He wasn't looking at me. He was still bare-chested, but now he was wearing a pair of gray pin-striped trousers and a black leather belt.

"I don't do any criminal law," he said as he threw

down his towel and took a white shirt out of his locker,
"so I don't suppose our paths will ever cross in court.
Where did you go to law school?"

I had a white shirt of my own in my hand. It was a
shortsleeved pullover knit with a little insignia over the
left breast. It was not the insignia of a polo player or an
alligator. "I didn't go to law school," I said. "I'm not a
lawyer."

Beneath the button-down collar of Skip's white shirt
was a red silk tie with a pattern of little blue diamonds.
He had one hand on each end of the tie and was maneuvering it back and forth to make sure it was in place
before he began buttoning his shirt. "Oh?" he said. "What
do you do at the district attorney's?"

I pulled on my own shirt. I grabbed my black Reeboks
off the floor of my locker and thrust my feet into them.
"I work as an investigator."

Skip sat down on a wooden bench and drew his own
shoes out of his locker. They were black and sleek and
each one bore a single small gold adornment. In the
expensive stores they were called slip-ons rather than
loafers. "Gee," he said, "we're always looking for investigators, even if it's just to serve subpoenas, that sort of
thing. You able to do any outside work?"

"I don't serve subpoenas," I said. I could have told
him that my title was litigation coordinator. I could have
told him that I probably had at least as many years in
graduate school as he did, and that I had the job I had
because I liked it. But instead I stared into my locker.

"Well," I heard him say, "if you ever think of branch-
ing out give me a call. I didn't mean it to sound like it
was just subpoenas. My firm does a lot of trial work and
there's always something going on. If you're half as good
at investigating as you are on the squash court I'm sure
we could use you."

The soles of his black shoes slapped against the floor as
he approached. "Here," he said, stopping.

I looked up. Skip was fully dressed now. He had his
pin-striped jacket to go with his pin-striped pants. He
was holding out his card, a card that made no reference
to the name "Skip."

"Call me," he said, "and let's get together for another game. Evenings are usually best for me. Today was just sort of a fluke."

"Righto," I said.

He held out his hand and I stood up to take it. In his slip-ons he was taller than I was in my Reeboks.

"See you," he said, removing his hand and turning it into a wave.

"Ciao," I said, doing the same, and waiting till he left the locker room before I crumpled his card and chucked it into the nearest wastebasket.

It was midafternoon by the time I returned to the office. I avoided everyone else and went directly to my desk, where I made phone calls and prepared a report on my interviews with Carpenter and Sarah Mitchell. I was waiting for the Keoughs' weekly Friday-night meeting to begin. I was wondering how Royster would act, and I was envisioning my own possible reactions.

But at five o'clock there was no call from John Michael's secretary, and at five fifteen I was the only one in the office. At five thirty I was on my way into Boston when I impulsively did a U-turn and headed back to the Patterson home. The afternoon had been a waste and the evening promised nothing ahead of me.

It was past six when I arrived at the rear entrance and I had no right to be surprised when my knock was answered by D. Dodge. He was, however, dressed in a cutaway coat and a pair of formal gray trousers, and in the short time since I had last seen him he had grown a pencil-thin mustache and changed his hair from yellow to black. Instead of being wavy, it was now slicked back close to his skull. His Chicletlike teeth now sported a slight gap and he had managed to acquire a pair of extraordinarily large ears. He seemed delighted with his new appearance.

"Dodge Patterson?" I asked, just to be sure.

"You injuh me, suh!" he cried in what was no doubt his best Southern accent. "I believe your attentions are directed elsewhere."

I looked over my shoulder to see what he meant before

I said or did anything further. I saw nothing which provided me with any clue. I looked back. Patterson was grinning.

"Clark Gable," he said. "How do I look?" He held out his hands and did a slow spin for me.

I nodded. "Kinky," I said.

"Aw," he said, "it's for the Halloween Ball at Bollingbrook."

"I had the impression you had given up Bollingbrook for Stonegate."

Dodge snapped his fingers. "The guy from the D.A.'s office," he said, pointing.

I said he was uncanny.

"Jesus." He patted his hair. "Didn't we talk enough already?"

"I just had a few more questions to ask of your wife. And as long as I have you here I wonder if maybe I could take a look at that sweater you were wearing the day Rebecca was killed."

"You're going to have to ask Rita Hayworth for that one. She's sent it to the cleaners."

"Is that who Mrs. Patterson is going as, Rita Hayworth?"

"Actually, I'm not sure who she's going as. She thinks a costume party means you try to see how glamorous you can look. I suspect, you know, she's not going to want to talk to you because she's still getting ready and we're supposed to leave here by seven thirty for the processional. It's really quite an event. They announce each couple by their costumes and so you have to give your identifications to the sergeant at arms, who's got to have them all in the right order so he can thump with his truncheon or whatever they call those long poles and say, 'Clark Gable and Rita Hayworth.' "

Dodge Patterson was quite pleased about the evening's prospects.

"So you are members of Bollingbrook."

"Not at all. We're going as guests of Molly and Dickie Barr. You've probably come across them in your travels through the back alleys of Woodedge, haven't you? They were friends of Becky's, I guess. I mean, as much as anybody was. Molly and Becky went to school someplace together."

"Wheaton."

"That's right. I went out with some of those Wheaton girls when I was in college."

"At Amherst."

"Right again. Our taxpayers' money is well spent, I see."

"Mrs. Patterson wasn't a Wheaton girl, was she?"

"Gretchen? Hah! Gretchen was a UMass girl, sharing the town of Amherst with me in my wild youth. I picked her up hitchhiking one day. I like to tell her she's been getting a ride off me ever since, but she doesn't always laugh. Anyhow, I mustn't stand here gabbing with you for very much longer and I'm really quite positive she's not going to have time for you herself before we have to leave, so maybe the best thing for you to do is come back another time." He started to close the door. "Call first," he said, and suddenly I was alone on the doorstep.

I walked slowly back to my car, feeling rather like an applicant who has just been turned down for a job. I looked up at the great house and thought of my father and wondered why the two of us always seemed to have such difficulty getting into the place.

My most direct way home was to follow Highland Street to Route 30, turn east on Route 30, and follow it to the entrance to the Mass Pike near the Marriott River Inn. It was also possible for me to get to the same place by turning off Highland at Fox Chase Run, which was a longer and more winding road. By choosing it, however, I was able to drive past the entrance to the Bollingbrook Country Club, and there I found my old friend Officer Browning directing traffic.

It was not a particularly difficult job for her. If she saw a Jag or a Mercedes or a BMW or a Cadillac she would point it through the club's gates. If she saw anything else she would wave it along the road.

She was trying to do that to me, but I insisted on stopping next to her and smiling at her. She was breathing heavily from the exertion of her arm movements and she was pretty annoyed that my little sports car was not responding appropriately to her efforts. Then she saw who I was and said, "Oh, it's you."

"Survived the repeated deaths of Mrs. Carpenter, I see."

She looked at me quizzically for an instant and then remembered. "Oh, God," she said. "That was a piece of work, wasn't it?"

The cars were beginning to back up behind us. Impatient rich people were honking their horns.

"I need a favor," I said.

She waved her hand at a few cars coming from the opposite direction. "Can you ask me later?"

"I need you to get me into this party."

"What, at the Bollingbrook? Are you out of your gourd?"

"It's part of the Carpenter investigation and I've got an idea how you can do it."

There were no more cars coming from the opposite direction and there was now a steady blasting of horns behind me.

"I can't talk to you now," Browning said, starting to move away.

"Wait," I said, thrusting my hand toward her. She glanced back impatiently, worriedly.

I said, "I'll park in the lot and when you're done out here come in and find me."

She nodded, perhaps because it was a way to get rid of me. I made the turn and parked in the most out-of-the-way spot I could find. I shut off the engine, flicked on the radio, and waited.

The clubhouse was built on a rise, overlooking the first and the eighteenth fairways. A paved path ran through a tunnel beneath a portion of the building so that people could drive their golf carts right to the edge of the parking lot. Officer Browning and I strode down that path and through the tunnel and I did my level best to match her pace.

"I'm only doing this because you tell me it's all right, Patt. Nobody said anything to me about any sort of departmental activity except directing traffic from seven to nine o'clock and from ten to one. So whatever it is you're doing, it's your responsibility. You're doing something you're not supposed to, I'm going to say you misled me, you misrepresented your authority to me."

"Now, what do you think, Elizabeth?" I panted. "Think I'll rip off the cake or something? You know what I'm working on. We're working on it together."

"I'm not officially assigned to that investigation. I had special-duty assignment one day, that's all. My job assignment tonight was simply to direct traffic and do street patrol. I have a bad feeling for this, I want you to know, Patt. I'm not in the habit of carrying out unauthorized operations."

She wouldn't look at me. It was enough of a commitment that she was doing what I asked.

We turned the corner at the rear of the building and found the right door. Officer Browning sucked in her breath and opened it. Immediately, we were surrounded by hustling waiters in red jackets and black bow ties. They were being directed by a stocky man in a long white jacket and a black bow tie. We made our way to him.

"Are you the head guy here?" demanded Officer Browning.

"I'm the director," responded the head guy, who was at least four inches shorter than Officer Browning.

"I've been requested by the district attorney's office to solicit your assistance." She looked at me out of the corner of her eye, checking to see if she had delivered her line correctly.

The head guy caught the movement and turned his attention to me. "I'm Patt Starbuck," I said. "We think it's necessary I bodyguard one of the people here tonight, a person whose identity I can't disclose to you for reasons of legal security." I let the idea sink in. It might have been a rock dropping through water, by the look on the head guy's face. "What the D.A.'s office requests is that you provide me with some minimal form of cover that will allow me access to the event upstairs."

The head guy looked at Officer Browning, who held his gaze admirably. He looked back at me. "You're not

going to punch people or anything like that, are you?" he
asked. "This is the Bollingbrook Country Club, after all.
We have our reputation."

"Mr. Director—"

"Mr. Prince."

"Mr. Prince, the thing about my position is that no one
is supposed to know I am here."

"How come nobody told me about this before?" he
said, directing his question to Browning.

I answered for her. "Because until just a short time
ago we thought we were going to be able to handle this
matter in an entirely different way."

The head guy nodded, waiting for the rest. Officer
Browning and I stoically gave him nothing. The head guy
nodded some more.

I entered the main ballroom of the Bollingbrook Country Club wearing a long white jacket, a black bow tie, a
white shirt, black trousers with satin stripes down the
sides, and a pair of black Reebok sneakers. Director
Prince had not been able to find me a pair of shoes that
fit. Tucked into my hip pocket was Officer Browning's
home telephone number. It was part of the deal.

The Bollingbrook Country Club was not quite what I
had expected. No place outside of Versailles would have
been.

My father had told me that his grandfather had been
one of the founding officers of the club. He said a picture
of his grandfather was on a wall somewhere and he
promised to show it to me one day when we were members. I had always had an image of my father and me in
matching white flannel pants, blue blazers, and rep ties,
approaching the picture with reverence and being greeted
by other club members who would exclaim such things
as, "I say, you're a dead ringer for old Patterson, wot?"

Less formulated in my imagination was an idea of the
layout of the club itself. I had assumed the dining room
would be elegant, the ballroom would be the size of a
football field, with balconies and gold columns and ballroom stairs cut from the finest Italian marble, but in
reality the two rooms turned out to be one and the same.

There were no balconies and no ballroom stairs. Walls were simply rolled back to create one elongated room with tasteful gray carpet at either end and an intricately parqueted dance floor in the middle.

The band was arranged on a very low portable stage set against a row of paneled glass doors that extended along the wooden portion of the floor. The band consisted of three black men, and they were the only black men in the room. They wore harlequin costumes that may or may not have been of their own choosing and they were doggedly playing music that might best be described as inoffensive Top 40 tunes of the past thirty years. For the most part, however, the band was being ignored. The Bollingbrookers milled about the round tables that were located everywhere but the dance floor. They formed concentric circles that rotated dynamically as they passed from table to table, commenting on each other's costumes and sipping steadily from glasses of liquor, wine, champagne.

The last Halloween party I had attended had been held at Barnacle Bully's, and the contrast was remarkable. At Bully's a man had come in with a cowboy costume that incorporated a pair of fake legs and made him look as if he were a dwarf riding a pony. Another man had come in wearing a chef's outfit and pushing a table-cart laden with goodies. One of the goodies was the head of his friend lying on a platter, an effect made possible by the long white tablecloth that covered the cart. Not everyone at Bully's had been so imaginative, but almost everyone had made his or her own costume and the overwhelming themes had been humor and creativity. These were not the results for which the Bollingbrookers strove.

Almost all the partygoers on this particular night had chosen to rent their costumes. Almost all the costumes were elaborate and pristine. Gentlemen tended to be dressed as historical figures: Henry VIII, George Patton à la George C. Scott, Emperor Nero, Napoleon, Admiral Nelson (you could tell it was Admiral Nelson because he only had one arm). Ladies were Southern belles, flappers, and all manner of royalty—dependent, it seemed, largely on the cut of their own figures.

And then there was Gretchen Patterson. I found her seated at a table with three other people directly across from the band. One of the people, of course, was Dodge in his Clark Gable disguise. The other two were Molly Barr dressed as a fairy princess with a little halo propped over her head, and a man in wire-rimmed glasses and a great white hunter's suit, whom I presumed to be Dickie Barr. They might have been a group of actors resting between takes at some type of "Hello, Hollywood" production: Rhett Butler, Jungle Jim, the Good Witch of the North, and Gretchen—who was definitely not Rita Hayworth.

Gretchen was Cleopatra. She wore a blue-black wig and a headband with the frontal figure of a gold serpent. She wore a gown that was white and satiny and molded to her body, except in the stomach. Her stomach was flat and smooth and provocatively beautiful as it showed bare through a huge diamond pattern cut in the dress. It was, in many respects, not much of a costume. In other respects it was the best costume there.

The group at Gretchen's table was occasionally chitchatting with passersby, but they were not talking a lot among themselves, and they were drinking heavily. Dickie looked drunk and bored. Molly kept scanning the room. Gretchen looked as if she could have been angry. Dodge just looked drunk.

I had taken up a position from which I could watch them without drawing their attention. I was behind the band's amplifiers, which were far too large for the kind of music that was being played, but which were perfect for my purposes. On the stage, the lead singer was trying gamely not to let it all out on a song by Gary Puckett and Union Gap. On the dance floor, several older couples were flailing away spastically at what they thought were the body motions of rock-and-roll dancing. One of the women, dressed as Queen Victoria, incessantly clapped her hands without ever once catching the beat of the music.

The whole scene was curiously lifeless and it surprised me because Dodge had been so enthusiastic about the party just a few hours before. I had expected wild things to be happening: mass dancing and chandelier swinging. Instead I saw such things as a man in a pirate's costume (cum eye patch) talking to a man in zoot suit about investments. "No, really, Henry, with its current P/E ratio I think Raytheon is vastly undervalued."

I thought, perhaps, the problem had to do with the age of the revelers. The Patterson group were among the youngest people there. Indeed, the majority seemed to be in their forties and fifties, with at least as many people older than that as younger. There was much tinkling laughter from the circulating women, and there were a lot of stationary men who looked as if they hoped their picture was not going to appear in their company's annual report. All in all, it was not much fun. It was not like a party at Barnacle Bully's, where you could be assured that sooner or later at least one of the women was going to lose the top of her costume.

Suddenly a voice at my elbow was telling me that Rollie needed something at the standing bar.

"Excuse me?" I said politely.

A young man in a red waiter's coat grimaced at the task of having to repeat himself. "Rollie," he said, gesturing, his voice rising. "Says he's got no barback. Says he's running outa soda water and champagne glasses."

I glanced at where he was indicating and Officer Roland Tagget of the Woodedge Police Department, wearing a red waiter's coat, acknowledged me with a sharp upward movement of his chin.

"You know him?" I said to the waiter. My eyes were still on Tagget, but I had not made any attempt to return his acknowledgment.

The waiter was cocky and quick to be annoyed. He could have used a better haircut, his watery eyes slipped around in his head like greasy little pellets, and his mouth hung open when he wasn't speaking. I knew guys like this. I knew them in high school when they used to sit in the back row and shoot paperclips. "A course I do," he said, smoothing his hair, rolling his eyes, letting his mouth smack as he spoke. "He comes in to work all the big parties."

"What else did he say to you about me?"

"He asked me what you were doing here."

"What did you say?"

"I said, 'Beats the shit outa me. I never seen you before.' I never seen a headwaiter standing around staring at one table all night long, either."

I turned away, wondering what I should do next. The waiter helped me with my decision. "So who are you, anyway?"

I moved quickly, grabbing his arm and hustling him toward the paned glass doors behind the band before he had a chance to figure out what was happening. I shoved open one of the doors and we stumbled onto a veranda that overlooked the golf course. Winston Churchill was there already, regaling a dance-hall girl with tales of corporate lust and greed: "And all the time I was exercising my warrants by proxy. Har, har, har."

The dance-hall girl was smoking a long cigarette and did not appear to care much for Winston's proxy, but she and her companion were more than happy to turn their backs on the help and I was able to sling my friend into the farthest, darkest corner.

I got my face real close to his. "Rollie tell you that you're interfering with police work?"

"Oh, God," he said, recoiling, "is that who you are?"

There seemed to be a fear factor associated with the law. I exploited it by wrapping my fingers around his bicep and shaking him for good measure. His head bopped back and forth. "Who you working for?" I demanded.

"What do you mean? I work for the club."

"And Rollie just sent you over to harass me? To try to blow my cover?"

"He sent me over to tell you to order someone to get the stuff he needs."

"Why didn't you do it yourself?"

"It's not in my job description."

I gradually released my hold on him. I asked if he knew the people I was watching.

He tried a shrug, a "you-didn't-hurt-me" kind of shrug. "Sure. Mr. Barr. He's a member."

"How about the other guy?"

"Mr. Patterson."

"How do you know him?"

The waiter was straightening his lapels. "Used to be a member."

"What do you know about him?"

The waiter's loose jaw swung from side to side. He was debating whether to make a smart remark. I could see it in his eyes. He settled for, "He's kind of a legend."

"What's that mean?"

The waiter was as far into the corner as he could go. We were close enough that someone coming onto the porch might have mistaken us for a couple of neckers. I backed off half a step. I stuck a twenty-dollar bill in the breast pocket of his red waiter's coat. A whole new personality blossomed before my eyes.

"For being a sleaze, man. He's like your classic clubhouse rat, you know what I mean?"

"I don't have a clue," I said, but already I was getting prickly heat spots behind my ears.

"The guy . . ." He shook his head. "The guy, the guy was like the worst tipper in the entire world."

My heat spots started to subside.

"But it wasn't just tipping, man. It was anything to do with money. The guy just never seemed to have any."

"How do you know that? Besides the tipping thing, I mean."

"How do I know that? How do you think I know that? I'm a waiter, man. Waiters hear shit. What do you think, we just deliver the drinks and don't listen to what people are saying? C'mon. The guy hangs around long enough and bets enough games, holes, drives—whatever—without paying off when he loses, people start to talk. After a while it was like a joke, you know? People start talking about being Pattersoned. You ask me, that's probably why he left the club. He couldn't get anybody to play with him anymore."

"Not even Wylie Carpenter?"

"Oh, Mr. Carpenter." The waiter brightened. "Sure, he'd play him, I guess. They always seemed to get along real good. Maybe it's because Mr. Carpenter doesn't give a shit about money, I don't know."

"What does Mr. Carpenter give a shit about?"

The waiter hesitated. "This on the same twenty bucks?"

I turned sideways so that instead of facing the man I was standing next to him. I leaned back against the rail with my arms folded, and the waiter did likewise, listening for my response. "It better be," I hissed, startling him.

After a moment of studying the floor in front of my feet the waiter sighed. "Pussy," he said, startling me.

I repeated the word, not sure if I had heard right.

"Pussy," he affirmed, nodding his head. "Best ass man I seen around here. Discreet, though, you know what I mean?"

"Oh, sure."

"Yeah." He had been looking at me to see if I did know what he meant, but now he went back to nodding. "You can tell, though. I mean, you catch the guy coming out of one of the pool cabanas with the tennis instructor, eleven o'clock at night, you don't gotta be any Einstein to figure out what's going on."

I agreed with him about Einstein, but the waiter was on a roll and he liked the power of being able to pass some inside information to someone who cared. Because we were standing side by side he got to speak out of the corner of his mouth, and he liked that too.

"I'd bet that old Mr. Carpenter musta stuck about half the girls who work here. My sister, I'm pretty sure he got her one time." He said that as if he was proud of it, and then explained, "She used to work in accounting."

"Ah, then it all adds up."

"What does?"

I quickly moved the conversation back on track. "What about Mrs. Carpenter, did she know what was going on?"

"What, her?" He dry-spit.

"No?"

"Well, she wasn't around a lot, and when she was, well, she wasn't around much then, either."

"What was wrong with her?"

"Loaded on something. You could ask anybody. I mean, I didn't see her that much, just at a few dinners and stuff, but it always seemed to me that she was in another dimension."

"Like she was on Valium, something like that?"

"Valium? Maybe. Sleeping pills, reds, downers, horse tranquilizers." His voice drifted off into silence.

"Did you ever hear she was playing around, having any affairs of her own?"

"Mrs. Carpenter?" He asked the question as though he were unsure we were talking about the same person.

I had to say yes to get him to continue.

"Nah. You wanna know what she was like? She was sorta like nothing, man. She was like this pretty good-looking lady, little big in the ass, who'd come to something like this thing tonight, drink up a fishbowl of liquor, and then just sit there with her eyes glazed over until it was time to go home. That's why, you know, a lot of people probably didn't blame Mr. Carpenter for all the fooling around he was doing. It was like, you know, everybody was sorta wondering what a great guy like him was doing married to a woman like her anyway."

"She was from one of the richest families in this area."

"Hey," said the waiter, making me look at him, "everybody in this place is from one of the richest families in the area."

Before I could say anything more, the door to the veranda opened and out marched little Mr. Prince.

"Oh, oh," said the waiter, breaking his casual pose and standing upright.

Mr. Prince made straight for us and stopped when he was five feet away. By all appearances, Mr. Prince was steaming mad. "You planning on working anymore tonight, Rodney?"

"Yes, sir," said the waiter, speaking out of the center of his mouth for a change.

"Then come on, come on, come on," cried Mr. Prince, clapping one hand over the other. "And as for you," he said to me, "you told me you weren't going to interfere with anything."

"I'm trying not to. He came up to me and started asking me questions. I didn't want to start a scene."

"You told me you were bodyguarding."

"I told you—"

"How can you bodyguard when you're out here?"

"I'm going right back inside."

Prince, looking at me dubiously, let me go.

From the moment I pushed open the glass door and stepped over the threshhold I could see the scene had changed dramatically. The band had picked up its tempo and was now joyfully working its way through an old Chuck Berry song called "Maybelline." The younger people had moved onto the dance floor and those who were out there seemed to be genuinely having a good time, especially one tall, formally dressed gentleman in big ears and a painted mustache.

D. Dodge Patterson was attempting splits. He was whooping whenever he tried one and he had more than a few admirers who were egging him on. Conspicuous by her lack of inclusion within that group was his wife. Cleopatra was ostensibly dancing with Dodge, but she had allowed several feet of distance between them and she was moving extremely conservatively. When the song ended and Dodge had struggled back to an upright position for the last time, everybody but she broke into rough applause.

The band segued into "My Girl," but Dodge was in the middle of a group of revelers who seemed to be making their way straight for the bar and Cleopatra was heading back to her table by herself. She was passing by the amplifiers when I stepped out from between them and slipped her into my arms.

She was not expecting the contact. She was not expecting to be grabbed by a man in a headwaiter's coat, but I had a good grip on her and after she said "What? . . . Oh . . . You!" she simply let me glide her around in a small circle. She even rested the heel of her left hand on my shoulder and then she slowly dropped her fingertips until they were touching me. When I looked into her face her eyes melted me and took the bravado out of my performance. Almost immediately I began to perspire and wish I had never been so bold.

"I don't think you're supposed to be here," she said.

I kept up the tatters of my smile.

"Should I scream?"

"Why? I have a disguise, just like you."

"And who are you? Hmmn?"

"Inspector Clouseau?"

"All right, Inspector. Are you here to solve the mystery of the missing chum? Or are you just moonlighting, picking up a little extra cash to supplement your county income?"

"I'm working." It was not much, as lines went, but it was all that came out.

"How disappointing. I thought you might say something romantic, like you had come to see me. Like you had bribed the powers that be, or hit some evil eunuch over the head and stolen his coat, all so you could have this dance."

"You're not far off," I murmured.

"Why? Was it so you could ask me more questions . . . or did you just want to hold me in your arms?"

She moved in closer to me. Her fingers moved a little further across my shoulder. All around us people were taking second and third looks. The band sang, "What could make me feel this way? . . . My girl . . ." And the perspiration rolled down my cheek.

"Oooh, you're so strong," she said, moving herself even closer to me, slipping her thigh between my legs and then letting it slip out again as if one of us had mildly misstepped, letting me feel how firm and smooth and warm she was beneath that satiny white dress. "And I see you've brought your pistol with you, too."

"I thought maybe you could tell me a few things about Rebecca Carpenter," I said, but the words came out as if I were gasping for air.

"Is that all you want?" she said, moving once more across me, letting her thigh slip once again. Her eyebrows arched.

"Well . . ."

"Catch me another time, Patt," she said, and suddenly she spun out of my grasp. I was alone in the middle of the dance floor in my borrowed waiter's coat and pants and my black Reebok shoes and a bulge that most definitely did not come from any pistol.

A vise clamped on each of my elbows. My head swiveled from side to side and I saw that two of the larger men ever to engage in the food service industry had hold of me. Their expressions reflected a rather determined sadness. As I looked forward again I saw on the very edge of the parqueted dance floor, but not standing directly on it, a very irate Mr. Prince.

Perhaps at any other time or place I would have smiled sweetly at him. As it was, however, I dropped my eyes and let his goons escort me through a parting sea of Woodedgians in fezes and wigs and robes and gowns. "Excuse me, excuse me, excuse me," the goons said, and I was mumbling right along with them. "Excuse me, excuse me, excuse me."

17

Saturday night I could not get out of going to the Keoughs' house. The invitation came in the form of a Saturday afternoon telephone call to my apartment by Jessica, asking if I would like to join them for Chinese food. Nothing fancy, just the Hansens were coming over and maybe I would like to get a date and come along.

"Sure," I said. "I'll bring Anita."

"Anita D'Orfio? From the office? Whatever for?"

I did not tell Jessica it was because I was feeling mean and nasty and vindictive. I just made noises to that effect.

"What about that redheaded gal . . . Desdemona? The one with the marvelous figure. You know who I'm talking about."

"Deirdre. She can't come. She already has a date."

"Well, there must be somebody you can bring. How about that lovely Asian gal you used to bring? Marilyn?"

"Mai Lin. And she won't come because Patty cornered her the last time and spent the whole night talking about hysterectomies."

"Oh, Patt, just come by yourself then. It'll be fun, I promise. Besides, I have something very special to show you. Something good."

So I went: but in recognition of my single status Jessica allowed me to arrive late and leave early. By the time I got there they were halfway through an eight-course meal, fresh from the cartons.

Jessica began the evening's surprises by answering the door wearing a pair of incredibly tight jeans. She was no teenage bubblebutt, but the jeans showed she was firm and round and they made me look at her when her back

161

was turned. They made me look at her as I followed her into the dining room, and I knew right away that was a mistake. Suddenly, instead of Royster being embarrassed because I had caught him humping his secretary the day before, I was the one who was blushing because he had seen me eyeing our boss's wife. Patty Hansen must have seen me, too, because already she was doing that crazy thing of looking back and forth from Jessica to me. As for John Michael, he acknowledged nothing. He was in the middle of a monologue when we walked in and he kept right on talking until he was done with what he was saying.

I sat and listened to John Michael and ate everything that was put in front of me without asking what it was. And when the food was gone and the plates had been cleared away and John Michael had finally shut up, Jessica pulled out the special thing she had to show us. It was a newspaper.

It was, to be specific, a copy of that day's *Walmouth-Nestor Courier*, and it was turned to the editorial page. "I don't suppose anybody bothered reading this," she said, pointing to a letter that was captioned, A DYNASTY ENDS IN SORDID MYSTERY.

John Michael, as was his due, got to read it first. When he was done he looked thoughtful and passed it to Royster. When Royster was done he looked thoughtful and passed it to me. Patty didn't count in matters that required us to look thoughtful.

The letter read:

A dynasty has ended with the murder of a beautiful and fabulously wealthy woman, and nobody seems to care. In the early morning hours of October 16, the body of Rebecca Chesley Carpenter was found on the seat of her late model Mercedes at a lonely turnoff in Woodedge. She had been strangled and sexually assaulted, and devoted readers of this newspaper will know little more than that and the fact that she had private funeral services in Woodedge three days later. Yet this woman was the last surviving member of the family that had virtually ruled Woodedge for most of the past 300 years. At least 13 generations of that great name have trod the lands of this town and now all that remains are the structures and grounds of the magnificent Chesley Estate on Bulham Road. One can only hope that Mrs. Carpenter's husband, assuming that's who inherits it, will not allow the estate to be broken up and sold as parcels to suddenly rich hockey players and computer jockeys. And while one is hoping, one may also be wondering why more attention hasn't been paid to this unsolved and exceedingly curious murder. Can it be that there are people even more important in Woodedge these days than Chesleys?

It was signed William Brown, a name that meant nothing to me.

"What do you think?" asked John Michael. He was wearing a white tennis shirt that was supposed to fit tight around his biceps and didn't. His lips were pursed, his pale face was drawn while he awaited my answer.

"It sounds," I said, waving my hand over it, "rather Sherlock Holmesian to me. I read all this 'trod the lands' and 'exceedingly curious' stuff and I want to say, 'Quick, Watson, get the dog cart. The game's afoot.' "

I grinned around the table at my own cleverness, but nobody grinned back. John Michael steepled his fingers in front of his face. Jessica and Royster stared at the tablecloth. Patty looked from me to Jessica and Jessica to me.

"Who is this William Brown, anyway?" I said.

"It's me, for God's sake," said Jessica.

Silence weighed heavily on the group for a moment and then John Michael said, "I kind of like it."

Royster said, "I really like it." He nodded his head at each and every one of us.

"I mean the concept," John Michael added. "When did you do this, Jessie?"

"I sent it in Wednesday."

"I like the Holmesian touch," said Royster, taking the newspaper away from me so he could look at it again. "That sounds the way one of those old Yankees in

Woodedge would write. 'Devoted readers of this news-paper,' I like that. Don't you, Patty?"

"What I can do now, you see," John Michael said, reaching out to get the paper from Royster, "is write a letter in response. 'In regard to the letter of Mr. William Brown, published in last Saturday's edition, let me has-ten to assure the people of this county that the shocking murder of Rebecca Chesley Carpenter retains the utmost priority in my office. Let me further hasten to assure Mr. Brown that nobody, no matter how rich or influential, famous or well connected, is above the law in Exeter County.' Something like that."

"I like it," said Royster, snapping his fingers.

"Get a little dialogue going," said John Michael. "Get him to write back, maybe."

"Where did you get the name, Jessica?" I asked.

She told me she made it up. "It sounded common enough."

"But if you use it again, somebody might go looking for him," I cautioned.

Everyone looked at me as though I was being pur-posely annoying.

"I can quote some statistics," said John Michael. "In Massachusetts last year there were one hundred nine murders, of which sixty-nine have been solved. Through the first ten months of this year the Carpenter case is the only murder in Exeter County left unresolved out of some eight that have taken place, a rate considerably better than that in the Commonwealth as a whole."

"You could even put in," said Royster, "that we have a suspect and intend to have the murderer in custody in a matter of, what, weeks?"

"What I thought we could do," said Jessica, leaning onto the table, "is get Miles Bell at the *Courier* to dig out some of the old unresolved murders in Woodedge his-tory. Run a series of articles on them; get the public thinking about murders among the affluent."

"It wouldn't be much of a series," I said, stilling the conversation and immediately regretting that I had spo-ken out loud.

Jessica, her body still bent, her head turned to face

me, demanded to know why not. I was, once again, the focus of everyone's attention.

"There have only been a couple. Around the turn of the century a woman named Mabel Norcross was found dead on the floor of her bedroom in the house she shared with her father and brother on Highland Street. On days when her father and brother were off working she was known to entertain a gentleman caller or two. She was known to do this because she had a neighbor who apparently had nothing better to do all day long than watch her and report what she saw to Mabel's father."

My audience stared.

"One day the brother left, the father left, the milkman was seen entering and leaving the house, one gentleman caller was seen entering and leaving, and a second gentleman caller arrived to find Mabel strangled to death.

"The father and brother claimed she was alive when they were there, the milkman and first gentleman caller claimed they had left without seeing her, and the second gentleman caller was the one who rang for the doctor. Since nobody could figure out which one of them did it they convicted the milkman. He went to the chair protesting his innocence and the story is that Mabel Norcross haunts the house to this day because she was never properly avenged." I offered a tentative shrug in case anybody was wondering if I really believed the story.

Royster took hold of his cup of tea and held it thoughtfully between the table and his lips. "How do you know all this stuff, Patt?" he asked.

I flipped my hand one way and then the other.

"You said there were a couple. What were the others?" He still had not tasted his tea. He still was holding the cup halfway to his mouth.

"A nude body was found in the snow near Bollingbrook about ten years ago. You can ask Ralphie about that one. Most mysterious thing about it was probably his investigation. He decided she was a prostitute from Boston that somebody had brought down the pike and thrown out of his car. Wembley wholeheartedly agreed and that was the end of it. They buried her as a Jane Doe."

"And you disagreed?" Royster said, regarding me curiously.

I shrugged. "What do I know? I wasn't even in this business at the time. Maybe it was the most incisive analysis of Ralphie's career."

Royster put down his tea, untouched. "But you've looked into it. And you looked into the Norcross murder. What, have you made some sort of study of murders in Woodedge?"

"Maybe you could work with Miles Bell directly on this, Patt," Jessica suggested.

"No," I said to both of them.

"I like those two you've told us about, Patt," said John Michael from his position at the head of the table. "Do you know of any more?"

"No."

"They don't necessarily have to be unresolved," he pressed. "I mean, technically, the Norcross one isn't unresolved. Think it would be worthwhile for one of us to go through the *Courier*'s archives?"

"I could do it," Jessica said. "I've got some time this week."

"You won't find anything," I said.

"Well, it won't hurt to look. I mean, between Wembley and Ralph, who knows what's gone down over there? They may have let things go as suicide—"

I spoke quickly, cutting her off. "There was one. About eighteen or nineteen years ago. A body of a man was found on a path that led up from the Charles and it was ruled to be suicide because he had been shot in the head with a small-caliber gun that was lying on the ground next to him."

"Any reason why it wouldn't have been suicide?" Royster asked.

I looked from one person to the other before deciding how to answer. "No note was ever found, the man didn't own a gun and wasn't known to have ever fired one, and the gun that was next to him was untraceable."

I may have spoken sharply. There may have been some edge in my voice that caused the subtle changes I

saw in their expressions, that caused them to keep looking at me long after I had finished.

"So you don't think the guy offed himself, Patt?" said
Royster, and whatever was in his voice matched whatever was in mine.

I fixed my eyes on his before I answered. "The medical
examiner said it was suicide and that was the end of it."

Suddenly John Michael popped his fist into his open
palm and we all got distracted. "By God, I like Jessica's
idea. But we don't need a whole history. We don't need
a series. All we need's that one Norcross story. You see
the parallels? Beautiful Woodedge woman, strangled in
her own environment while her male guardian is nowhere
to be found. Same question in both cases about what the
victim could have been doing in the place she was at the
time she was killed. Same question as to where the male
guardian was. Old Mr. Norcross, was he upset his daughter was whoring around? How about Mr. Carpenter, was
he upset his wife may have been climbing aboard the
yardman? The milkman took the fall back then, is the
yardman taking the fall now?"

John Michael gestured enthusiastically, encouraging us
to see what he was seeing. "The husband and the father,
the yardman and the milkman . . . and lurking behind
everything is the question of steamy, bawdy, untold sex.
Huh? I like it, I like it, and I can see Miles Bell liking it,
too."

Everybody around the table got into liking it so much
that I didn't have the heart to tell them I thought it
stunk.

18

To the casual observer, there would have been nothing unusual about a man bumping into a woman with a small child in the parking lot of the Woodedge post office on a Monday morning. If the observer was not so casual, however, he or she might have noticed that the man had been waiting in his little gray-green Alfa for almost two and a half hours, and that he did not get out of his car until a dusty Country Squire station wagon pulled into the lot and lurched into a parking space. He or she might have noticed that the woman sprang from behind the wheel, ran around the car to the passenger's door, quickly unbelted her child, and then started to hurry into the post office with one hand holding onto the child and one hand holding her coat closed—only to draw up short when she saw who was standing in front of her.

"I thought I'd see you sooner or later, Patt," Gretchen Patterson said to me. Her hair was blowing in the wind, blowing away from her head and making her face stand out by itself as a thing of dark and complex beauty.

The sky was overcast in a mishmash of gray colors. The leaves that had been so pretty just the week before were now brown and crisp and blowing past us as if they were late for an appointment. I was cold from my long wait in my little car and I was afraid my nose was starting to run so I kept sniffing and nervously touching it. I was grinning and sniffing and touching my nose and not saying anything.

"You caused quite a stir the other night," she said, with a beguiling flick of her head. "Everybody was so solicitous of me after you left, you'd think I'd been assaulted or something. Old Mrs. Ransom, who usually only talks to me at Christmas, asked me if I wanted to lie down in the women's lounge."

"Did anybody ask who I was?"

"Of course. I told them I didn't know."

"But I must have been recognized. By your husband, perhaps, or Molly Barr."

"Dodge was getting a drink when it happened, and you must not have made much of an impression on Molly."

"She was more interested in a tennis instructor named Cliff the day I saw her."

"Ah, Cliff. Well, that explains it."

"You people in Woodedge seem to live such interesting lives."

"Not really. That's why someone like Molly has a Cliff."

"Is that why someone like Becky had a Dougie Rasmussin?"

"My, we cut right to the bone, don't we?" Gretchen was smiling at me, but her son was pulling away from her. He was also making horrible noises.

Little Ian Patterson was three or four years old and did not deserve criticism, but I was thinking bad thoughts about him nonetheless. I said, "How would the little tyke like a nice cup of hot chocolate while his mommy and I share a little conversation?"

Gretchen looked at her watch. "It's just eleven thirty. Adolfo's will be opening if you want to go there."

I had been thinking of the Brigham's ice cream parlor, but I put on a brave front and told her Adolfo's would be swell. In my mind I was remembering the twenty dollars I had impulsively popped into the waiter's pocket the previous Friday night and I was wondering if I would be able to justify to the office the expense of a lunch for three at Adolfo's.

"Then why don't you go and get us a table," Gretchen said, "and Ian and I will join you after we get the mail."

It was not hard getting a table at Adolfo's at eleven thirty-five on a Monday morning. I was even given one by the window so I could look out over the patio with its un-used tables and umbrellas. And then I sat alone,

sipping from my water goblet and playing with my silver-
ware and trying to decide if the fun-loving Mrs. Patterson
had made a fool of me once again. But then, finally, just
as I was about to get up and leave, she and her child
arrived, and I didn't know whether to be angry that she
had taken so long or grateful that she had actually come.
I chose to act grateful.

Gretchen brought the freshness of the outdoors with
her as she dug her way out of her coat and stripped Ian
of his. I watched her shoulders and her breasts move
beneath her tan sweater and I found that I actually was
grateful.

"Do you come here often?" I asked.

"Adolfo's? Never. The post office? Every day. How
about you?"

"The post office? Oh, yeah, sure. I like to be on the
spot in case some new commemoratives come in."

Gretchen looked at me strangely, perhaps not realizing
what a funny guy I could be. She arranged her napkin on
her lap and tried to keep Ian from squirming out of his
seat. She buttered him a piece of bread from the basket
that had been brought to our table shortly after I sat
down, and put it on his plate. When the waiter came
within singing distance of us she beckoned him over and
quickly ordered Ian a glass of apple juice and herself a
Dubonnet. I ordered a vodka grapefruit so I could be
one of the party.

"That must have been a terribly humiliating experience
for you," she said suddenly. "Friday night, I mean."

"Well . . . ," I said, feigning magnanimity.

"No. It was very cruel of me." She broke off a piece of
bread for herself and then broke off a piece of that and
buttered it. "Especially since I knew how you would
feel."

I laughed. "How could you? We've barely even met."

"I can tell. We're a lot alike, you and I. We both
absolutely hate the idea of failure . . . we just go about
dealing with it in different ways."

"What is this?" I said, my grin only halfway intact.
"Are you trying to psychoanalyze me?"

"You didn't think this was a one-way street, did you?

You didn't think you got to go unexplored while you picked my brain?"

"Of course I did. I'm the investigator."

"You don't look at me like you're an investigator." She gave a quick glance at Ian and then leaned across the table and whispered, "You look at me like you want to get in my pants."

I choked. I spit little flecks of bread all over my napkin as I hurried to cover my mouth. I was bent over hacking when the waiter arrived with our drinks and obsequiously asked if he could be of any assistance. I tried to wave him away.

"Does this mean you're not ready to order, sir?" he asked.

Gretchen told him to come back in five minutes. Ian, meanwhile, was in hysterics. He thought it quite funny to see a grown man in such distress.

"Something went down the wrong way," I tried to explain, clearing my throat.

"Sure it did," Gretchen said.

I looked up quickly and she disarmed me with a smile.

"Don't you want to get in my pants?" Her leg touched mine beneath the table.

I dabbed at my mouth.

"I can ask you that, you see, because I know you won't say yes. And even if you did say yes you wouldn't do anything about it. You wouldn't put yourself in that position."

"And why wouldn't I?"

"Because you aren't sure I'm serious. I might turn you down. Reject you." She withdrew her leg. "Your idea of dealing with failure is to keep yourself from ever letting it occur. That's where you and I differ. My idea is to make sure it never does occur."

I took a long sip of my drink and tried to figure out why she was saying these things to me. "Do you really know who I am?"

"Patterson Starbuck. My husband's second cousin, once removed, or something like that. Removed in more ways than one, I might add."

"How did you know?"

"My father-in-law told me. He recognized your name right away. In fact, he told me I shouldn't have let you in the house. 'Once a Starbuck gets in your house,' he said, 'you've got to call the police to get him out.' "

I grimaced. "And Dodge, does he know?"

"Not from me."

"Why not?"

Gretchen toyed with her Dubonnet. She looked at her menu. For the first time she averted her gaze. "I don't know why," she said, not really expecting me to believe her.

"His father must have told him."

"His father and he don't talk, despite whatever appearances they have given you."

"This is where I get to say 'Why not?' again."

Gretchen's smiles came easily when she wanted. She had a way of pointing her chin and catching your eye as she flashed her teeth, and suddenly you were swept away to places you hadn't meant to go. I had almost forgotten my question when she said, "Well, I guess it's no secret that Dodge hasn't quite fit the image that old Frost set for him."

"Image?"

"Sure. Andover, Amherst and all that. Frost expected his only son to come home with a glittering and glorious career and instead he came home with me, the peasant of Lowell."

I wasn't sure if she was putting me on. I couldn't conceive of Gretchen Patterson as a peasant. I couldn't imagine her coming from a working-class city like Lowell. I couldn't understand any man not being exhilarated just to be in her presence and have her smile at him.

"Oh, yes," she said, reading me. "That greatly upset Frost and Florence, Dodge's mother. I was not what they had envisioned at all. They looked at me and saw sex and lust and youthful indiscretion. 'Wait a little while, Dodgie, and you'll grow out of this phase. You'll meet someone of your own kind and you'll realize how transient impetuous infatuation can be with a daughter of immigrants from the mill city.' " Gretchen sang the imitation happily, as though it had been traumatic enough at the time, but did not hurt anymore.

She busied herself for a moment tidying her son. "What they didn't understand," she went on, "was Dodge. The ironic thing is, I didn't understand him either—but for totally different reasons."

The waiter reappeared. Gretchen ordered scallops doré for herself and lobster bisque for her three-year-old son. I ordered coquilles St. Jacques, without being sure what it was, and the waiter bowed as though we had made excellent choices and went away. A busboy immediately took his place and filled our water goblets and placed before us a schooner dish of celery and carrot sticks and black olives. Then he went away.

Gretchen said, "Dodge managed to get himself into law school at B.U. and I took a job as a cocktail waitress in Copley Square so I could be near him." She half-shrugged.

I full-shrugged back.

"Becoming a waitress wasn't exactly why I worked my way through school. But I kept telling myself it was all temporary. That it would all work out in the long run. We lived together the whole three years he was in law school. And that, Florence Patterson would tell you if she were still alive, is where her little Dodgie went wrong. The truth is, of course, that the framework of Dodge's life had been laid long before I came on the scene. It wasn't me who steered him onto the path of penury and frivolity."

"Penury and frivolity?"

My question was meant as a comment on her choice of words. They were not the words of the urban peasant she was claiming herself to be. But her great dark eyes seared me when she heard my slightly mocking tone, and her own voice cracked when she spoke back. "Well, you're the detective, what do you call what you've found out about him?"

I sat whiplashed, unsure of what she meant; feeling a bit like a student who has to come up with an excuse for failing to do his homework.

"What did you think," she pressed, "when you found us all living together in his father's home?"

"I thought," I said, pausing to clear my voice, "that it was a big house with plenty of rooms. I thought that Dodge would be inheriting it anyway when his father dies and that maybe Frost needed you there until then to help him run the place."

"Boy," she said, making a grab for Ian just as he was about to crawl onto the table, "are you misinformed." She managed to get Ian reseated, his nose cleaned, and a stalk of celery and a stick of carrot placed in his hands with an admirable economy of motion. "Dodge's grandfather Gordon left that house to both his sons. Frost got it first because he was the oldest, and Parker was none too pleased because he figured he had the most kids and he should get it. Still, the way it was left, when Frost dies the house goes straight to Parker—and Parker has four daughters who are going to inherit it from him."

"Where's Parker now?"

"Oh, kept up on the relatives, have we?" She was smiling warmly again, ingratiatingly again, sucking me in again. "He's fit as a fiddle in Palm Beach. Living with his third wife and waiting impatiently for his brother to die."

"The house isn't that nice," I said.

"Listen, any house in Woodedge these days is that nice. A house with that much land and that many rooms is worth well more than a million dollars."

I shifted about uncomfortably.

"Besides," Gretchen said, her head cocking to one side, her hair cascading over her shoulder, "as I understand it, the Pattersons put tremendous personal value on the old homestead."

"My father had a lot of emotional reasons for wanting to get in that house," I said, "if that's what you're referring to."

She nodded. "The house, it was originally built by Frederick Patterson, wasn't it?"

"Yeah. Then he built another house for his son John and left this one to his son Alfred. I'm from John's side of the family. Dodge is from Alfred's."

"And what happened to John's house?"

"He left it to my great-uncle Frank, who sold it and

moved away." I neglected to mention how many times Frank had sold it.

"Leaving you out in the cold."

"It was long before I was born."

"And yet you're still resentful."

"I'm not resentful."

"Oh."

The bisque came. Gretchen and I received little cups of heated clam broth to prepare us for our main courses.

"You're the one who sounds resentful," I said.

Gretchen put down her cup and stared at me. "Well, can you blame me? Here I am, an outsider in this town full of snobs, trying to go around pretending not only that I'm one of them, but that everything is jim-dandy in my home, which doesn't belong to me, where I'm not wanted, and which is soon going to be taken away from me."

"It seems to me you fit in just fine."

"Oh, c'mon, Patt, be real. Look at my skin coloring. Listen to my accent. I could never be one of these people in a lifetime of trying. But that's not important. What's important is that my son fit in; and as long as we're living here, as long as we keep up the image, he will."

"Why's that important?"

Gretchen dropped her forearm rather loudly on the table. "I can't believe you, of all people, are asking me that, Patt. Wasn't it your father who moved his family into the Patterson place? Wasn't it your father who used to hide in the trees after that, scheming to get back in? Didn't he keep returning even after Gordon Patterson bought a gun and took a shot at him? Even after Frost and Parker chased him through the woods? Why, Patt? Because he knew what it's like to live here and live someplace else. He knew that you live here and you have land and room and privacy and a sense of personal identity. Maybe you look at living in West Nestor differently than he did, but if it's anything like where I come from you share your room and you share your building and you share your street, and your identity comes from being one of the people in the neighborhood. You know what the biggest advantage of that is? It means you don't get your car stolen by somebody who lives on your block."

Gretchen continued to stare at me until she realized I was not going to respond, and then she added, "Like I said, maybe I'm confusing you with what I've been told about your father. But it seems to me I understand what he wanted. He knew the difference between being somebody and not being somebody—and he knew about the arbitrariness that can cause a person to be in one position or the other."

Suddenly her head fell into the palm of her hand. Just as suddenly Ian stopped playing with his soup. "Mommy, are you all right?" he asked, and when he got no answer he looked at me accusingly.

"Hey," I said softly, reaching over to touch her shoulder. She shook me away and I quickly looked around the room to see if anyone was noticing us. No one was. I leaned closer and said, "Gretchen, why are you telling me all this?"

"I suppose," she murmured, "so that you would understand."

"I understand. I understand . . . it's just, I'm not sure why we're talking about it."

"I meant understand what I've done. I meant understand why I'm so scared."

Little pulsations began to race through my body. I sat very still.

Gretchen Patterson's face remained covered by her hand and her hair. She did not appear to be looking at anything other than the white linen tablecloth.

"Are you all right, Mommy?" Ian asked again.

She assured him she was. She straightened up again. She smiled bravely and told Ian to eat his soup. He explained that he didn't like it because it had yucky things in it. In the midst of receiving Gretchen's confession I found myself distracted by the nearly full bowl of lobster bisque and feeling pained at the waste of nine dollars and fifty cents.

"Why is it you're scared, Gretchen?"

"What is that, Ian?" she said, directing her son's attention out the window. Ian practically stood on his chair to see, his head tilted back, his eyes scanning. Gretchen quickly turned to me. "Because I've been having an affair with Wylie Carpenter."

She was trying to collect my reaction and I was trying to remain as unreactive as possible. A silly line came into my head. "Oh, yes. Frightfully bad spot, that." But I said nothing. In truth, I was having difficulty knowing what to do with the information.

She shrugged. It was an easy, athletic, undulating motion that swept across her shoulders. "I still am, I suppose, though of course we haven't seen each other since all this happened."

"Is it that bird, Mommy? The one with the thing in its mouth?"

"No, no, sweetheart. Keep looking."

She let her son get up and put his hands on the windowsill so that his back was to us. "You see why I had to tell you before you found out on your own? I mean, I know the types of questions you've been going around asking and I know why you have to do it—to get all the relevant information inside that big circle you were telling me about. But something like this, if it were made public, either Ian and I would be thrown out of the Patterson house or we'd be ostracized from Woodedge society forever."

"Ostrich, Mommy?"

"No, honey. Keep looking."

"Yet it seems to have been all right for your husband to have an affair with Wylie's wife," I said cautiously.

"What was I supposed to do? Leave him? Tell him to pack up and get out of his father's house? This is the very thing I'm worried about, ending up on my own with my son and no place to go. Dodge may have his shortcomings, and I'm sure you've found out about plenty of them if you're doing the job I think you're doing, but he's all I've got. I mean, when I learned what was going on between Dodge and Becky I wanted to kill them both. But what good would that have done me? I lose Dodge, do you think the old man's going to take care of me?"

"You're speaking figuratively, of course. About killing them."

"Of course. Although I was so humiliated when I first found out that the thought crossed my mind. But leaving Dodge, what's that going to gain me? The rest of Woodedge is not going to welcome Ian and me with open arms, even if we could afford to stay here. Dodge is our ticket and we're all perfectly well aware of it. So, again, what could I do? I tried talking about it with my father-in-law, but all he did was make me feel as though it must be my fault. I realized if I was going to protect myself I'd have to do it on my own."

I nodded. I agreed. I was not in control of this conversation.

Gretchen checked on her son, who was still searching the patio and the sidewalk and the street for whatever his mother had told him to find. She said, "So I went to Becky and I insinuated myself with her. And we became friends, she and I, and because Wylie and Dodge were already friends we began to do things as couples. The idea, you know, the idea I had was just to make us all so close that I wouldn't have to worry about Dodge and Becky anymore, but what became clear after not too long was that . . . well, Wylie and Becky didn't have much of a relationship. It probably wasn't even as good as Dodge's and mine. Which, I suppose, is why she was available to Dodge in the first place."

She looked at her glass of Dubonnet, which was only half gone, and said, "Becky, you see, had a bit of a dependency problem. She was always on Valium, Librium, whatever she could get hold of, and when she drank, which was often, she would just sort of zone out. Wylie, on the other hand, is somebody who always wants to be on the go, who always wants to be doing something. And whatever they once had between them, well, it just didn't seem to be there anymore."

"Like with you and Dodge," I said, and then I was ashamed of myself because there was almost a strain of hope in my voice.

"Is it the sign, Mommy? Is that it?"

"No, it's not the sign, Ian." And then she said no to me, too. "Dodge and I haven't reached the point that the Carpenters did. The problems we're having have to do with external things. Neither one of us is very secure about who we are or what we're doing right now. Dodge, as I'm sure you know, hasn't been very successful as a lawyer. His credit, both personal and financial, is pretty much used up. He's tied to his father and yet he almost hates his father. So what he does is, he resorts to the things he does best, that he's most comfortable with. You know, golf, tennis, carousing. And all those things keep him away from his father, away from home, and away from me. I'm left behind, feeling unwanted and out of place, and all of a sudden one of the most prominent men in town is paying a lot of attention to me. He's telling me that I'm beautiful, that I'm intelligent, that I'm interesting." Her voice trailed off.

"And that man is Wylie Carpenter?"

She took a deep breath and sighed. It was a sigh of affirmation.

Our meals arrived. Mine was on a seashell. It was covered with an orange sauce that looked like Welsh rarebit. I gazed at it, only half assimilating what I was seeing.

"Were you," I said, as she started to eat, "with Wylie on the night his wife was killed?"

Gretchen kept her dark eyes on her plate and waited until she was done chewing before she answered. "No. I was out shopping that night. In fact, I was out looking for something for the Halloween Ball."

"Was there someplace special you usually met him?"

Gretchen hesitated. "That's not really important, is it, Patt? I mean, the affair doesn't have anything to do with what you're investigating and I'm only telling you about it so you won't stumble on it and cause my whole marriage to blow up in my face."

"But now that I know about it, I can't just ignore it."

Gretchen had been carving a scallop. Her knife and fork went very still. "Why not? It doesn't have anything to do with anything unless you think Wylie could have killed her because of me." The word "killed" was mouthed silently after a quick glance toward Ian.

She must not have gotten the reaction from me that

she wanted. Laying down her utensils, she said, "I'm suddenly sorry I told you anything at all."

I didn't want her to be sorry. I wanted her to look at me again with some kind of indication that she liked what she was seeing. "You know, if a guy is having an affair, it can explain things other than murder."

"What does Wylie need to explain?"

"He's got a couple of hours that night he can't account for."

"If that's the case then I won't have any choice. I'll say I was with him."

I didn't respond. I looked for the good parts of my coquilles St. Jacques.

"Because he didn't do it, Patt. He wouldn't have had any reason to. I mean, he could have walked away from that marriage at any time. He didn't need her money, there weren't any kids . . . What motive would he have for killing her? At a lovers' lane, of all places?"

Suddenly Ian cried out with delight. "I see him, Mommy. I see him." He began pounding on the window with the heel of his hand. "It's Daddy. In here, Daddy. Daddy!"

"Oh, my God," Gretchen said, sliding over quickly to grab Ian's hand before he caused any more commotion. As soon as her fingers closed around her son's arm her expression froze. She waved her hand unenthusiastically. "He's coming in," she said, and her lips barely moved.

She spun back to me. "You won't say anything, will you? Promise me you won't say anything."

Her beautiful features were carved with anxiety. Her voice was desperate with emotion.

"I've got nothing to say."

The tenseness went out of her shoulders. Relief flooded her face. Everything about her told me I was a hell of a guy.

My back was to the door, but I knew when Dodge Patterson entered the restaurant. Gretchen beckoned him as if she had been saving his seat. Ian called to him. I turned and watched him unbutton his topcoat and smooth back his hair and register only mild surprise when he saw me dining with his wife and son.

"Dodge, you remember Mr. Starbuck," Gretchen said.

"Yes," I said, half-rising and holding out my hand. "Patt Starbuck, D.A.'s office. We've talked a couple of times."

"Sure," he said, giving me a cold hand to shake. "Still investigating?"

It was, I thought, a funny question to ask, but I laughed as though we were both being charming, and said, "Oh, they let us ask our questions over lunch every now and then. Won't you join us?"

I swept my hand toward the empty seat next to me, hoping he would say no and tell me that he had some errand he had to run, someplace he had to be. Instead, he looked at each of our meals and said, "Fine. That would be great."

The waiter, who had been hovering ever since Ian had beaten on the window, moved in for the order as soon as Dodge had taken off his coat and sat down.

"Let me see," Dodge said, "that lobster bisque looks good." And before I could point out that his son's was almost untouched, he had ordered a nice big bowl for himself and the waiter had scurried away like a thief in the night.

19

On Tuesday morning I went for a walk in the woods beneath the overlook where Rebecca Carpenter's body was found. The overlook itself was a turnoff, a hundred yards wide, bellying out from a little country lane called Ivanhoe Road. It was one of the highest spots in Woodedge and it provided a fine view of the Charles River. This being October, there were a couple of cars from New York at the overlook when I arrived. This being morning, there was fog lifting off the river, obscuring the view for the consequently embittered visitors from the Empire State.

"It always look like this?" one man demanded of me.

"Ay-yuh," I told him, and scrambled over the stone wall that separated the parking area from the wooded slope.

There was a path that was difficult to follow for about twenty yards because of its steepness. Then it went into the trees and spilled onto a cart track that was strewn with leaves and twigs and horse droppings. I had been on this track when I was a boy and I knew that if I followed it one way it would lead to a set of cairns that my father told me were built by the Norsemen hundreds of years before Columbus. If I took it the other way it would lead down to a mud pond, where my father and I had once spent an afternoon digging for buried treasure that he had read about in a book. At the pond the cart track would intersect a path that led up from the river. It was the path my father used to take in order to get from Nestor to Whitehall Road after Gordon Patterson obtained a restraining order keeping him from coming within a mile of the family property.

Whoever killed Mrs. Carpenter could have gone downhill to the lake and then followed the path to the river if he wanted to get out of the woods as fast as possible. From the river it would have been a short climb to either Route 128 or the turnpike. I turned the other way and started walking toward the cairns. It was the way Wylie Carpenter would have gone if he was trying to get back to the Stonegate Country Club.

I walked for no more than five minutes and then I stopped. The track was no different now than it had been when I was a child. It twisted and turned and was rutted from horse hooves, and it would have taken an expert woodsman to have followed it all the way to Stonegate in the dark.

I looked in the direction of the pond and memories came back to me as sharp as if I were seeing them in a movie. The path that led by the pond was straight and smooth. I had walked it dozens of times with my father, usually with him lost in thought, gripping the fingers of my hand so hard I wanted to cry out from the pain. I remembered the sounds he made as he walked. His grunting sounded in my ears. It became heavy breathing, and then it became panting and then I realized it was me who was making all those noises. I was standing in the middle of an otherwise deserted trail, surrounded by trees and ferns and bushes, and I was hyperventilating.

There was a conference table in John Michael's office and when it was fully occupied it held eight people. On Tuesday afternoon there was only one seat open. At the head of the table sat John Michael, with his cheek resting against his fist and his arm hooked over the back of his chair. Along one side of the table sat Royster, Detective Lieutenant Libby, and Woodedge Police Sergeant Roselli. Along the other side sat Chief Tuttle in a wrinkled gray business suit, Inspector Lester in a loud check sport coat, and Officer Tagget in a uniform considerably different from the last one I had seen him wearing.

They were waiting for me. They were all unhappy, or uncomfortable, and acting as if it was my fault.

John Michael did his best to lighten up the proceedings. "Jesus, Patt. You look like you just learned Ted Kennedy was going to be driving you to the ferry."

A few of the soldiers dutifully laughed. It was always best to laugh at John Michael's jokes, especially when they dealt with the Kennedys.

"You're not exactly a festive gathering yourselves."

"Yes, well . . ." John Michael let go of the back of his chair and inclined forward so he could rest his arms on the table. "The chief asked for this meeting so he could bring to my attention some of the things you've been doing in connection with the Carpenter investigation."

"You must have been at it for a while."

"About an hour. I left word for you to join us as soon as you came in."

"I was out in the woods behind the overlook."

John Michael shifted his eyes to Chief Tuttle, who looked down the table at Roselli.

"We've combed that whole area," said Roselli. "There's nothing there. No sign of any flight, no pocketbook, no nothing."

The chief turned back to John Michael as though something significant had just been announced. "You see?" he demanded, his jowls flubbering up and down.

John Michael nodded. "Wembley wants me to take you off the investigation, Patt. He says what you're doing is at best duplicative and at worst counterproductive. He says you're upsetting a lot of people in Woodedge."

I waited for some sort of hint as to which way John Michael wanted me to go.

"For example, he says you crashed a fancy dress ball at one of the country clubs last Friday night."

I could feel myself blushing, but I fought the urge to look at Tagget. I fought the urge to look at anything other than John Michael's face.

"Was that part of your investigation?" he asked.

"Yes."

"You didn't tell us anything about that when we met on Saturday night."

"There wasn't anything to tell."

"Wanna tell us now?"

"I was hoping to learn something from people who socialized with the Carpenters. I considered it an undercover operation. Somebody blew my cover."

The looks went around the table: John Michael to Tuttle to Tagget and back to Tuttle. "I understand you blew it yourself," said the chief.

"In any event," John Michael declared quickly, "the chief seems to feel you have your focus a little too narrowly set. There are a couple of reasons why this is important, Patt. One is the general social-political reason, you understand that. The other is that Inspector Lester has just come up with some valuable information that could turn this case around." He pointed at Lester and spoke his name.

The inspector flipped open a little spiral notebook, cleared his throat, and shifted his position so as to address me without looking at me. "On Sunday, the twenty-seventh of October, I located Rasmussin, Douglas A., and spoke to him by telephone. He confirmed that he was hired by Mrs. Rebecca Carpenter on or about the first of September to assume temporary employment at the Carpenters' place of residence, number six Bulham Road, Woodedge. Affirmative that conditions of employment included termination on the fifteenth of October and that was clear to all concerned. Emphasis on 'all,' " he concluded with a flourish.

"How," I asked, "did you locate him, Les?"

"First-class detective work," he said, cutting his eyes away from me and barking out a laugh that sounded like "arf, arf, arf."

"He called his mother and she called you, is that it?"

Lester stopped barking. "Something like that," he said, wiping his mouth.

"Then you called him back."

"Yeah."

"In California."

"Area code 213."

"So you don't even know if it was him you were talking to."

"Oh, it was him all right."

"Is he coming back here?"

"Didn't ask him. Didn't want to scare him till we could get out there to have a go at him face to face."

"That's what we were talking about when you came in, Patt," John Michael said. "We're trying to decide what to do next. Les and the chief would like Les to go out there to interview Rasmussin and talk him into coming back. I'm wondering what you think about that."

"I don't know. Is Les planning on interviewing him as a witness or as a suspect?"

"Well, we bloody well know what you'd do," snorted Lester.

I sighed, showing infinite patience with my pillory. "Les, all we've got on Rasmussin so far is that he disappeared on the day Mrs. Carpenter was killed."

"And she was found in the kind of place only someone like him would take her," chimed in the chief, nodding his great fleshy head.

"Personally," I said, trying to catch John Michael's eye to make sure I was heading in the right direction, "I don't think we've sufficiently explored all our other options."

"Like Wylie Carpenter, you mean," said the chief.

"Not just him."

"Who else is there?" cried Lester. "Mrs. Mitchell?"

"Well," I said, because everyone was waiting for me to come up with a suggestion, "there's Dodge Patterson."

Chief Tuttle sucked in his breath. His face turned red and his meaty jowls began to quiver again.

John Michael put his elbows on the table. He put his hands together and then brought his chin down slowly to rest on his fingertips. He wanted us all to know he was giving full consideration to what I had just said. "You think he might be a suspect because he and Rebecca Carpenter had once been lovers."

The chief groaned. He put his hand to his forehead.

"I was thinking Wylie wasn't the only one wearing a white club sweater that day, and he wasn't the only one missing from the club for a couple of hours that night," I said. "I was thinking Dodge grew up in Woodedge and is as likely as anybody to have an expert knowledge of those woods behind the overlook."

The reaction around the table was palpable. Everyone stirred, adding body movements in support of John Michael's spoken question: "Meaning?"

"That it's possible to use the trail behind the overlook to get to the river, and it's also possible to use it to get to a lot of other places in Woodedge. That's why I was checking it out this morning."

John Michael hesitated. Now it was he who was watching me for signs. He spread his hands. He brought them back together in a soft clap. He smiled, "So what did you learn?"

"Simply that unless the killer was completely familiar with the woods there was no way he could have used them to get back to Stonegate. Not even if there was a full moon, which I understand there wasn't."

"What about using the woods to get to the river?" demanded the chief. "Do you deny the murderer could have done that?"

"It would have been easier," I admitted, and the chief started to look pleased. "On the other hand," I said, putting an end to that reaction, "if it was Rasmussin you're thinking about—indeed, if it was anybody who was robbing Mrs. Carpenter or trying to make it look like a robbery—why didn't your men find the pocketbook somewhere? No thief this side of San Francisco would go running through the woods at night with a pocketbook flopping over his arm. He'd take the wallet out and throw the rest away."

John Michael casually flicked his eyes at Royster, who spoke up for the first time. "Let's put the whole thing into perspective," he said, affecting the voice of reason. "If the kid did it, Rasmussin, what's he going to take her up the overlook for? He can rob her and kill her a whole lot more easily—"

"Unless it was a mistake," interrupted the chief. His eyes were wide. The top of his head was inclined slightly forward. "Unless he took her there for sex, she fought him off, he strangled her by mistake, and then he just grabbed her pocketbook because he knew he would need money in order to make his getaway." He nodded, encouraging others to nod with him.

"Well, what about the sweater fiber we found?" demanded Royster.

"Forget the sweater," the chief snarled back. "Patt's already knocked that out."

John Michael was doing some maneuvering with his lips. They went in and out, over and under each other. He turned to Roselli and Tagget. "How far did you guys search for that pocketbook?"

"All the way to the river," said Roselli, nodding with his boss.

"Beyond that," said Tagget. "All the way to the turnpike. Then all the way along 128 in both directions for a couple of miles. We checked anyplace we thought he could have gone to hitchhike."

John Michael contorted his brow as though he had just come to a difficult decision. "I think I've heard enough for right now, so I'm going to adjourn the meeting and ask the chief and his men to excuse us."

The chief was taken completely by surprise. "What about Patt?" he stammered, pointing a stubby finger at me.

"I'm satisfied for the time being, Wembley. If there are any more incidents like the one Friday night, you be sure to let me know and we'll deal with it then. But I'm going to let him continue with the investigation as he sees fit."

"What about my bloody trip to California?" yelped Lester, and his tone was so sharp that the chief forgot his own problems long enough to lay a trembling hand on Lester's garishly clothed arm.

In a few seconds Lester was pushing back his chair along with the rest of the cops. There were mumbled good-byes and Roselli and Tagget carefully replaced their chairs under the table and then the four men clumped to the door, where the chief turned and made one last appeal.

"I assume I'll be hearing from you?" he said.

"Of course," John Michael said, giving him a smile of blatantly false reassurance.

I watched the door close behind the police entourage and when I turned back I saw that John Michael was studying Ralphie as though trying to remember why he had not booted him out as well. Ralphie hunched forward in his seat, eager to be a part of whatever was about to happen.

"Ralph, tell Patt about the other evidence you boys have just come up with."

Panic streaked across Ralphie's face.

"The credit-card receipt." John Michael made a boosting motion with his hand.

The panic was washed away in a flood of relief. "Oh, yeah," he said, still looking at John Michael. "We traced the murder weapon, the scarf. It was purchased from a place called Burberry's by credit card, signed by Mr. Carpenter on Saturday, the twelfth, three days before she was killed."

I did as Ralphie had done and spoke directly to John Michael. "Now wait a minute," I said. "You think Wylie Carpenter went to the trouble of purchasing 'the murder weapon,' as Ralph calls it, from Burberry's? You think a scarf from Zayre's wouldn't have done the trick just as well? You think he couldn't have used one from the hall closet, maybe?"

Libby spoke up. "We couldn't find any other scarfs in the house. And this one was brand-new. That's what made us suspicious."

I let the remark pass. We all did.

"The fact is, it was done," said John Michael. "Consider what we've got. The man's very wealthy wife is killed. Regardless of how independently wealthy he is, she's got a damn fine piece of property for him to inherit. Okay, that's point one." He held up his index finger. "Point two is, he can't account for his time on the night she was killed." His middle finger went up. "Point three, the weapon, such as it is, was just purchased by him." He waved the three fingers at all of us generally and at me in particular. "So we've got the weapon, we've got the motive, and with his absence we've got the framework for his method."

"Meaning he parks his wife's car at the overlook early

in the day, somehow gets himself home and then drives
to the club, plays golf, plays cards, leaves the clubhouse
to murder his wife and drive her to her own car, and then
drives back to the clubhouse and acts as if nothing
happened."

John Michael beamed with pleasure that I had remembered and incorporated his theory so exactly. Ralphie,
however, was completely lost.

"Does this mean you think Carpenter really did it?" he
asked.

John Michael answered him by speaking to me. "I
think it's time we took that idea to the grand jury."

Startled, I said, "What about Rasmussin?"

John Michael waved the name away.

"And, well, you haven't even looked into Dodge
Patterson."

Royster's booming voice broke the silence that followed. "What possible motive would he have had? What
would he possibly have to gain?"

There was more silence. Glances were exchanged between Royster and John Michael.

"I can't answer those questions," I said finally. "I can
only tell you that the path behind the overlook also can
be followed to the Patterson home by someone who
knows what he's doing."

"As well as everywhere else in Woodedge, I think you
said."

"Some places easier than others."

John Michael sighed. "All right." He fixed a stare on
Ralphie. "Let me talk to these guys alone, will you,
Ralph?"

Ralphie looked as if he had just been stabbed, but he
did as he was asked and shambled to the door.

When he was gone John Michael put a locker-room
grin on his face that did not quite match the burn in his
eyes. "Hey, what's the story, Patt? You a little queer for
this guy Carpenter, or what? It seems every time we
come up with something on him you try to knock it
down. Tell me, am I missing some vital point here, or
what?"

"It's just, I don't see where we've got enough to prosecute him."

John Michael threw out his hands. His lips opened in a smile that was meant to show a willingness to cast any disagreement in friendly terms. "That's the beauty of the grand jury system. If there's not enough, they'll tell us so. Carpenter's rights are safe-guarded by the grand jurors themselves. But it's up to us, hell, it's our duty, to give them the information they need to make that decision. The grand jury's made up of people on the street, Patt. You know that. And right now the people on the street want to know what we have on this case. I think we ought to tell them."

I answered with my eyes pointed at the table. "John, you don't haul a guy before the grand jury unless you're damn sure he's the right man."

"And I'm damn sure of it in this case."

"I think you're moving way too fast."

"I'm not moving fast enough. That's the problem. You see the papers today? I can't get Constantinis off the front page. He wants to have an international architectural competition for his goddamn theme park now. You know what's going on here?" He sat forward, lurched forward. "I've got it figured out. This is a grandstand play he's making, right? He's going for something and he's going for something big. The only big office that's coming up for election next year is the congressional seat. Huh? You see what I'm saying?"

A feeling of amazement slowly spread over me. "You think Jim Kilrain's going to step down? He's only in his fifties, isn't he?"

"Who knows with Jim Kilrain? He and I aren't exactly asshole buddies. I mean, he comes from goddamn Waterford, so who's likely to know what he's got up his sleeve? Constantinis, that's who. And Constantinis isn't pushing that silly Watertowne Plantation out of civic-mindedness, believe me."

Royster shook his head and made clucking noises to show John Michael that he believed him.

"Can you imagine going to Washington, Patt?" John Michael asked, his eyes shining.

"I can't imagine you needing an investigator in Washington, John."

"What do you mean? I'll need something. I'll need you. We're a team, the three of us. Where I go, you guys go."

"And right now where I go is California, is that what you're about to tell me?"

"Hey, and you're gonna complain? The chicks and the sun and the beaches?"

"And Dougie Rasmussin."

"Who's going to turn out to be the key to this case if he's handled right. If I send somebody out there to meet with him I want to be damn sure I know what I'm getting. Follow me?"

He issued penetrating looks that went to both Royster and me.

"Think I can trust Stanley Lester that way?"

He took our silence for the answer he was expecting.

"Not on your life. His loyalty is to that fat shit Tuttle and Tuttle would probably plead guilty himself if he thought it would save one of his precious citizens. You see the way the guy goes crazy because you ruffled a few feathers over there in rich-person's-land, Patt? Well, fuck him. Fuck all those guys. We're gonna do this on our own and we're gonna do it right. If we bring Carpenter before a grand jury we've got to make sure we get an indictment. If we get an indictment we've got to make damn sure we can get a conviction. Now," he paused. "Any reason I can't count on you, Patt?"

"No," I said.

"Good." He paused again, studying me. Then he turned his blue-eyed gaze on Royster. "Any reason I can't count on you, Roy?"

The question surprised me almost as much as it did Royster. He had to clear his throat to get out his denial.

"Good," said John Michael. "Then I want Patt to go out West and if he brings back what I think he will then I want you to handle the grand jury proceedings personally. Snap, Crackle, and Pop. Patt, you, and me, right? We'll take care of this thing from start to finish, right?"

Royster muttered, "Right," and then swiveled his head

quickly as if he expected to see some sort of sign pass between John Michael and me.

"Good," said John Michael for the third time. He got to his feet, looking at his watch. "Then that will do for now. Except, Patt, you might want to stick around for a minute or two so we can discuss how we're going to go about approaching Rasmussin." He lowered his watch. He looked at me in all innocence as if it were my feelings he did not want to offend. "That all right?"

I said yes and Royster very slowly and very silently made his way out of the room.

John Michael took a deep breath. He pushed his hands into his pockets and began jingling his keys. He was still staring at the door when he said, "You two don't like each other very much, do you?"

I fought back the urge to say "No shit," and instead told him, "It's not that big a deal, John."

"No," he said, walking around the table toward me. "I think it is. If it's true, I mean. I depend on you two guys one hundred percent and I can't have you backstabbing or bickering or setting each other up. I trust you as much as I trust Jessica, and, believe me, that's a lot of trust. My life's an open book to you. You want something? Let me know. You need something? It's yours. But I expect the same thing from you guys in return. Complete candor. You know what I'm saying?"

"I know what you're saying. I'm not sure why you're saying it."

I was still seated. John was standing next to me, over me, jingling his keys just a few inches from my face. I was glad when he turned away and walked back to his desk.

"Do you have any reason for believing Roy hasn't been candid in his dealings with you, Patt?" He was bent over, looking through piles of paper.

"Not really." My shoulders were hunched. My voice was on edge. I was not prepared to unload on Royster, not at this time and place, not gratuitously.

John Michael found the piece of paper for which he had been searching. He straightened up while he read it. He spoke without lifting his eyes. "Do you have any reason for believing he's not . . . well, let's use the word 'faithful'?"

The word immediately conjured up images of Royster planted in his secretary, slapping his belly against her bottom; but the context of the question, the tone John Michael was using, told me that he was not asking about Royster's sex life. "No," I said, truthfully. "I think Roy Hansen is a born second-in-command. I think he's your Ed Meese. Your Bob Haldeman."

"The road to my ruin, in other words."

"No. I mean I think he's completely loyal to you. I think he considers your interests his interests. I just don't think he considers my interests to be necessarily the same, that's all."

"Interesting," said John Michael, his brow wrinkled in thought.

After a while I stood up. The motion made John Michael approach me.

"Who," he said, "do you think is most likely to be unfaithful to me?"

When he was close enough, when he saw I wasn't going to answer, he handed me the piece of paper he had retrieved from his desk. It was plain typing paper with no date, no salutation, and no signature. In the middle of the page, in a typical IBM script, it read:

John—
Someone close to you is unfaithful.
Watch out.

"I got that the day you were up in Wylie Carpenter's hometown and I've been holding on to it just to see if there'd be any follow-up. There hasn't. But it's still made me wonder. You don't suppose Roy would be selling us out in any way, do you?"

I remained silent, staring at the typewritten words.

"The only reason I'm asking that, Patt, is because I realize how tricky this Carpenter situation is. It could wipe me out politically if we're not careful. That guy's going to be able to pay for the best defense money can buy and we can't afford to take even the slightest chance."

"I don't think you're taking a chance with Roy, John."

He slipped the letter out of my hand. "And you," he said, holding the letter between us as if it were a Bible on which I was supposed to swear an oath, "the same goes for you, too?"

He looked worried, as if he did not know what my answer would be. I smiled. If he had been a less formal man I would have clapped him on the shoulder. "Yeah," I said.

"You'll go to California and question the kid—Rasmussin, I mean—and you'll get what we need?"

"I'll get what I can."

"We need to know if he was sleeping with Carpenter's wife and we need to know if Carpenter knew about it."

"I understand."

"And once you've got everything you can get I want you to do whatever it takes to convince him to come back here to testify."

"I'll do my best, John."

"Good, Patt. I knew I could trust you."

20

I stood in a phone booth at Logan Airport with a pen in my mouth. The pen may have been coincidental, but I did not remove it when my call was answered and when a man said "Hello?" I talked around it, using a high-pitched, stuttering, nervous voice that I had not planned on using at all.

"Is Mrs. Patterson there? Mrs. Gretchen Patterson?"

"No, this is Dodge Patterson. May I help you?"

I had had more than enough of Dodge Patterson's help when he crashed our lunch. He had told me nothing of significance and his presence had kept Gretchen and me from communicating on any significant level.

"No, no," I said. "I call back." I used the same high-pitched, stuttering voice.

When I hung up I was sweating profusely. I was sure that he had recognized me, sure that I had made a fool of myself. Thirty-eight years old and I was playing kid tricks, making anonymous phone calls to women and pretending to be somebody I wasn't.

Doug Rasmussin had taken a room in a place called the Apart-Lets in a city called Venice. I rented a little car at the Los Angeles airport, tossed my overnight bag in the trunk, and drove there in a matter of minutes. I was disappointed it was so close.

I had been in California once before. I had gone out to see my high-school girlfriend—girlfriend of sorts—Mary Marie Gastonatto, shortly before I started working for the D.A.'s office. She and her sister Angeljean had moved to Newport Beach and, although I had not seen her since my father's death, I had accepted her invitation to visit. It was a mistake. Mary Marie had changed. Her sister had changed. I, apparently, had not.

I had arrived in March and my accent and winter pallor had immediately set me apart from their Southern California friends. I, on the other hand, had failed to appreciate their successes. I had not understood the value of their small condominium within walking distance of the Pacific. I had not admired Mary Marie's breast implants or Angeljean's black boyfriend, who majored in cool and inevitably took Angie, as she was now called, behind closed doors whenever I was around. He was not impressed with my job as an insurance claims supervisor, and neither Angie nor "M" was interested in it either.

"M" was now a sales rep for a sportswear manufacturer. She wore beautiful clothes that emphasized her new cleavage and she drove a little Fiat convertible that looked better than it ran. She was not used to planning where to go or what to do. She was used to having her dates plan for her, and I had no ideas beyond Disneyland and the beach. She said one was too old and the other too cold. I went home early. It seemed better than going to Disneyland alone.

Doug Rasmussin had fared better than I had on his first trip to the West Coast. Venice fit a certain California image for New England guys like us. It had stucco, Spanish-style buildings; elaborate murals painted on public walls; boys towing surfboards behind bicycles, and girls on rollerskates; fancy cars and sporty cars and cars with long sailboards on their roofs.

The building at the address I had been given was boxlike and six stories high. It was ugly, in and of itself, but it was just a few blocks from the ocean and I had learned on my last trip the value of that. I parked my car on the street and did not bother to put any money in the meter since I did not care if the rental company got a ticket, and suspected that neither did the rental company.

I walked through a plain door, over which was painted the word "Apart-Lets," and entered a small lobby. In the lobby was a long unframed mirror that occupied one wall. It was cracked in the lower left-hand corner, cracked clear through so that one piece was separated from the rest. Beneath the mirror were a handful of mismatched chairs arranged around a heavy blond coffee table that bore the marks of a thousand burning cigarettes.

There was a narrow bookcase against another wall. It had four bookshelves and not enough books to fill them. One of the books was volume E of an encyclopedia. Another was entitled *Learn to Swim*.

The only other furnishings in the lobby were an oval braided rug that had lost most of its color, a pay telephone, and a blackboard where someone had written in a large scrawl, "Mitch call home." A different hand had written beneath that, "E.T. wants you."

There was a metal door with a push bar and the word STAIRS stenciled on it. A Bullwinkle sticker obscured the letter I. Another door led to an elevator that was unmarked with words, lights, or floor indicators. Next to that door a reception counter was recessed into the wall. A Japanese lantern hung above the counter. A poster of a middle-aged Ronald Reagan holding a giant sausage was on the wall behind the counter. Taped onto the poster were the words EAT MY MEAT!

A desk clerk looked at me from a chair behind the counter. It was an armchair and because he was sitting down his eyes were barely higher than the countertop. When he wasn't looking at me he was watching a tiny black-and-white television propped on the seat of a straight-back chair.

"Can you tell me what room Mr. Rasmussin is in?" I asked him.

The clerk was dark-haired and dark-skinned and had a jet-black mustache. He concentrated his gaze on the television screen. "Never heard of him."

"Guy's just moved in the past couple of days. Good-looking guy." I pointed a finger to my cheek, where Rasmussin's dimple would be.

"Don't got no guys like that. This a family sort of place."

"This is a family sort of guy. Comes from back east. I think he hitched out here."

"Show me your credentials." The clerk still was not

looking at me. He was watching a commercial in which Florence Henderson was pitching Wesson oil. It was a good commercial, I knew, but it lost something on a tiny black-and-white TV.

I said, "I don't got to show you no stinking credentials."

The clerk said, "Try 317."

As I turned to the elevator he said, "It's broken."

As I turned to the metal door with the word STAIRS and the Bullwinkle sticker on it he said, "Don't try to spend the night or I charge the dude twelve bucks."

I walked the two flights of stairs. I found room 317 on a dimly lit hallway that smelled a little of stale cigarette smoke and a lot of cooking tomato sauce. I knocked politely on the door to 317 and nothing happened. I knocked harder and nothing happened. I banged on it once out of frustration and suddenly a voice said, "Yeah, yeah," and pulled it open. Before me was the man in the photo on Mrs. Rasmussin's mantel.

It was after noon, but Doug Rasmussin had still been in bed. I knew this because he answered the door with a sheet wrapped around his otherwise naked body. I also knew it because there was a woman lying in his bed. She had tousled hair, she was still asleep, and, since Dougie had taken her sheet, her bare ass was pointed straight at me. There was a tattoo on one of her cheeks. It was a beautiful ass. It was an admirable tattoo.

The room reeked of alcohol and sex. It was a fairly good-sized room and it contained a kitchenette that had its own mini-refrigerator, two-burnered stove, sink, and linoleum floor. There was some shelf space, a couple of drawers and cabinets, and a breakfast counter that served as a room divider and that had two vinyl-topped stools tucked underneath it. Next to the bed, next to the woman on the bed, was a maple nightstand that held an empty bottle of tequila, some remnants of a lime, a knife, a salt shaker, and two bar glasses. On the floor were some pants and some socks and some panties, a shirt and a blouse. Dougie Rasmussin squinted at me, trying to figure out who I was.

I told him. "Patt Starbuck. I'm from Walmouth."

Dougie's jaw dropped. He rubbed his face. He looked

back at his friend, who wasn't moving. He looked at me again. He said, "Walmouth. Jees, that's great," and he seemed to mean it.

I had been prepared for a lot of reactions. I had even been prepared for flight. But Dougie Rasmussin shifted his grip on his sheet and stuck out his right hand for me to shake. "How j'ya know I was from Walmouth?"

"Because I've come out here looking for you." I showed him the card that I had declined to show the desk clerk.

"Shit, what's this mean?" Dougie said, and for a moment he looked worried. It was, however, not the kind of worry that comes from fear.

"You talked with a cop the other day about the death of Rebecca Carpenter, didn't you?"

"Wow! You came all the way out here to see me because of that?"

I was beginning to gather that Dougie did not realize he was a suspect in the murder. "Didn't Inspector Lester tell you someone would be in touch with you?"

Dougie scratched his head. Despite his puffy eyes, unshaven face, and unkempt hair, his appearance was rather appealing. His torso was smooth and muscular, but he carried himself loosely, in an unthreatening, natural sort of manner. He looked like a guy who liked people and expected them to like him. I suspected he would make an excellent salesman.

"He told me, you know, that she died. Listen, you want to come in? Sit down?"

We both glanced around. His naked friend was still on the bed, but there was a black vinyl Danish modern chair in one corner and Dougie pointed to that. "You can sit there and I can sit with her," he said.

We did as he suggested. He shut the door first and then kind of hopped back to the bed. He apologized and said they had had something of a party last night. He pulled a brown blanket over the sleeping woman and sat down on the edge of the bed.

"I just met her," he said. "Imagine that? She asked me to dance. That doesn't happen back in Walmouth, huh?"

I suddenly felt very old, very staid, and very middle-class. But Rasmussin was looking at me as if he and I were two peas in a pod, just a couple of freewheeling young men come out to California to party and seek our fortune.

"She says her name's Laraine. You know what she is? She's a singer in a rock-and-roll band. Look." He got down and scrambled around on his knees until he pulled something up from under the bed. "Leather pants," he said, holding them up for me to admire.

His delight was not the kind you could resent or mock. It was too genuine. He was too anxious to share it. I was beginning to ache in the pit of my stomach.

"How did you get out here?" he asked.

"I flew, Dougie. I just got off the plane."

"That's amazing, isn't it? What did it take, five-six hours? You got up this morning back in Walmouth and now you're sitting here. It took me, what, about twelve days to get out here. But you shoulda seen some of the people I met. Talk about wee-yud. I got picked up by this one guy, he told me he'd just gotten out of jail. You know why? You won't believe this. He got arrested for screwing a dead girl . . . Seriously."

Dougie Rasmussin looked at me with amazement, his eyes reflecting all the wonder of the universe. "You know why he got let go? Because the charge against him was screwing a dead person in the street and the judge says to the D.A., 'What's the evidence this man knew the woman was dead?' And the D.A. said, 'Well, it's against the law to screw anybody in the street.' Judge smashes down his gavel. Says, 'Can't charge him with that. That'd be double jeopardy. Case dismissed.' "

Dougie waited for my reaction.

I shifted my legs so that one was over the other. I said, "Dougie, didn't Inspector Lester tell you that you were wanted for questioning in connection with the death of Mrs. Carpenter?"

Dougie's head bobbed as if he had just been tagged with a glancing blow. He kept a portion of his grin intact. After all, he had just told me a story. "You're shittin' me," he said at last.

"What did he say to you?"

"He asked me if I was the Douglas Rasmussin who

came from 1429 Merrymount Ave. and if I had worked for the Carpenters."

I nodded because he wanted me to.

"He asked me when I had left the Carpenters and I told him, you know, whenever it was. Then he asked me when was the last time I seen Mrs. Carpenter. I said the morning of the day I left. She gave me my check and said good-bye and all. There wasn't anything wrong with her then."

"There wouldn't have been, Dougie. She was strangled to death."

Dougie gulped. I could see his Adam's apple move. "How?"

"With a scarf."

"Whose?"

"Her own."

"That's funny. I don't remember her wearing scarfs."

"This was a new scarf."

He nodded. "Oh."

"What else did Inspector Lester ask you?"

"Only, you know, did the Carpenters know when it was I was planning on leaving and I said, 'Yes, of course.' "

"And did he ask you who hired you?"

"Oh, yeah," Dougie said quickly. "Mrs. Carpenter."

The woman on the bed stirred. She lifted her head and peered at Dougie. It seemed to take her a long time to focus. "Arggh," she said, and dropped straight down onto the mattress again. Dougie patted her. He rubbed his hand up and down her back to make her feel better.

I said, "Dougie, why did you leave when you did?"

"Huh? Oh, because it was all planned that way. I mean, Mrs. Carpenter came to me one day and said she'd heard I'd done some yardwork and she needed somebody, you know, because she'd just had to let her people go." He turned away, checking on his friend again. I had the impression he wanted to get off the subject.

"You told her you could do it?"

"Sort of. Well, for a few weeks anyhow, and she said that was fine. We agreed I'd work until October fifteenth and that would still give me time to get across country before it got too cold."

"You had already decided you were definitely going to come out here?"

"Yeah. Uh-huh."

I said, "How did you know Mrs. Carpenter?"

"Oh, from the pool. At Stonegate."

"Dougie." I unfolded my legs. "She didn't belong to Stonegate."

"Yeah, but she'd come out sometimes. With a friend or somebody."

"Which friend?"

"I don't remember."

"Gretchen Patterson?"

"Yeah. I guess. Sometimes."

"Can you think of anybody else?"

Dougie's eyes were rolling. He was trying. "No," he said at last.

"Were you friends with Gretchen Patterson?"

"Not really. No."

"You taught her son to swim, didn't you?"

"That's how I knew her."

"But Mrs. Carpenter, you were better friends with her, were you?"

"We became friends, yes."

"What kind of things would you talk about with her?"

"Oh, yard things. Property things." He nodded. "Stuff related to my job."

"Did she seem to like the job you were doing for her?"

"Seemed to." Dougie was rubbing his bed companion again. It required him to keep his eyes on her back.

"Did she seem to want you to leave?"

"No. No. She said I was doing good."

"You think she would have kept you on for as long as you wanted?"

"Yeah."

"So it wasn't her idea for you to leave when you did."

"No, it was my idea—you know, October fifteenth."

"Then I'm a little confused, Dougie, because, you see, I talked to some of your buddies at Balducci's, some of the guys on the softball team, and they told me the woman you were working for encouraged you to come out here."

"Oh, yeah." He stopped rubbing. "She did some of that, too."

"These guys said she kept drilling it into your head that you were never going to amount to anything as long as you stayed around Walmouth."

"That's true." He waved an index finger at me, indicating he remembered now.

I cocked my head. I squinted one eye. I asked the next question as though it were a really hard thing for me to do. "What kind of reasons did she give for telling you that?"

Dougie Rasmussin took a moment to tuck in his sheet to make it look more like a toga. "Oh," he said, his chin pressed against his neck as he looked down at his handiwork, "she'd just always tell me how important it is to decide what you want and then go out there and make it happen. She liked to say nothing's ever going to come to you if you sit there dreaming about it."

"And did she explain what she meant by that?"

Dougie blinked, as if he did not understand what was unclear about what he had just said. "She asked me, you know . . . if I could have any job in the world, what would I choose."

I nodded, encouraging him. "What did you tell her?"

"I told her, if I could have any job in the world, I'd like to have Johnny Carson's. Have a job like his, you know?"

"And did she think that was something you could do if you came out here?"

Dougie, to his credit, eyed me closely to see if I was serious. "What it did was, it got us talking. Like, what was it about his job that I liked and could I get to do some of that same stuff in other jobs. And her big thing was—"

"Whose?"

Dougie ran his fingers through his hair. "Mrs. Carpenter's. Her big thing was that I was never going to take the chances I needed to take as long as I kept hanging around with the same guys at the same places. It wasn't the guys or the places so much as it was being comfort-able, you know what I mean?" He laughed. "I mean, she told me the one way I could make sure I wasn't never gonna get in movies or television or anything like that was to keep hanging around Balducci's. That's why she said I gotta come out here."

The woman, Laraine, was stirred by Dougie's laughter. She curled her hands into fists and pushed herself into a kneeling position. Her face was thin and her features were rather sharp, but her eyes were an intriguing green and they were set off nicely by the dark, stringy curls that fell into her face. She looked at me as though I had caused her a great deal of pain. "What is this bullshit?" she said.

"Hey, babe," Dougie told her as he slipped his arm around her shoulders, "this is a guy from back home."

He had such an innocent, engaging way about him that I actually found myself angered when Laraine shrugged him away. She crawled to the edge of the bed and stood up, stark naked. Her legs were long and thin. Her breasts were long and thin. Her waist was narrow. Her thatch of hair was very black and obviously sculpted.

"Where the fuck are my pants?" she demanded, and Dougie tossed them to her. She was starting to put them on when she leaned over and picked up her panties. They were red and they were torn. "Jesus," she said to no one, "what happened to these?"

"You want some breakfast?" Dougie asked her.

The woman gave him a withering look. She picked up all her clothes and walked into the bathroom and shut the door.

Dougie turned to me, undiscouraged. "How about you?"

I said, leaning forward, my elbows on my knees, "I'm amazed, Doug. You're the first person I've talked to who actually seemed to have any kind of conversations with Becky Carpenter."

He shrugged. "She was nice enough."

"You're pretty good with women, aren't you?"

He caught my eye. He grinned modestly but quickly looked away again, as though he did not want his secret to get out.

"Was she interested in you?"

We heard the toilet flush. We heard the shower start. Dougie said, "She liked me okay."

"Did your relationship go beyond work?"

There seemed to be something on Doug Rasmussin's knuckles that required his complete attention.

I said, "The woman was killed, Dougie. She died the day you left Massachusetts. She was found at a lovers' lane with her pantyhose ripped and her neck broken and there are people who think you did it."

Dougie's head snapped so fast and so far his own neck could have broken if it hadn't been so muscular. "Cut the shit," he said.

"No shit. This is serious business. I wouldn't be here if it weren't. Rebecca Carpenter was an important woman and somebody killed her and somebody's going to fry for it."

"Well, it won't be me." He was adamant.

"What do I have to prove it wasn't you?"

He had raised his jaw, folded his lips together. He had to unfold them to talk. "I could sleep with her anyplace I wanted. I didn't have to take her to no lovers' lane."

"Where did you sleep with her, Dougie?"

"Outside under the trees. In the caretaker's cottage. In her own bed once when Sarah wasn't around."

"Who knew that you were lovers?"

"Nobody got it offa me."

"What about the boys at Balducci's?"

"Oh, yeah, well . . . I guess I said some things to them."

"Do you think her husband knew?"

"Once I started working there him and me never really spoke. I'd see him sometimes, but he'd just kinda look at me."

"Like he was looking for something?"

"Sorta."

"Had you ever spoken to him before you worked for him?"

"Oh, yeah. We used to talk all the time at the club."

I was digesting this information when the bathroom door opened and Laraine stepped out toweling her hair. She had on her black leather pants and a white blouse of the style where the shoulder seams hung halfway down her arms. She spoke as she walked toward us. "Anybody still up for breakfast?"

We ate at a place that served breakfast around the clock. At three in the afternoon there were a good number of people in need of eggs and pancakes. Most of these people did not look as though they had just gotten off work.

I did my best to be circumspect around Dougie's friend Laraine, but I was not altogether successful. When Dougie got up to go to the men's room she lost no time in asking me the big question.

"You a cop?"

"No."

"You act like a cop."

"I do not."

She shrugged. We were in a booth and she sat back in a two-point position with her arms folded across her breasts, her long thin breasts that I knew were lurking just beneath the surface of her blouse. "Then why're you hassling the poor dude?" she asked.

"I'm not hassling him."

"I heard the questions you were asking him. You think he did something."

"I don't *think* he did anything. I want to know what he did."

"Why?"

"It's my job."

She was enjoying this. I could tell by the smirk that was building on her face. "Just exactly what is your job, if you're not a cop?"

"I coordinate litigation for a bunch of lawyers. I help them prepare their cases."

"What kind of lawyers?"

"Public lawyers."

"You mean like government lawyers? Like district attorney lawyers?"

"Something like that."

"Oh, brother," she said, and her smirk blossomed.

I had been about to take a sip of coffee, but now I put my cup down. "What's that supposed to mean?"

She raised her leg, her knee bent, and put her foot down flat on the bench next to her. It was a provocative way to sit and it made me look at the long leather rise of her calf and the long leather plummet of her thigh. The pants were supple but very tight, and they hugged her as if they were her own skin. "It means," she said, "why would anybody want a job like that?"

I looked down at my plate and what was left of my eggs and hash browns. There are few things uglier than egg yolk on a plate and I smoothed the remnants of my hash browns around to cover the yellow as much as possible. "It can be interesting."

"What, getting involved in other people's misery?"

"I don't look at it that way."

She dropped her hand behind her. She slid further down in her seat. "How do you look at it?"

"I look at it as a job, just a job. Somebody gets hurt, somebody gets killed—somebody's got to figure out who did it, make sure he doesn't do it again."

"But it doesn't work, does it? You capture one person, it doesn't stop someone else from doing the same thing."

"So what's the alternative?" I offered her a smile, not because I felt like it but because I wanted to get out of the conversation. "I don't have any illusions about putting an end to crime, if that's what you're talking about."

"What do you have illusions about?" She was still slouched, still leaning back. Her foot was still on the bench and her knee was still in the air.

"Nothing," I said.

Now she sat up. Her black leathered leg went beneath the table. "Don't you have illusions about helping people? Saving society? Making the world a better place? Isn't that how you justify going around doing what you're doing—scaring the shit out of everyone, asking them questions, setting them up for arrests?"

"Look . . . Laraine . . . if it's any of your business, I don't do the arresting and I don't make the decisions as to who gets arrested, okay? I try to find evidence as to who did what, and when I get it I bring it to the prosecutors. What they do with it is their business."

"And you don't give a damn what they do with it, is that what you're saying?"

"That's right."

Laraine's mouth opened. Her tongue ran between her parted teeth as she stared at me thoughtfully. "So, then . . . you don't really care whether what you're doing is helping anyone or not."

Exasperated, I answered too loudly. "Hey, if a crime's committed and I come up with the evidence that solves it then I've helped everybody. Everybody."

The conversation stopped at the table next to us. The diners looked over. I looked down at my plate again. "Now, can we talk about something else?" I said softly. "Please?"

But Laraine persisted. "Does it ever bother you, the people you hurt along the way?"

"I told you, I just gather the evidence."

"Would you gather evidence against somebody you knew wasn't guilty?"

"It's not up to me to determine if someone's guilty."

Laraine leaned forward. Her green eyes held mine. I thought she was going to ask me another question and I leaned forward to meet her. "You know what I think?" she whispered. "I think you're a fascist."

I straightened slowly and tried not to look to see if the people at the next table were still watching us. "So," I said calmly, "what do you do for a living?"

She gave my question the time needed to make it perfectly clear that I wasn't getting away with anything. "I heard Dougie tell you," she said. "I'm a singer."

"You, ah, between bands or just between gigs?"

"What makes you think I'm between anything?"

"Because," I said, dropping even the semblance of politeness from my voice, "if you were making any money you wouldn't have spent the night in Rasmussin's shithole of a room."

She swallowed, but other than that she never moved and her eyes were still the green shafts they had been. "Maybe I've got a husband or a boyfriend. Maybe I live too far away to go home. Maybe I was just too drunk to know the difference."

"Maybe," I agreed. "On the other hand, you haven't been in any hurry to leave and the afternoon's almost gone."

Laraine's features, narrow to begin with, took on a pinched appearance. "You know what I think?"

"Yes."

"How could you?"

"Because there's not that much to know."

Suddenly Dougie was back at the table, standing next to us with a big smile on his face. "How're you guys doing?" he asked.

Laraine told him. "Your friend's an asshole."

Dougie looked crestfallen. His loyalties were clearly divided between his girlfriend of one night and his fellow Walmouthian. He wanted us to like each other. He wanted to say just the right thing. "Oh, gee," he declared. It was not enough.

Laraine shoved her way out of the booth. She put her hand on Dougie's chest and shoved him a bit, too. "You want to stay with him, you stay. I'm leaving."

Dougie watched her stride toward the door. Everyone in the place, it seemed, watched her stride toward the door. People were leaning out of their seats to watch her go.

Dougie made up his mind quickly. It may have had something to do with the exquisiteness of her walk, the perfect sway of her hips in her tight leather pants, but he made a grab for his wallet and told me he had to go after her.

I reached out and caught his wrist before he was able to get the wallet out of his back pocket. "Dougie, I've got to finish with you."

"What do you want?" he said, looking pained.

"I want you to come home to testify."

"But I just got out here."

"We'll provide you with a round-trip plane ticket. You come home, you tell a grand jury what you told me, you can fly back the same day."

Laraine had hit the sidewalk. Through the restaurant's

plate-glass window we could see her turn and walk in the opposite direction from the Apart-Lets. "Who'll I be testifying against?"

"I can't tell you that. I can only promise that you won't be the focus of the grand jury's investigation."

"All right," he said, not looking at me. "I'll do it."

"You'll be coming back to the Apart-Lets tonight?"

"Yes . . . no. I don't know. It depends on Laraine."

"But I can reach you there?"

"Yeah. Just leave a message with Zorro at the front desk."

"Good. You run and catch her then. I'll take care of the tab."

"I can pay."

"It's all right. Go. Run."

In a moment I was alone, remembering how much I hated being alone, wondering what it was about me that brought out the worst in the women of California, and deciding that I probably wouldn't carry out any plan I may have had to give Mary Marie Gastonatto a call after all.

21

John Michael struck quickly. On the Monday following my return from the West Coast he had Wylie S. Carpenter arrested at his place of business, Woodedge Savings and Loan. It was a staged arrest, with the three Boston television stations waiting on the street with their Minicams to record a grim-looking Inspector Stanley Lester, resplendent in a green and yellow plaid sport coat, leading out a handcuffed, ashen-faced Wylie. The cameras on the six- and the eleven-o'clock news clearly showed the horror-stricken employees of the savings and loan gathered at the doors and windows as their boss was guided by his elbow down the walk to a waiting patrol car.

John Michael defended his choice of arrest locations at a little celebratory gathering at his house that evening. "I could have done it at one of his clubs in front of all his hoity-toity friends," he explained. "What do you think he'd rather do, lose a little business or bring shame down on his peers?"

Jessica, who was wearing a low-plunging V-neck cashmere sweater that revealed a hitherto undisclosed array of freckles on her chest, wanted to clink glasses with everyone. She hit mine, she hit her husband's, she hit Royster's, and then she kind of waved her glass in Patty's general direction because Patty was standing behind Royster and looking down at the carpet.

"You could have arrested him at his home, I guess," I said.

I had, everyone knew, argued against an arrest at all. I had suggested that the grand jury be used as an investigative body looking into the murder without a named suspect. "That way," I had said, "we can get Wylie himself to testify without him pulling a lot of Fifth Amendment crap." But John Michael had overruled me. He had said we didn't need Wylie to testify, all we needed was me.

Now John Michael listened to my latest complaint, subtle though it was, and stared into his glass of Pepsi. "That long driveway," he said. "A parade of cars going up there could have tipped him off. I couldn't take any chances on what he might do. It's a lot safer this way."

Inasmuch as Wylie was an accused scarf murderer, I well understood the vast array of household weapons he might have brought to bear on the Woodedge Police Department. I could picture Lester cautioning his mates, "Keep him away from the bureau. That's where he keeps those bloody chokers. And don't let him near his golf bag."

But everyone else was murmuring agreement and Royster suddenly exclaimed, "You know what I can't believe is who he got for a lawyer."

When we had decided to go ahead with the arrest we had spent a good part of Sunday afternoon speculating on who Wylie might get to represent him. Names of all the top Boston attorneys had been thrown out alongside those of the brighter lights of Exeter County. No one had ever once mentioned Phil Burns, and yet that was who showed up at the arraignment.

"He won't keep him," John Michael assured us.

"He was probably the only guy Wylie could get on a moment's notice," Jessica added. "Right now Wylie's probably meeting with Joseph Oteri or F. Lee Bailey."

"I hope he gets Lee," John Michael said, squeezing his face into a little pocket of flesh and shuffling his feet. "Imagine the attention we'd get if Lee came into it?"

"On the other hand," Royster replied, "Burnsie showed up at the arraignment looking reasonably sober. Maybe he'll fool Wylie." He chuckled and showed everybody his white teeth. In a spontaneous gesture that more than anything else revealed the euphoria he was feeling he grabbed his wife around the shoulders and hugged her to him.

Patty rocked stiffly onto one foot, was forced to nuzzle

into Royster's neck, and then rocked back again. She looked at me. She looked at John Michael. Her cheeks flushed.

I said, to get everyone's attention away from her, "Old Burnsie didn't do so bad today, getting Carpenter out of there on a hundred thousand dollars' bail. Not really what you'd expect for a rich man and a capital crime."

"Yeah, what did he have to post, a ten-thousand-dollar bond?" said John Michael. "He probably paid for that out of what he had in his wallet."

Royster slurped his grin a little tighter. He was focused on John Michael. "Ah, we didn't really fight Burnsie too hard on that. We knew Wylie Carpenter wouldn't be taking off anywhere. Not a prominent citizen like him."

"Let's hope he's prominent enough to make the goddamn *Courier* forget about Constantinis for a day or so," said John Michael. "But I suppose with my luck the stock market will fold tomorrow or the Russians will invade Maine or the governor will be caught exposing himself to a group of schoolchildren in New Bedford."

"Still," said Jessica, gathering glasses for a new round of drinks, "you don't want Wylie's conviction to be a foregone conclusion. If everybody thinks he's guilty from the moment he's arrested, there'll be no story to tell."

John Michael slapped his forehead. "Oh, my God, I just had an awful thought."

We all turned to him in alarm. The word "What?" came out of all our mouths.

"What if we get him indicted by the grand jury and the sonofabitch pleads guilty?"

"Then," said Royster, hooking his thumbs in his armpits and mugging around at all of us, "I guess I'll be the one who runs for Congress."

He may have been expecting more laughter than he actually got; but Patty was too busy watching me, and I was too busy watching John Michael and Jessica. And they were too busy catching each other's eye.

It is entirely possible that there are people charged before grand juries in Massachusetts who are not indicted. I may even have read about some from time to time. The odds, however, are not in favor of the subject of the investigation.

The Exeter County Grand Jury had been impaneled for twenty-seven days of their thirty-day term when Royster Hansen presented them with the case of *Commonwealth* v. *Carpenter*. The grand jurors knew why they were there. They sat, twenty-three of them, in sixteen fixed jurors' chairs and seven broad-bottomed wooden armchairs in a sealed-off corner courtroom on the second floor of our building on Court Street.

They were bored for the most part. They were mostly of retirement age and overwhelmingly working-class in appearance. There were fourteen men and nine women, including one black, but no Asians or other discernible minorities. If any of them came from Woodedge they were doing a good job of disguising it.

I am told that they perked up considerably when Royster informed them of the matter involving Mr. Carpenter. And since Mr. Hansen was ungoverned by any judge and unhampered by any opposing counsel, he could describe the action in pretty much any way he pleased.

The Annotated Laws of Massachusetts provide that the only persons who may be present during a grand jury proceeding are attorneys for the commonwealth who may be convenient to the presentation of evidence, the witness under examination, the attorney for the witness under examination, "and such other persons who are necessary or convenient to the presentation of evidence." In the grand jury proceedings involving the case of *Commonwealth* v. *Carpenter* it was determined by the attorney representing the commonwealth, Royster Hansen, that no other "such persons" except the court reporter were necessary. It was his show and my only knowledge of what actually took place came while I was on the stand being examined under oath by Royster.

The one problem of which I was aware came with respect to Dougie Rasmussin. When I called him several days before he was scheduled to appear, I was told by Zorro, the desk clerk at the Apart-Lets, that he was not there. I had anticipated this situation and had gone out of my way to avoid it by leaving Zorro a ten-dollar bill.

Zorro, however, remembered the ten dollars. He remembered me. He would have been more than happy to earn another ten dollars by telling me where Dougie had gone, but he didn't know, because Dougie had simply moved out and had left no forwarding address. He had done it when Zorro was not on duty and there was nothing Zorro could do.

"That's not insurmountable," said John Michael, cracking a pencil between his fingers when he learned of Dougie's disappearance. "You can present hearsay evidence before a grand jury. It doesn't invalidate the indictment."

And so my task, guided by the leading questions of Royster Hansen, was to tell the jurors not only what I had seen and determined, but what I had heard. I was on the stand only ninety minutes, but by the time I was done twenty-three members of the Exeter County Grand Jury had reason to believe that Wylie S. Carpenter's wife was having an affair with Douglas Rasmussin, that Wylie had lied when he told me he did not know Rasmussin was leaving the state on the fifteenth of October, that Wylie's presence could not be accounted for during a period of two hours on the night of the fifteenth, and that my investigation—and my observations of Inspector Lester's investigation—indicated that Rebecca Carpenter had been placed in the front seat of her Mercedes after she had been killed. This last item, of course, was not so much what the investigations had indicated to me as it was what they had indicated to John Michael, but the distinction was not required to be made in my answers to Royster's questions.

Other matters were left to other witnesses, but I apparently did a good job in my role because Royster lost his head for a moment on the night after my testimony and actually complimented me. In any event, on the thirtieth and final day of the grand jury's term they handed down a bill of indictment charging Wylie S. Carpenter with the murder of his wife, Rebecca Chesley Carpenter.

22

John Michael got the attention he was seeking, or some of it anyway. The *Courier* put the indictment on the front page, but it was put at the bottom and the caption read, WOODEDGE MAN TO STAND TRIAL IN WIFE'S MURDER.

The Keoughs had been hoping for a good deal more. They thought the case should have had enough notoriety to mention Carpenter by name in a headline. They thought the article should have been more explosive and they were quite upset by the negative slant they perceived from the reporter, a woman named Lia Chapin whom none of us knew.

The article read:

An Exeter County Grand Jury has indicted Wylie S. Carpenter for the October 15th murder of his wife, Rebecca. Mr. Carpenter, 48, reigning golf champion of the Bollingbrook and Stonegate Country Clubs, is a director of Woodedge Savings & Loan and a prominent member of Woodedge society.

According to Deputy District Attorney Royster Hansen, the motive in the killing of Rebecca Carpenter, 40, was a combination of greed and revenge. "Mr. Carpenter discovered that his wife was having an affair," said Hansen. "His method for dealing with that left him in a position to inherit her multi-million dollar estate."

Mrs. Carpenter was the sole child of the late financier and art patron Walter Chesley, and the last survivor of a family whose influence spans the history of Woodedge, dating back to the arrival of

217

Reverend Thomas Chesley in the year 1700. Her body was found in the front seat of her automobile at an overlook off Ivanhoe Road. She had been strangled with a scarf her husband was known to have purchased three days before.

Mr. Carpenter, who is currently free on $100,000 bail, could not be reached for comment. However his lawyer, former District Attorney Philip Burns, was succinct in his response to the indictmemt. "It's bull——," he said. "Pure and absolute bull——. It is the product of a totally inept legal system."

Many of those who know Mr. Carpenter appeared stunned by the charge. "Wylie wouldn't hurt a flea," said Gerard Whitman, president of Whitman Orthopedic Supply Company, and one of the town's largest employers. "He has been devastated by the death of his wife and I can't believe he had anything to do with it. The whole thing smacks of a witch hunt to me."

Trial has been set to begin on January 6th and Burns vowed it would go forward that day. "We're not waiving Wylie Carpenter's right to a speedy trial," he said. "We don't think the D.A.'s office has anything on this man and we want his name cleared as fast as possible."

"The money angle," John Michael screamed, throwing the newspaper at Royster so that Royster had to raise his hands to keep from getting hit in the face. "You had specifics you could have given that reporter, whoever the hell she is. The sixty-three-million-dollar inheritance. The twenty-five-acre estate on Bulham Road, the mountaintop retreat in Vermont, and the twelve-room cottage on the ocean in Osterville. You should have called Freddie Murray, he would have known how to write the story. But if you didn't, if you got this broad, you should have at least had enough sense to give her a hook, something she could use to make her story better than the next person's story. Give it to her, goddammit, Roy. Give it to her."

Jessica, who had brought the newspaper to us, was

trying to mollify her husband. "I think what John is telling you, Roy, is that you don't waste an opportunity like this by summing everything up with a phrase like 'multimillion-dollar estate.' Isn't that what you meant, honey?"

Jessica, once again, was dressed differently than I had ever seen her. She was wearing a black sweater with a few colorful horizontal stripes, a black leather skirt that ended above her knees, and black stockings. She had fine legs and she looked good. But I appeared to be the only one who was noticing.

John Michael was carrying his rant around the room. "The reporter's got to fill up her space. You don't give her enough to do it and she's going to keep calling other sources until she's got enough. The more people she calls the less control we have over what she writes. It's as simple as that."

Royster was fuming. When he spoke only his bottom lip moved and only his bottom teeth showed. "I called Miles Bell directly. This is who he had call me back. I gave her the story and this is what she did with it."

John Michael, from across the room, whirled and said, "No written press release?"

Royster drummed his fingers.

"You couldn't manage to write one for the crime of the decade?"

Roy drummed harder. "I figured, I'd give her the story as fast as I could. The indictment comes down at two o'clock, I'm on the phone to Miles at two-oh-five. She's back to me at two-fifteen. I know she's going to talk to Burnsie and it seems to me the most important thing is to get our version to her before the evening edition comes out."

"So it's five o'clock now and the evening edition is out and whosever's version she's got it ain't yours. How do you suppose she got ahold of this other guy that fast? The big shot? Gerard Whitman?"

I spoke up. "He was one of the guys who was playing golf and cards with Wylie that day."

"I know who he is, for Chrissake. But how did she?"

"She's probably one of those gung-ho types," Royster

muttered after a long silence. "Thinks she's breaking Watergate or something."

John Michael came back to the table. "We want her to think that way, Roy. We want her digging. But we want her digging up what we know is out there." He was trying to be reasonable now, trying to control his temper. "We don't want her getting blanket statements from us and then having to go elsewhere to get her details. You don't have time to write a press release? Then find out what her favorite booze is, and send her a case of it."

Royster's lips pursed and unpursed.

"Maybe," said Jessica, advancing on us tentatively, "we should call Miles and try to get this girl taken off the story. Ask him to put Freddie on it."

John Michael massaged his jaw a while before saying no. "I don't know. This Lia Chapin may be just what the doctor ordered if we can feed her the right stuff. Let's just play it cool with her for now. Except, Roy, if she contacts you again, you put her right through to me and let me talk to her."

Royster said nothing.

"Got it?"

Royster said yes.

The Keoughs were not the only ones upset about the newspaper article. There was a message waiting for me when I came out of the meeting. Gretchen Patterson had called and wanted a call back.

"Hi," was all I said when I reached her, but she knew right away who it was.

She was trying to modulate her voice. "How could you have done this?" she asked.

I told her I didn't do anything.

"But I explained to you that Wylie couldn't possibly have killed Becky, Patt, and here the newspaper says you've gone and indicted him."

I didn't correct her. I didn't say I didn't indict him. I said, "All you told me was that Wylie didn't do it. You didn't tell me why."

"The why is simple. You just have to know the man."

Once again I had an opportunity to tell Gretchen how little my opinion counted in the office's prosecutorial decisions. Once again I tried to impress her with my silence on the subject.

She caught her breath. "What if I were to tell you that I know where he was during those missing hours you're so concerned about?" The words were said slowly, as if each had been individually selected.

"Are you going to tell me he was with you?"

"Yes."

"You told me before he wasn't."

"I lied. I was afraid." She hesitated. "I told you why I didn't want any of this to come out. I thought, you know, it wouldn't be necessary."

"And now you're willing to testify?"

"Now I'm willing to tell you the truth about that night."

"That may not be good enough."

"I think we should meet."

"When?"

"Now."

"Where?"

"You know where the Marriott is?"

When I was a child growing up in West Nestor, the Marriott River Inn did not exist. The land on which the Marriott River Inn now stands was occupied by Algonquin Park, a very clean and rather leisurely-paced amusement area that offered an array of nonvertical rides, the usual games of chance and competition, boating facilities for the River Charles, an outdoor movie screen that showed mostly free travelogues, a fenced-in bear den, and a number of grassy picnic areas. There was also a ballroom, where teenagers and young couples would go on Friday and Saturday nights to see crooners such as Mario Lanza.

About the time I entered junior high, Algonquin Park was closed and the rides, the games, the movie screen, the bears, and the ballroom all disappeared in favor of a paved parking lot and a huge multi-unit structure that eventually became the Marriott River Inn. The boating stayed, as did one or two of the picnic areas. Neither kept much of the ambience of Algonquin Park.

By the time I was thirty-eight, however, by the time I approached the River Inn on a cold November night, it looked immensely inviting. Its red neon shimmered its reflection off the water. Its lobby looked busy and affluent. People hurried to and from its doors wearing nice topcoats and wool scarfs. A doorman looked happy to be of service. "Ah," he said, when I told him where I wanted to go, "the apartments!"

He directed me to a separate building, where I rode a wood-paneled and carpeted elevator to the third floor and trudged down a quiet and pleasantly decorated hallway. I found the number 397 and stood for a moment before knocking.

I stood long enough to finish the Velamint I was chewing, to run my hand through my hair, to think weird thoughts: like whether I should have brought a bottle of champagne; like how I was going to react if she was dressed in something revealing, or if she was dressed in nothing at all.

I knocked, the door opened, and Gretchen Patterson was wearing a long cable-knit sweater and a black turtleneck jersey over a pair of plain black slacks. She might have been dressed to go to the supermarket or her son's mighty-tots soccer game. But her dark hair tumbled over one shoulder, her dark face looked at me anxiously, and I found her immensely alluring.

"Patt," she said huskily, and if she had opened her arms I would have moved right into them and swept her off her feet and carried her back to whatever unseen bed lay behind the door she was holding closed against her leg.

"Hi, Gretchen," I said softly.

"I'm glad you came," she said in that same deep, almost breathless voice.

She pushed open the door to reveal a mini-apartment with a galley kitchen, a small dining area, a living room, a door that led to a bedroom, and a little boy sitting at a desk painstakingly drawing on a piece of paper. "Welcome," she said.

I stepped inside. Ian barely glanced up. The feeling coursing through me was beyond disappointment. It was one of foolishness. "Is this yours?" I asked.

She put her finger to her lips and rolled her eyes back toward her son.

It was a comfortable enough apartment, equipped with everything an American living space requires, as well as a few extras, like a bar and a VCR attached to the TV and a set of wall bookshelves stocked with paperbacks. The furnishings were serviceable and solid and looked fairly expensive, but they were totally undistinguished and there was no artwork or knicknacks or anything other than the paperbacks that reflected a personal touch. I walked into the galley kitchen because Gretchen was directing me that way. It had a coffeemaker and an electric can opener and a Waring blender on otherwise immaculately empty counters. Gretchen walked to the steel sink, turned, and took up a leaning position against it. She put one fingernail between her teeth and looked at me. The light here was brightest, perhaps the brightest in the whole apartment, and it would have been harsh to most women in their mid-thirties, but it only offered Gretchen's skin as a study in perfection.

"What is this?" I said, taking up a lean of my own, my hands in my pockets, the base of my spine against the countertop.

"It's Wylie's place. Woodedge Savings and Loan's place. It's where they keep visitors, special guests, and so forth." She was whispering. "There aren't many of those."

"So this is where you and Wylie meet?"

Her great dark eyes flicked in the direction of her son, sitting behind a wall and out of sight. "Every week . . .for a while." She dropped her voice even lower. "Until Becky died."

"You were able to get away every week without—"

"I'm able to get away when my father-in-law watches Ian. He'll only do that if he knows exactly where I'm going. It was okay to go to Becky's—good family, you know—or maybe to the Woodedge Woman's Club because his wife was a member there."

"What, exactly, is the Woodedge Woman's Club?" I asked, unwilling to let that valuable bit of information pass by no matter how confused I was on every other issue.

But Gretchen waved away my inquiry. "Oh, it's absolutely nothing. Clare Ransom's wife Emily founded it to indulge her philanthropic instincts and guarantee herself a place in heaven."

"But what do you do there?"

"Nothing. They have lectures once a week and an annual antique sale and they plant the flowers in front of town hall and I may be the only active member under fifty."

"Becky wasn't?"

"They don't serve booze."

"Molly, Hannah . . . ?"

"Wouldn't be caught dead there."

"Then why would you?"

"To get me out of the house on Tuesday nights. I'd go to the lecture or whatever they were having, or say I was, and then slip away for two-three-four hours to meet Wylie."

"So that's what happened that night Rebecca was killed. You said you were going to the Woman's Club and Wylie threw his card game and here's where you ended up."

Gretchen raised her fingernail to her lips again. She looked at me for a moment before answering. "Basically."

I shifted my position, nodding, crossing and uncrossing my legs, glancing around the brightly lit kitchen. "What is it, about ten minutes from Stonegate to here? Fifteen maybe? Doesn't leave much time for foreplay."

It was a shot, a dig, and Gretchen took it. She checked to see what she had done to her nail. "Things weren't always ideal," she said. "I don't imagine they ever are."

"Do you love him? Wylie, I mean."

Her eyes stayed on her nail. "I don't know," she said. Suddenly she pushed away from the counter. "I have to go to the bathroom. Will you excuse me for a minute?"

She left without waiting for an answer and I stayed behind, staring at the blank walls and almost blank counters. A little noise, something like a sigh, reminded me of

Ian's presence and I wandered into the living room to see what he was doing.

He was working hard with his crayons and paper. He had his little face set seriously and he ignored me even when I was leaning over his shoulder. The scene he was coloring showed trees, lots of them, an oversized red bird, and a big patch of blue that I took for a body of water. It was not bad for a child his age.

I know how to talk to kids. I said, "Whacha got there, Ian?"

"It's the pond my mummy takes me to."

"That's neat, Ian. Is that red bird a cardinal?"

"No. A woodpecker."

"A woodpecker! Do you have woodpeckers in your yard?"

"We see lots of them when Mummy takes me for walks."

"Really?"

The boy tilted his head and stuck his tongue out the corner of his lips to work on a particularly tough coloring spot. "We got lots of places to walk where we live." He lifted his crayon and admired what he had accomplished.

"I guess you're very lucky, then."

"No," he said. "There aren't any other kids around."

His mother came out of the bathroom. She saw us talking and motioned me to return with her to the kitchen.

"I'll see you, Ian," I said, but as I walked away Ian called after me.

"Here's the woodpecker's house."

"Good, Ian," I said without looking.

"My mummy knows where it is."

"Good, Ian."

"It's not far, you know."

I had to call back from the kitchen. "That's good."

"It's on the path behind our house."

This time I did not answer out loud. Gretchen had entered the kitchen from the other side and we exchanged silent smiles about her chatterbox son.

"You take him out in the woods often?"

"What else am I supposed to do with him all day long? I take him with me wherever I go. Like here. I can just see him telling his father now. I'm really going to have to come up with a good one to explain this."

"Why did we come here, Gretchen? Why bring him? Why bring me?"

"I had to bring Ian because it's not Tuesday and I had no excuse to get out of the house without him. You . . . because I don't know what else to do. I tried before, you know, convincing you that Wylie didn't kill her, and it didn't work. I thought maybe if I gave you the evidence, let you see for yourself, you could drop this whole lousy prosecution."

"I'm afraid it's not that easy, Gretchen."

She threw up her hands in a sudden, exasperated gesture. "Why isn't it? It doesn't take any genius to see what's going on here." She froze. The flash went out of her eyes and she slowly lowered her hands. "I'm sorry," she said. "It's just, I thought, coming here and everything I told you before, well, I thought it would be obvious that Wylie's covering up for me."

"With his life, Gretchen? He's covering up your social embarrassment with his life?"

"You don't know Wylie," she said, shaking her head.

"I don't know anybody this side of the Middle Ages who would do that unless he's an idiot."

"Why? Don't you believe in commitments? Doesn't anybody ever depend on you to do what you say you're going to do?"

Now it was my turn to wave my hand. I did it in a rolling motion.

"Because that's what Wylie's doing for me, keeping his commitment. He promised when we first got involved that no matter what he would never let anybody know about our affair. Sure, nobody expected this was going to happen, I grant you that, but if there's any way, Patt, any way that he can be cleared without having to expose me in front of the whole world, he's going to do it. I'm begging you, Patt, begging you for your help." She moved in closer as she spoke and I could smell the sweetness of her breath as she looked up into my face.

"You're asking me to go to the D.A. and get him to drop the charges against Wylie because I have found his alibi—even though Wylie won't admit to it and even though the person he was with won't testify to help him."

Gretchen clasped her hands together. She closed them on my chest. "You can do it, can't you? I mean, you're the one running the investigation—not him. You're the one who's supposed to figure out what happened, who the suspects are, who should be charged. If you don't give him the evidence he's not going to be able to do it on his own. And if you tell him you've learned Wylie couldn't have done it he's got to listen."

I put my hands over hers. She was clutching my shirt and I was trying gently to make her stop.

"They have secret witnesses, don't they? Can't you say you've learned where Wylie was from a secret witness?"

"I'll try, Gretchen. But I don't think he's going to buy it. And if I tell him I've got a witness he's going to want to subpoena you and then one way or another you're going to be blown out in the open."

My words did what my fingers hadn't. She let go of my shirt. "Then you'll have to talk him out of it," she said, backing away only inches. "Now that you know the truth, now that you know what really happened and what will happen to me if the truth gets out, you'll have to convince the D.A. on your own that Wylie didn't do it. You have ways. You can make him believe you."

Her eyes held mine, held me, until I had no doubt what was going to happen next. I leaned just a tiny bit closer and her mouth was under mine, against mine, opening into mine. We didn't put our arms around each other, we just hung there, our lips touching, lingering, and falling away. Both of us looked to see if Ian was still on the other side of the wall and then both of us looked back at each other.

This time when we kissed my arms did go around her, my hands went under her sweater, under her jersey, and slid, glided, across her skin until one of them was in front of her and cupping her small, firm, bare breast. My knees went weak and I pulled her even closer to me. I ran my fingers down to the hard curve of her crotch. "No," she said, but then her tongue was driving into my mouth. She was holding my face between the palms of her hands and I was opening her slacks and peeling them away from her hips. "No," she said again and tore herself away.

She took a step backward, and then another. Her thick dark hair was tossed wildly. Her sweater had fallen so that it was bunched on one hip and her hard, flat belly was exposed all the way down her open zipper until it disappeared beneath the emerald strip of her panties.

I moved toward her and she put up her hand, holding it at bent-arm's length. Her hair was covering half her face and one black eye burned me with a warning to stay back.

"Ian," she called out.

"I'm in here, Mommy."

She looked in his general direction. "Everything okay?"

"Yes."

"Draw me . . . draw me the picture of the fish in the pond. Draw me a lot of pictures and then yell to me when they're ready." Her eye came back to me. She threw her hair away from her face. She turned and hit the overhead light. "C'mere," she said.

She had moved to the corner formed by the wall and the refrigerator. "Get behind me," she said, and I, with visions of what I had seen in Royster Hansen's office, did as I was told.

She pushed her slacks and her emerald underwear down her thighs. I wanted to do it myself. I wanted to see how tiny her panties were. I wanted to touch them and take them all the way to the floor. But I was opening my own pants, and it was enough that she was backing into me, pressing her ass against me and letting me feel its cool, rounded firmness against the burning heat of my cock.

"Do it, Patterson," hissed my dark princess as she rose up on the toes of one foot and balanced herself with a hand on top of the refrigerator and a hand pulling down the front of her sweater. "Do it," she said, flinging her head back against my shoulder, keeping her eyes on the doorway through which Ian could appear at any moment with his latest effort of color and imagination. "I am," I said as she arched her spine. And then suddenly she had let go of her sweater and reached her arm up behind my neck and pulled my head forward until my face was next to hers and her tongue was once again stabbing at my mouth. "Do it," she cried as our bodies twisted in ways they may never have been meant to go. But her lips were against mine and her breath was pouring into my throat and I was promising her that I would. I was promising her anything that she wanted.

23

John Michael was in his shirtsleeves and his tie was loosened. It was unusual to see him that way in the office. He usually kept on his suit jacket and had his tie knotted and pinching at his neck at all times. But then again, John Michael was not usually in the habit of preparing cases for trial.

He had the transcripts of the grand jury proceedings spread out in front of him. He had the various investigation reports scattered across the floor around his chair. He had a scowl on his face. He was not buying my attempts at subtlety.

"It's a little late in the day to be wondering if maybe we shouldn't be looking for someplace Wylie might have gone instead of killing his wife."

"I'm just saying, John, when you were having the asset check done on him, you didn't try to find out what residential properties his S and L had. You know, maybe they had an apartment or a condo or something where they put up friends and visitors. Maybe that's why Wylie can't or won't account for his time that night. Maybe he was there with somebody's wife or daughter."

"I'm not buying it, Patt."

"Then you better watch out Burnsie doesn't come up with it for a defense, John. Let you set up your whole circumstantial evidence bit and then come in on defense and blow you out of the water with some bimbo who says, 'Oh, yes. Wylie-kins couldn't have been killing his wife because I was humping him for the whole two hours he was out of sight.' "

The blood drained from John Michael's face. "When did you come up with this, Patt?"

"I've been thinking about it."

"When you were supposed to be thinking about where in hell Dougie Rasmussin has gone and how the hell we're going to get him back? Is that what you mean?" John Michael kicked himself away from his desk. His chair rolled over two or three files and a couple of yellow sheets of notes. "This whole fucking case is going down the tubes, Patt, and I'm beginning to wonder whose fault it is." His voice had risen shrilly.

I considered beating a retreat for the door behind my back. I shifted my feet.

John Michael moved faster. He smacked the intercom on his telephone and screamed at his secretary. "Get that asshole Lester in here as fast as you can. Tell him to bring a toothbrush, if he's got one, because he's going on his bloody California trip." He punched off the intercom and thrust a finger at me. "And as for you, pal, you just make sure Burnsie doesn't come up with any bimbo— married, professional, or any other kind. Got it?"

There was not much sense in arguing. "No sweat," I said.

I met Gretchen in the post office parking lot. It was cold enough that windshields were frosted, cold enough to see our breath in front of our faces, cold enough to keep our hands in our pockets while we spoke.

I told her there was no change. The prosecution was going ahead as planned. I told her that it was up to her now, that if she knew Wylie was innocent and he wasn't going to clear himself then she was going to have to come forward and do it for him. I said there wasn't anything more I could do.

"Why?" she asked. The end of her nose was red and her eyes were watery from the wind, and she still was beautiful. "It costs you so little and it would cost me so much."

"Look, it's not enough for one person to say that something happened because somebody else told him it happened. The only one whose testimony counts for anything is the one with the actual knowledge. That's you. If you're going to save Wylie you do it now or you do it at trial—and I've got to know if you're going to do it at trial."

"I can always do it then." She shook her head. "But the moment I do it all else is lost."

"Gretchen, you can't wait till trial. You're playing with Wylie's life by doing that. You'll just be increasing the notoriety of the whole affair. You've got to decide now if you're going to be testifying."

She took a deep breath and looked far off into the distance, to where a row of leafless trees formed a splintered outline against the bleak gray sky. "I won't be testifying, Patt. Like you, I've gone as far as I can." She cut her eyes to me to see if I understood, and then she looked away again. "I lied to you," she said.

The wind picked up. It blew open my coat and made my teeth start to chatter. I plunged my hands into my coat pockets and pulled it tight around me.

"Do you think," she said, "it's okay to lie sometimes? If you know something is right and the only way you can make sure it comes out right is to lie, do you think it's all right then?"

"Are you going to tell me that you really weren't with Wylie after all?"

"I was supposed to be. We were supposed to meet like we usually did on Tuesday nights, but if you'll check you'll see there was no lecture at the Woodedge Woman's Club that night. The speaker canceled and my father-in-law is the one who took the phone message. The only way I could get out alone was to tell Frost that I had to go shopping for a costume and that I couldn't do it with Ian tagging along. That meant I had to buy something. My idea, you know, my idea was that I could get over to Shopper's World in Framingham, get something quick, and then get back to the apartment in time to meet Wylie. But it took longer than I thought. I couldn't find anything and all of a sudden it was nine o'clock and the stores were closing."

"Did you call him and tell him you weren't coming?"

"No, because I kept thinking I'd only be another ten

minutes. You know how that goes. By the time I got there it was nine thirty and he was gone."

"How do you know he'd been there?"

She looked down and pawed a crack in the pavement with the edge of her boot. "I just knew. He'd always been there before when he said he would and there was just, you know, his presence. I could feel that someone had been there a short time before I was."

"Have you asked him?"

"Yes. He told me he waited until after nine and then just assumed I hadn't been able to get away."

"Did he ask you to lie for him?"

Gretchen's attention snapped away from the crack in the pavement. "No! In fact, he forbade even to mention the apartment because he knew we couldn't prove anything about that night and he thought our affair would only make things look worse for him."

"But you decided to tell me anyhow."

"You're the only one." Gretchen's hair blew into her mouth and she had to hold it back with one hand. Her fingers were different colors from the cold, white and pink and red. "I knew that you were the person putting everything together and I thought that if I could just explain it to you . . . show you what really happened . . ."

"Gretchen, you don't know what really happened."

"I do," she protested, releasing her hair and grabbing my arm. She searched my face. "I know he didn't kill her. He couldn't have killed her. I mean, if somebody is absolutely convinced of that it seems to me that she shouldn't just stand by and watch a man get railroaded. It seems to me she ought to pursue every possible option to convince others."

Gretchen's fingers crept downward on my sleeve until they made contact with my bare wrist. They slid then and touched the palm of my hand. They were warmer than I thought they would be. They made my fingertips close over hers. I found myself snorting and saying, "And so you used me."

A little smile came over her face. It was not a friendly smile, just an acknowledging one. "In a strange way,

Patt, you were the only one I could trust enough to lie to."

"Well," I said, "I think that option's over. In fact, I think you've about run out of options."

Her smile became braver. It became more fixed. She said she understood that now.

24

On a Thursday morning in mid-November Woodedge Police Inspector Stanley Lester took off for L.A. in search of the elusive Douglas Rasmussin. On the following day he telephoned the District Attorney's office to inform us that he had located the Apart-Lets. That was the good news.

He had, of course, not found any trace of Dougie, but that was only part of the bad news. He had gotten into a fight with Zorro the desk clerk and Zorro had called the police. The L.A.P.D. arrived and were not impressed with the fact that Lester purported to be a brother officer from Woodedge, Massachusetts. The patrolmen who responded to Zorro's call were unfamiliar with the concept of reciprocity as it pertained to Woodedge and they refused to allow Lester to speak with any of their superiors. Lester wanted John Michael's help.

He also wanted us to know that he was embarking on a search of L.A.'s rock-and-roll clubs for my friend Laraine. He was worried about the costs of some of these clubs and wanted to make sure he was going to be reimbursed.

On the evening of the day Lester called, my mother's neighbor Mrs. Graham was rushed to the hospital with a heart attack. While she was going down Harry Kelsey was scrambling for his life across my mother's porch, and before the paramedics had her out of her house Charlie Curren had chased the cause of their problems all the way to Balducci's Tavern.

Just before her heart attack Mrs. Graham had been sitting at the table in her kitchen, gazing out the window at the street. It was the warmest room in her house and on cold nights she would often sit there until the "good shows" came on television. She would sit there and drink tea and try to remember who was who and when they had come.

At some point she noticed the large, dark American-model car parked against the curb across the street, but her eyes weren't good enough to be able to tell if anyone was sitting in it. "I wouldn't have expected it," she told us later. "It was so cold."

Kelsey had arrived at my mother's house around six, well after dark. He had waved to Mrs. Graham and she had waved back. She saw him start out of the house at just after seven, on his way to the fish market to get the lobsters he and my mother had on reserve. He opened the front door and pushed open the storm door and then my mother called after him to pick up some extra butter. His head was turned and he was backing onto the porch when the first gunshot exploded and a bullet whacked into the wooden doorframe next to his fingers.

He knew right away, instinctively perhaps, what it was. He dove to the floorboards as a second shot shattered one of my mother's front windows. The bullet would later be found in the back of her sofa. Her divan.

Kelsey, looking for some cover, was crawling on his elbows and knees. He was trying to get behind some rose bushes and vines that could do nothing to stop a bullet but that made him that much harder to see. The porch light was on and Kelsey was a big target, but the shooter kept missing.

Four shots went off before Charlie Curren was out on his front steps firing back. The dark American car turned out to be an old Chevrolet Chevelle, and Charlie, who knew what he was doing, hit it easily. The first bullet that cracked a window caused the driver to leave a thirty-foot strip of rubber in his wake. By the time the Chevelle had found taction, Charlie, in his T-shirt, sweat pants, and wool socks, his .38 police special clutched in his hand, was already running for his Trans-Am. Nobody took shots at anyone in Charlie Curren's neighborhood and got away with it.

For the entire five miles from my mother's house in

West Nestor to Balducci's in Walmouth, Charlie chased the Chevelle. He had given it a considerable head start, but Charlie proved to be adept at tailing, a skill that somehow surprised none of us. Charlie managed to guess the right direction, and then he went through stoplights, through stop signs, around cars in intersections and on two-lane roads; and when the Chevelle finally was able to lose him on the back streets near Walmouth Center, Charlie was able to find it again, hidden in a lot behind Balducci's. He did all this with his .38 pressed against the steering wheel. That may not have been too bright, but Charlie was at least smart enough not to go into Balducci's with his gun. Later he told us he would have gone in if he'd had something on his feet besides just his socks, but as it was he contented himself with taking down the license number and calling it in to his mother, who ran it across the street to the investigating Nestor police officers. Charlie was not the sort who would call the police himself.

The license plates turned out to be stolen and the Chevelle unregistered and no one emerged to reclaim it before the police arrived to relieve Charlie from his vigil; whereupon they promptly arrested poor Charlie for possession of an illegal firearm. Once again Charlie called his mother, and his mother called my mother and my mother called me—and that was how I first learned there had been a shooting. Until then she hadn't wanted to worry me.

By the time I arrived on the scene the police had developed a theory. A sergeant on the Nestor force named Mulcahey had been in touch with his Walmouth counterparts to pass along the original information relayed through Charlie's mother about the sniper's vehicle being found behind Balducci's. Mulcahey had then sat down with a somewhat shaken Harry Kelsey and tried to extract from him any connection he might have with Balducci's. What Mulcahey got from Kelsey was softball. What Mulcahey determined was that someone at Balducci's had tried to kill Kelsey because he was a rival softball player.

"You ever slide real hard into one of those guys?" Mulcahey was asking when I showed up.

I handed Mulcahey my identification. He knew my name and picked up the relationship between my mother and me in a remarkably short period of time.

"Do you think," Mulcahey said, his eyes narrowing, his bald dome flushing with thought, "those shots could have been meant for you?"

"Why?" snapped my mother, her face set as if this were an insult, a crazy thing to say. "Why would they be?"

I told her it wasn't such a wild idea, that maybe the shots had come from somebody I had helped to put in jail.

"I was thinking more about the Woodedge murder case I hear you been working on," said Mulcahey, while my mother gaped at me in astonishment.

Just then a call came in to Mulcahey announcing that the Walmouth police had blocked off Balducci's and nobody was getting out unless he could identify himself.

"Let's go," I said, sliding my hand under Mulcahey's elbow.

"What Woodedge murder case?" said my mother.

"C'mon, Mr. Kelsey," ordered Mulcahey.

I put up my palm to keep Kelsey in his chair. "I know the place and I'm damn sure Harry didn't get a look at whoever was doing the shooting. We don't need him."

Kelsey protested because he was not going.

My mother protested because I was.

I was very stern with both of them in front of Sergeant Mulcahey.

Three people had come out of Balducci's since the police had arrived, according to Walmouth police Sergeant Garimundi. None of them was considered a possible suspect, including the man who was standing in front of the bar waving his arms around in the air and shouting about his civil rights. That was Buzzy Balducci himself.

Garimundi calmly sipped coffee out of a paper cup that bore the logo of Mister Donut. "Claims nobody went running in, nobody went running out. Claims he didn't notice who was in the joint at any time. Claims he don't know the names of any of his customers."

"Well, I know a couple. Let's go in and see what we've got."

Garimundi shook his head. "What d'ya think, I got shit for brains? I went inside as soon as I took care a your friend Curren. Nobody there but this guy. 'Evenin', officer,' he says, like I come in for a couple a wet ones before I finish my rounds." Garimundi snorted. It left his upper lip gleaming in the night light. "A sink fulla dirty glasses, half a rack a balls on the pool table, seats of the barstools still warm, and the only people we seen coming outa there are two broads and this joker."

"There must be another way out."

Garimundi slapped himself in the eye. He let his hand stay there and turned to look at Mulcahey. "This guy," he said, tipping his head at me, "has gotta be a detective."

I walked away from Garimundi and Mulcahey and went over to confront Balducci. The tavern owner was without a jacket, but his arms were moving so rapidly and so frequently that he gave no sign of being cold.

"You," he said, when I got close enough for him to recognize. "I knew you was a cop. Oh yeah, all your talk about fixin' tickets. I knew it. I just knew it."

"I'm not a cop," I said, stopping when I was just outside of arm's length. "I'm a friend of Kelsey's and someone you know just took four shots at him."

"Ooh, slander," said Balducci. He put both hands to his mouth and screamed up and down the street, "Slander. He's slandering my good name."

I waited until he was done. "Tell me how Dougie Rasmussin fits into this, Buzzy."

"Hey," said Balducci, "I'll tell you." He motioned me closer until he was able to speak directly into my ear. "Eat shit, pig," he whispered.

I straightened up slowly as if he had just given me valuable information. I looked him in the eye. His was a triumphant, spiteful look; one that told me he would not mind clouting me, doing serious damage to me for the sheer joy of it. "You don't care that some asshole just tried to kill Kelsey, the best damn softball player in the whole city?"

"Maybe Kelsey should watch who he hangs around

with." Balducci checked to see who was near, and then
leaned in closer again. "Maybe it wasn't Kelsey he was
shooting at."

Now Balducci took his time straightening up. "Yeah,"
he said, nodding, his near eye bright and unblinking.

"Let's suppose," I said, "that there was some guy who
hangs around your bar. Let's suppose he isn't all that
smart and he did take a couple of shots at Kelsey thinking it was me . . . why do you think he might do that?"

Balducci's warrior's grin slowly transformed itself into
one of smug self-satisfaction. "Maybe," he said, "he was
pissed off because you lied to him about the parking
tickets."

Jessica Keough was wearing a one-piece red jumpsuit
that seemed to have been tailored to her figure. It swelled
where she swelled. It was taut where she was taut. I
thought it a rather unusual outfit to be wearing in her
home at eleven o'clock at night, but I had called to say I
was coming and it was possible she had gotten dressed for
company.

The two of us were leaning over John Michael's shoulder as he sat at the desk in the study of his house. His
desk faced the window and so we had to lean over his
shoulder in order to follow the police reports he was
reading. Jessica had one hand on the back of his blue
leather chair. She had one hand resting lightly on my
back as I bent forward with my elbow on the desk. Her
right leg was against my left one. The inside of her right
leg was against the inside of my left one. I was trying not
to make any big thing out of it.

John Michael held up one of the reports. "They ask
this woman who came out of the bar, Janice Neeley, why
she's covering an attempt to murder somebody in cold
blood. 'Hey, those people,' she says, 'what are you going
to do?' They ask her doesn't she care that there's a
potential killer running around loose. She goes, 'I'm from
Walmouth. We keep to ourselves.' " John Michael threw
down the report disgustedly. He turned around. Jessica
slipped her leg away from mine.

"This is the kind of thing we're up against," he said.

"Parochialism. This points up how important it is that the people of Walmouth see me as one of their own. We get the right jury for Carpenter and we can make it a matter of us against them. I see this kind of attitude," he thumped the report, "and I'm thinking, 'You're in trouble, Carpenter. Not only do you come from Woodedge, but you weren't even born around here.' "

"John," I said, pushing all the reports back in front of him. "This was my mother's boyfriend got shot at. On my mother's porch. There's every reason in the world to think he was a mistaken target, that it was me who was supposed to get shot."

John Michael leaned back in his chair. He looked at me with sympathy. "I know."

Jessica stepped around to the other side of her husband's chair so that we could talk across the top of John Michael's head. "How do you figure it, Patt?"

I took my time trying to marshal the words for the jumbled ideas in my mind. "Balducci's is Dougie Rasmussin's place. If he needs somebody back here to do something, that's where he's going to call. The one guy Rasmussin's had direct contact with, face to face I mean, is me. He talks with me, he bullshits me, he splits. It's possible he hears we're back live and in person looking for him on the West Coast and he's afraid we're closing in so he decides to eliminate the guy he thinks is orchestrating everything."

John Michael raised one pale eyebrow in a show of tempered significance.

"Yeah," I said, "I don't buy that either. That brings me to the next possibility, which is that someone wants us to think that Rasmussin is trying to kill me."

"Or maybe even has killed you," John Michael said, his face stretched with concern.

"Yeah."

"And the most likely person that would be," he went on, "is Wylie Carpenter. He knows Rasmussin is our only other suspect. Hell, he set him up that way in the first place, committing the murder on the day Rasmussin left for the Coast. So now he's desperate, see? Desperate times call for desperate measures. If he can get us to make the connection between Rasmussin and you getting shot then maybe he can get himself off the hook."

John Michael began pressing his fingertips together. "So let's think it through. There's no real reason why Rasmussin would panic when Carpenter's already scheduled to stand trial. But let's say Carpenter realizes he's up shit creek without a paddle and is looking for any way he can to create doubt. Hmmn? You with me? Now what would make him think . . . that we'll think . . . that Rasmussin's responsible?"

"The bar?" said Jessica, raising her shoulders and making a silky sound with her jumpsuit as her arms moved against her sides.

"The bar. Consider the cleverness. We don't actually know if anybody from the bar did it. All we know is that the car that was used was found parked near the bar. Whose bar? Rasmussin's bar. What do we assume? One of Rasmussin's buddies must have done it."

Jessica interrupted. "But if nobody from the bar actually did it, why did they all run away?"

John Michael grabbed the police reports, held them up for us to see, and then let them fall back to his desk. "Cops arrive and first thing they do is make a commotion arresting Curren. He starts yelling about the sniper inside. You think it's just a coincidence the two women came out? Bullshit. That's what they do in bars like this. Send the women out to discover what's going on."

I marveled silently at the breadth of John Michael's knowledge of the ways and mores of drinking establishments.

John Michael surveyed us with a professorial eye. "All right, now, any other reason why Carpenter might think we'd blame Rasmussin for this little episode tonight?"

Jessica thought hard. "The timing?" she said.

"Exactly." John Michael's finger soared upward. "And how would Carpenter have known that now, I mean tonight, was the perfect time to get us focusing our attention on Rasmussin? Because there's a bloody little South African in a loud sport coat running around Los Angeles at this very minute making inquiries about Rasmussin. And how does Carpenter know that? Because somebody tipped him off, by God. We have a leak in our organization."

"Wembley Tuttle," I said softly.

"I wonder," said the district attorney of Exeter County. "I wonder if he's the only one being unfaithful."

Almost immediately the inside of my left leg began to burn. For some reason, I dared not look at Jessica and I trusted she was not looking at me.

Down below us John Michael was still speaking. "You know, if it's only Wembley, I can deal with that. Because I know where he's coming from and I don't really depend on him to be any more than what he is. What I couldn't take would be betrayal from somebody I trusted. I mean I really couldn't take that. In fact, I think there's probably no more base crime than to betray somebody who you've encouraged to count on you or trust in you or depend on you. Because that's really a conscious decision, to betray someone, and if you'll do that you'll do anything. You know what I mean?"

He didn't wait for an answer. He sighed instead, and said, "I guess I'm just going to have to be more careful."

25

My mother's house was placed under twenty-four-hour police surveillance. John Michael offered to arrange the same service for my apartment, but I declined and satisfied whatever fears I had by watching for tails and varying my routes home.

There were no further attacks and no success at learning the identity of Kelsey's assailant. The lack of both served to reinforce John Michael's belief that the shooting at my mother's house had been nothing more than an attempt on Carpenter's part to deflect our attention toward Rasmussin.

"In fact," he said to me one day, "I'm convinced Carpenter wasn't trying to kill you. I'm convinced his plan was to shoot at you and miss just so he could set up the Balducci-Rasmussin connection."

John Michael was smarting from the fact that he had called Lester home early from California. He wanted me to understand that this had been a magnanimous gesture on his part—one made in an abundance of caution and out of the most deep and abiding concern for my mother's safety. He wanted me to know that he regretted it.

Lester, once he returned, made no bones about the fact that he blamed me entirely for his truncated trip through rock-and-roll paradise. He complained to Wembley that I was responsible for his failure to find Dougie Rasmussin, and Wembley took up the matter with Royster, who began to ask me how my mother was doing on a near daily basis.

John Michael, meanwhile, began to prepare for trial in earnest. Unlike his subordinate attorneys, he had the

244

luxury of concentrating on just one case—and the fact that he was concentrating on this one made it far and away the most important thing in the office. He had Libby running in and out and Lester running in and out and me running in and out, and he had us all running at different times.

Monday-evening squash games were canceled, Friday-evening meetings were canceled, no impromptu gatherings were held; and I found myself cranked into an unusual state of anxiety as I watched mysterious assignments being handed out to Lester, who was of no mind to share them with me, and Libby, who acted as though everything he was given to do was the absolute key to salvation. When alone in John Michael's presence I began to search for some sign of approval, or even disapproval, that I could address. I tested him with jokes and concentrated on his eyes when we spoke; but his smiles did not linger, and his expressions remained distant or preoccupied. Occasionally I went so far as to ask him what was wrong, but his answers were uniformly meaningless: "Nothing," or "Everything."

Yet my insecurity as to John Michael's new circumspection was nothing compared to Royster's. He had taken to popping into his boss's office on almost any excuse of news, to laughing boisterously over any remark that vaguely approached the realm of humor, and to staring at me with great concern whenever we happened to cross each other's path.

As for Jessica, her appearances in the office suddenly became very infrequent. On the few occasions when she did appear during the last few weeks of the year I could not help but notice that her recent penchant for tight and shimmery clothes seemed to have been abandoned in favor of a return to more traditional tweeds and wools. The New Year passed without her usual invitation to "join the Keoughs in a glass of holiday cheer," and then I did not see her again until she showed up in court for her husband's opening address to the jury—wearing a conservative dark blue knit suit, gazing with rapt devotion throughout John Michael's spiel, and generally act-

ing as though she had every confidence in the world in
what her husband was about to do.

Philip Burns had hair like pumpkin guts. It was a weak
and unpleasant orange color and it tended to be stringy
and stay plastered close to his round skull. Burnsie's
brown eyes floated about in their sockets as if they were
not as well tethered as other people's. His skin had a
glistening quality to it that made him look as if he was
constantly perspiring. These were not the physical char-
acteristics one would expect in a successful trial lawyer.

But Philip Burns's mind, when not pickled, was fairly
astute. He also had a wonderful voice, a quick laugh, and
a sense of humor that never seemed mean or aggressive.
People mocked Burnsie, but he managed to get away
with a lot because he was genuinely likable, and those
who knew him best did not underestimate him after they
told their jokes and did their imitations.

The Keoughs were the exceptions. They believed all
the jokes and repeated the ones they did not make up
themselves. John Michael regarded Burnsie as an idiot
and Jessica reinforced that idea at every opportunity.

John Michael's disrespect for his predecessor was apparent from the outset of the Carpenter trial. It was
manifested in eye rollings and quick little tightenings at
the corners of his mouth, paper shufflings when Burnsie
was talking, and failures to respond when Burnsie was
asking him questions.

The two men were a study in contrasts. Burnsie's yellow and brown tie was knotted just below the top button
of his slightly rumpled shirt. His brown suit had a slight
tear on the seam leading out of the back vent, and his
brogans could have used a better shine. He was constantly looking for things, putting on and taking off his
reading glasses, licking his fingers whenever he turned
pages, being distracted by almost any other noise in the
room. John Michael, however, wore an immaculate gray
suit, an immaculate white shirt, a bright red silk power
tie with fancy little blue figurines, and black calfskin
loafers that would have passed a Marine drill sergeant's

inspection. He had everything in place and everything under control.

When John Michael needed something he simply extended his hand and a junior attorney named Mary Alice Devon handed it to him. When he wanted a question answered he had only to turn around and Lester and I were right there in the front row, ready to lean forward to the bar and supply him with whatever we could. If he was stuck on some legal nicety he could always send one of the office interns scurrying to the library or, if necessary, to Royster Hansen.

The jury to which these two men were playing was the product of ten days of scrutinous questioning that had eliminated everyone but housewives, retirees, and employees of the phone company, Boston Edison, the post office, and the city, state, and federal governments. Twelve jurors and four alternates, and not one of them was from Woodedge. They looked pleased to have been chosen. They looked happy to be off work or out of the house.

The judge presiding was a little man named Victor LoBianco, and his assignment to the trial had caused John Michael a certain amount of concern. Nobody was ever sure what Victor was up to. He tended to keep his head down and write notes throughout trials. He tended to grin at inappropriate times.

He was grinning when he called the trial to order on the first day after completion of jury selection. He was grinning for the jurors, and for the spectators who filled about three-quarters of the gallery, and for the television camera he had allowed into the courtroom. After his introductory remarks he turned stiffly in his chair and pointed grandly at John Michael. "Are you ready, Mr. Keough?"

John Michael rose carefully to his feet. He gave one last glance at his notepad and then strode out in front of the jury with nothing whatsoever in his hands. He introduced himself for the umpteenth time and explained to the jurors that he was the district attorney for Exeter County and that he was conducting this prosecution on behalf of the people of the county.

The jurors, primed by the long selection process, by

the words of the judge, and by the presence of the television camera, were ready to act like jurors. When John Michael thrust his finger at Wylie Carpenter, sitting at the defendant's table next to his lawyer, they turned to stare as if they had never seen him before. When John Michael produced a scale relief model, previously cleared with the defense and showing the relationship of Stonegate Country Club, the overlook off Ivanhoe Road, and the Carpenter estate on Bulham Road, the jurors nearly bolted from their seats to get a better look.

John Michael spoke for an hour. His words rolled, he never repeated himself, he segued from one bit of information to another, and when he was done it was all perfectly obvious that Wylie S. Carpenter, trapped in marriage to an unfaithful wife and trying to secure her fortune for his own, had diabolically plotted and carried out Rebecca's murder to coincide with the disappearance of the family's young caretaker, Douglas Rasmussin.

The change in the prosecution's theory was due entirely to the inability to produce Rasmussin at trial. "You'll see," John Michael had said when I asked how he was going to get around the fact that Wylie was at least a millionaire in his own right; and that, plus a wink and a sly grin, was all that I could get out of him.

The commonwealth's first witness in its case against Wylie Carpenter was Officer Roland Tagget. He identified thirty-six photographs of the scene of the crime and described in scrupulous detail what he had observed. He introduced blow-ups of a couple of the photographs, one of which clearly showed the formerly pretty face of Rebecca Carpenter contorted in the agony of death by strangulation. He made use of the scale model for demonstration purposes. And then he explained how he had accompanied Sergeant Roselli to the Carpenter home to meet with Mr. Carpenter.

It was this last point that Burnsie homed in on. He asked a few questions about whether Tagget had moved the body and whether he had disturbed any evidence at the scene, but mostly he cross-examined on the issue of what Tagget knew about Wylie Carpenter.

"You say you went to his house?"

"Yes sir. Number six Bulham Road."

"You wouldn't really call it a house, would you? More of a mansion?"

"It's pretty big, yes sir."

"And six Bulham Road, that's really an estate, isn't it?"

"I guess it is, yes sir."

"Did you know it was the Chesley family estate?"

"I heard of it, yes sir."

"Uh-huh. And Mr. Carpenter, had you heard of him before?"

"I didn't know him, but I guess I knew there was a Mr. Carpenter."

"Know anything about his background, where he came from, how he happened to marry Rebecca Chesley and move to that house, anything like that?"

"No sir."

"Uh-huh. You certainly didn't immediately suspect Mr. Carpenter when you found his wife's body, did you?"

"No sir."

"Did you even know that was his wife? Did you know right away that was Rebecca Carpenter?"

"No sir."

"How did you find that out, that this woman, this dead body was Rebecca Carpenter?"

"I radioed in the license tag on the vehicle."

"You didn't look at her driver's license, her wallet, anything in her purse?"

"No sir."

"Why not?"

"I didn't find a pocketbook."

"A wallet?"

"Didn't find anything."

"Money?"

"Nothing."

"Uh-huh. I see. When you got to the Carpenter . . . estate, did you check to see if her pocketbook was there?"

"That's correct."

"And was it?"

"Mr. Carpenter couldn't find it."

"Was it there, Officer Tagget?"

"I don't know. I couldn't find it either."

"To your knowledge, has it ever been found?"

"Not to my knowledge."

Burnsie looked as if he were bewildered. He raised his hands halfway from his sides and let them fall back against his flanks. His face was scrunched as if he were about to ask a question that was going to challenge the very heart and soul of everything that Officer Roland Tagget had ever said in his life. But then he backed off. He returned to his seat and almost sat down before he caught himself.

"One final thing, Officer. Now, you've testified that you're a trained policeman, police academy, nine years on the force and so forth . . . You've testified that you examined the body when you found it and that you interviewed Mr. Carpenter that night along with Sergeant Roselli . . . Tell me, based on all that, did you form an opinion that night that Mr. Carpenter had killed his wife?"

Tagget glanced toward John Michael for help, but John Michael did not want to disturb the cool persona in which he had cast himself. He made no motion to object and gave no sign that he cared in the slightest about Tagget's answer.

"No," said Tagget.

Burnsie pressed on. "There was nothing in his demeanor, nothing in his appearance that made you suspect that night that he might have killed his wife?"

"No sir."

"Well, when was it then that you decided he did kill his wife?"

"Objection."

"Sustained," said LoBianco. "Counsel approach the bench."

John Michael rose looking faintly disgusted. Burnsie immediately assumed a perplexed air, as though he was baffled by the consternation he had caused. LoBianco grinned heartily at the jurors, letting them know that this was all part of the great game of law in which we were all engaged.

*   *   *

To say that Wylie Carpenter wore a brown suit to court on the first day of testimony would be like saying Babe Ruth was a ballplayer. Wylie's suit was the deepest, richest brown I had ever seen. It was cut perfectly to his shape and it never seemed to bend, fold or mutilate no matter how he moved. His grayish hair was combed in a longish, yet perfectly neat fashion. His nails looked buffed to my untrained eye, and his skin was as tanned as if he had spent the Christmas holidays in the Caribbean. He remained quiet throughout the day, and his only visible reaction to anything that was said came when he picked up his pencil and occasionally jotted down a casual note.

I noticed the jurors stealing peeks at him from time to time. I noticed that the women jurors tended to let their gaze linger.

Sergeant Francis Roselli described what he had seen when he arrived at the overlook. He confirmed that virtually all prints had been wiped clean. He identified the scarf that had been found wrapped around Rebecca Carpenter's neck. He testified as to its chain of custody and it was admitted into evidence.

Then he explained how he had traced the scarf to its point of purchase from Burberry's just three days before the murder. He identified the charge slip that was used to make the purchase. He read the imprinted name on the charge slip. He read the signature. He read them both as Wylie S. Carpenter.

John Michael let this news sink in while he strode around the courtroom with his hands clasped loosely behind his back. Then he started Roselli in on a new line of questioning. Yes, Roselli affirmed, to his observation this was a death by strangulation. No, he did not think the strangulation had occurred there at the overlook or even in the car in which the body was found.

More blow-up photographs were produced and Roselli used a pointer to go over them with the jury. He explained about the lack of damage to the inside of the car and he walked the edges of expert testimony by describing the expected thrashings of a garotted woman.

Finally, John Michael asked Roselli about any testings he had personally done and the sergeant got out a series of notes and calculations and interpreted them for the jurors. It was exactly 3.6 miles by roadway from the Carpenter home to the overlook. It was exactly 2.5 miles from the overlook to the Stonegate Country Club. The distance from Stonegate to the Carpenter home, by the fastest roadway route, was 4.9 miles. Roselli had driven between all these points, at night, keeping within the speed limit, and it had taken him approximately twenty eight minutes to go from Stonegate to the Carpenters' home to the overlook and back to Stonegate.

John Michael had Roselli make a loose diagram on a large piece of artist's paper and mark off the distances and the times between the three points. Then he offered the diagram into evidence and looked slightly amazed when Burnsie waved it in without objection.

Burnsie was far more interested in finding out what Roselli knew about the missing pocketbook. He wanted to go over Roselli's notes of his interview with Mr. Carpenter. He wanted to know if he suspected Mr. Carpenter right away. He probed Roselli as to what he knew about the Carpenters before the night of the murder, and he seemed satisfied when Roselli said all he knew was that they were rich and lived on a nice piece of property.

"What," demanded John Michael that night as we gathered in his office for the first time in weeks, "is that drunken old bum up to?"

Royster, who had been trying to pour everybody a glass of bourbon, discreetly put down his bottle of Harper's.

Jessica said, "He doesn't know, John. That's what's so wonderful. You're running circles around him."

John Michael, who had taken off his suit jacket, who had his hand wrapped around a warm mug of coffee, and who was getting ready to spend most of the night preparing for the second day's testimony, glanced up eagerly and said, "Do you think so?"

Jessica and Royster answered simultaneously. "Yes," they sang. And John Michael looked very pleased.

26

Dr.Marshall Havens, Exeter County Medical Examiner, led off the second day of testimony. He confirmed that it was death by strangulation and gave his best medical estimate that it had occurred between nine and ten p.m. —closer to nine, he thought. He was given the scarf that had been admitted into evidence and he demonstrated how he thought it had been used. He demonstrated as though the murderer had been face to face with the victim.

Havens confirmed that blood alcohol had tested at .18 and noted that legally drunk in our state was considered to be a .10. He also admitted that toxicology testing had revealed a large amount of Valium in Mrs. Carpenter's system, but he was unable to quantify it. "However," he said, clearing his throat for emphasis, "ten milligrams of Valium, the conventional dose, is generally deemed to be the equivalent of two strong drinks."

"And while you can't quantify exactly how much Valium she had, you can state that it was more than the conventional dose, is that right, Doctor?" asked John Michael.

And Havens, who was a bit of a ham, harrumphed and smiled and said, "Oh, my, yes."

On cross examination, Burnsie, now wearing a herringbone suit so bold it was practically striped, produced a plastic model of a human head and torso. He handed Dr. Havens the scarf again and asked him to strangle the model. Havens knotted the scarf on the model's neck, grabbed it on both sides of the knot, and wrenched it in opposite directions.

"Take much strength, Doctor?"

"Some."

"Doesn't have to be a male athlete's strength to snap that hyoid bone, does it?"

Havens studied the model for too long before saying no.

Burnsie asked him to stand behind the model. He asked him if the model could be strangled from that position. He asked Havens to demonstrate and Havens did, just as I had done for Lester some weeks before. "Any scientific or medical evidence that you're aware of that disproves the killer was behind Mrs. Carpenter as opposed to in front?"

Havens, concerned that he was not doing his best job for the county and John Michael, mumbled his answer.

"What's that, Doctor?"

"No."

"Oh," said Burnsie, as though surprised. He pointed to the torso with his wooden pointing stick. "Your autopsy, it included the liver, did it?"

"It included the liver, yes, Mr. Burns."

"And, in lay terms, how would you describe that liver?"

"In lay terms? Well, in lay terms it was enlarged."

"In an advanced state of cirrhosis, would you say?"

"Advanced state? No. Cirrhotic . . . yes."

"More than you would expect in a woman of forty years?"

"Well, as to what I expect, I have seen some amazing things over the course of my career, Mr. Burns."

"This was a diseased liver, wasn't it, Doctor?"

"Diseased? I guess you would say that."

"Diseased due to a history of alcohol abuse?"

"Due, I would say, to consumption of more alcohol than was good for her liver."

"Over what period of time?"

"It wasn't overnight, Mr. Burns, if that's what you're getting at."

"Yes, Doctor, that's exactly what I'm getting at. No further questions, Your Honor."

Havens was followed to the stand by the bartender from Stonegate. In the afternoon came Teasdale, who among other things identified Wylie as wearing a white

V-necked sweater that day; and then Whitman, who turned out to be unexpectedly combative in the defense of his friend. In reality, however, Whitman's attitude did Wylie Carpenter little good. By the time he was off it was clear that every minute of Wylie's life was accounted for between two and eight p.m. on October fifteenth, and none was accounted for from eight until almost ten.

In the normal course of events it did not seem extraordinary that John Michael followed Teasdale and Whitman by having D. Dodge Patterson as his lead witness on the third day of testimony. Still, I was somewhat surprised when Dodge came into the courtroom. He had been part of my sphere of responsibility and I had not been aware that John Michael was planning on calling him. I also was not prepared to see Gretchen accompanying him.

She was wearing a purple hat that was broad-brimmed and almost flat, and when she removed her heavy wool cape I saw that she was wearing a matching purple dress. She was breathtaking in the purity of her beauty and I must have reacted in some way because Jessica wanted to know what it was I was looking at.

She discovered quickly enough, and she did it without me saying anything. "Who's that?" she demanded.

We were standing at the rail, Jessica and I, waiting for things to get started. Jessica was wearing a tweed suit that flattened the curves of her breasts and her buttocks. Her hair was pulled back. Her wool coat was over her arm. She looked exceptionally severe and almost masculine.

"Gretchen Patterson," I said.

The two of us watched her make herself comfortable.

"Dodge's wife?" There was a distinct note of concern in Jessica's voice, one that made me shift my glance to her and wonder why her brow was wrinkling and her eyes were narrowing.

"Yes," I said.

"South American?"

"Beats me. She was born in Lowell."

Jessica's forehead smoothed slowly. A touch of a smile came to her lips. "Pretty," she said, and turned away.

*   *   *

The direct examination of Teasdale had taken only about twenty minutes. The direct examination of Whitman had taken about an hour. John Michael's questioning of D. Dodge, however, covered the entire morning session.

Dodge was not without his charm, and faced with the cool and efficient presence of John Michael he tended to affect a loose and slightly bemused appearance, as though he was very willing to help but didn't know what help he could possibly be. He dipped his head and smiled at the jury and got them to smile back. He sat forward easily at first, and sat back relaxed and comfortable after a while. Every now and then, however, I saw him glance at the courtroom clock on the back wall.

John Michael established Dodge's background, education, and profession, and then established that he had spent the afternoon and evening of October 15 playing golf and cards with Wylie.

"You consider yourself to be a good friend of Mr. Carpenter's, don't you, Mr. Patterson?"

"Yes, I do."

"Known him for a number of years?"

"Pretty much ever since he moved to Woodedge."

"Went to his wedding, didn't you?"

"As a guest of Becky's, I suppose."

"After that you grew close and stayed close."

"I guess that would be fair to say."

"In fact, you could say that Wylie Carpenter has been something of a model for your life, couldn't you?"

"A model? Well, no, I wouldn't say that."

"A mentor?"

Dodge laughed. "On the golf course he has certainly tried to be. But other than that, we're just friends."

"You do admire him, don't you, Mr. Patterson?"

"Sure."

"And wouldn't you say that he has been a major influence on you over the course of, say, the past ten years?"

"This is all very vague, Mr. Keough. A major influence? Sure, like any friend would be. But I'm not clear as to what you're getting at."

"Wouldn't you agree that you have tried to be as much like Wylie Carpenter as you could over the past ten years?"

"Really, you know, I find that impossible to answer." Dodge looked to the jury and gave a very small shrug. "I admire him, I'd like to play golf like he does. . . . He's a smart, generous, personable guy. I could do a whole lot worse than be like him."

"Mr. Patterson, where were you on the night of October fifteenth between the hours of seven and nine o'clock?"

"Playing cards in the clubhouse at Stonegate."

"You played a Mr. Ben Butcher in the first round of cards, and you played Gerard Whitman in the last round. What did you do in between?"

"I don't know. Got something to eat. Watched television. I might have taken a shower."

"You didn't go home to see your wife and child?"

For the first time, Dodge squirmed. "No. Ah, as I recall, my wife was out shopping and my son, ah, probably was in bed. My father would have been watching him."

"You know Rebecca Carpenter was killed that night?"

"I do."

"You knew her from childhood, didn't you?"

"I did. She was a little older than I."

"You regarded her as an attractive woman, didn't you?"

"Very." Dodge folded his hands. His eyes narrowed as he tried to figure out where John Michael was going.

"You were able to observe Rebecca over the course of her sixteen-year marriage. Did you, from your perspective, regard her marriage as a happy one?"

"Objection," said Burnsie. "Calls for speculation or expert opinion, which this witness is not qualified to give."

"Overruled," said Judge LoBianco, grinning.

Dodge said "Yes" in answer to the question.

"Based on what you were able to observe, did you feel that fidelity on the part of both partners was essential to that marriage?"

"Objection."

LoBianco grinned at the ceiling. He grinned at his notes. "Overruled," he said.

Dodge fidgeted. "I don't know," he said.

"Based on what you were able to observe, did you interpret the marriage as being important to Wylie Carpenter?"

"Yes."

"You knew the house, of course. Six Bulham Road?"

"Yes."

"How long had you known them to live there?"

"Couple of years."

"Where did they live before that?"

"Gladstone Road."

"Big house?"

"Mmm—modest. Ten rooms, maybe."

"Not as big as six Bulham Road."

"Not by a long shot."

"Not an estate."

"No."

"How did you refer to six Bulham Road? Does it have another name?"

"I don't know. The Chesley Estate."

"Who lived there before the Carpenters?"

"Rebecca's mother. Rebecca grew up there with her parents. The place dates back to Squire Chesley, I think."

"And so Rebecca and her husband, Wylie, moved onto the estate when Rebecca's last surviving parent died?"

"Rebecca inherited it, yes. They sold the Gladstone Road place."

"And at this time, when they moved onto the estate, was Wylie Carpenter working? To your knowledge?"

"Well, he had an ownership interest in the savings and loan."

John Michael nodded. He waited until all eyes were on him and then, speaking deliberately, said, "Are you aware of any infidelities on the part of Mr. Carpenter over the course of his marriage?"

Burnsie unleashed a torrent of objections. LoBianco quickly summoned the two counsel to the bench and the three men engaged in some animated whispering. I kept my eyes on Dodge and Dodge kept his eyes on the floor of the witness box.

"The objection's overruled," announced LoBianco as Burnsie stormed back to his seat and John Michael, one hand in his pants pocket, meandered over to a spot in front of the jury box.

Dodge opened his hands. "I don't know for certain," he said.

"Is that because you never saw him in the act?"

"That's right."

"But you saw him in situations which led you to conclude that he was having extramarital relations, is that right?"

"Objection."

"Sustained," said LoBianco, pumping his pen as if Burnsie had just said the right word or guessed the right number.

"Mr. Patterson, do you have any personal knowledge of infidelities on the part of Mrs. Carpenter over the course of her marriage?"

"No," said Dodge firmly.

John Michael's chin shot up. He stared hard at Dodge, who stared hard back. "Didn't you yourself have an affair with Rebecca Carpenter?"

"I never did." Dodge was still staring, but a light seemed to come on in his eyes and he slowly twisted his head so that he was no longer looking at John Michael. He was looking at me.

John Michael took a step forward. His voice rose a degree louder. "Mr. Patterson, where *were* you on the night of October fifteenth between the hours of seven and nine o'clock?"

"Objection," shouted Burnsie, laboring to his feet. "Asked and answered."

"Sustained," said LoBianco, waving him down.

"Did you see Mrs. Carpenter at any time on that night?"

Dodge was no longer trying to be charming. He was frustrated and angry and suddenly fighting a battle he had never anticipated. "No, I didn't."

"Do you know of anyone who can verify where you were between seven and nine that night?"

Dodge leaned forward. He bit his lip. "I was not with her."

"Did you see Wylie Carpenter at any time between seven and nine o'clock that night?"

"No, I didn't."

"Did you leave the premises of the Stonegate Country Club at any time between seven and nine o'clock? At any time before ten o'clock that night?"

"No."

"Do you know if Wylie Carpenter did?"

"No."

"You did not leave the premises, you did not see Wylie Carpenter, do you agree that Wylie Carpenter could not have been on the premises between seven and nine?"

"No."

"Why not?"

Dodge hesitated. His eyes went from John Michael to Wylie to Gretchen in the back of the courtroom. Then they returned to Wylie and rested there. "Because I wasn't anyplace he could see me. Or I him."

John Michael, who had been all set to bury Dodge, stopped with the words of his next question stuck in his mouth. He walked back to his table. "Where were you, Mr. Patterson?"

This time there was no objection from Burnsie, who was leaning on his elbows, peering over the top of his reading glasses, seemingly as anxious as everyone else for the answer.

It took Dodge a very long while to respond. "There are some rooms at the club," he said. "Some members' rooms. I was in one of them."

Silence followed. Then LoBianco, clearing his throat, said, "Since nobody else seems to be going to ask it, what's a members' room, Mr. Patterson?"

"They're overnight rooms."

LoBianco wrote down that information. "By overnight you mean they have a bed in them?"

"They're basically for use by visiting officials or members who find themselves in sudden need of . . ."

"Overnight accommodation?" offered the judge helpfully.

"Yes sir."

The silence resumed. Nobody, it seemed, was looking directly at anybody else. Finally, the judge asked John Michael if he had any further questions.

John Michael, standing at counsel's table, staring down at his papers, said, "I assume you have some independent corroboration that you were in one of these rooms between seven and nine."

Dodge nodded. Very softly he said yes.

"Who were you with, Mr. Patterson?"

"I was with Shawna . . . I don't know her last name. She's employed in the dining room at Stonegate as a waitress."

John Michael met this revelation head-on. "I think," he said, his voice loud and distinct, "that now would be a good time to break for lunch, Your Honor."

John Michael was mad and he had a very difficult time containing his anger until everyone else was out of the courtroom. He occupied himself by smashing papers into unneeded piles; and then, when he and I and Jessica and Lester and Mary Alice Devon were the only ones left, he wheeled on me. "What kind of bullshit is this, Patt?" he demanded.

"I told you he was missing for a couple of hours. I don't see what difference it makes that he was with some girl—"

"That's not what I'm pissed off about, goddammit." John Michael pushed his face to within inches of mine. The hate in his expression was so unexpected, so intense, that for a moment I had a primitive urge to shove him away.

"You told me," he said, spit flying out of the corner of his mouth, "that Patterson had an affair with Rebecca Carpenter. I counted on that to explain what happened with Rasmussin. How am I going to prove she's a fucking slut whore now?"

"John," I said through clenched teeth, "I just told you what Dodge's wife told me. Just because he denies it now—hell, he denied it when I confronted him."

"But he's under oath now. It's one thing to deny something like that to a stranger, but I've got him up on the stand. He's a goddamn attorney. Think he's going to perjure himself over something like that?"

"His wife was here," I said, gesturing. "Why not?"

"Because"—John Michael drew himself up straight so that we were nearly on eye level with one another—"he just admitted that he was shacked up with some waitress whose last name he doesn't even know as recently as two and a half months ago. You think he's going to admit to that in front of his wife, in front of everyone, practically gratuitously, and then deny something she supposedly already knows about?"

I spent some time clearing my throat.

"Gimme a break, will ya, Patt?" he said, and his voice was almost sad.

Eventually he turned and looked at Stanley Lester. "Go out to Stonegate, find this Shawna woman," he said. "I want a complete statement from her. I want to know if this was a regular thing they had going, or what. I want to know if she also did it with Carpenter that night, or if she ever did it with him. I want to know what she knows about Carpenter's whereabouts and I want to know the name of every other woman who could possibly have been involved in anything like this. Got it?"

Lester practically saluted. But before he bolted for the door as fast as his little immigrant legs could carry him, John Michael held up one hand and asked me a question without looking at me. "I'm assuming this isn't something you've done already, Patt."

I told him it wasn't.

John Michael flicked his hand and Lester was off. His eyes sought out his wife's and he shook his head by moving it to one side and then bringing it back very slowly. His mouth was fixed in a lipless grimace and it stayed that way until he addressed Mary Alice. "This could be the whole ballgame," he said, "if Carpenter's protecting the reputation of some little golf-course slut by refusing to say where he was."

"You want to ask for a recess?" she said. Her square Irish face was worried and sympathetic and ridden with the desire to be of any service she could.

"Not on your life," he told her. "There's still a possibility they don't realize we've been hurt. And even if they do, I'm not going to give them the satisfaction of acknowledging it. We'll play it out for now." He grinned forcefully. "Who knows? When you've got a lemon you can always make lemonade."

"What do you want me to do, John?" I asked.

He stopped grinning. He turned back to the table and began stuffing his little piles into his briefcase. "I told you weeks ago to make sure this kind of surprise didn't happen. 'No sweat,' you said. Remember that? Well, I'm sweating now, Patt." The briefcase slammed shut. He hauled it off the table. "Kind of makes you wonder, doesn't it?"

He started up the aisle with Mary Alice hot on his heels. That left Jessica and me with nobody to look at but each other. She was searching my face and I was searching hers. And then she too turned and followed her husband up the aisle, her heels clicking resolutely on the tiled floor.

27

Gretchen Patterson returned in the afternoon. She sat in the same row, the same seat, but no matter how many times I turned, no matter how long I stared at her, she would not let me catch her eye.

Up on the stand, Dodge Patterson was being gently manipulated by Burnsie. Yes, during the nearly four hours they spent out on the course he had had plenty of opportunity to engage in conversation with Wylie Carpenter and he had noticed nothing unusual about his demeanor. Wylie had shot his typical fine game. They had entered the clubhouse together, had a drink together, sat down at the same time to play cards. If Carpenter had acted peculiarly in any way it had escaped Dodge's attention. And yes, Carpenter was definitely back in the clubhouse before ten, or at ten, or near ten—Dodge couldn't be sure of the exact time, but he was sure that Carpenter was acting no differently then than he had earlier in the evening. The thing that stood out in his mind was that they had been bantering back and forth and the bartender had been trying to get them to leave. And then Dodge had walked Wylie to his car.

Dodge volunteered that last bit of information, knowing that it was important.

"You recognized his car?"

"Yes sir. A gray Jaguar XJ-6."

"You saw him get in it? Saw him drive away?"

"That's right."

"No reason to think his car hadn't been sitting right there in the parking lot ever since two o'clock in the afternoon?"

Dodge started to answer and then hesitated. His mouth was open, but his eyes had gone off to one side. John Michael slowly raised his head. He put his pen between his lips and he leaned far back into his chair.

Burnsie, recognizing a mistake, said, "I'll withdraw that question. That's an unfair question. It calls for speculation."

"I object to counsel's argument," said John Michael calmly. "I don't see anything unfair about the question. Mr. Burns has made his bed, now let him lie in it."

"Well, you know, Judge—"

But LoBianco was in full grin. He waved Burnsie quiet and told Dodge he could answer the question.

Dodge said, "I don't know."

"What was that answer?" asked John Michael, turning his ear as if he was a little hard of hearing.

"I don't know."

Burnsie winged the next few questions, trying to get everyone's mind off whatever it was that had caused Dodge's equivocation, trying to restore the sense of synchronization that he had initially established with the witness. Throughout, John Michael sat patiently, twirling his pen between his teeth, until finally Burnsie ran out of questions and sat down awkwardly, his body betraying the uncertainty he felt at turning Dodge back over to John Michael.

"Why," said John Michael, "did you walk Mr. Carpenter to his car?"

"I don't recall."

"Was he too drunk to walk there himself?"

"No."

"Too emotional or distraught?"

"No."

"Didn't he know the way?"

"He knew the way."

"Was his car on the way to your car?"

"Yes."

"Where was his car located?"

"Near the clubhouse."

"How near?"

"Very near."

"The closest space to the clubhouse?"

"I guess."

"Where was your car?"

"Further away."

"How much further?"

"The corner of the lot."

"The back corner?"

"I suppose you'd call it that."

"Why did you park there?"

"It was the only space available when I arrived."

"And what time was that?"

"One forty-five, maybe. Maybe one fifty."

"Was that before or after Mr. Carpenter arrived at the club?"

"Objection!" hollered Burnsie.

LoBianco looked down. "If you know," he instructed Dodge.

Dodge looked at the judge as if he had been hoping he would say something else. He looked back at John Michael, who now had a glint in his eye, a glow to his face, like a predatory animal moving in on his quarry.

"You arrived the same time Mr. Carpenter did, didn't you, Mr. Patterson?"

John Michael could not wait for Dodge's answer. He took a step closer. "You actually saw him arrive and you saw him park his car, didn't you?"

Dodge gripped the end of his chair. "I might have the day confused."

"But what you don't have confused, what you remember now, is that on the afternoon of October fifteenth you saw Wylie Carpenter park his car in a different space than the one it was in when you walked him out at ten o'clock. Isn't that right?"

Dodge Patterson's eyes rocketed to Wylie Carpenter, who sat at the defendant's table with his own eyes downcast. "I don't remember," he said.

John Michael was happy. John Michael was excited. He was practically raving at Mary Alice Devon, telling her they had to get Lester on the stand right away. "We've got to get the testimony in about the white sweater fibers he took from the driver's seat of Rebecca's car. The jury's going to know then what's going on."

"What about the lab tech?" she said. "Aren't we going to need him to match the fibers in the car with the ones in Wylie's sweater?"

"Of course, of course. But we can put him on after. The jurors are going to know the moment we hold up Les's little baggie. Then we get Mrs. Mitchell up there. She testifies how Wylie came home before he went to the club and we just fill in the gaps. He came home, he took his wife's car up to the overlook, he walked back, he drove his own car to the club. Right? Boom, boom, boom, boom."

Mary Alice began frantically pawing through her notes.

"He plays golf, he plays cards, he takes off at eight to go back to his house. You with me, Mary Alice? Boom, boom, boom . . . gurgle, gurgle, gurgle. Back to the club, shoot the shit with old Dodgie, the moron, and the only mistake he makes is he parks his car in the wrong goddamn place." John Michael beat a drumroll with his open hands on the surface of the counsel's table.

He glanced around the empty courtroom until his eyes came to rest on me. His drumroll slowed to a halt. "Didn't you think to ask him that question, Patt? Didn't it ever occur to you to ask Patterson if Wylie's car had been moved?"

Mary Alice grabbed his sleeve. "But John," she said, reading from her notes, "Sergeant Roselli said it was three point six miles from the overlook to the Carpenter home."

"By roadway, Mary Alice, by roadway." He nodded to me, his face creased peculiarly with a smile that was not a smile. "But that's not the only way to walk from the overlook to the Carpenters', is it, Patt?"

The wooden railing, the fence that is sometimes known as the bar and that separates the audience from the participants in a trial, was between us. I was standing alone on my side and Mary Alice and Jessica and John Michael were all on the other side. My hands were in my pockets and I was not sharing in the general good feeling that was being disseminated as a result of Dodge's unexpected gift of information.

"There's a trail that runs behind the overlook, isn't there, Patt?"

"Yes."

"That trail goes a lot of places, doesn't it?"

"I've told you that before, yes."

"Take it one way and it leads to Stonegate."

"That's right."

"Take it another way and it goes to the Charles."

"Yes. That's what Roselli did."

"But if he had turned west instead of east it would have led him right to the Chesley Estate."

"Not really."

"How long a walk would it be by the trail? Two miles?"

"It's just a path," I said. "It runs from the Charles River to Whitehall Road, but the Chesley Estate is beyond that."

"What are you saying, Patt? That you can't get from Whitehall Road to Bulham Road, where the Chesley Estate is?"

"No. I'm just saying that the path ends there. You want to get from Whitehall to Bulham you've got to walk along Highland Street for another half a mile."

"How come you never told me you could do that, Patt?"

"Do what? Walk from Whitehall to Bulham?"

John Michael shook his head without letting his eyes move. "Walk from the overlook to Wylie Carpenter's home by cutting through the woods. It wouldn't be that hard in the middle of the day, would it?"

"Like I said, the path really doesn't go there."

"How long would it take in daylight for someone like you? For a middle-aged athlete like Wylie Carpenter? Twenty-five, thirty minutes?"

"I haven't been on that path in many years."

"Not even as part of your investigation?"

"That wasn't really what you asked me to do."

"Lester walked it. He discovered the path and found his way to the Chesley Estate using a map and compass."

"He's a helluva man, that Lester."

"Did it in twenty-eight minutes."

"Sounds like Lester has all the qualities of a good dog," I said.

"Like devotion to a task?"

"I suppose."

"Like loyalty to the person he's working for?"

"Lester's switched loyalties from Wembley to you, has he?"

"Like faithfulness?"

"There's that word again."

John Michael's pale brow curled. His tight little mouth became as thin as a pencil line.

"Oh, c'mon, John," I pleaded. "We've been over all this before."

John Michael smacked his way through the gate and came up to where I was standing. He moved rapidly, with his hands hanging straight down by his sides and curled into fists. Mary Alice and Jessica watched us with their mouths open, as if they were ready to start screaming the moment John Michael and I came to blows. But I did not react to John Michael's advance and by the time he came to a halt his expression had changed.

He took a breath and then gently tucked his hand inside my elbow and guided me out to the corridor, where the two of us assumed positions with our backs against the marble wainscoting. "It's times like these I wish I smoked cigarettes," he said, without looking at me.

He put his hands behind him and spread his feet. "I'm under a lot of pressure these days, as I guess you can tell. A lot of things just aren't quite working out. Almost, you know. Just enough to keep me going. But nothing's quite the way I wanted it."

"Sometimes," I said, "it's best not to want too much."

John Michael's head had been squared to the floor. Now he looked up sharply. "That sort of sums you up, doesn't it, Patt? I mean, a guy like you is not going to sell me out because there's nothing you really want in this life, is there?"

I shrugged. I had not expected my remark to have

much significance beyond being a bridge between his thoughts.

"No, really. You're every bit as smart as I am, we're about the same age, we come from the same area—yet look how different our lives have become. I guess you kind of take things as they are, while I'm always out there trying to make them be better. I don't mean that to sound as if I'm putting you down for that, God knows I'm not. I'm just trying to figure out—you know, you get to certain times in your life and you just have to stop and ask yourself if any of what you're doing is worthwhile. Maybe you found the right answer early on. I mean, for each of the things I've accomplished I can think of a hundred reasons why I shouldn't have bothered. This whole thing about being district attorney is a good example. It looks great, it sounds great, but, Jesus, the pressure's never off. A guy doesn't become D.A. in his early thirties and then stay in that position for the next forty years. You've got to move on to something else and get public attention to do it, but meanwhile every little thing you do is open to potshots from the entire community."

John Michael pushed himself off the wall and then let himself fall back again. "That's why I've always valued you and Roy so much. With you guys I could form my own little insular community where I could really be myself. Where I could show my weaknesses, my ignorance. Where I could afford to make mistakes. That's why . . . that's why I'm so sensitive about this anonymous letter I got . . . coming when it did, you know. Coming when I've got this big case in which everything seems to be just slightly off center. All the pegs are just slightly larger than the holes they're supposed to go in. Or slightly smaller."

Some people came walking down the corridor, lawyers with lawyer briefcases. They were talking happily until they saw us and then they cut off in midsentence, perhaps midword. "John," said one of them as he passed by, and the others all nodded and smiled nervously. John had a nice smile for each of them.

As their footsteps drifted away John Michael said, "The combination of things has just naturally made me paranoid. By this point everybody knows I've made a commitment to this case and with the possibility of Kilrain's congressional seat hanging out there, that just ups the stakes to infinity. In other words, if there's one time in my life somebody could screw me up for good it's now. I fall on my face, Kilrain announces his retirement, and fat Constantinis waltzes in."

John Michael shivered at the prospect. He crossed his arms in front of his stomach. "So the case keeps slipping away. And I'm wondering why. And the letter comes. So I start to watch things a little more closely and suddenly the smallest remark, the smallest gesture, the smallest mistake seems to take on added significance. You understand where I'm coming from, Patt?"

"No, not completely, John. I've never liked the case to begin with, you know that. But I'd never do anything to sell you out. And neither, as far as I can tell, would Roy. As for Lester—"

"He's doing what I ask him to, that's all I can say about him."

"Fine. If that's what you want, if that satisfies you, fine. I personally don't trust him, but I don't think he's trying to screw you on this case. I don't think anybody's trying to screw you. I don't know where the letter came from or what it means, but if I were you I'd just forget it."

"Fine," said John Michael, once again pushing off the wall and this time turning to face me. He held out his hand. "Then will you forgive me?"

"Hey," I said, taking the hand in my own, "there's nothing to forgive."

28

Stanley Lester turned out to be an excellent witness for the prosecution, although he did not appear right after Dodge Patterson. John Michael elected to go first with Mrs. Mitchell and then with Mrs. Marconi. Although not making a direct issue out of it, John Michael quite successfully used them to create the impression that the relationship between Mrs. Carpenter and Douglas Rasmussin extended far beyond what would normally be expected between an employer and an employee. And then he called a CPA named Dandurand, who had greasy hair and the personality of a frog, but who nevertheless was able to explain in painstaking detail the multiple millions of dollars of assets, the $63 million of assets, that were about to befall Wylie as a result of the death of his wife.

When Lester did make it to the stand he remained for two full days. Much of what he said was an elaboration, an exaggeration, or simply untrue; but he said everything well and he said it with a mixture of confidence, enthusiasm, and foreign intrigue that made him seem quite credible. Burnsie, with his rumpled suit and his local-boy manner, could not break him, and on more than one occasion his cross-examination technique allowed Lester to enhance his facts with his opinions.

By the time the two counsel had been through direct, cross, redirect, and recross, the story seemed clear enough. The bonvivant golfer Wylie Carpenter had grown tired of his life with the increasingly reclusive, aging, alcoholic, pill-addicted heiress, who may or may not have been having affairs right under his nose. He selected the day when her handsome young yardboy was leaving for California (to which Lester claimed to have traced him, trailed him, and lost him). On that day he came home for lunch, removed his wife's car and drove it to the overlook, walked back through the woods to get his own car, and then drove off to the club. That night he sneaked away from his card games, strangled his wife with the scarf he had recently purchased, delivered her body to her parked car, and then returned to the club as if nothing had happened. And now he was $63 million richer and free to frolic with the waitresses at the country club.

John Michael allowed himself to be photographed emerging from the courthouse and looking triumphant.

In his opening statement, Burnsie had lamented the sad state of affairs that had caused his client to be made to account for what he had done simply because of who he was. He had extolled Wylie as a pillar of the community and had hinted at the dark forces who were setting up Wylie for their own personal reasons. A tissue of lies, he called the commonwealth's case, transparent in its intent and based on nothing more than a desire for sensationalism and character assassination. I naturally assumed Burnsie was directing his remarks at John Michael, and therefore was completely taken by surprise when he announced that he was calling me as his first witness.

I was sitting in the front row between Lester and Jessica Keough and all three of us reacted as though we had just been bolted to the backs of our seats. "What the bloody hell?" cracked Lester, and Jessica, if she didn't use the same words, meant the same thing.

John Michael literally rushed the bench. He started from his seat with an objection, but he kept moving closer and closer as he spoke until he was whispering and gesturing heatedly and LoBianco had to signal Burns to join them.

The talk at the bench led to talk in the audience. Jessica was leaning in close to me, so close her hair was touching mine. She was asking me why Burnsie would possibly be doing this and I was trying to tell her I had no idea when both of us, without a single word to indicate we would do it, turned our heads and looked into the row behind us.

Patty Hansen was sitting only a couple of feet away. Her hair, as always, was hanging over her forehead, dropping in front of her eyes. She was wearing a heavy, fur-collared coat, and she was holding thin brown gloves in one hand.

"Hello, Patty," Jessica said, in a voice that asked what she was doing there when she had never attended a trial before, why she was sitting there without making her presence known, and whether there was any reason why she was looking so furtive as she let her eyes flick back and forth between us.

"Is Mr. Starbuck in the courtroom?" called out Judge LoBianco.

"Yes, sir," I said, turning front and waving my hand.

"Ah." LoBianco grinned and I had the sinking feeling I was in trouble. "You may take the stand, sir."

Burnsie had never been what I would call a friend. When he was district attorney I worked for John Michael and John Michael worked for him and it was a rare occasion when we had direct contact. He never ordered me to do anything, he never praised me, and he never yelled at me either.

Now he was looking at me in that peculiar way attorneys have when they are pretending for the jury they know nothing and yet are almost robotically anticipating certain answers.

"Good afternoon, Mr. Starbuck."

"Good afternoon."

"That's Patterson Starbuck, you said when you were being sworn in?"

"Yes."

"Is Patterson an old family name?"

Burnsie's orange hair was matted down. His face was round and flushed. His mouth was round and it opened like a little hole in his skin when he spoke. Of all the objects in the universe, Burnsie's face looked most like a catcher's mitt.

"Yes," I said.

"Are you, by any chance, related to D. Dodge Patterson, who testified, when was it, last week?"

I looked out at the audience. The benches were about half full. I saw Lester and Jessica and Patty Hansen. I saw Ralphie Libby sitting next to a uniformed Chief Wembley Tuttle. I saw Gerard Whitman, the loyal friend, sitting with Bud Teasdale. I saw the television reporter and the television cameraman, who had not been there since the first day of testimony, and I knew that something was up and that at least a couple of those people knew what it was.

"We're some sort of cousins," I said.

"How are you employed, Mr. Starbuck?"

"I'm what's known as the litigation coordinator for the office of the district attorney for Exeter County."

"And what exactly is the litigation coordinator?"

I nailed Burnsie with my eyes. "Well, Mr. Burns, I'm not exactly sure I'm the right person to define the title since I believe you had a hand in making up the position when you were district attorney, but as I understand it I'm a public investigator employed by Exeter County to investigate crimes and to assist the county attorneys and police in their investigations and presentation of the evidence. In my capacity I assist and supplement the role of the state police, in particular Detective Lieutenant Ralph Libby, who is assigned to the Exeter County office as an investigator."

Burnsie chuckled. It was meant to cover the fact that I had, in a very small way, embarrassed him. It was also meant as a sign to me, a precursor of what was to come.

"As litigation coordinator, do you report directly to Mr. Keough, over here?"

"Sometimes. I report to the attorney assigned to handle the case on which I'm working."

"And you're given a good deal of discretion in your investigations, aren't you? Mr. Keough delegates authority to you in that regard?"

"I guess that's correct."

"And on days when you're not working on a particular case assigned to a particular staff attorney, you regularly report to Mr. Keough, don't you?"

"You could say that."

"In fact, I could say that you and Deputy District Attorney Hansen are part of a sort of kitchen cabinet for Mr. Keough, couldn't I?" Burnsie asked, his voice rising.

"You could . . ." I waited a beat or two until Burnsie had started to milk his self-satisfaction, and then I said, "It wouldn't necessarily be true."

The titters I drew probably did not make the remark worthwhile. Burnsie merely plunged on.

"You assisted in the preparation and investigation of this case, didn't you? Assisted Mr. Keough, I mean?"

"Objection," shouted John Michael in perhaps his loudest voice of the trial.

"Overruled," said LoBianco without looking up.

"Approach the bench, Your Honor?"

"No."

John Michael bit his lip and I answered that I had.

"In fact, you were in charge of the investigation?"

"No. Detective Lieutenant Libby was in charge."

"Did you ever, at any time, receive any direction regarding this particular investigation from Detective Lieutenant Libby, didn't you?"

I hesitated, wanting everyone to know that the question was ambiguous, but Burnsie bulled ahead without waiting for an answer.

"In fact you never did, and in fact you carried out your investigation right through the indictment of my client by effectively bypassing the state police and Detective Lieutenant Libby, didnt you?"

The first nodules of fear began to cluster inside my chest. "No," I said, but Burnsie didn't care.

"How many times did you question my client without Detective Libby being present?"

"Twice, that I recall."

"How many times did you read him his rights?"

"Objection," said John Michael.

"Overruled."

"None. He wasn't under arrest or even a suspect when I interviewed him."

"When did you determine he was a suspect?"

I needed to think about it and in order to do that I had

to remove my eyes from Burnsie. I did not like removing my eyes from him, not until I knew what he was going to do with me up there on the stand. "When at the end of my second interview I ascertained that Mr. Carpenter was unable to account for approximately two hours of his time on the night of his wife's murder."

"Did you ever find out where he was during those two hours, Mr. Starbuck?"

The question pierced me. It made me go cold and clammy. I said, "Not really," and the words did not sound as if they were mine.

"What does that mean, Mr. Starbuck: not really?"

"Well . . . I was told—"

"Objection," said John Michael. "Hearsay."

LoBianco considered his notes, looked down at me and said, "Were you told whatever you are about to say by Mr. Carpenter?"

"No."

"In that case, the objection's sustained. Don't answer what you were told by somebody else."

"I can't answer any other way, Judge."

LoBianco showed me all his teeth. "Then you can't answer at all. Next question, Mr. Burns."

Burnsie held his right elbow in his left hand and ran his right index finger up alongside his cheek. "You conducted interviews of other people besides Mr. Carpenter in carrying out your investigation, didn't you?"

"Yes."

"How many of those people were you told to interview by Detective Lieutenant Libby, the man you said was in charge of the investigation?"

"None."

"Aside from my client, did you at any time consider any of the other people who you interviewed to be a suspect in the killing of Mrs. Carpenter?"

I remembered Lester's line that everybody was a suspect and I probably chose not to use it simply because it had come from Lester. "Yes," I said.

"Who?"

Once again John Michael rose to his feet with an objection and once again there was a lengthy conference at the bench. It ended with John Michael delivering me a quick, unhappy look.

"You may answer, Mr. Starbuck," declared the judge. "However, I caution the jury that any answer this witness is about to give is not evidence of the truth of the matter asserted. In other words, it is not evidence of the guilt or innocence of any person. It is merely being allowed in as part of the defense's case in support of their claim of bias or prejudice on the part of the prosecution."

Involuntarily, my head snapped, my mouth fell open. I was so totally unprepared for such a remark that I compounded its effect. And LoBianco, with a curt nod, simply acted as though he had done me a favor.

"Mr. Starbuck?" said Burnsie. "The judge told you to answer the question."

"Suspects could have been anybody, Mr. Burns. You know that."

"Ah, what I know is beside the point. You didn't, for example, consider Mr. Whitman, sitting back here, to be a suspect, did you?"

I looked at Whitman with his arms folded and his face defiant. "No," I said.

"Or Mrs. Mitchell?"

"I didn't really, no. Not once I met her."

"Well, then. Who did you consider a suspect?"

"Mr. Carpenter."

"Only Mr. Carpenter? Right from the start, is that what you told Mr. Keough? That my client did it?"

"No."

"Then who else did you consider, Mr. Starbuck?"

"Douglas Rasmussin."

"Ah, the missing caretaker. Where was he from?"

"He was from Walmouth."

"I see. And as part of your investigation did you interview Mr. Rasmussin?"

"Yes."

"In Walmouth?"

"In Los Angeles."

"So you found him there?"

"Yes."

"Mr. Starbuck, weren't you working with Inspector Lester on this investigation?"

"We were each conducting investigations."

"And weren't you keeping in contact with each other? Weren't you sharing information with each other?"

"Yes. We were."

"Well, Mr. Starbuck, you were present when Inspector Lester told us how he traced Rasmussin to California and then could not locate him once he got out there. Didn't you tell the inspector where he was?"

"I did. But Mr. Rasmussin apparently had moved without leaving any forwarding address."

"So the only one who ever met with Rasmussin in connection with this investigation—these investigations— was you."

"That's right."

"And you determined on your own . . . what? That he was no longer a suspect?"

"I determined . . . I reported my findings to Mr. Keough and he made whatever determination there was."

"Based on what you told him?"

"Yes."

"And did you tell Mr. Keough that Rasmussin ought to be arrested?"

"No."

"Did you tell him that Rasmussin ought to be let go, disregarded, ignored?"

"I believe I told Mr. Keough he had testimony that may be of use in this trial."

"May be of use in the trial against Wylie Carpenter, is that what you're saying?"

It was and it wasn't. I glanced at John Michael for some indication as to how to answer, but he did not seem to be sensing the danger of this line of questioning. "I meant of use in any trial concerning the murder of Rebecca Carpenter."

Burnsie backed off. He took a walk behind his table and tilted his head to look at the ceiling for a while. "You would agree, wouldn't you, Mr. Starbuck, that at the point the district attorney decided to seek an indictment of my client he had concluded that Douglas Rasmussin was not a suspect?"

"I guess I'd have to, yes."

"And by that point, whenever it was, you had told him your opinion of Douglas Rasmussin, who some time prior to that had been a suspect?"

"Yes."

"And as of that point in time nobody else had interviewed Rasmussin?"

"Actually, Inspector Lester talked to him by phone before I met with him."

"But since then, nobody else has interviewed Rasmussin?"

"As far as I know."

"And nobody knows where he is? Nobody has seen him since you allegedly did some months ago?"

"I can only tell you that I don't know where he is."

Burnsie clenched both fists in front of his chest. "So you would agree then that the dismissal of Douglas Rasmussin as a suspect in the murder of Rebecca Carpenter necessarily had to come as a result of your say-so and your say-so alone?"

John Michael at last saw what Burnsie was doing, but by the time he voiced his objection the damage was done.

Burnsie barely waited until the word "Sustained" was out of the judge's mouth before he was back at me again. "You personally orchestrated the indictment of Wylie Carpenter, didn't you?"

"I don't know what you mean," I said. I wanted to loosen my tie, but I was afraid of how it would look.

John Michael, still seated, was contending that I was being badgered. LoBianco was smiling and telling Burnsie not to badger me. Burnsie was not even listening.

"You didn't care who was found guilty of this murder as long as it was one of the wealthy people of Woodedge, one of the gentry, one of the people you aspired to be. Isn't that right, Mr. Starbuck?"

My feet lost all their feelings. They were empty cylinders at the bottom of my legs. My back was cold. It was nothing but a framework of bones. My facial muscles wouldn't work. I could only stare and listen as John Michael snorted his incredulity at such a question.

"Who first suggested Wylie Carpenter to Mr. Keough as a suspect?" demanded Philip Burns.

John Michael stopped arguing. He looked at me and made no effort to stop my answer.

"Me, I suppose," I said.

"Who first suggested Rasmussin?"

"I don't remember."

"It wasn't you?"

"It may have been Chief Tuttle."

"Did you ever suggest anyone other than Wylie Carpenter?"

"I don't know."

"Oh, really? Well, tell me, Mr. Starbuck, didn't you also propose Dodge Patterson as a suspect?"

My throat was very dry, almost too dry for me to speak. I knew that the defense had a legal right to our investigation files, I assumed Burns had been through them, and I was damn sure they said nothing about me suggesting Dodge as a suspect. I had only mentioned it orally in meetings, in front of people like John Michael, and Jessica Keough, and Ralphie Libby and Royster Hansen. With the exception of Royster, they were all here today. "Yes," I said. "I naturally considered it because—"

"Your cousin?" roared Burns. "Your own cousin?"

"He's a distant cousin and that shouldn't have affected my objectivity."

"No," said Burnsie, adjusting the knot in his tie. "No, it shouldn't."

"I object to counsel's argumentative comments," said John Michael, getting halfway to his feet and pointing at his opponent. He had stopped taking notes. He had stopped looking as though nothing that Burnsie did could possibly faze him.

LoBianco solved the instant complaint easily enough. "Don't argue," he told Burns.

"Just how distant a relation are you, Mr. Starbuck?"

I took a moment, as if calculating what I had known

since I was little more than a toddler. "Our great-grandfathers were brothers."

"I see. The Patterson family name is an old one in Woodedge, isn't it?"

"Yes."

"The Patterson family was one of the original founding families, wasn't it?"

"Yes."

"Sixteen forty?"

"That's when they first settled, I believe."

"So you and Dodge trace your roots back a long way together?"

"Yes."

"And did you grow up in Woodedge along with Dodge?"

"No. I was born and raised in West Nestor."

"I see. And where were you educated?"

I asked for and received a cup of water from the bailiff, a weightlifter named Pupulski. He and I knew each other slightly and he made eye contact with me when he handed me the water. The contact was meant to tell me to hang in there.

I drank all the water before I answered. "Nestor High School. I received an associate's degree from Walmouth J.C. and a bachelor's degree from UMass-Boston."

"Anything else?"

Burnsie well knew what else. "I have a master's degree in American civilization from Brown University."

"Anything else?"

"I completed some course work toward my Ph.D. in American civ at Brown, but I didn't write the dissertation."

"Really?" he remarked, as though he had never read my résumé. "And what did you intend to do with a Ph.D.?"

"I was never sure. That's why I dropped out after one year."

"Was that the only reason you dropped out?"

"I had financial reasons, too." I remembered to look at the jury. And to smile. "It cost a lot of money to go there."

No one smiled back.

"You were paying your own way, were you?"

I reached for the water cup again and saw that it was empty. "Yeah," I said, withdrawing my hand.

"That's a rather admirable record, Mr. Starbuck, working your way all the way up from our local junior college to a doctoral program at one of the most prestigious universities in the country. You must have worked very hard."

I said nothing. There was no question, he got no answer.

"Tell me, did that cause you any feelings of resentment that you had to drop out so close to your goal because you didn't have the money to pay the rest of your way?"

"Objection," said John Michael, but he said it as if he did not expect to win the point.

"Same reasons as stated at the bench," responded Burnsie as if he did.

LoBianco nodded. "Overruled."

"It wasn't really my goal, Mr. Burns. That was one of the problems. I had this professor at UMass who more or less sponsored me for the program and I—"

"What was your goal, Mr. Starbuck? To work as an investigator for the district attorney's office?"

"It's an honorable job, Mr. Burns," I said softly.

"Well, what was your job before this one?"

"I was a claims supervisor for Northeast American Way Insurance Company."

"And how did you happen to go to work for Northeast American Way?"

I knew at that moment where Burnsie was going and I wanted to scream at John Michael to stop it. But John Michael was sitting almost in a slouch, his legs stretched out in front of him, saving his precious objections, sparing himself from the mini-defeats of Judge LoBianco's rulings.

"My father," I said, "was an agent for the company."

"I see. A self-made man, was your father?"

"Yeah."

"So he did not inherit any of the Patterson family holdings."

"No."

"And you did not have any inheritance? Nothing to help you pay for schooling at Brown?"

"No."

"Did that cause you any resentment, Mr. Starbuck: the fact that your cousin Dodge grew up in Woodedge in a beautiful home and got to go to Andover and Amherst College and get his law degree from an expensive private university, all without ever having to work?"

"I didn't even know Dodge. I never met him before this investigation."

"And when you did meet him, did you introduce yourself? Did you tell him you were his cousin?"

"No."

"Why not?"

"I didn't think it was relevant."

Burnsie reacted as though this was a very surprising answer. He bent his elbow and touched his finger to his lips and then took it away and gently shook it at me. "Your branch of the family had certain claims to the Patterson holdings, didn't it?"

"I don't know what you mean." But I did. And John Michael still was not moving to help me.

"Didn't your father lay claim to Dodge Patterson's home in Woodedge?"

I looked directly at John Michael. I spoke directly to John Michael. I watched as Mary Alice jostled him with her arm to get him to pay attention to me. "I still don't know what you're talking about, Mr. Burns."

"Didn't your father once occupy that house, Mr. Starbuck? Didn't he, in fact, move his whole family in there while his relatives were away on vacation?"

John Michael threw up his hands. "Your Honor, what does this, even if true, have to do with the facts of this case?"

"I'll tell you," said Burnsie, dropping any pretense of being the innocent questioner. "It has to do with the fact that this man, this Patterson Starbuck, had a motive for everything he did: for orchestrating the investigation, for making his allegations, and for influencing the district attorney to his conclusions. And that motive was, pure and simple, one of revenge, jealousy, and retribution against the whole town of Woodedge for a longstanding family grievance."

John Michael was bellowing indignation at Burnsie's tactic. LoBianco was glaring at both attorneys and slamming his wooden gavel to get their attention. "Gentlemen," he shouted, "get yez both up here." Then he remembered the television Minicam now whirring away and he looked directly into it and clamped his lips grimly together.

The three men were so excited I could hear them as they leaned across the bench and whispered within inches of each other's faces. "But, Your Honor," John Michael was protesting, "this is crazy. Wylie Carpenter isn't even related to him."

"He tried to pin it on his cousin, he couldn't do it, so he turned his venomous attack on his cousin's best buddy," snapped Burns. "He hates 'em all anyway because they're all rich and they all have what he doesn't."

And LoBianco was talking right back at them, stepping on their words, possibly not even listening to what they were saying. "If either one of you makes another outburst like this I'm censuring you. Got me? Because right now I'm on the verge of declaring a mistrial."

"Let me pursue this line, Judge. You'll see—"

"It's not the line, counsel. It's your argument that I'm ripshit about."

"I'll watch it, Judge."

"You do."

Then LoBianco straightened up and smiled into the camera. "The jury is to disregard Mr. Burns's last remarks as they constitute argument and, as I have told you before, what counsel says is not evidence. However, the question may stand and Mr. Starbuck may answer it." He shifted his smile to the jury and regarded them paternally, as though everyone was happy now.

I let the camera continue to roll for a long time before I agreed that my father had once occupied the Patterson house.

"And wasn't your father banned from going near that house for a period of some years after that?"

"A restraining order was issued, yes."

"An order obtained by his mother's cousin Gordon Patterson?"

"Yes."

"Dodge's grandfather?"

"Yes."

"So, would you say there was a family feud between the two branches, the Starbucks and the Pattersons?"

"No, I wouldn't."

Burnsie was rather skilled at getting in his next question before I had any chance to explain my answer to his last. He spoke quickly, saying, "Your father continued to go near the house even though he was restrained by court order, didn't he?"

I wanted the water again. I looked at Pupulski and signaled and he nodded. "I don't know," I said.

"In fact, he used to approach the house on Whitehall Road from the rear, following a path up through the woods; and in fact he was chased away from the grounds at gunpoint on at least one occasion by his relatives—your relatives—wasn't he?"

I watched Pupulski drawing the water from a bubbling cooler. "He may have been," I said.

"What was that?" Burnsie cupped his ear and put a pained expression on his face.

"I said, he may have been."

Philip Burns lowered his hand and stood very still. "And in fact, Mr. Starbuck, your father took a gun to that house himself one day, didn't he?"

Pupulski, starting back, trying not to spill his paper cup of water, stopped cold.

"No," I said, but I did not hear the word come out of my mouth.

"And that day he was found shot to death on the path behind the Patterson house, wasn't he?"

The courtroom was very, very still. Everyone in it seemed to understand my answer even before I gave it.

Burns, his voice now nearly as soft as mine, said, "And although it was ruled a suicide, you always thought that your father's death was brought about by one of the Pattersons, didn't you?"

As though he was a caring physician whose only concern was my interest, Philip Burns leaned in closer. "What's your answer, Mr. Starbuck?"

"The answer," I said, the words catching in my mouth, "is that what you're asking, what you're implying, is disgusting. I think it's so far beneath normal standards of human conduct, what you're doing, that you've made me sick to my stomach."

Somebody, somewhere, suppressed a nervous giggle. It wasn't John Michael. He was staring at me in shock. Most everyone else was not looking at me at all.

"I see," said Burns, leaning back again. His arms were folded, his hands were tucked under his biceps. "Well, then. Let's go back to a different area. Wouldn't you consider yourself, Mr. Starbuck, to be the single greatest influence on Mr. Keough's decision to prosecute my client?"

Pupulski delivered my water. There was apology written all over his face.

"No."

"Who was then? Jessica Keough?"

John Michael's head popped up. A look of disbelief crossed his boyish features. "What's he doing bringing my wife into this?" he demanded.

"It's relevant, Judge," said Burnsie quickly.

"No," said John Michael, bouncing his pencil off his table. "I want to know what he's doing bringing my wife into this." He had gotten to his feet and Burnsie instinctively moved away from him.

"Explain, Mr. Burns," ordered LoBianco.

"Let me withdraw the question, Judge, and ask this. Mr. Starbuck, you didn't protest when I used the term 'kitchen cabinet' a while back. You understood that to refer to John Michael Keough's little informal group of closest advisers, didn't you?"

"I suppose."

"And that group consists of you, Roy Hansen, and Mr. Keough's wife, Jessica, am I right?"

"There he goes again, Judge."

"The questions so far are all right, Mr. Keough. Let's just see where he's going with this."

I said, "Insofar as I know what you're talking about, Mr. Keough has on occasion called the three of us together for advice."

"And you were present when Mrs. Keough advised her husband with respect to this case, weren't you?"

"Your Honor, this is outrageous."

"Sit down, Mr. Keough."

"You would agree she had an influence on him in his decision to prosecute Wylie Carpenter."

"I can't agree or disagree. I don't know."

"And you had an influence over Mrs. Keough, didn't you?"

John Michael was too stunned by the question to object. I looked to the audience, where Jessica's eyes were as big as Christmas ornaments. Then, behind her, I saw the twitch of a head, a sweep of stringy brown hair; and by leaning to one side I was able to see the face of Patty Hansen, and I was able to see that her expression was one of pure glee.

"I don't think so," I said slowly.

"Weren't you . . ." Burnsie hesitated. His mouth formed a circle, closed, and opened again. ". . . In fact having an affair with Mrs. Keough—"

Whatever his last words were they were drowned out by John Michael. With a sudden shot of his arm he knocked half his files and papers and books to the floor. "Is that outrageous enough for you, Judge?" he said shrilly. "Accusing my wife of adultery in the middle of a goddamn murder trial?"

Mary Alice Devon was unable to keep her hold on John Michael's coattails and it is possible he would have gone after Philip Burns in front of everyone if Pupulski's muscle-bulging frame had not magically appeared between them.

Burnsie, now that he could see he was safe, was trying to explain himself to the judge. "But why can't I ask a question like that? It's the same thing he asked of Dodge Patterson."

"He's gotta be drunk," shouted John Michael over Pupulski's shoulder. "Everybody knows he's a drunk. That's how come I've got his job."

Pupulski slipped his massive arm around John Michael's waist and lifted his feet off the floor. The judge was pointing the handle end of his gavel at Burns and telling him that he was censured.

"Just make him answer the question," Burnsie was pleading, his sweaty hands spread wide. "And then if he says no you can censure me."

"You're censured now," LoBianco hollered. "You're censured, you're in contempt, and you're going to jail because this is a mistrial, Mr. Burns, and you have caused it."

His gavel smashed down on the bench. Burnsie kept arguing, John Michael kept hollering, and all the while the television Minicam kept rolling.

29

It is best not to want too much. John Michael had said that was my creed. It is best not to want. My father wanted. Too much. John Michael wanted and now I was suffering the consequences. Betrayed by everything I never stood for.

I lay on my bed in my anonymous Commonwealth Avenue apartment listening to the sounds of late-night Boston pass beneath my window. Snow tires made squishing noises as they rolled over salt-marked pavement. Occasionally a radio would crackle. Rarer still was the cry of a human voice. I could hear them, those human voices, but in the hours I lay awake they only drifted my way once or twice or maybe three times. Just enough to remind me that there were people out there in the darkness, people with jobs and families and problems that had nothing to do with me and my humiliation. Just enough to remind me of my favorite sound ever, the sound of children playing outside as night was coming on.

That was the sound of my childhood, when the world was mine, when I was going to grow up to be a great ballplayer—or at least rich and secure, honored and honorable. It was an indistinct memory, but the strongest one I had: my friends' voices calling to me in the growing darkness, our ways lit by the last vestiges of twilight, by th occasional streetlight, by the glow of familiarity of everything in the neighborhood. And when it was finally too dark to stay out I would rush into the house, still full of energy but ready to be made safe and warm and full by my mother.

She had never wanted too much, my mother, and I had

always believed her to be the most stable person I knew. When my father was with us she made the best of the situation by adopting his dreams and complaints as her own. When he was gone she put them behind her, as though they had never existed, and there was no further reason to speak of Woodedge or Pattersons or suicide, estates or heirlooms or inheritances. From then on she only mentioned my father's name in connection with good things or simple things, such as the way he laughed or the foods he liked; and I would listen and say nothing because she seemed happiest keeping memories on that level and because neither of us wanted to open the doors to the world of hurt he had left behind.

She had called me after the evening news and she had asked me if there was anything she could do. I thought of a hundred funny lines: make me a bowl of chicken soup, yell at mean old Phil Burns, ask Kelsey if he can get me a job on the loading dock. Remind me in the future to pay more attention to miserable women like Patty Hansen. "No," I said, "there's nothing you can do." And she had said, "Well, at least they kept you in the background."

I had, of course, been in the background throughout. Yet that had not kept me from serving as the means by which the Keoughs sought to achieve their fame, Carpenter and Burns their defense, Patty Hansen her revenge. All of them had exploited me because they had wanted so much more than I. Or perhaps they had done it simply because I had let them—because I had confused wanting with caring and had told myself I had no need of either. Or perhaps they had recognized what I had not: that there were things that I wanted, things that I had wanted so much they had made me blind.

That last thought bothered me more than any other. It made me unable to sleep no matter how long I lay in bed.

It was still pitch dark when I got dressed. I put on wool socks and blue jeans, a T-shirt, a flannel shirt, and rubber-soled boots. I splashed water on my face and brushed my teeth and then I put on a parka and gloves and went downstairs to warm up my Alfa. I sat sipping instant coffee and listening to the good morning voices of the radio news readers and when the coffee was gone and the car was warm I drove out to Woodedge and parked by the side of the road before the sun came up.

At seven o'clock there was enough gray light for me to be able to get out. The snow on the sides of the road and beneath the trees was covered with a breakable crust that looked like ground glass. The driveway on which I started walking was rutted with ice, some of it blue, some of it almost yellow. I followed it to the old wooden barn, slip-sliding even on my rubber soles.

When I was a boy I thought that the barn must hold wondrous things. Viewed from the path at the rear of the property it had the potential for haylofts and rope swings and horse stalls. In reality it proved to be a makeshift garage and storage area, occupied in the middle by the two family automobiles and on the sides by the wreckage of the sixties and seventies and perhaps the eighties: an old refrigerator, a sink, a broken couch, crates of moldering books, empty oil cans, and rusting machinery parts. There were other things, more modern things, things that looked new enough to work, like a riding lawnmower and a snowblower and shovels and garden utensils; but I was interested in trunks and cabinets and cartons and whatever would make a good hiding place.

I found it in a cardboard barrel choked with strands of metal and broken chunks of Sheetrock. The metal strands were probably part of an old bedframe. I had to hold them out of my way with the back of my arm and shoulder so I could reach to the bottom, so I could move aside the pieces of Sheetrock. I was bent over, almost handcuffed by what I was doing, and I did not hear the doors move or the footsteps behind me. I only heard a voice tell me to straighten up slowly with my hands empty.

I did as I was told, my hands held high.

"It's you, isn't it, Mr. Starbuck?"

I admitted that it was.

"Give me one good reason why I shouldn't shoot you."

"Because then people might start asking questions you don't want to answer." I turned very slowly. "Particularly if you leave your gun next to my body."

Frost Patterson was dressed for the cold. He was wearing a three-quarter-length coat that would have allowed him to survive a Arctic night. Its fur-lined hood peaked above his bald head and shadowed the colorlessness of his haughty, unforgiving face. In one hand he held a gnarled cane, and the only thing that made him look dangerous was the pistol he held in his other hand. It was a medium-caliber automatic, the kind that a frail person like Frost could use with some accuracy over the distance of twenty feet or so that separated us.

There was a slight tremor to his body, one that I could not remember seeing before, but his voice was flat, almost resigned. "Your father was a pest, Mr. Starbuck. A pain in the ass. But I didn't shoot him. He did that himself, and I always suspected he did it on our property as a final little element of whatever game he thought he was playing with us. I suspect he did it hoping somebody would think it was one of us. My brother or me, maybe. But it wasn't."

"People will never know, though, will they?"

He laughed harshly. "People don't care."

"They might if you shoot me now."

"On the contrary. They'd know exactly why I had to shoot you now. You've come here to do my family harm because you've got this crazy idea that I shot your father. It all came out in court yesterday, didn't it?" There was nothing pleasurable about the grin on Frost Patterson's face. It may not even have been a grin. "The news didn't bother to show it all. It was only interested in covering the sex and violence angle, the question about your affair with the district attorney's wife and Keough's assault on that other lawyer there. But Wem Tuttle came by last night and told me what really happened. He told me what led up to that farrago. He told me to watch out for you, that you might be coming out here after Dodge next." He grunted at Wembley's prescience.

I slackened my hands. "What would I be doing out here in the barn that could possibly harm Dodge?"

"Planting something."

"What if I wasn't planting anything? What if there was something that was already here that would be evidence as to who killed Rebecca Carpenter? What if there was something here that would help to clear Wylie and make sure he isn't retried for the murder?"

"Wembley says there's no way Keough will try him a second time. He says the whole case is in shambles, that Wylie's lawyer discredited you and proved it was just some kind of a vendetta on your part. He says Keough's publicly disgraced himself and the judge actually did him a favor by declaring a mistrial." Frost paused and I could hear him wheezing until he got his rhythm going again. "He says the only thing we have to be careful of is you trying to pull something. That's why I was watching for you. Been up all night."

"Frost, what if Rebecca's pocketbook is in this barn? What if it's in that barrel I was just looking in? Wouldn't that mean anything to you?"

"It would mean that you put it there. It would mean that you're twice as dangerous as I thought you were because now I have to wonder how you got it."

"What if I didn't put it there, though? What would that mean to you?"

"You did put it there," he said, his voice rising, cracking, making me instinctively thrust my hands higher. "You put it there to frame my boy. You're going to say he did it to get money to pay off his gambling debts, or maybe because of the affair he had—"

"Your son didn't have an affair with Rebecca. That was just something your daughter-in-law told you to cover up her own affair with Wylie."

Frost's tremor became a shimmer. His gun moved up and down, but it stayed trained on me. "Gretchen?" he said.

"Why are you so surprised? Did you think she and your son had such a wonderful marriage? Dodge may have looked darn good when he was a twenty-year-old preppie, but not when he's an indebted thirty-five-year-old with no inheritance and no future. What did you think, that a woman like Gretchen was going to be satisfied forever just because she got the Patterson name? Think again, Frost. The Patterson name doesn't mean shit in this day and age."

Frost was thinking. I could tell by the trembles.

"She and Wylie used to meet on Tuesday nights at the River Inn. You remember Tuesday nights, that's when she told you she was going to the Woodedge Woman's Club. Only she didn't go to either the club or the inn on the Tuesday night that Rebecca was killed."

"She went shopping," Frost mumbled.

"Maybe. But she also went to the Carpenters' house. Maybe she told Rebecca they were going to go together. They talked earlier that day on the phone, you know, and Rebecca probably needed a costume, too. It would make sense that Rebecca would have put on her new scarf if she thought she was going out. People don't tend to wear scarfs if they are staying home alone, do they? But I don't know exactly what went on, Frost. I can only tell you what I think happened: that Gretchen went to the house, that either Rebecca was loaded or Gretchen got her loaded, and that Gretchen strangled her with her scarf—probably from behind, probably while she was sitting in a chair somewhere so that when she kicked out or fought back she wouldn't leave any marks on Gretchen or anything else."

Frost cleared his throat with a rattling noise that I took as a sign to continue.

"She hauled Rebecca out to her own car and manipulated her feet to make it look as if that's where she died. Then she drove her up to the overlook and walked back to the Carpenter house by way of the woods. We were stumped by that part for a while, but then I remembered what your grandson had told me about taking walks in the woods with his mother. Ian even had a picture of the pond you have to go by if you walk from the overlook to your house. Gretchen could have done it with a flashlight if she knew the trail. Once she got here it was just a matter of walking along the road to the Carpenters', picking up her car, and getting back home to bed before Dodge returned from the club."

"You're guessing, Mr. Starbuck," Frost said, but there was not a great deal of conviction in the way he said it.

I lowered my hands. I put them all the way down "Perhaps on some things. Not on everything. If that pocketbook is here it's going to substantiate a lot. You see, as long as it's missing the possibility exists that the killer took it because he needed the cash that was in it. It helps make a logical suspect out of the caretaker who disappeared the day Rebecca was killed.

"Gretchen knew that caretaker very well, Frost. She orchestrated his hiring by the Carpenters. She knew Rebecca liked good-looking, athletic men, and that Rebecca was lonely and unhappy and being ignored by her husband. Gretchen set up the dismissal of the Marconis, who had been with the Chesley family for years, and she convinced the lifeguard at Stonegate to go to work in their place until the fifteenth of October and then take off for California. The Carpenters probably never knew he was leaving. He probably never knew why he couldn't tell them, but Douglas Rasmussin's a stupid kid and he would do whatever Gretchen wanted because Gretchen knows how to manipulate men—all sorts of men. Even now I imagine he's been in touch with her and she's responsible for him making himself scarce. And this is the point, Frost . . . her plan was to set up Rasmussin as the suspect, even the scapegoat if necessary, so that her lover Wylie wouldn't be in any jeopardy for what she did. Taking the pocketbook was part of the plan."

Frost said nothing He just stared.

"The police have combed the woods looking for it and can't find a trace—which makes sense because she wouldn't have wanted to have thrown it away along the trail leading here. But once the trail ended, once she had to walk along Highland Street, she wouldn't want to be seen carrying a dead woman's purse, would she? And she had to pass right by this barn to get to the Carpenters', didn't she?"

The old man's eyes flicked to the barrel behind me.

"I've got more, Frost," I said. "It's all circumstantial, but I think it'll mean something to you."

Frost licked his lips. It was an ugly sight.

"I don't know how much Wembley said to you, but the cross examination of me yesterday was based on a lot of inside information, information Phil Burns shouldn't have had. Some of it came from a leak inside the prosecution team, but not all of it—not the personal stuff about me. There were things brought up that I've never talked about with anyone—that nobody else would know, or suspect, or put into words except you, Frost. And you didn't call up Wylie's lawyer and tell him, did you? You wouldn't have had any reason to. I mean, you weren't planning on marrying Wylie and sharing his newly inherited sixty-three-million-dollar estate, were you?"

Frost blinked. It was something that seemed to take him an extraordinarily long time to do. "Gretchen's married to my son," he said weakly.

"She'd asked you a lot of questions about me, hadn't she? Starting with that day I first came here to interview her, when you told her never to let a Starbuck in the house, you gave her all the dirt about my father, I bet."

"She asked me some questions." The skinny old tongue came out and went around his lips again. "I told her some things."

"Did you tell her where I lived?"

He moved the gun from side to side. It was a way of shrugging. "I told her your father lived in West Nestor. I told her your parents' names and she could have looked the address up in the phone book, I suppose."

"And she could have sent a hit man there, too, couldn't she?"

Frost Patterson's head drew back. "That's preposterous," he snorted, and the old contempt returned to his eyes.

"Why?" I said, speaking quickly in case he was deciding he did not have to listen to me anymore. "Somebody went out to my mother's house in November and put four bullets into the front of it in an attempt to shoot me. I don't know if I was supposed to get killed or not, but I know everyone was supposed to think Dougie Rasmussin was responsible because the gunman used a stolen car that was abandoned behind Dougie's favorite watering hole in Walmouth. The one thing I can be certain about, Frost, is that Dougie didn't have any reason to shoot me—not then, anyhow. Not just after Wylie had been indicted. So who else is there at that point? Not Wylie.

The time to take out an investigator is before he hands in his evidence. Doesn't do you very much good to eliminate him after you've already been indicted. The only one who still had reason to fear the investigator, who knew the investigator had information about her that nobody else had, was Gretchen."

"Sounds to me," Frost said, clearing his throat with a rattling sound, "as though you're throwing mud against the wall, Mr. Starbuck."

"I don't imagine she ever gave you the spiel about how tough it was growing up in Lowell, about how you had to get to know your neighbors just to keep them from stealing your car, but she gave it to me. If she needed a stolen car she knew where to go. She might have gotten the driver along with it, or she might have just gotten the car and taken the shots herself. She might even have used that gun you've got in your hand."

There was an added tremble in Frost's arm as he glanced at the gun. His glance became a stare, as if he was remembering something or seeing something that he was not sharing. "How," he said at last, "are you going to prove that it was my daughter-in-law who did any of these things?"

"I can't prove it. Like you said a few minutes ago, my credibility is shot. But find the pocketbook and you can judge for yourself."

The old man thought about what I was saying. "And if I find it, I should tell Wylie, is that what you want me to do?"

"I suspect he already knows. I suspect that's why he refuses to tell anybody where he was for those two hours on the night of the fifteenth. Wylie, from everything I've been able to learn, considers himself an honorable man. But he's got a confused sense of honor. It's all bundled up with notions of chivalry and machismo and dignity. He's not going to be making accusations or offering up someone else to save himself. But he has to know. If he and Gretchen ever professed love for each other, if they ever talked about marrying, then he has to wonder why she never joined him at the River Inn on the night his wife was killed."

"Is it possible . . ." Frost hesitated, trying to decide if he should say the next words. I helped him.

"That he was involved? I don't know. There are some things that point to it even now. The scarf, for example. Was it just a coincidence he bought it three days before it was used to kill Rebecca? The police haven't been able to find any other scarves in her wardrobe, her house. How did she happen to be wearing one that night? Was it something he told Gretchen would be there? Or did he even give it to Rebecca? It cost a hundred and fifty dollars, maybe he gave it to Gretchen. He wouldn't necessarily have intended her to use it the way she did, but at the very least it would mean he knows she did it.

"There's something else that troubles me about Wylie. He claims not to have known Rasmussin before he started work, but he did. Maybe he helped Gretchen set up Rasmussin. Maybe, on the other hand, he's just figured out how she set the kid up and he's trying to protect her. These are things I can't possibly know for sure.

"That's the dilemma I have, Frost. People shouldn't be able to get away with murder. Not even beautiful people or talented people or rich people. Not even if their victims are murdering themselves with alcohol or drugs or self-pity. Not even if the victims are obsessive or emotionally disturbed. But at the same time someone who is charged with enforcing the law is not supposed to be going around trying to convict people unless he can prove beyond a reasonable doubt that they did it. There has to be something in the middle. There has to be some kind of pain and punishment in other people knowing that you did it even if the law can't prove it.

"It's all in degrees, Frost. If Wylie won't explain himself, that's not enough to put him on trial, but he has to suffer the doubts and suspicions that go along with keeping silent. And if you know somebody did something as awful as murder, then you either make other people know it as well as you or you share in the guilt."

Frost started to clear his throat again. He started deep down in his chest and by the time it came out of his mouth it had become a cough. Being the well-mannered Yalie that he was, he covered his mouth with his gun hand. But I didn't move. "And you think," he said, looking at what he had done with the gun, "that if the pocketbook, Becky's pocketbook, is in here we'll know for certain?"

"I would. Whether it's enough for you isn't for me to say. But I'm giving you the opportunity to find out. And I'm giving you the opportunity to watch Gretchen and Wylie to see what happens between them. And if nothing does, then I'm still giving you the opportunity to watch Gretchen. Whether you decide to discuss it with Dodge is your decision."

Frost thought it over. His blue eyes flicked once more between me and the barrel. "Tip it over, Mr. Starbuck," he said.

I turned. I walked around so that the barrel was between Frost and me. I carefully lifted out the metal pieces and dropped them so that they clanged onto the wooden floor. The noise made Frost jump, but he kept his attention on the barrel. I squatted and pushed and the barrel tipped over and its contents spilled onto the floor. Sheetrock and bolts and odd-size pieces of wood tumbled out. There was no pocketbook. I looked inside. I swept the barrel with my hand, but it was not there.

"It's somewhere, Frost," I said. "Maybe she loaded it with rocks and threw it into the pond that night. Maybe it's been destroyed between October and now. But I doubt it. I think it's still here and I'm willing to keep looking if you are."

Frost Patterson stared at the mess on the floor for a long time. Little clouds of Sheetrock dust were still swirling around our feet and I was still squatting. "I think," he said, "you've done enough, Mr. Starbuck. I think you should go now."

I got to my feet, nowhere near as thrilled as I should have been at being freed from the immediate prospect of dying; and knowing, too, that I had nothing more to argue with Cousin Frost. I walked outside, but I made it only as far as the yard, where I stood for several minutes staring at the house with all its branches and additions, all the twists and turns that had never been contemplated by the original builder. It once had been a beautiful place, I suppose. Now, like the Patterson family itself, it was showing its age.

I was starting to turn away when I saw a figure appear at an upstairs window. I saw what looked like a sleeveless cotton undershirt and for an instant I thought it was Dodge. Then I saw the outline of the breasts, the smooth flow of the neck, the dark skin, and I knew it was Gretchen.

She moved closer, until she was right against the window and I could see the look of surprise, of disbelief, on her face. She started to raise her hand as if to wave and then slowly her eyes shifted to the barn behind me. I had been listening to the sounds of Frost Patterson moving things around, opening and closing doors, but those sounds had gone silent now.

I looked over my shoulder just as Frost emerged into the early-morning light. His gun was out of sight, his cane was tucked under his arm, he was limping along on arthritic joints. And cradled in his arms like a newborn baby was a woman's black leather purse.